Praise for Jesse

'Has ... ined ... ... and delightful twists and turns at every corner'
Buzzfeed

'Whip-smart, original and so funny, I found
it impossible to put down'
Beth O'Leary

'I loved the plot. Hugely entertaining'
SJ Bennett

'Utterly clever, deeply funny, and altogether charming'
Emily Henry

'Charming, refreshing and delightfully subversive'
The i

'Nothing short of genius. Highly recommend'
M. W. Craven

'A gloriously screwball crime caper which
will have you snort-laughing'
Red

'A fantastic puzzle that will have you hooked'
Jonathan Whitelaw

Jesse Sutanto is the author of books for children and adults. She is the author of YA novel, *The Obsession*, and *Theo Tan and the Fox Spirit*, the first book in a middle grade series. *Dial A For Aunties* was her debut adult novel and won the 2021 Comedy Women In Print Prize.

Jesse received her Masters from the University of Oxford. She grew up in Indonesia and Singapore and currently lives in Jakarta with her husband and two daughters.

You can find out more about Jesse on her website www.jesseqsutantoauthor.com and follow her on Twitter @thewritinghippo and on Facebook and Instagram @JesseQSutanto.

Also by Jesse Sutanto
Vera Wong's Unsolicited Advice for Murderers

The Aunties series
Dial A For Aunties
Four Aunties and a Wedding

YA
Well, That Was Unexpected

I'M NOT DONE WITH YOU YET

JESSE SUTANTO

ONE PLACE. MANY STORIES

HQ
An imprint of HarperCollins*Publishers* Ltd
1 London Bridge Street
London SE1 9GF

www.harpercollins.co.uk

HarperCollins*Publishers*
Macken House, 39/40 Mayor Street Upper,
Dublin 1, D01 C9W8, Ireland

This edition 2023

1
First published in Great Britain by
HQ, an imprint of HarperCollins*Publishers* Ltd 2023

Copyright © PT Karya Hippo Makmur 2023

Jesse Sutanto asserts the moral right to be
identified as the author of this work.
A catalogue record for this book is
available from the British Library.

ISBN: 9780008558765

MIX
Paper | Supporting
responsible forestry
FSC™ C007454

This book is produced from independently certified FSC™ paper
to ensure responsible forest management.

For more information visit: www.harpercollins.co.uk/green

This book is set in 9.5/15.5 pt. Brother by Type-it AS, Norway

Printed and Bound in the UK using 100% Renewable Electricity at
CPI Group (UK) Ltd, Croydon, CR0 4YY

To Laurie Elizabeth Flynn, my soul twin, without whom
I wouldn't have had the courage to even start this book.

When did you first realize you're not normal?

PART ONE

Chapter 1

TWENTY-SIX YEARS AGO

Aunt Claudette, she's the best. So everyone says. By everyone, I mean my mother. My mother loves Aunt Claudette because she is always ready to help out with "the cutie pie," i.e., me. "Cutie pie" is the first clue that should tell you that my mother doesn't give a shit about me, because really, how fucking generic a pet name can someone get for their only child? She can't even be bothered to come up with a more unique pet name, one that's tailored to fit me. No, I remain known as "cutie pie" up until even my idiot mother can't pretend that I'm cute anymore.

But anyway. Back to Aunt Claudette. Not technically my aunt. She's just an elderly neighbor who Mom swears loves me like "her own." Her own what? Aunt Claudette never had kids. And the thing about Aunt Claudette is, she doesn't look after me out of love, no matter how much Mom would like to believe she does.

Sure, maybe she did it out of love at first, when I was little enough not to have any personality. When I really was a generic little cutie pie. But now that I'm seven, I realize she's not looking after me because she cares about me. She does so because she cares about what I would do if I'm not being watched.

This morning, Mom made me cocoa pancakes for breakfast before rushing out the door to get to work. Cocoa pancakes, not chocolate pancakes. She'd read that unsweetened cocoa powder is full of antioxidants, so today, my pancakes come out brown as shit and tasting no better. I hate the color brown. That's what my hair is. Mom sometimes tries to call it "chestnut" or "chocolate," but we both know it's neither of those things. And here are my pancakes, the same disgusting mud-brown as my hair. I can drown the pancakes in syrup, but the only syrup allowed in the house is agave, which tastes like melted plastic. Clint Eastwood nudges my foot. The name's a joke that stuck—Clint is a loyal rescue mutt of an indeterminate age, but he looks about as old as God. I look into his trusting face and tear a tiny bit of shit pancake off. His stumpy tail wags, and he stands on his hind legs and paws my knees with a desperate whine.

But before I can give him the piece of pancake, Aunt Claudette rushes in like a hurricane and grabs my wrist, almost painfully. "What are you doing, child?"

I gaze at her. I have huge hazel eyes. Whenever people describe their eyes as "hazel," it's always brown. But mine have that warm honey hue that make people do a double take. They're also stupidly big and round. Legit Bambi eyes. I widen them now, because I know that's what people do when they're taken by surprise. "Clint is hungwy," I say.

Most people, including my own mother, would soften and say, "Aww," at that. But Aunt Claudette's mouth thins. I've miscalculated. She knows I'm too old for such mispronunciations. "Hung-ree," she says. "You know how to pronounce it properly."

I do.

"And you know Clint isn't allowed chocolate. It's bad for him."

It's not even a huge amount of cocoa. Not enough to do any permanent damage, only enough to give Clint the runs. I was going to really enjoy watching Mom clean up after Clint's diarrhea.

"I'm sorry." I cast my Bambi eyes down. All of my picture books show kids doing that when they're sorry. "I forgot." I look up at Aunt Claudette again, and this time, I've weaponized my Bambis—they're shining with tears. "Please don't be mad at me, Auntie."

That's something I'd learned from Jayden, Mom's current "special friend." Whenever they argue, Jayden looks at Mom a certain way and says, "Don't be mad at me, babe," and she sighs and her shoulders slump in defeat, and even at the age of seven, I know what a conniving asshole Jayden is, because telling someone not to be mad is putting all of the responsibility on them. *Sure, I may have done something wrong, but YOU do the labor of getting over it.* Jayden may be a grade A asshole, but he's taught me some really great tactics. And women fall for that shit all the time.

Even Aunt Claudette is no match for it. She flushes, her eyebrows coming together, and she quickly says, "Of course I'm not mad at you, angel," and I know for sure she's mad because she knows I'm no angel. Then she taps a palm against her fat thigh and says, "Here, Clint," and herds Clint away. Away from me. I shrug, running a finger down the edge of my butter knife. I fleetingly entertain the thought of plunging the point of that knife someplace soft and warm, someplace with a steady pulse, so the blood would come out in a rhythmic spurt. But I could never hurt Aunt Claudette. She's special. She's the only one who can always see right through my bullshit, and she loves me anyway, which just goes to show how flawed humans are.

She may as well love a cockroach.

Chapter 2

PRESENT DAY
SOUTH SAN FRANCISCO, CALIFORNIA

The thing about crazy bitches is there's usually some man who's pushed and prodded and gaslit her to that point.

I've never been a tidy person, but I like the idea of it; I enjoy the feeling of having tidied up, of sitting in an uncluttered room with a cup of tea and a good book. I like it enough to spend some time at the end of each day putting things away. I never get the room to "pristine," because I've been raised with clutter and never quite got the hang of cleaning, but I put in enough effort to make sure the space is livable. Ted, on the other hand, is an all-or-nothing guy. When I ask him to help declutter, he'll say, "Why bother? It's all just going to get messy again." If he can't have perfection, then we may as well live in a hovel.

This evening is no different. After dinner (in front of the TV so we won't actually have to make conversation with each other), Ted shuts himself away in his man cave for a round of Fortnite—apparently, it's not just for twelve-year-old boys; it's also for thirty-seven-year-old men—while I putter about the house putting away our daily bric-a-brac.

6

Normally, I wouldn't mind it, but today, our neighbor Kimiko had stopped by to "borrow" some flour (I say "borrow," but Kimiko is always coming by to borrow cups of sugar, or an egg or two, and not once has she returned anything), and while she waited in our foyer, Ted had said, laughingly, "Sorry about the state of the house. Jane's just really messy like that."

I'd come out of the kitchen then, carrying a Tupperware of flour, and said with more bite than I'd intended, "What? I'm not the messy one here."

Ted had raised his arms in a theatrical way, eyes wide, and laughed. "Whoa, it's okay, babe. I don't care that you're messy."

"But I'm not—" I caught it then. The shrill tone of anger in my voice that sounded like cracking glass. I stopped myself, but I could tell that Kimiko and Ted had both caught it too.

Kimiko had left pretty quickly after that, not bothering to stay around for a chitchat like she usually does. Which was just as well, because it gave me a chance to nip down to the basement and be alone. Lock myself away so I could cool down before I did something I'd regret. Something irredeemable.

Now, as I pick up Ted's half-drunk glasses of water and tea from the coffee table, my resentment mounts. Why is it always down to me to clear away all this shit? The random remnants of our daily lives—socks on the floor, pens and bits of paper everywhere, a half-eaten sandwich abandoned on, of all places, the TV cabinet. And I wouldn't mind it so much if Ted weren't such a fucking asshole about it all, if he'd at least acknowledge that I put in more effort than he does. I may be messy by nature, but I'm trying, and he's not seeing it, or maybe he's refusing to. Maybe he enjoys pushing my buttons, seeing how far he can twist the dials before I crack and show anger, like this morning,

7

so he can say, "Geez, why're you getting so worked up over nothing?" He'd do his little incredulous snort and share a look with whoever he's talking to, and in the end, I'm always the crazy bitch who shoveled molehills into my own Mount Everest.

I can feel the old anger rising up again. I don't want to have to go down to the basement for the second time in a day, so I fling down the balled-up Fortnite T-shirt I'd picked up and stride out of the living room and into the dining room, where my laptop lives. Let Ted deal with his own mess.

Taking a deep breath, I sink into my chair and turn my laptop on. I scroll through Twitter for a while, losing myself in the usual cacophony of intense emotions. Everyone on Twitter is always either manically happy or completely enraged, and it makes me feel a bit better. More normal. When I get tired of all the virtual yelling, I switch over to check my email.

And that's when I see it. A newsletter from the *New York Times* with their latest bestseller list. The words scream at me through my computer screen, flashing in huge capital letters, neon bright.

Well, okay, the *New York Times* doesn't ever do anything that's as uncouth as screaming, and they sure as hell do not do headlines in huge caps and neon colors—what are they, the *Daily Mail*? But they might as well have, because there, right in front of me, is her name. Surely, it can't be written in plain black font; it's radiating with so much light. Blindingly bright, like the way she was. And just seeing those two words, that beautiful, uncommon name of hers, is enough to swallow me whole again. I'm whisked back into the common room at Pemberton, nervously skirting the edges of the crowd, biting my nails as I watch her hungrily.

Thalia Ashcroft.

In Greek mythology, Thalia was a Muse. Someone who inspired others to write. To create.

This version is no different. Even back at the program all those years ago, our classmates were drawn to her, always buzzing around her like bees swarming the queen, wanting to drink from the well of inspiration. Hands always touching her, a pat on the shoulder here, a brush on the arm there, as though she were Jesus and they were lepers desperate for a cure. I detested them all, not because I judged them for their insipid personalities, grown lazy and bland through privilege. No, I couldn't give two shits about our classmates. But I despised them their audacity. The way they felt entitled to be near her, to converse with her as though they were even close to being on the same level as she was.

No one was on the same level as Thalia the Muse, Thalia the Beautiful, Thalia the Perfect.

And now here she is again, her name right there in front of me, blasting her way back into my life in the most Thalia-esque fashion. Right at the top of the *New York Times* bestseller list.

New this week

A MOST PLEASANT DEATH
by Thalia Ashcroft, writing as May Pierce

The squeak of creaking plastic wrenches me out of my reverie. With a start, I see that I've been squeezing my mouse so hard that it has cracked in my hand. I peer down at the mouse. It was a bargain buy, made in China, cheap and unloved. Just like everything in my house, yours truly included.

If Ted knew I think this badly of the house his parents helped us to get, he'd have a go at me. And I suppose I should be grateful for it, thankful that his parents, unlike mine, are generous enough to help out with the down payment. But Ted's a contract data analyst and I'm a midlist writer, and the house is just a bit beyond our means. The mortgage alone is almost crippling. Almost, but not quite. Enough that each month, when we make the payment, I feel embittered that we have to pay so much for a house where I don't even have my own study. Ted's man cave doubles as his office, so he's just fine and dandy, but me? I have to make do with the communal spaces. The spaces that are dominated by his mess.

So I write at cafés. Of course, the tech boom in the Bay Area means that a cup of coffee costs me an arm and a leg and half a kidney, but it's worth it to give me a few precious hours away from the house and the mess.

I wonder if Thalia writes at cafés too. No, I reject the thought as soon as it surfaces. I can't see her at a hipster café with a mocha latte next to a rose gold laptop. No, Thalia isn't the type to soak up attention like that. Even back then, I could tell she hated it, hated that she was the sun and everyone else was a sunflower turning their wide, open faces toward her, feeding off her warmth.

She'd write in her apartment. Or maybe a house? My heart leaps to my throat, forming a lump as I open up a new tab and type down her name. Each letter a heartbreak.

T-h-a-l-i-a A—

I don't even get to finish before Google finishes the search for me. Because of course, she's the only Thalia worth Googling. My chest squeezes into a jealous fist. How many have done this search before me? I've done it so many times, but until now, I have only ever been able to find a ghost. Hits that were years old—a few blurry Facebook photos of her from college, from high school. Nothing from our master's course, certainly. After what happened in our year, Oxford had extended its powerful hand and crushed everything, scrubbed every last bit of news until all that remained were the ramblings of a couple of local tabloids. Nothing that anyone of consequence would pay attention to.

But now, oh my god. So many hits. A Goodreads page. An Amazon page. And a website. How is this possible? How have so many hits sprouted up without my knowledge? In the early days, I used to do a search for her name obsessively. She used to blog. I'd read and reread her posts in my room, devouring every word, marveling at the elegance of her writing. Then that final formal had happened, and Thalia disappeared. I often wondered if Oxford had been responsible for scrubbing her off the Internet too. And, years later, I've moved on, sort of. My search became more sporadic.

And now, here she is.

The tip of my tongue edges out, moistening my lips ever so slightly. I press down on the inside of my wrist, noting my heart rate. Slightly elevated. The way it gets whenever there's anything Thalia-related. I swallow and move the cracked mouse so the cursor hovers over her website. I watch as the arrow turns into a pointing hand.

Our time at Oxford flashes before me—the heavy, damp English air, the wet cobblestones, the books—oh god, all the books—the feverish writing, the heady wine and sweet cider, and the blood. By now, I'm breathing heavily, the way I always do when my mind wanders over to that blood-soaked night. I lick my lips again before biting down hard enough to taste a metallic tang, as though my body can't wait to go back to

11

that night, the night that should've bound me to Thalia. The night I lost her.

But here she is, after all these years. And this time, I'm going to do things right. I'm not losing her again.

I grip the mouse tight, until it squeaks in near death, and I click Enter.

Chapter 3

NINE YEARS AGO
OXFORD, ENGLAND

The sky in England is different from the sky in California. It's the first thing I notice when I walk out of Heathrow. It seems lower somehow, and even though it's a beautiful English summer day with wispy white clouds frosting the deep blue sky, it feels slightly oppressive. Or maybe it's just my mood. I'm nervous, and when I'm nervous, I get cranky, which is bad. Really bad. Because I can't control my anger like the normals do.

Mom has never bothered taking me to see anyone, because she insisted nothing was wrong with me. She'd say things like, "Why do white people come up with so many mental health issues? All of a sudden, everybody has mental health issues. It's all made up so they can medicate us and take our money." I think she just didn't give a shit, but tomayto, tomahto. It doesn't matter, anyway. Early on in my teens, I researched my condition and diagnosed myself with the help of Dr. Google.

Pretty sure I'm a sociopath. I'm not ashamed of it; in fact it's something I quite like, and I carry the thought in the recesses of my mind like a lucky charm, returning to it the way one might stroke a rabbit's foot once in a while. Caressing it mentally. My own little touchstone. Sociopath. As long as I can identify it, I can deal with it.

Sociopathy.

Antisocial Personality Disorder.

Behaviors: antisocial (check), deceitful (check), hostile (check), irresponsible (okay, check), manipulative (I suppose, though I'm not as good at it as I'd like to be), aggressive (yeah).

The thing that most people don't know about sociopaths is that we do actually get lonely. At least this one does. It's hard to explain. I don't like people—I don't know how to be interested in them the way everyone else seems to be. But god, I wish they'd like me. Not much luck in that aspect though.

But England will be different. It's the whole reason I chose to do my master's here instead of California. California is basically the worst place in the world for antisocials. It's too loud, too sunny, too fucking friendly. Everyone gets revved up on kale smoothies and cocaine so I can't even get a tub of hummus without the Trader Joe's checkout lady grinning at me and calling me honey and asking me how I'm doing and what are my plans for the weekend? Californians just can't help themselves. If I stayed there any longer I was bound to kill someone.

Just kidding. Sort of.

So I researched the world's rudest, unfriendliest places. Top two are apparently Russia and France, which I dismissed because I don't speak French or Russian. And then there it was. Number 3: United Kingdom. What do I know about England?

1. Surly people (Yay, means I should fit in perfectly. Maybe they won't notice that I'm a sociopath?)
2. Gloomy weather (If even the English find me too surly for them, I could blame it on the weather!)
3. Terrible food (. . . or I could blame it on the food.)
4. Brilliant writers

The last bit has been the deal clincher for me. I've always wanted to write for a living. When I was little and magazines were still a thing, I'd daydreamed about writing for them. It seemed very glamorous at the time. I'd pictured myself in New York City, a place teeming with people just as vicious and cruel and empty as myself. Not a single person is allowed to be bubbly in New York City; I was sure of it. I'd wear sky-high heels and lipstick the color of a gaping wound and stride around with a cigarette hanging from my lips, getting paid to talk to people, manipulate them into giving up information, and then write down my observations in the most wickedly delicious way.

But then the Internet swallowed up the magazine industry whole and I just couldn't bring myself to write for online news sites. All those bright colors and dementedly cheerful headlines:

TEN LOL-WORTHY PUPPIES!

SEVEN SMOOTHIES WORTH BUYING A BLENDER FOR!

FIVE WAYS TO TELL WHETHER YOU'RE A SOCIOPATH!

To be fair, I actually found the last one useful.

The thought of my impossible New York dream rankles me, even now, so many years after its death. I give myself a little shake. Whatever, forget New York. I'm in England, for god's sake. I locate the bus headed to Oxford and pay the driver.

"Which stop?" he says.

"Um." It takes a moment to recall the name that had been included in the welcome email. "Glow-chester?"

"Nope, sorry, don't know that."

I frown at him and peer at the sign above the bus, which clearly says "OXFORD." "This is going to Oxford, right?"

"Yep," he says, and turns away from me.

Jesus. I'd been warned that people here would be unfriendly, but this guy is on a whole other level. A familiar tendril caresses the depth of my guts. Oh no, please. Don't lose your temper here. Do not. I take a deep breath and snap the rubber band at my wrist. The rubber band is one of the things that my extensive research had suggested as a method to control my sociopathic rage. A literal way to "snap" myself out of the spiral that would otherwise grab me like a riptide and fling me into dark oblivion, leaving nothing but broken detritus in my wake.

It works, most of the time. My stomach settles and I step aside to open up the welcome email on my phone. I was right; it says right here: Gloucester Green.

I wait until the elderly man boards the bus before approaching the driver again. "Hi, it says here my stop is Glow-chester—"

"Nope," he says, beckoning at the next passenger to come up.

The slick caress again. My cheeks grow warm. Oh no, I'm going to lose it right here, less than an hour after arriving in a foreign country where I'm supposed to make my fresh start.

16

"But it says right here—"

"I think she means Gloucester Green," a female voice says from behind me, pronouncing it Gloss-ter, "and I think you knew all along what she meant."

I turn around and that's when I see her. The most beautiful girl I have ever laid eyes on outside of Instagram. My mouth parts, and all of the bubbling anger that had been ready to erupt just moments ago dissipates. She looks like she might have mixed ancestry, too, though unlike the uneasy way that the different lineages have converged on my face, Thalia's features are a work of art. She looks like a literal angel. Gold hair that looks like threads of pulled sunlight, huge, huge eyes—distracting, so distracting. But it's not the face that arrests me; it's the kindness in it. Like she's the long-lost best friend you didn't know you had and she knows every gross secret about you and doesn't judge you for it. She makes me want to make a motherfucking friendship bracelet for her and buy one of those obnoxious heart necklaces that say "best friends" when you put them together.

She quirks one corner of her mouth up at the bus driver in what I can only describe as an empathetic smirk. "Come on, luv, let's stop messing about, okay?"

She sounds very clearly American, but somehow she carries off "luv" with so much flair that the bus driver is obligated to give a grin in return.

He winks at me and says, "Ah, just messing with ya. Off you go, then. Two for Gloucester Green, is it?"

"Yep," the girl says, and cocks her head at me. "Let's go, before this cheeky bugger decides to fuck with us again." She winks at him as she says this before hopping onto the bus.

The driver roars with laughter, and I clamber up after her.

Already my mind is going at breakneck speed, analyzing every microsecond of the encounter. It's what I do most times I have an awkward encounter with people.

Was that a normal interaction? Did I react in a socially acceptable manner? How would a normal person behave? How would a bad-tempered normal person behave? What might I have done differently to pass under the radar next time?

As though reading my mind, the girl turns her head and gives me a rueful smile. "You okay? He was an asshole, wasn't he? I bet he thought he was being real cute too."

My mouth drops open but nothing comes out. It's not that my mind's empty; on the contrary, there are way too many thoughts zipping around in it. Chief among them: What should I say? I'd nearly blown my cover of normalcy just moments ago, and as much as I hate to admit it, I'm rattled. I've burned so many bridges back in Cali. People I thought were my friends ghosted me. I can't let that happen here, not at my laundry-fresh start.

I've stayed silent far too long. I know it. The atmosphere thickens the way it always does when I know I'm not Being Normal. I stare helplessly at the girl, feeling that old heat travel up my chest and onto my cheeks. I wish she'd end my suffering and leave me alone already.

Instead, she slides into a seat, scooting over so she takes the window seat, and then cocks her head at me. "Come on, the bus will get full soon and I don't really wanna sit with some random stranger."

"I'm a random stranger," I blurt out.

God damn it.

Sociopathic tendency #57: Lacks filters.

She laughs, and it's the best laugh in the world. Very different from the manic, need-for-attention-driven shriek-giggles I got used to in California. It's low and husky, a laugh so soft I know it's meant for my ears alone.

"True, but I just saved you from that asshole out there, so I think you owe me one," she says.

I swallow, gripping my bag with sweaty palms, and slide in before I can talk myself out of it. This close to her, I can smell her scent. Lavender and the musky, tired smell of travel. It's a surprisingly pleasant combination, one that relaxes me. If I were a cat, this is where I'd retract my claws.

"I'm Thalia," she says.

Thalia. What a beautiful name. Different. Unexpected, with a hint of foreign flavor. Again, I find myself wondering about her lineage.

As though reading my mind, she adds, "It's Greek. Half my ancestors came from there; the other half came from Italy. Of course, this was, like, five generations ago, so don't ask me anything about either place, aside from the food." She grins sheepishly and my mind goes blank. Like her, I know nothing about my ancestral heritage. I don't even speak Chinese. A similarity, a bond fusing us to each other.

No. This is not how normal people think. We've just met. There is no bond. I focus instead on her name.

It suits her perfectly, and I realize she must have parents who love her and know her the way I wish my mother knew me. Parents who cared enough to find the perfect name for their little girl. Parents that are very much unlike mine.

"I'm Jane."

"I love that name."

I roll my eyes and instantly regret it. Why am I so thorny?

19

But Thalia smiles, seemingly unperturbed by my bitchiness. "No, really. You know *Jane the Virgin*? I love that show. Ever since season one, I loved the name Jane."

"Never saw it." A small lie. My mom watched it religiously with my aunt, and I'd sometimes catch snippets of it. It enraged me—the saccharine-sweet, fairy tale–perfect relationship between Jane, her mother, and her grandmother. And the fact that my mother, the woman who couldn't give a tiny rat's ass about me, loved the show made me even angrier. I wanted to put my hands around that fucking show and crush it.

"Yeah? What shows do you watch?"

The mention of *Jane the Virgin* has angered me enough to let my guard down a little, so I look Thalia straight in the eye. "I like dark shows. Shows that aren't afraid to kill main characters. Shows that have a healthy body count. *Breaking Bad. The Walking Dead.* Those kinds of shows."

I fully expected *Jane the Virgin*–loving Thalia to stop talking to me then and there, but instead, she laughs and says, "I think you and I are going to have a lot of fun together, Jane."

It's meant to be. We were meant to meet this way, with her rescuing me from the London–Oxford bus driver. Meant to sit next to each other for over one hundred minutes, our elbows a mere hair's breadth away from touching. With each bump the bus takes, my elbow kisses hers, and I am dying a sweet, slow death.

I steal glances at her as the miles are eaten up beneath us. While men lust after the soft, bulging parts of the female anatomy—the breasts, the ass—we women notice the hardness. The places that signify control. Discipline. The clavicle, the shoulder blades, the cheekbones. Thalia's collarbone is defined in a way that makes me swallow. I imagine myself running a finger along its hard length, from the bottom of her neck all the way to her shoulder, where it juts out into a single knife point. I want to press on it with my index finger and feel the solidity of it pushing up against me. I want her lovely bones to cut into my skin.

I don't understand it myself; I'm quite sure I'm not sexually attracted to women, but there's just something about Thalia that captures my attention, clutching it tight in a sweaty grip that refuses to let go. I'm ashamed of my inability to cast my eye away, as though I were a creepy man breathing heavily into the mouthpiece of a phone. Maybe it's the fact that somehow, the mixed ethnicities have rewarded her and punished me. My nose has a bump on the end, rodent-like, my lips chapped, with a slight overbite. Though we're about the same height, Thalia seems taller because she carries herself straight-backed, while I slouch and try to hide from the light. Maybe, if I'd had a more loving mom, a present dad instead of a dead one, I could've been more like Thalia. Mom's voice floats up to the surface, a bubble popping in toxic waste, releasing noxious fumes. *Still rejecting the Asian side of you? Still worshipping white people, wishing you were them?*

"I can feel you staring."

My breath catches in a painful rush, and I practically plaster my entire back against the seat. Fuck shit fuck. "Uh." Half a second to catch my breath, compose myself. *Don't get caught being a creep, Jane.* "I was just looking at the scenery."

Fortunately for me, the scenery outside is somewhat decent. Definitely worth looking at as opposed to the inside of a crowded bus. We're going past a bucolic setting of rolling hills, complete with flocks of sheep grazing lazily, their movements so slow it's like we caught them in a portrait as we rush past on the freeway—no, sorry, the motorway.

Thalia laughs under her breath. "I'm just messing with you. Sorry. I've been told I have a terrible sense of humor." She looks out the window before I can reply, which is a relief because I have no idea what to say to that. A second later, she glances back at me. "So, Jane. What brings you to Oxford?"

I have an answer to that, at least. "I'm here to attend the master's program at Pemberton College."

The Oxbridge universities operate like no other that I know of. They're each divided into various colleges, instead of operating as a single university, a fact that had been a source of confusion as I navigated my way through the complicated applications. But whatever, it doesn't matter which college I attend, as long as my final diploma says Oxford bloody University.

"Oh my gosh," Thalia breathes, her clavicles rising and falling. Mesmerizing. "Wait, don't tell me. The Creative Writing program?"

Again, that painful rush of breath. I'm going to develop asthma if I'm not careful. "Uh. Yeah."

Her entire face lights up. "No way! That's what I'm doing too." Her mouth stretches into the most beautiful smile. "Holy shit, Jane. We're going to be classmates."

I don't really know what to say to that. Part of me wants to crawl into a hole, but a small part of me is writhing with joy. I don't realize I'm biting my lip until I taste the salty tang of blood.

"What do you write?"

I lick my lips before I answer, wondering if there's blood visible on my mouth, if I've given myself away. But Thalia is still smiling a smile so innocent it physically hurts me to look at it.

I can't help but get a flashback of Mom, tilting her head down in the way that she does to show anyone watching that she's had a long day's work. I never know how she's able to convey exhaustion and put-upon-ness with just a turn of the head, but there's my mother. I pretend not to see her; most of the time, we pretend the other person doesn't exist. Then the sigh comes. *Still doing that writing thing, are you? When will you learn, Jane? Those things are for rich white folk. Not people like us. People like us, Jane, we do honest work.*

By "honest work" she means menial labor—work that breaks our bodies apart bit by bit. I often thought of how, throughout history, the bodies of people of color have been destroyed and fed in little pieces to rich white people to swallow, and they won't stop, not even when there's nothing left of us to give.

Mrs. Crawford's niece is due to give birth in September. She asked about you again, asked if you'd be available.

You know I won't be, I bite out. *I'm going to school.* A mistake. I should've stayed silent.

Mom has been working her whole life for people like Mrs. Crawford; people who have children and then decide they don't actually like kids that much, so enter my mother. She does everything for those kids—feeds them, bathes them, hugs them tight when they cry. The kids reward her by forgetting her name as soon as they become old enough to not need a nanny and she moves on to the next family. Over the years, I've watched my mother scurry around at the beck and call of the rich—"Can you work this weekend? We've been invited to the Robertsons' lake house for the weekend, for an adults-only hunting session, and Bella is so sensitive, we couldn't bring her anyway—you know how it is." The kids are always "sensitive" or "precocious," never "needy as fuck" and "spoiled as shit," which is really what they are. She gives and gives, her back becoming more hunched as she bends to pick up carelessly strewn shoes, bends to carry tantrum-throwing toddlers, and bends to kiss the feet of the Crawfords and Robertsons of the world. Good, honest work.

School, she snorts. *School for writing, who ever heard of that? Throwing good money away to learn how to dream your life away. It's not our way, Jane. If you insist on spending money on higher education, then go for proper subjects. Accounting. Medicine. Things you can make an actual living from.*

And I type extra loudly so she'll know I'm ignoring her, that unlike her, I haven't given up dreaming of a better life. That I'll write a thousand different novels if that's what it takes to save me from my mother's life. That there is no such thing as "our way." It's always grated at me, the way that my mother assumes that I am just like her. I'm not all Chinese like my mom. I'm half-white, and just because my father's gone, it doesn't mean that part of me is magically erased.

I've stayed quiet far too long. Thalia is still looking at me with an expectant smile, so I quickly say, "Uh. I write fiction. A bit of poetry. You?" I add, shifting the conversation back at her. I've read that this is how normal conversations go. One person asks a question; the other one answers and fires back another question. Back and forth, a verbal game of tennis that most people seem to find so natural but often leaves me lost and exhausted.

"Same," she says. "What sort of fiction do you write?"

Stories about death. Stories where good people are forced to do bad things. And then find that they actually enjoy it. "Um, everything, really. I dabble in this and that."

"Still trying to find your voice," Thalia muses. "Yeah, that's how

24

I feel too. I've tried writing both lit fic and genre, and I haven't quite decided where I feel most authentic."

Stop. Staring.

It's impossible not to, though. Not when she's speaking my truth. Authenticity is so hard to come by, and it's what I've always strived for in my writing. It means everything to me, because I can't be authentic anywhere else but on paper.

"I'm really hoping the program helps with that," she continues. "Maybe it'll help both of us find our voice, huh? I bet your voice is really special, Jane. Powerful." Her eyes meet mine, and I can't look away. I wonder what it would be like to lose myself in them, to plunge my fingers into the golden silk of her hair and feel her skull underneath my skin, only a thin layer of bone separating my hands from her brilliant, perfect mind.

Chapter 4

PRESENT DAY
SOUTH SAN FRANCISCO

Her website is beautiful. Clean and elegant, all of its focus on her book. *A Most Pleasant Death.* What a title. I read the description, which teases my skin into gooseflesh.

Marie and Sylvia used to be the best of friends. The kind of friendship that only comes once in a lifetime. It's just too bad that Marie had to move away, making the two friends drift apart. But when the two are reunited years later, they pick up right where they left off. Marie is now an Instagram star documenting her every move. Sylvia is quickly absorbed into Marie's frenetic, glamorous world of yacht parties and exotic trips. She even starts becoming Insta-famous herself. Everything's wonderful, or is it? When Marie gets involved in a shocking scandal, Sylvia quickly becomes trapped in her best friend's mess. The fans turn into trolls, with many of them lobbing death threats at both Marie and Sylvia. As everybody's obsession about Marie grows to a fever pitch, Sylvia has to go back to the past and discover the true

reason why Marie had to move away so abruptly all those
years ago, and what her supposed best friend is hiding.

No matter how I keep reminding myself to breathe, I keep losing my breath. *The kind of friendship that only comes once in a lifetime.* Now I'm no longer squeezing the mouse so hard. In fact, my hand is shaking. I snap the wristband a couple of times and try to control my breathing. It's us. I know it's us. She's written about us.

SHE WROTE ABOUT US!

The words flash in my head like one of those casino machines when you hit jackpot and it lights up with the accompanying *ding-ding-ding*! Us! She wrote about us! Flashing in neon lights, on off on off. Us! All these years, she, too, hasn't managed to leave me in the past. This is Thalia trying to get me to come back to her. This is a love letter written to me.

I try to get my breathing back under control as I click on her About page, but I don't know why I bother because there's a huge picture of her, and by god, she is perfect. Her hair is a shade lighter than it was in Oxford—an icy blond instead of the honey I was used to. It suits her, just as early thirties suits her. She's lost the baby roundness of her cheeks, and her cheekbones jut out in a way that makes me swallow, a way that I'm sure most runway models would kill to have. Her eyes are the same though. Impossibly large, ringed with heavy lashes and looking somehow innocent and yet knowing at the same time.

Thalia Ashcroft, writing as May Pierce, is the author of
A Most Pleasant Death. *The psychological suspense novel sold at a competitive seven-house auction, and its film*

27

rights sold at a five-studio auction before being won by Sony Pictures. Director Ambrose Wells and Oscar-nominated actress Margaux Thomas are attached to the film, which is reported to start production next summer. The book is due out in August of this year.

Her bio tells me next to nothing about her, but holy shit, her debut is a big book. A lead title. Those two words—"lead title"—are what most writers lust over. Every year, thousands of books are published by traditional publishers, but most of these books are midlisters—books that will only get the minimum backing and publicity, if any. Only a small handful of all published books are what are called the "lead titles," and these are the books that get everything—front placement at bookstores, magazine and newspaper ads, radio, TV, and online interviews with the author, pitches to Oprah's and Reese's book clubs in the hopes that they might pick these books out of the endlessly high mountain of books submitted to them every month. In other words, "lead title" is mecca for us writers. I've never even dared to dream about getting lead status at a Big Five publishing house. Not I, midlister at a small indie press who writes flaccid lit fic that nobody reads. Literary fiction is highbrow, often difficult to read because every sentence is full of hidden meaning. Virginia Woolf. Toni Morrison. Authors who don't make it easy for the reader; we're not here to spoon-feed the masses. In the past, I had dreams of being one of the great lit fic writers of my generation, but ever since I lost Thalia, I've lost whatever magic touch I had that made my writing shine. My teachers and classmates at Oxford used to celebrate my work, but now, after I've released two lackluster books, none of them ever bothers to respond to my emails. I have been forgotten.

In the News section of Thalia's website, I see that her cover reveal happened in *Entertainment Weekly*—yet more evidence of her publisher splashing out on her. I scroll further down and find the Publishers Marketplace announcement back when she got her book deal.

> *Denise Hazuki of Story House has bought, in a seven-figure deal, at auction, Thalia Ashcroft's debut adult suspense,* A Most Pleasant Death. *Pitched as* Gone Girl *meets* The Best of Friends, *the story follows a married couple after the husband goes missing, triggering an investigation of his seemingly perfect wife and the mysterious best friend who has recently reappeared. Agent Beatrice McHale brokered the deal for North American rights.*

Seven figures. Holy shit. I'd been expecting six figures, but this. This is out of this world. Most of us only ever dream of six figures. I spend time lurking on several writing forums, and the threads that discuss dreams and goals only ever have people posting about how they dream of one day getting a six-figure book deal. And even then, usually you'd get other writers snarking back and saying stuff like, "Keep dreaming." Us writers are a petty, insecure bunch. But the point is, no one has ever dared to say, "I wish I could have a seven-figure deal one day." You'd get laughed out of the forums.

But here she is, after a nine-year disappearance—not even a trace of an update online—screaming back into the public sphere with a unicorn deal. I can't help but laugh a little. That is SO Thalia.

I go to her Contact page and my mouth turns into a desert.

A contact form. My fingers hover over the keyboard. I don't know if I can do this. What would I say?

Hey, it's Jane. I know you wrote about me. About us.

No.

Hiii, it's Jane! It's been forever!

No.

How are you? It's Jane. I've been looking for you ever since—

No.

I can't write to her through a goddamned contact form. I've imagined us meeting again a thousand different ways—most of them cheesy meet-cutes like reaching for the same box of cereal at the same time, or crashing into each other on the sidewalk, our bodies slamming and recognizing each other before our minds catch up. Not a single one of my dream scenarios had me reaching out to her over a clinical contact form—*Contact Me! I love to hear from my readers!*

I'm not your reader, Thalia. I'm me. Jane. Your Jane.

I go back to the Home page and scroll down, and aha! There's a list of social media icons. I click on Instagram, because I need to see her first and foremost. So badly that my mouth is actually watering. As though I haven't eaten in years and my body knows it's about to nourished.

This account is set to private. To follow, please send a follow request.

NO. WHAT?

Why even bother having an Insta account if you're just going to set it to private?

The world is painted red for a moment. I'm gritting my teeth so hard that I hear the clack in my ears. I force my jaw to unclench. Take a deep inhale. Exhale. Another inhale. *It's okay, Jane. It's fine.*

Her profile picture is the same as the one on her About page. And she has—wow, she has over fifty thousand followers. Practically an influencer. I swallow, my cursor hovering over the Follow button.

But then I think of my Instagram page. I see it through her eyes. Fifty-six followers. Six posts, all of them mundane, all of them half-assed. Limp posts about my books at the behest of my publisher, who can't be bothered to market the books themselves and gaslit me into doing my own promotion. My profile picture a painfully awkward shot that had taken Ted four seconds to take on my secondhand Oppo phone. He'd offered to take more, but he'd also said it in a faux generous way: *I'm slammed with projects, babe, but I could pull an all-nighter if you want me to spend more time on your author photos?*

Like I could accept after he put it that way. Not sure why taking ten minutes to properly photograph me meant that he'd then have to pull an all-nighter, but if I asked him that, he'd give that sigh. Ted has The Sigh mastered. It somehow conveys every emotion a sigh has ever managed to convey—disappointment (*I expected you to understand, Jane*), exhaustion (*not this again, Jane*), and resignation (*okay, Jane, you win. AGAIN. Because this is my life, isn't it? Yes dear, no dear, I'll take the trash out, dear*). The Sigh means that he's won, because he's about to be magnanimous to placate his nagging shrew of a wife. So of course I say no, it's okay, this will do.

I could have taken photos of myself, I suppose. But just the idea of it makes my skin crawl. Even the term for it, "selfie," sounds unbearable, a stain on my generation that we'll never be able to wash off. So there's my sad Instagram page. Might as well be a giant stamp on my forehead that says: FAILURE.

I close the Instagram tab and go back to the list of social

media pages that Thalia's on. Twitter. She's got about fifteen thousand followers on it (I have one hundred), but her Twitter bio says: I'm not active on here. This is just for book updates. Instagram is my jam! Follow me on there @ThaliaAshcroft.

A small laugh escapes me. Follow her on Instagram. Well, some of us are trying, Thalia.

I close Twitter and open the third and last social media page: Facebook. The same profile photo appears. I scroll down and my heart stops, because this is it. A post about SusPens Con (ha, very cunning), a convention for suspense/thriller authors in New York City that takes place six days from now. And Thalia's going to attend. The post says: "Can't wait to see you there!"

I can't wait to see you there either.

I approach this carefully. Patiently. I make a cup of Ted's favorite hot drink—chai. He's white, not Indian, but he loves loving things from other cultures because it's so very progressive, so very NorCal. Here I am, my whole life spent trying to fit into white American culture, and all of a sudden, to be not-white, to be a person of color, is trendy. What a name, "Person of Color"—like whiteness is a blank canvas that you start with, and along the way, some of us are splashed and come out stained. But now, being stained is cool, so men like Ted are scrambling to show how worldly they are. The same people who, as kids, told me my lunches were "weird" and "stinky" now lecture me on the health benefits of tempeh and matcha.

Ted's turned his nose up at things that he thinks are too basic—the pumpkin spice lattes that I like, the American cheese I used to buy (now we buy feta and camembert and queso, which he pronounces "koo-ay-sow"), the Red Delicious apples

I like for their mealy texture and the way that I can masticate them with a forceful tongue (apples are too American for Ted, though he'll settle for Fujis if we must). I watch from the sidelines and wonder if maybe part of the reason he was so attracted to me in the first place is because of my not-quite-whiteness. I'm different enough to be exotic, but not so different that it scares him. Of course, if I were to even broach the edges of the subject, Ted would be horrified. *You really think I would marry someone just because they're—ugh—exotic?* He can't even say the word without choking on it. One time, I bought a bag of "exotic mixed nuts" from Costco, and Ted snorted and said, "Exotic? I thought we'd done away with that word." *It's a fucking bag of nuts, Ted*, I wanted to say, but I didn't, because then he'd tell me I don't get it, because I'm "white-passing," therefore I don't understand the struggles of real POC. He loves this term, "white-passing." Often uses it to remind me I'm just as white as he is, and thus am just as unequipped to tackle the gnarly, tangled subject of race as he is.

But this isn't the time to ruminate. I must focus. Eyes on the prize. I pour the tea, its fragrance spicy with cloves and cardamom, into Ted's favorite mug, and put a Trader Joe's dunker on a side plate. As a last-minute addition, I sprinkle a pinch of cinnamon on top of the chai.

I carry the offerings to his study, pausing after I knock, for him to say, "Yeah?" I go inside and have to swallow my anger again, because Ted's office is pristine. Bright and airy, not a single sheet of paper cluttering the space. Everything slotted neatly into its assigned place.

So Ted, the guy who has never lifted a finger to help me clean the rest of the house because he's always claimed he doesn't mind clutter, evidently DOES mind clutter, and not only that, but he knows how to fucking clean. He just doesn't do it because why bother when you've got your wife, basically an unpaid live-in maid?

But never mind that, I remind myself. That's minor stuff. Don't focus on it. We've got bigger things on our minds, don't we? So I plaster a smile on my face—not too big or he'll get suspicious.

He barely looks up from his big computer screen (a splurge he had deemed necessary for analyzing numbers, though honestly I think it's more to do with Fortnite). "I'm kind of busy—" Then he sees the chai and the side plate with the stupidly huge dunker on it and his eyebrows lift a little. "Wow, this is a nice surprise."

I suppose it is a nice surprise. I don't tend to come in here with tea and a snack. A small coil of guilt tightens in my chest, which makes me resentful. Did he say this is a "surprise" to drive home the fact that I don't often do things like this? To highlight what a negligent wife I am? No, I'm being too sensitive. Or am I?

When did every tiny thing between us turn into a barb? I hate to admit it, but it's probably my fault. In the early days, after the wreck that was Oxford, I'd contorted myself to fit the image of a normal, happy person because I needed to fill that void so badly. And when I'd met Ted, I'd fooled him. I kept up the charade for about a year after we got married. Then I got lazy. Let the mask slip a few too many times, and slowly, we changed from partners into adversaries. I wonder if he knows what I really am, and he's pushing so he can expose me.

"Thanks," he says, looking genuinely pleased as he slurps his tea. "What's the occasion?"

I shrug. "Just thought it would be nice."

"Well, it is." He looks at me quizzically before replacing the look with a smile. "This job's turning out to be a lot more complicated than I expected." He leans back with a sigh (not a sigh meant for me, so it's not The Sigh) and dunks the biscotti in before chewing it noisily. "How's your day going?"

I make myself nod. "It's okay. I was just looking up book events, and there's a book con that I think could be good for my career."

Ted's eyes flick toward mine, and my hackles rise. Oh shit. I wasn't careful or casual enough. He knows I'm here for something. My defenses clap into place, ready for his attack. "A book con?" he says.

He knows what a "book con" is. Bastard.

"You know, a book convention? Everyone in the industry will go—publishers, authors, agents, booksellers, librarians, reviewers . . . It's a great opportunity to network with other industry people." Good job, me. That's a great way of describing it—a smart business move.

Ted nods. "Oh, okay."

That's it? I wait another few seconds, but all he does is dip more of the dunker in his tea before taking another big bite and chewing carefully. Okay, so he's not even going to meet me halfway. He's making me say it, spell it out for him.

"There's one in New York that I want to go to," I blurt out. God damn it. *Have more fucking filters, self.* As soon as the words are out, I think of half a dozen ways I could have worded it better. But it's too late now. I've given Ted exactly what he needed, and he's not going to waste it. Of course not.

His eyes widen and he straightens up in his seat—*gosh, Jane, I'm shocked!*—and he places his tea and cookie on the table. Not so shocked that he's forgotten about the drink and snack, I see. "In New York? Like, New York City? The East Coast?"

How many fucking New Yorks are there? He really has to drive home how far away this con is.

"Yeah," I say in the most neutral voice possible. I am Switzerland. I will not be swayed.

"Sweetie, that's—" He pauses, then there it is. The Sigh. Except this one also conveys, in addition to all the other emotions, impatience (*we've been over this, Jane, why do you have to be so thick?*). "That's out of our budget."

Know what's really outside of our budget? I want to hiss. This fucking house. The way it dominates all of our income, its cumbersome presence sucking every available cent and giving me nothing in return. An overgrown backyard we hardly use, despite Ted's insistence that we would use it one day. His parents are avid gardeners; every month there's a new offering from them—a basket of yellow-green apples, a punnet of apricots, a bag of heirloom tomatoes, bulbous and ugly and disturbingly warm from the sun. And with each gift, there is an attached comment. "You kids should grow your own too! It's so rewarding!" With a pointed look at me, because Teddy Bear is just so busy, isn't he? They literally call him that—Teddy Bear. He pretends to hate it, but he adores the name and resents that I haven't picked it up, that I still call him Ted, or worse, Theo sometimes.

I would rather live in an apartment. I'd lived in an apartment with Mom for most of my life, and living in a house seems wrong, like wearing borrowed clothes. Mom had died in her apartment three years ago. A stroke. Her neighbor called to complain about the smell, and that was when they found her, two days before I was due my weekly visit. If she'd been living in a house, I would've been the one to discover her. We're not built for houses, Mom and I.

I push the thought out of my head and focus on the discussion. "It's a good investment for my career," I say. He likes this word, "investment." Uses it for all of his splurges. The stupidly expensive computer, the gaming chair, the adjustable standing desk that he never, ever stands at.

I can see him considering whether he should deploy The Sigh again. He thinks better of it. For now. "I know how much this writing thing means to you . . ." This writing thing. I try not to dwell on it. Instead, I brace myself for the "but."

"But . . ." He winces like what he's about to say is physically hurting him. *Look how much pain you're putting me through, Jane.* "I just don't think it's quite there yet, you know?"

I shake my head. No, I don't know, you fucker. I'm not going to make this easy for him. I'll watch as he struggles through the next few sentences, watch him prettify the words that are meant to cut me down.

"Well—" Now he sighs. It's not The Sigh, just a small one. An "I'm trying" sigh. "It's just—look, please don't take this the wrong way. But you're a midlist writer. What was your last advance for?"

He knows what my last advance was for because he adores how tiny it is, how insignificant it is compared to his freelancing fees. So I don't say anything. Let him say the numbers, rolling them in his mouth like peppermint candy to be savored.

"What was it, two grand?"

"Two thousand three hundred." Dammit. I wasn't going to say it, but I fell for his bait.

"Two thousand three hundred dollars," he announces with a satisfied nod. "Broken up into three payments."

This is how most publishing payments work. They're broken up into as many chunks as possible—the signing payment, the delivery and acceptance payment, and one last chunk when the book is actually published. Eight months it took me to write the book, a book about a depressed suburban housewife that is never going to earn out, never going to make me another cent. Ted likes to remind me that I am privileged because I can afford to write full-time thanks to him.

"A ticket to New York City at this time of the year is going to set us back what, five hundred dollars?"

Ha. I've prepared for this, you asshole. "Actually, only about a hundred if I fly budget."

He frowns. He hadn't seen this coming. Then he rallies, "Sweetheart, I don't think you should fly budget. That's not safe."

"I looked up their safety ratings"—I did not—"and they seem really good."

"And where would you stay? New York's expensive."

"No problem. I would stay outside of the city and commute in. I found places for around fifty bucks a night—"

"No, those places won't be safe. I can't possibly let you stay there."

All these nos disguised as concern. I want to scratch him, peel the skin off his face so I can see the thoughts oozing underneath like toxic mud. He just wants to keep me here, tethered to his side so he can always be the superior one of the two of us.

"And then there's the cost of food and travel and . . ." Here it comes, The Sigh. And it's a good one this time. He's been building up to it. It conveys the world. When it's done, he looks deflated and sad and empathetic. "I'm sorry, sweetie, but I just don't think we can afford it. We can't justify the cost of sending you to a con."

I make it out of his study and down to the basement just in time before I snap.

Chapter 5

NINE YEARS AGO
OXFORD, ENGLAND

Pemberton College is one of the smaller of Oxford University's colleges. But smaller doesn't mean any less impressive. Thalia and I wheel our luggage across the cobblestones from the bus station, about half a mile away from the college. I can't help but notice how nice her luggage is compared to mine—hers a sleek black Samsonite, mine a ratty thrift store affair, the fabric patterned with seventies-style roses and vines. Every step across the uneven cobblestones makes the wheels rattle. I'm half expecting them to pop right off, leaving me to heave it up onto my shoulders and stagger all the way to my fancy new college. I wonder what Thalia would do then. Leave me, probably. I won't blame her. Or rather, I will, but only secretly, and the blame would be tinged with so much want that it wouldn't matter anyway.

I shake my head. Try to focus on the beauty that's around me. There's so much of it, even all the way back at the bus station. Who's ever known a bus station to be beautiful? But Gloucester Green is surrounded by Gothic Revival–style buildings, so different from the laid-back, slouching buildings I got used to in

California. Everything around us is built in that same elaborate style, all impressive stone buildings with stained glass windows. Huge red buses trundle down the narrow streets, charming English names emblazoned on their sign boards: Kidlington, Almond Ave, Cowley Road.

I am charmed by it all, in a way, but in an even bigger way, I'm too absorbed by Thalia to really take in any of it. I sneak glances at her as we walk, trying to inhale the tiniest details about her. The way her hair turns into spun gold when the late afternoon English sun hits it. The way she licks her lips, moistening them ever so slightly with her impossibly pink tongue. Her lips are pouty in the way that most girls would have to rely on fillers to get; two full pillows that speak of innocent lust. If I were a guy, I would be obsessed with those lips.

Ugh, what is wrong with me? Why would I think that? But there's something about Thalia that makes me want to defile her, to see her kneeling before someone, her face awash with lust and shame, tinged with anger underneath a thick layer of pleasure, begging for more.

"Phew, I was not expecting such a long walk," Thalia says, and I nearly jump because holy shit, what the hell was going through my mind?

"Uh, yeah, me neither." I take in a deep breath of the brisk Oxford air to try and un-crazify my crazy thoughts. Even though it's only the start of autumn—mid-September; the end of summer, really—Oxford has a head start on the weather, and already I can smell the breath of winter on the edge of the wind.

"Still, I guess it's a nice walk," Thalia continues. "Though if I break the wheels of my luggage, my mom's going to murder me."

There's a beat before I realize it's my turn to speak instead of staring at her like I'm hoping to see the insides of her. "Yeah, same." I go over the words I just said, making sure they're appropriate under the circumstances, that I haven't just given myself away.

"Your mom's a bitch like mine?"

That startles me enough to snatch me out of my anxiety spiral. I don't know why it should; it's not like I know Thalia. We met two hours ago, and the whole bus ride here, we only made small talk about the master's course. Why should I be surprised that she doesn't like her mother?

Because. In the past two hours, I've concocted this entire image of Thalia. Thalia comes from a family with 2.5 children and a golden retriever–Lab mix named Ginger or Biscuit or Cookie. Definitely some kind of food, anyway. Her mother is a "homemaker," not a housewife. She makes rhubarb tarts from scratch, using locally sourced butter that comes wrapped in wax paper and twine. Her father is an architect / lawyer / finance manager who owns a little bachelor pad in the city so he can work late nights and fuck his secretary without staining the high–thread count sheets at home. Mom knows about it but turns a blind eye; she's benignly happy in suburban heaven, plus she can twist Dad's guilt into a new pair of princess-cut diamond earrings, or maybe an emerald necklace surrounded with leaf-shaped diamonds. She hasn't decided yet. Thalia is the baby of the family; you can tell because she's so innocent and unspoiled. Totally unprepared for the likes of me. Ripe for the plucking.

But now, with that one little question, Thalia's ripped apart this image I've built of her family. I can't tell if that pleases or angers me. I don't like having to rearrange my thoughts, to reorient them like this. It's confusing. Unnerving. And what do I say to that? It's not normal interaction to call your mother a bitch, especially not to someone who's effectively a stranger, surely? I want to encourage further interaction without revealing too much of my own bitch of a mother.

"I can relate to that," I say finally. I read once that this is something you say as a form of commiseration, an updated version of "I understand." Saying, "I understand," opens you up to backlash, because you can't, in fact, "understand" what someone else is going through, not even when you've gone through the same thing yourself. Because everyone processes things differently. Or some such bullshit, I don't know.

It works, anyway. Those porno lips stretch into a smile. She has a dimple on her left cheek. I hadn't noticed before because I'd been sitting on the other side of her, but wow, that dimple. "I had a feeling you might," she says.

I'm about to ask her more about her mother, her father, and her 1.5 sibling(s), but Thalia says, "I think we're supposed to turn right here," so we do, down a narrow side street, and suddenly, Pemberton is there.

It's like going through some enchanted passageway. The noise of St. Aldate's is muffled by the closely packed buildings, and Pemberton is so much bigger than I'd expected. What the hell have I landed myself in? I'd read that it was one of the smaller Oxford colleges, meant only for graduate courses, large enough to house only a hundred students. About fifty more students live off campus, but I've scrimped and saved, existing only on ramen, and taken out staggering loans. I had to have the full Oxford University experience. No off-campus apartments for me. I wonder where Thalia's staying, and the thought sends a jolt of excitement through me. Maybe we'd be roommates, and I'd be able to observe her all the time, catch a glimpse of her shedding that skin of perfection at night, because there's no way that anyone can be this wholesome, this brilliant, all the time. But no, I recall belatedly that Oxford only has single rooms, a fact that I had celebrated when I found out months ago, but now detest because it means there is no chance of Thalia and me rooming together.

There's a giant wooden gate at the entrance of Pemberton, and a side door carved into the gate that has been left open. I let Thalia go through first, because I'm half-certain guards are going to swarm us at any second and tell me I'm a fraud who needs to be deported back to the US. Right through the gate is a guard's office with the words "PORTER'S LODGE" above it. We go inside, and a self-important guard wearing a black suit and a bowler hat says, "New students, are we?"

I am, technically, a new student here, but when this man in a black suit and a black hat asks that, the answer screams out of my head, leaving me with Mom's voice. *What do you think you're doing, sweetie? Going to that posh school with the posh kids? You're going to the same school the kids I raised go to. They're gonna know you're not one of them right away.*

I know she's not wrong. When I was little—I don't know how old, but definitely too little to be left alone at home—Mom was called in for a weekend because the people she worked for had to travel someplace suddenly. An "emergency" golf trip, maybe, or an "urgent" ski trip, who knows. They needed Mom to come in to take care of their kid, and they didn't care that she had to find a caregiver for her own kid on such short notice. None of the neighbors or the aunts could watch me, so after she came to the end of her frantic search, Mom got this determined look and said, "You'll just have to come with me. You and Nectarine are about the same age. You can play with each other."

These kids' names are always some such ridiculous ones—some sort of fruit, or a color (always Blue, never Pink, to show defiance toward gender roles), or an emotion (one of them was called Jubilation).

Anyway, Nectarine took one look at me and knew I was "the help." The entire weekend, we "played together" as in she'd play with her toys while I waited patiently, at the end of which she'd point to the mess and say, "Clean." And I'd clean.

"So cute! You kids play so well together," Mom said, and I'd think, *You stupid bitch*.

The worst part of it was how naturally picking up after Nectarine had come to me. I didn't even hesitate when she'd point and tell me to bend over and clean up her mess. Go on my hands and knees and gather the strewn Duplo blocks. Inside, I seethed, wanting to fling myself at Nectarine and claw at her little face, feel my fingernails rip apart her soft, moisturized skin. But my body listened to her demands without a fight. It knew, even then, that I belonged to one class of people, and that there I would stay.

This guard—this Oxford porter—is looking at me like he knows exactly what I am. Like he knows I'm only able to afford being here by taking out massive loans and grants. I swear he's this close to telling me to go round the back, to the entrance for "the help." Thank god I have Thalia with me. She says, "Yup!" and gives him one of those smiles and you can just see the spell working on him. He blinks, his stern expression melting away, and his wrinkled cheeks turn rosy.

"Just uh—write your names down in this book here then, luv." He pushes a guest book toward us.

I watch her write her name down. Thalia Ashcroft. An elegant cursive spelling out an elegant name, nothing as stupid as hearts over the i. She hands the pen to me, her fingers brushing fire across mine, and I have to swallow before writing my own name down. Jane Morgan. A name as plain as I am, the letters ugly and stark underneath Thalia's cursive.

"Through this way," the porter says to us—to Thalia, really; he can't take his eyes off her either, as he leads us outside of the porter's lodge. "This is the Old Quad. Built in the fourteenth century. Have you seen anything more beautiful?" He points to a pristine quad surrounded by ivy-covered sandstone buildings on all sides. Both Thalia and I shake our heads obediently. I haven't, actually, been anyplace this impressive. The buildings around us look like a palace from a fairy tale, bursts of flowers hanging beneath every window. "Here you are: this is Highgate Hall, and the common room is right in there. All right then?" He smiles at us, twinkly eyes still on Thalia.

"Thank you," she says, shaving another ten years off his face. I swear he practically skips away from us.

"I think he's in love with you."

She barks with laughter, and I wonder what's so funny about what I just said. I'd merely pointed out the truth. Luckily, I'm saved from having to say anything because a woman greets us at the entrance of Highgate Hall.

"Hello! I'm Becca, your resident advisor. Which course are you here for?"

"Uh—" I can never just reply when a stranger asks me a question like this, even though I know the answer already. My brain

45

always has to add in an extra syllable just to buy myself that split second of time to put on my mask, make sure I'm presenting okay.

"The MFA in Creative Writing," Thalia says easily.

"Brilliant," Becca says, leading us inside Highgate Hall. The interior is just as stunning as the exterior—high, vaulted ceilings, hardwood floors covered with giant Oriental rugs, and Renaissance paintings adorning the walls. Becca goes to a large table, where an array of name tags and envelopes awaits. "Right, here we are. Names, please?"

We tell her our names, and she locates our materials. "The envelopes contain the keys to your rooms—I see both of you are rooming at Downing—and a welcome packet with information about the college and Oxford in general, that sort of thing. Let me know if you need anything, all right?"

"Great," Thalia says. "Thank you."

Becca has fallen under Thalia's spell as well, and it makes me want to scratch out her eyes. Seeing everyone fall for Thalia isn't easy to stomach. She's mine, not theirs.

"You'll have your induction seminar at the Sawyer Room at four o'clock, where they'll tell you about the process of matriculation and everything. And then right after that we'll have a welcome reception and dinner. You can go up that staircase there; there's a bridge that leads straight to Downing. Welcome to Michaelmas!"

The names and terms of everything are making my head swim, and I want to grab Becca and scream at her to talk in plain English. What the hell is "matriculation"? What's "induction," and why is she welcoming us to "Michaelmas" and not Pemberton? I snap my wristband before the curl of anger can overcome me and I actually do end up assaulting my resident advisor my first day here.

"Cool, thank you," Thalia says, and with that, she turns and walks toward the staircase. We lug our heavy bags up the stone steps, the sounds of our rapid breaths echoing in the cavernous stairwell. Once we're on the second floor, Thalia drops her bag with a loud sigh, turns to me, and whispers, "What the fuck is Michaelmas?"

I laugh, and it's the first genuine laugh I remember doing. My world is a whirling, broken mess and I don't belong anywhere, but Thalia is the eye of the storm, where everything is still and silent and I can finally breathe.

There is an actual fireplace in my dorm room.

It's no longer usable, of course, and instead of logs, there is a small bookcase sitting inside it, but still. It's a fireplace. Inside my dorm room. There's even space for a sofa and coffee table in addition to the expected single bed and study desk. And there's a sink in one corner of the room. What kind of bougie dorm room has a sofa set and a fireplace? All this for one student. Back home, there was no student housing at the community college, and when I transferred to Cal State for the final two years of undergrad, I was assigned a dorm room that would've been shared between me and two other girls; a recipe for disaster, so I'd opted to stay at home instead. Not the college experience I wanted, but freaks like me don't deserve the traditional college experience, and we sure as hell don't deserve a solo room with a fireplace in it.

The moment my door clicks shut, I abandon my heavy luggage and fling my purse and papers on the coffee table before striding across the room and opening the bay windows. Oh yeah, did I mention the room has actual bay windows? It overlooks the Old Quad, and the whole thing is so pretty I don't quite know what to do with myself. I stand there for a long while, watching students trickling in through the front gate. None of them is escorted by the porter, I can't help but notice. I guess we just got the special treatment because of Thalia.

Thalia. My breath comes out in a choked rush. I'm suffocating with need for her. Though need for what, I can't say exactly. Do I want to fuck her? Is that what all this is about? The thought of Thalia and me entwined in bed—in my new single bed—our sweat-damp bodies writhing against each other, makes me shiver. I'm not into girls. I—

A knock at my door, making me jump and sparking irritation like a jolt of electricity. I snap around, teeth gritted. I've just been on a long journey, I'm in a foreign country and a foreign college, and I just need one fucking moment to recenter myself so I don't fall apart. Is that too much to—

"Jane? What are you wearing?" Even muffled by the door, Thalia's voice carries with it the musical quality that I've come to love. "I can't decide what to wear to the dinner. You've got to help me."

All of the irritation melts away, replaced now with anticipation. Then, with it, a sudden barrage of anxiety. Oh god, this is it. We'll meet others at the induction, whatever that is, and then the welcome reception. Our course mates, or maybe even Pemberton students from other courses. Many people. My palms turn slick. I don't want to meet them. Not right now. Not ever. I want to exist in a place where it's just me and Thalia.

I cross the room and open the door. Fuck, it's hard to remember to breathe at the sight of her.

"Yes?"

"Have you decided what to wear to the welcome dinner?"

"Oh, right. No." I glance at the mirror above the fireplace. I look exactly how I feel—travel-weary and irritated by the world. My oversize jacket is rumpled, my hair flat with grease, whatever minimal makeup I had on rubbed off during my journey here. With a sinking feeling, I realize something that mortifies even me: I don't have anything that's appropriate for a "welcome reception." I hadn't expected anything formal. In college, we all existed in hoodies and torn jeans or yoga pants and Uggs, and during finals week, some of the other kids even showed up in their pj's.

I must look as lost as I feel, because understanding dawns on Thalia's face. "Come on," she says, grabbing my hand. "You can wear one of my dresses."

I open my mouth, about to resist, because no way, I'm not one of those girls who have female friends that they can swap clothes with. But she doesn't give me a chance to protest before she pulls me along, saying, "Oh, this is so exciting. I'm so glad we met each other, Jane. I'd be so lost without you otherwise."

She wouldn't. The thought is laughable. I would've been lost back at the Heathrow bus terminal, but Thalia swans through the world like she belongs everywhere, and everyone opens their arms to take her in, because who wouldn't? But I'm helpless to resist, letting her guide me the way a faultless little child guides a slouching beast in fairy tales, confident in their ignorance of what they drag behind them.

Her room is right across from mine, nearly identical except her bay window overlooks the Chapel Quad instead of the Old Quad. Somehow, in the time I spent just staring vacantly out of my window, Thalia has unpacked her belongings and put personal touches to her room. Books adorn the space—a handful placed in her bookcase in the fireplace, a few more on the mantelpiece, and yet more on the floating shelves above her study desk. Her bed no longer has the standard woolen blanket on it; instead, a fluffy white duvet rests like a cloud over it, complete with a crimson silk runner. It actually looks like a hotel bed instead of a dorm bed, and the small touch transforms the room completely.

"Have a seat," Thalia says, walking to her closet.

I perch hesitantly on her sofa, noticing that she's also draped a soft, rich blanket over it. I run my hand across the blanket, marveling at the softness. It's like touching pure wealth.

"That's my favorite blanket," she says, smiling over her shoulder as she rifles through her closet, and I snatch my hand back as though she's just caught me going through her underwear drawer. Luckily, she's turned back to face the closet and doesn't see me flinching. "What do you think of this?" She brandishes a dress the color of sunshine.

"No," I say flatly, and then immediately regret it. That came out a lot more brusque than I had intended. I never want to be rough with you, Thalia. I clear my throat, modulating my voice so it doesn't come out so raw. "Thank you, but it's not very—it's too—I can't—"

She watches me struggle for the right words for a second before coming to my rescue. "No, you're right. You're too sophisticated for such a bright color."

Sophisticated? I start to protest, to correct her—you're wrong, there's nothing sophisticated about me!—but she's already rifling through her closet again.

"This one," she says, and I want to protest because *I don't belong in your clothes, Thalia, I really don't*, but my words die in my throat at the sight of the dress she holds up. It's the color of old, dark blood. The kind of dress that promises danger and class in equal measure. The kind of dress I have always secretly wondered how I'd look in, except of course I've never had the money to buy one, nor do I have any events to attend in one.

"Yes, this is so you," Thalia says, striding across the room and placing the dress in my hands. She walks back to the closet, humming, then turns around with a frown when she notices the lack of movement on my part. "What's up? Come on, we don't want to be late."

She expects me to change here. In front of her.

"Oh," she says, reading my mind again. "I won't look. I'll be facing this way, searching for something for myself to wear."

Is this what girls do? Change in front of one another? Parading one's flaws like that? Unbearable. But I don't want to offend, so I stand up, feeling suddenly gigantic, aware that the room seems to have shrunk in the past thirty seconds. But true to her word, Thalia isn't watching me. She doesn't care what my body looks like. This is normal. Be normal.

I take off my rumpled shirt with slightly shaking hands, feeling goose bumps sprout across my bare skin as the cold air kisses it. My breath sounds so loud in the cramped room. My bra hikes up as I pull up my shirt, and for a horrifying second, my left breast almost pops out from underneath. I catch it in time, and now I truly am out of breath, like I've just run a marathon.

"Oh, I would kill for those abs," Thalia says, and I jerk around and sure enough, she's looking. She's LOOKING.

I should feel betrayed, but she's looking at me with admiration, and the small, sick part of me wants to arch my back so she can see more of me. Instead, I turn away from her, cheeks burning, curling in on myself as I yank on the dress over my head.

"I'll help you with the zip."

"No!" The word rips out without warning. I want to catch it, ram it back in my mouth, and swallow it, but it's too late.

"Okay," Thalia says, easy-breezy like I didn't just shriek at her like a crazed animal. "Just let me know if you need help. What do you think of this one? Too Alabama-housewife-at-country-club?"

"Uh, I don't know." I can't think. My mind's a mess, thoughts whizzing past and crashing into one another. I struggle into the dress, my limbs too long and ungraceful to move fast. I feel like a praying mantis. Once it's on, I realize with dawning horror that I do, in fact, need help with the zipper. "Um—"

She doesn't need me to say the words out loud, and for that small kindness, I love her even more. She simply crosses the room and puts one hand at the small of my back. All of my senses are zeroed in on a laser point of focus—Thalia's hand on my back. Then she pulls the zipper slowly up, up. My eyes flutter close. The barest caress of her fingertips across my skin, a trail of sensation I feel more acutely than anything I've experienced.

"Done."

Air floods my lungs. The world resumes spinning on its axis. Birds are chirping once more. Done, and just like that, her fingers are no longer on my skin, leaving me cold. I turn around slowly, my gaze on my feet.

"Oh, Jane," she breathes. I look up and the first thing I see are her eyes, like a lake. Like a mirror. I could get lost in them. "You look amazing."

There is no way in hell I look anywhere close to "amazing," but

Thalia doesn't give me a chance to reply before she takes the hem of her sweater and pulls it over her head. I've just resumed breathing, for god's sake.

Her body is creamy bronze, a stark contrast to the violet lace bra she wears. Her breasts are small but high, and I really need to stop staring, but I can't. Not while her ribs are right in front of me, each curved bone ever so slightly visible under that satiny skin. A gentle curve I could take a hundred years to trace. So different to her hip bones, which jut out like knife points. Her belly is so taut that there's a depression between her jeans and her skin, just enough for a fingertip to dip in. I swallow hard, and the sound is thunderous in the small room. God, she must have heard. I need to leave.

But Thalia is standing in nothing but panties, and you do not leave the room when this is happening. She shivers, smiling. "Gosh, it's a lot colder than back home, isn't it?" She doesn't wait for a reply before she pulls out another dress from the closet and shrugs it on. A forest green dress that brings out the creaminess of her skin and makes her hair shine like melted gold, off the shoulder so her clavicles are still in my face. She cinches the waist with a thin black belt, highlighting her tiny waistline, and I have never seen anyone make looking gorgeous so effortless.

"Come," she commands, and I don't even hesitate before I do so. I walk to her, each step bringing me closer.

"Sit. Let me do your makeup."

Ah. Right. Makeup.

I'm only used to doing makeup that makes it look like I'm not wearing makeup. Makeup that's worn to blend in, not stand out. But I feel helpless as I sit there and Thalia takes out a bag filled with brushes and lipsticks and powders. She dabs and smooths and draws, my face her canvas, and each touch leaves me wanting more. And when she uses her ring finger to rub lipstick on my lips, I nearly lose it, nearly jump up and grab her, relishing the frightened squeak she would surely make, like a rabbit that belatedly realizes it's stepped into a steel-toothed trap.

I jerk up to my feet, my heartbeat a roar of thunder. *Get it the fuck under control, Jane.*

"Whoa, you okay? Did I hurt you?"

The question makes me snort. No, Thalia, you did not hurt me. How ridiculous for the rabbit to ask if it has hurt the wolf. "No, I just—sorry, I—I'm not used to people touching me." Isthatnormalisitokaywillitoutme?

"Oh." A small line appears between Thalia's eyebrows for one second before it clears. "I'm sorry, I should've asked you first. I didn't mean to be so pushy. I get that way sometimes, so please let me know if I ever make you uncomfortable, okay?"

She's blaming herself. She, Thalia, a completely normal, friendly person, thinks she is at fault for my sociopathy. I don't know what to say to that, so I just shrug and nod. "Okay, yeah."

"Cool. Can you give me like five minutes to finish putting on my war paint?"

I would give her the rest of the time I have in this world if I could. I nod and head toward the window. I pretend to look out and enjoy the scenery, but the whole time, I can't stop sneaking glances as she applies things onto her already perfect face, wondering what it would be like to touch her, to run my fingers down her cheek, her mouth, and that incredible, thin neck of hers.

Chapter 6

The memory of that first day with Thalia possesses me. I can't believe I was about to let Ted derail my goal of getting to New York. I guess the years have just worn me down a lot more than I had thought. But when it comes to Thalia, nothing's too much, no cost is too great. When I'm done in the basement, I climb up with a purpose. My mind is swirling with images of Thalia—her laughter, that rumpled silk hair of hers, the way she looked at me sometimes, an all-knowing look underlaid with the ghost of a playful smile. And I think of how I had twined a scarf around her neck and squeezed and squeezed until she turned red, and my heart thrums taut and I can barely get back up fast enough.

I walk briskly to the bedroom and take out my jewelry box. It's mostly cheap things in here—Ted likes to adorn me with cubic zirconia. I don't mind; jewelry is frivolous, and I have no space in my life for frivolity. Ted's parents are the epitome of frivolity; every week, his father buys a rose for his mother, and every week, she somehow resists telling him he's an unimaginative moron and acts like she is surprised and delighted by the single rose.

The same thing, every week, for over forty years. I don't know why she hasn't killed him yet.

I rummage around the fake diamonds until I find the pieces I'm looking for. A ring and a necklace. The only things I have left from Oxford. My stomach clenches at the sight of them. The diamonds on both are ridiculously large. If Ted were to see these, he'd assume they're fake, just like everything else in the box. Which is precisely why I've tucked them in here, to hide in plain sight. Because these, like my time at Oxford, are painfully real.

The necklace is a simpler piece—a thin white gold chain with one huge diamond flanked by two smaller ones. The ring, on the other hand, is a monstrosity. A square-cut diamond the size of a cough drop. I select the ring and slide it into my pocket. It's too ostentatious for me to ever wear, so I might as well get rid of it. I only call out to Ted that I'm going to the store when I'm already halfway out the door, so he can't come lumbering out of his study and ask me to pick up some soy ice cream or whatever. He says, "Hmm?" but I don't wait to reply.

I drive down the street before I stop and look up jewelry shops. There's one fifteen minutes away from here. I click on directions to get there, and when I arrive, I take my time deleting my search history. Just in case Ted decides to be smart for the first time in his life.

The shop assistant takes one look at the ring and glances up at me again, his eyes wide.

"Please wait a moment, ma'am," he says, before going to the back room. He comes back out with an older man with wiry white hair and glasses with what looks like a tiny microscope attached to one of the lenses. The old man asks, very gently, "May I?"

56

I nod and watch as he inspects the ring. Then the worst happens. He asks, "May I inquire where you procured this ring?"

"Procured." Not "bought" or "who gifted you this ring." My guts turn into snakes and I almost throw up then and there. I snatch the ring from the velvet tray and mutter, "Never mind, I've changed my mind. I won't be selling this after all. It's a family heirloom."

"Wait, please, ma'am—"

But I can't. I need to get out of here before the walls close in on me. I rush out, half expecting a cage to slide down on me as I head for the front door, but nothing happens and I walk out into the late-afternoon sunlight without anyone chasing after me. Outside, I don't even pause to catch my breath. I half run until I'm safely round the corner before I stop.

Stupid, stupid! I need to be more careful. What was it that gave me away? I slip the ring back into the inside pocket of my bag and smooth down my hair. Glancing up, I catch my reflection in a store window. That'll be it, then. I don't look like someone who would be in possession of such an expensive piece of jewelry. I'm in loose-fitting jeans and a shirt and ratty cardigan—my "midlist author who's given up on life" outfit.

It's too late to go home and change now, so instead, I look up pawnshops. Here in South San Francisco, there's a depressing number of them around. I pick the one with the highest number of star ratings and drive over there.

I've never been to a pawnshop before, and the only things I know about them are things I learned from the movies. It's surprising how close reality resembles the movies. The pawnshop clerk inspects the ring for a few minutes, glancing up at me and back at the ring, frowning. I swallow, try to look less shady. Not sure how, but I try to channel my innermost wealthy-white-lady-who-just-happens-to-want-to-pawn-off-a-magnificent-ring aura. Finally, he punches some numbers into a calculator and slides the calculator through the little slip hole under the bulletproof sheet separating the two of us.

I look at the number on the calculator, and a laugh burbles up my chest and into my throat, where I manage to swallow it back down. Well, holy shit. Ten grand. It would more than cover my airfare as well as accommodation and food and still leave me with a sizable amount to do whatever I need to do. I want to jump and scream, "YES!" but I've watched enough shows to purse my lips and say, "Is that all? Never mind, then."

In the end, I walk out of the pawnshop with twelve thousand dollars. I only allow the grin to take over my face when I'm outside of the shop. Twelve thousand dollars. It feels like a huge fuck you to Ted, though I'm not sure why that is. I practically dance my way back to the car.

Back at home, I move sneakily past Ted's office and into the bedroom, where I stand, for a minute, wondering where to hide my wad of cash. That's the problem with twelve thousand dollars; it's thick and heavy and kind of a challenge to hide. I'm about to head for the closet when the door clicks open and in comes my husband, trying to give me a goddamned heart attack.

"What the fuck?" I say.

"Everything okay? You look like you've just seen a ghost."

The hallway outside of our bedroom is made of old, rickety wood. It creaks like a demon with a grudge, and at night, when I wake up needing a glass of water, I have to step very, very carefully at specific spots to avoid waking Ted. Ted, on the other hand, never gives me the courtesy of picking the non-creaky spots; when he goes to the kitchen in the middle of the night, he makes sure I know it.

But now, when it matters, he's able to make his way through the creaky hallway as quietly as a fucking cat.

"I'm okay. You just surprised me a little, that's all." My hand's still in my bag, clutching the thick envelope. I have to consciously tell my fingers to unclench and instead, to reach for something else. Anything. They brush up against my phone, and I grab it with relief and take it out. *I was just taking my phone out of my bag, Ted, no biggie.*

"Where did you go?" Ted says in this ultracasual way that tells me there's nothing casual about his question.

"Oh, I just went to Safeway. Just wanted to get some . . ." Some what? "Stuff. Some Swedish Fish." I hate Swedish Fish. I don't know why that popped into my head.

"I thought you don't like Swedish Fish." It comes out as an accusation, which immediately makes me bristle, because if there's one thing I can't stand, it's my husband using that tone of voice with me.

"I just had a sudden craving for them." How many times can I say the word "just"?

Ted looks at me, and for a second, I wonder what made me agree to marry this man. We never had the same chemistry that Thalia and I had. I never wanted to carve my name into the curves of his heart the way I fantasized doing with Thalia. I never had the need to leave an imprint of myself on him. I think back to five years ago, when I met him at the most basic of all places—a Starbucks.

Someone had taken my drink, and Ted had seen my confused, about-to-be-enraged expression and bought me another latte.

And I remember thinking then that here's a nice, safe person. I've had enough of my own un-niceness, of the disaster I had left Oxford in. I was only in my twenties, but already my life had been a series of mishaps and tragedies. I was ready for nice and safe, and if ever there were two words to describe Ted, they're "nice" and "safe." Of course, over time the veneer of niceness became abraded, whether by natural wear and tear or maybe he'd rubbed against my sharp edges one too many times. Now, as I look at him, I realize that those two qualities that had attracted me to him have turned into the bars of my jail cell. He's still nice, but in a very conscious, calculating way that serves to highlight my own lack of niceness. And he's still safe, but it comes in the form of this cumbersome house, which we will only manage to pay off seventeen years later, its presence holding us back from making any brash financial choices. I'm in a prison made out of polite words and a steady mortgage, and the bars had descended so gently that I hadn't felt them coming.

I know what he's about to say before he says it, and there's a moment where I see myself lunging at him with something sharp—maybe the letter opener that had ended my time at Oxford prematurely. I see the glinting point of it pressing into his skin, making a small indentation at first, and then finally breaking through, its tip parting the skin silkily, so smoothly that not a sound is made as it goes past skin and fat and into flesh and bone. Not a single sound.

Then he says it and breaks the spell.

"Can I have some?"

He doesn't like Swedish Fish either; nobody likes Swedish Fish, and he's only asking me this because he knows that I haven't, in fact, been to Safeway, and I haven't, in fact, bought any Swedish Fish.

"They were out." And if he drives to the store to check, then I will know that our marriage is truly over.

"Aw, that's a shame. Okay." He stays there for a second too long, still watching me with those watery blue eyes of his—who would've known that blue eyes could look unattractive—then he turns, scratching his belly, and slouches out of the room. The wooden boards sing as he treads on them. Just like that, he's once again magically lost the ability to walk without making noise.

I wait until he's out of earshot before releasing my breath. Jesus, that was close. I open up my underwear drawer, then shut it again. Too obvious. I go into the bathroom and open up cabinets and drawers before finally spotting the boxes of tampons that I buy in bulk at Costco. Perfect. Ted is the kind of guy who winces every time the subject of menstruation comes up, as though it's hurting his delicate senses. He'd never look in here. I open one of the giant boxes, stuff the wad of cash in it, and tuck the box in the farthest reaches of the cabinet.

Later, I wait until after dinner (massaman curry; nothing as basic as pasta, though Ted complains that I have put too many cloves in) before I skulk off to the bathroom and then come hurrying back with a somewhat excited smile on my face. Not too excited, mind, because we don't want Ted to get suspicious.

"Hey, guess what?" I hate the way my voice sounds—so artificial, so conscious of itself.

Ted glances up from the TV. He's watching a food travel show on YouTube where some white guy is in rural Vietnam eating bugs. We've never been to Vietnam, but the other day, I heard Ted saying to his friends over Fortnite that he loves authentic pho, the kind you could only get at alleyways in Saigon. How the hell would you even know what authentic pho from the alleyways of Saigon tastes like, I wanted to scream, but I restrained myself, because that's what marriage is about. Restraint, control, folding myself up into as tiny a square as possible. "Look what they're eating, babe," he says, turning back to the TV. "Look how huge those water bugs are. Revolting. I mean, no disrespect, of course." Of course not. Never any disrespect from Ted, the woke white man.

I lick my lips and swallow. Try again. "So I just got a sort of exciting email from Toni. You know, my agent."

"Oh?" Ted brightens up and finally gives me his full attention. "Did your last book earn out?"

The knife in my gut twists. He knows my sales have been lackluster. The idea of earning out my measly advance is laughable, given how little publicity my publisher has given my books. He's only making that his guess to set the bar impossibly high, so that when I inevitably fail to meet it, we'll both know what a disappointment my writing career is. What a disappointment I am. It's his way of putting me back in my place.

Normally, this would enrage me enough to pick a fight with him, bicker over stupid shit like him leaving his crap everywhere, but tonight, I won't be distracted from my goal. Not when the goal is Thalia. So I force a smile and say, "No, I haven't earned out."

He sighs, but before he can turn back to the TV, I quickly say, "But I emailed Toni about the possibility of going to SusPens Con, and she thought it was a really great idea."

"Hmm," he grunts, already getting swallowed up by the video, in which the Woke White Guy is explaining to us that bugs have a ton of protein and are really good for you, so we should get over our fear of them and start crunching down on their hard little bodies.

This is good, actually. Since he's not really paying attention, I don't have so much heat on me. I let the words out in a rush. "Anyway, she emailed my publisher and they agreed and said they're going to pay for my trip and my tickets to the con."

"Wait, what?" Now I've got his attention. He actually presses the Mute button, plunging us into sudden deafening silence. There's nothing acting as a buffer, and I find it disconcerting, like, *sorry, Ted, I know I asked for your attention but I don't actually want it, or rather I don't want a hundred percent of it, maybe just sixty percent so your bullshit radar doesn't ever ping.* "Did I hear you right? Harvest Publishing is sending you to a con? On their dime?"

I'm trying hard to get a read on his emotions, picking apart his words and his tone frantically to gauge just what he's thinking. Is that sarcasm I detect? No, I think he's genuinely surprised, and why wouldn't he be? It is surprising. Harvest is a small independent publisher, not even one of the big indies but a small one whose advances average low four figures. That's not the kind of house that can afford to send its midlist authors to cons, especially cons that are on the other side of the country.

I don't know if Ted's aware of all these semantics, and my whole body is taut, waiting to see if he'll spot it, if he'll smell the whiff of bullshit. And what he might do if he were to detect it.

Slowly, dreadfully, my head inches forward. Then back. A nod.

And then suddenly he's up from the couch, this big bear of a man coming at me, and everything inside me shrieks. If I had a knife in my hand I would have stabbed him with it and called it self-defense, and I wouldn't have been lying.

But I only stand there, rooted, because the saying "flight or fight"? It's wrong. It's flight or fight or fucking freeze and that's me; that's what I've always done. I freeze and my husband comes at me and he—

Hugs

Me.

It takes a while for my brain to catch up and process the thing Ted is doing and feed it to the rest of my body so that my limbs stop mid-flail. It's a hug. A hug. Something you do to someone you like.

I close my eyes and let myself thaw, just a bit, leaning into his embrace. It's not unpleasant, hugging my husband. He smells familiar—vanilla sugar and something musky, a distinctly male odor. I let my breath out, sagging into him.

"Wow, I'm so happy to hear that," he murmurs, shifting.

I feel it then, him getting a semi, pushing against my thigh. I want to shove him off me.

"You fully deserve this, Jane," he says.

I don't push him away. Instead, I smile at him and nod.

"Didn't I always tell you to ask Toni for things? She works for you. Remember that, babe."

"Mm-hmm."

"I'm coming with you, okay?" It's not a question. It's a statement disguised as a question, and if I were to say no, there would be a price to pay later. "We'll make a trip of it, stay somewhere nice. Go to Lombardi's."

A trip of it when just hours ago, there was absolutely no money in the pot to spare for this. I want to rail at him, to push my fingers into his eyes until I can feel the squish of his brains against them, and then yank them out, unravel the curls of his brains so I can read his mind and see just the sort of shit that's floating through it.

I want him to stop talking, I want me to be able to celebrate this moment of possibility without the weight of his idiotic words clumping down on it, making it sag and strain. I've earned this. I've outsmarted him and he can't stand it; that's why he wants to shove his way into this, to spoil it all somehow.

But it doesn't matter. He can come. I don't care. As long as I can see Thalia in the flesh, hear that throaty voice of hers, I will be okay. I will bear it. I will go through anything for her.

Chapter 7

NINE YEARS AGO
OXFORD, ENGLAND

The welcome dinner isn't as bad as I had feared. No, it's much worse.

I thought it would be bad when Thalia and I walked out of Downing and ran into a clot of students in the Chapel Quad. They all smiled at us, and one of them said, "Off to the reception dinner?" Obviously we are, asshole. As though there were anyplace else we might be going at this time, dressed like this. But Thalia smiled back and then did the unthinkable—she introduced herself, and then me, and before I knew it, we were swallowed by their group.

And so here I stand on what's apparently one of the most beautiful quads in Oxford, wearing a dress that doesn't quite fit me, grasping a glass of chardonnay like it's a lifeline. Oh yes, there's wine and canapés set out at the quad, where we're doomed to mingle before dinner begins. My first ever cocktail hour. I've never attended a cocktail hour before. One does not go to such things on one's own, and I've always been on my own.

The small group of students has swelled into a crowd. An actual crowd of people, all of them mingling, lots of straight-toothed smiles, and the conversation. The conversation!

I catch snatches of "Belize for the summer—" and "undergrad at Yale—" and "Boston Consultant Group—." Who went to the better school for undergrad? Who's got the better job? Whose penis is bigger, yours or mine?

I cast a desperate search for Thalia. She's abandoned me. We'd been standing next to the canapé table when an attractive blond guy had approached her and asked her which course she's taking. She'd answered for the two of us, which I didn't mind. In fact, I appreciated it. But then as the conversation stretched unbearably, more and more people had joined in, and I had taken a small step backward because groups of people are dangerous, groups of people are like wolf packs, and yet more people had buzzed toward us, no doubt attracted by Thalia's presence, and I took another step back and another step back and before I knew it, I had been spat out of the group.

I finish my glass of wine and walk toward the table to discard my glass. I should stop drinking. I don't do well with alcohol. My inhibitions aren't there to stop me from doing stupid things, dangerous ones.

"There's always one," someone says.

I look up to see a slightly pudgy girl with mouse-brown hair. She's wearing a black dress that's probably been marketed as the LBD, but it looks all wrong on her, the capped sleeves highlighting the pallid flab of her arms, the material cheap and shiny so it highlights every roll and bulge. She's drinking red, and when she smiles at me, I see that it's stained her teeth, making her look monstrous. It's like looking in a mirror. I have no idea what she's talking about, and neither am I interested in knowing, so I don't reply. Instead, I pick up another glass of white.

She takes my silence as an invitation to keep talking. "That girl," she says, nodding at the swarm of Pemberton students with Thalia dead center. "There's always one, isn't there?" A long sigh, followed by a deep gulp of wine. "The golden girl."

I hate the way the words sound rolling out of her sloppy mouth. Dirt-smudged and bored, like Thalia isn't anything special, like she isn't one in a million. One in a billion.

The heat of rage caresses me deep in my belly. I snap the wristband.

"What's that?" she says, watching me from the sides of her bullfrog eyes. "Do you have anxiety?"

I take a long sip of wine so I don't have to answer, but it doesn't matter anyway. The charmless girl is still talking. I think she likes that I'm silent. I think she's used to people ignoring her.

"My sister's like that," she's saying, "except she just flicks her own arm. Not organized enough to always wear a wristband."

Huh. That's actually a good solution for the times when I snap the wristband so hard that it breaks, leaving me untethered. Uncaged. I make a mental note of it.

She gives a brittle, eager smile before taking another swig of wine, and I realize that like me, she's nervous.

"I'm Pam, by the way. What's your name?"

I don't want to give her my name, but I'm trapped. I'm here to make a fresh start, and fresh starts don't involve walking away mid-conversation with your schoolmate, even if said schoolmate is as interesting as a piece of chewed gum.

"Jane." One-word answers. That's safe.

"Jane." Her smile turns even more eager, if that's possible. "I like that name. Down-to-earth. Like Pam, I guess. I feel like everyone here's got some fancy name—they're either exotic or, like, one of those long, old ones. You know—Hubert Weatherby the Third."

That gets a smile out of me, because among the throng of people who had swarmed me and Thalia at the canapés table, there had been a "the Third." I think he was a Robert though, not a Hubert. I'm sure there's a Hubert here somewhere in this crowd, and perhaps a Rupert or two.

"Which course are you doing here?" Pam says. She's actually clutching her wineglass with both hands, strangling the stem with her pudgy fingers. I'm torn between pity and secondhand embarrassment for her.

"Creative Writing."

"Ooh, that one's intense, I hear."

Is it? My stomach twists, whether from the alcohol or from anticipation, I don't know. But an "intense" course that involves Thalia sounds like something straight out of my darkest dreams.

"I hear that every year, about a quarter of the students flunk out of the course."

What? I hadn't even been aware that you could flunk out of a Creative Writing course. "How do you flunk out of a Creative Writing course?"

Pam shrugs. "By writing badly, I imagine."

I suppose it seems obvious when she puts it that way.

"I'm doing the master's in Women's, Gender and Sexuality Studies."

I have to stop myself from snorting out loud, because of course she is.

"I'm kind of really nervous about it, are you? I'm from March? You know it? No, of course you don't. It's a small town outside of

Cambridge," she says apologetically, as though the fact that she came from a small town is a personal affront to me.

"I'm from Oakland." San Francisco's armpit, a half-abandoned, half-industrial city that's being threatened by gentrification, if the techbros can be bothered to colonize Oakland. My own answer startles me, because I usually tell people I'm from San Francisco. Why admit to Oakland when you can cover yourself under the sheen and sparkle of SF? But something about Pam is so sad and honest that it compels me to drop the act, if only just a little. I hadn't expected English girls to be like Pam, so unworldly and unattractive. I suppose I've only ever seen the ones on TV, the English Roses fed on a diet of poetry and wine.

"Oakland, that's nice," Pam says, nodding like she knows of it. Nobody who isn't Californian knows of Oakland, but she's trying so hard. It makes me feel a tad better, being with someone who's even more out of place than I am. Though, with a nasty jolt, I realize then that I don't know if Pam does look more out of place than I do. I look down at the dress I've borrowed, by far the most expensive thing I have ever worn. It doesn't fit me well; Thalia's waist is smaller than mine, so her dress is ungracefully tight around my midsection, squeezing so that my lower belly bulges out. My boobs are bigger than hers, so the chest section is also tight, showing the lines where my bra is slicing into my skin, squashing my boobs like grotesque balloons. The thought hits like a fist. I'm no better than Pam.

I'm about to make my excuses and rush back to Downing to lock myself in my room for the rest of the evening when I become aware that the crowd is suddenly headed toward us. Because Thalia is leading them here. I sense Pam turning rigid with fear at the advancing crowd.

"There you are," Thalia says, and truly, she is dazzling in all senses of the word. The nearness of her knocks every other thought out of my head, and I am left confused and off-balance. "I've been looking for you."

Pam stares at me with mouth slightly open. I'd been feeling slovenly only moments ago, but now, as the subject of Thalia's smile and Thalia's kind attention, I feel myself unfurling once more, blooming from deep inside the rotten core of me.

"I'm Thalia." Thalia extends a hand toward Pam. I can't help noticing how slender her wrist is compared to Pam's. How Pam's meaty hand completely swallows Thalia's. The sight of it sends a thrill down my back. So thin, so snappable. After she shakes Pam's hand, Thalia turns to her side, and that's when I notice the girl standing way too close to Thalia. A girl I hate on sight.

"And this is Ani," Thalia says, pronouncing it Ah-nee, and not Annie.

Ani is Asian, and she is everything I'm not—tall, slender, her features flawless.

My entire being wants to cringe away from her. Growing up, my Asian-ness was the source of poverty, the reason for everything that was lacking with my life. I was used to Asians like my mother—women with bedraggled hair, stooped shoulders, faces lined with bitterness and need. I was used to rejecting it, to running away from it. But Ani is unapologetically Asian, and fabulous. Unlike the rest of us, she's not wearing a dress, but a navy blue jumpsuit that hugs her slim figure, the kind of expensive outfit that is all elegant clean lines.

She looks down her nose at me and Pam, her dark eyes lined with eyeliner so sharp it looks like it could cut me, and there's a gnawing in my stomach, because I am just now realizing that Ani is grouping me together with Pam. Whatever magic had captured me today and fooled me into thinking I might be on the same level as Thalia, under Ani's aloof, derisive gaze, it dissipates, and I am thrown to the curb, exposed for the fraud I am.

Everything goes by in a bit of a daze after that. I'm vaguely aware of making our way across the Chapel Quad and into Haygrove Hall, aka the dining hall. It's styled like a medieval great hall, complete with an arched roof with hammer beams, large bay windows, chandeliers, and wood-paneled walls, on which hang portraits of disapproving white men. In other words, yet more hallowed, ostentatious wealth that serves to remind me of how much I don't belong.

Worse still, at some point, Thalia says to Pam, "I love your dress. Prada?"

And she flushes with pleasure and nods eagerly. Prada. And here I had thought it was a cheap dress from one of those Chinese websites. But no. Pam—fucking Pam—is wearing Prada. The thought that if I hadn't bumped into Thalia at the bus station, I would've come here wearing a dress from Ross Dress for Less makes bile rise up my throat.

We're seated at long tables, each place set with three plates and three different glasses. I'm about to slide into the seat next to Thalia when Ani slinks in between us with a smooth, smiling, "Oops, sorry." I end up sitting next to Ani, with Pam on the other side of me. I can't believe we're all doing our master's when it feels so much closer to high school than even college did.

"So, Jane," Ani says. My name comes out poisonous from her dark plum lips. She touches the tips of two fingers to her chin, and a giant sapphire ring glints on her index finger. "Thalia tells me you're doing Creative Writing as well."

"Yeah. You?"

"MBA. Cursed to help out with the family business. You know how it is."

I don't know how it is, actually. I'm about as far from knowing how it is as humanly possible. But I'm saved from having to answer when a server comes bearing two bottles of wine, one red and one white. Ani cocks an eyebrow at him, and he smoothly pours the wines into our glasses.

"Cheers," Ani says lazily, lifting her glass of red wine. I lift mine, too, and manage to spill a little bit over the side. The corner of Ani's mouth crooks up. I amuse her. I want to run away and hide. I want to smash my wineglass and push the sharp edges into her porcelain face, see which one cracks first—the shard of glass or that fake face of hers?

"This year is going to be so fun," Thalia says, leaning toward me and holding out her glass. "Bottoms up, everyone!"

Ani doesn't take her eyes off me as she downs her glass in one long, smooth swallow, and though I almost choke, I end up draining mine as well.

It was a trap. Of course it was a trap. I should have known, the way Ani's eyes never left mine, the languid, predatory gaze crawled over my skin, her mouth curved into a constant smirk. The way she made sure my glass was always full.

By the end of dinner, I can barely walk back to Downing. The only saving grace is that everybody else seems just as sloshed as I am—Pam keeps talking about how "pissed" she is, and Thalia is looking more flushed than before. There's a guy—Edward; of course there's an Edward here—who's taken it upon himself to "make sure you ladies get back all right." He has his hand on the small of Thalia's back, a sight that sickens me. But before I can lunge forward, put myself between sweet Thalia and Edward the creep, Edward the would-be date rapist, Thalia turns, catching my eye, and says, "Jane and I live on the same floor. We'll be okay, won't we, Jane?"

I don't remember the walk up the stairs in Downing. Next thing I know, I'm falling asleep without bothering to wash off the makeup that Thalia had applied on my face, my head swimming in nauseating circles, my room spinning, hating myself. Last thought that crosses my mind is if Thalia's back in her room okay. I try to recall if I'd deposited her like a lost treasure safely in her room before stumbling back to mine, and then the darkness descends.

I can barely choke down the breakfast buffet the next morning. I sit at the far corner of the massive dining hall, avoiding the morning crowd, and force myself to eat one of the roasted tomatoes and drink a glass of OJ—vitamin C is good for hangovers. I'm about to leave the hall when the doors swing open and in come Thalia and Ani. They're chatting easily, and the sight of them sours my already queasy stomach. I almost vomit, literally. They came in together. Together, as a single unit. I hunch further into the corner so they won't see me, my cheeks blazing hot.

How did that happen? I scramble through the tangle in my mind, trying to sort out the events of last night. Thalia and I had staggered back to our rooms together. There was laughter. Who was laughing? I remember talking, though the actual words themselves now escape me. I have no fucking clue what I might have said to her. Something awful? Something that might have repelled/alarmed/scared her? *Don't be scared of me, Thalia*, I want to scream until she promises that she isn't, that we're still the best of friends, forever and ever, amen.

Had she stolen out of her room after that? Tiptoed past mine—careful, don't wake Jane the freak—and gone to meet up with Ani? There's nothing quite like the exquisite pain of being excluded, your presence purposefully blotted out. After careful deliberation, we have deemed you, Plain Jane Morgan, unworthy of our company.

What was it that had finally dealt the killing blow, that had strangled the blossoming friendship between Thalia and me? The answer comes naturally, quickly. Ani. Ani has whispered some poison into Thalia's ear in a bid to steal her from me, and it worked.

I sneak out of the dining hall like a rat and scurry all the way back to my room. Only when I've shut the door do I let myself unravel, leaning against the door and breathing deep. I snap the wristband and think of Ani. Ani, with her black-painted eyelids and her elegant clothes and long limbs, which, like a spider, she has wrapped around my Thalia.

The shatter of glass wrenches me out of my black state, and I realize that I've thrown my coffee mug across the room. Shit. I hadn't even noticed that I'd taken a coffee mug from the dining room. Coffee is dripping in light brown rivulets down the wall, and I really should mop it all up, but I don't have time. This is the first day of my master's course, and I'm not going to let Ani ruin that too. Forget Thalia. Forget everyone. I'm not even here to make friends; I'm here to learn the craft of writing. I grab my things—a new spiral-bound notebook, my favorite pen, and a folder full of coursework material that had cost an annoying amount to print out, and I hurry out the door, trying not to think of what I might say when I see Thalia in class.

Our first class plunges us into the deep end. Boom, straight away a fiction workshop. There are fifteen of us in total, ranging from early-twenties to the oldest student who is in his sixties. I'm supposed to admire that he's pursuing higher education so close to death, but instead, it makes me uncomfortable. They're all well dressed, lots of leather shoes and boots and what the English would call "smart" button-down shirts. Sharply tailored Burberry coats and shiny leather handbags with neat stitches and logos that are small enough to be subtle, but not so small that you can't read the "Prada" or "LV." Nothing so crass as monogrammed logos all over the bags, oh no. We're writers, after all.

The tables are set in a U, with the teacher's desk at the center. I hesitate, trying to figure out where to sit for minimum attention, trying not to make it too obvious that I'm waiting to see where Thalia is going to sit. She swans into class last, right before it begins, and her presence brightens up the room. All that golden hair and dewy skin and Colgate smile. All heads turn toward her, but she doesn't seem to notice. She's used to being the center of attention, neither loves it nor hates it. She spots me, and her smile widens. While everybody watches, she crosses the room straight to me. The sixty-year-old man has taken the seat next to mine, but she smiles sweetly at him and says, "I'm sorry, is it okay if I take this one?" and he shifts one seat over with a friendly, "Of course, luv."

And now here she is again, next to me, close enough for me to smell her. My heart twists and twists, and I feel like I could die from the nearness of her, but Thalia is ignorant of the quiet death I'm going through. My mind is a mess of jagged questions, slicing their way across the soft folds of my brains. Did you ditch me so you could party with Ani? Did you spend the night with some guy? Did you fuck him? Did you, did you?

"Hey, didn't see you at breakfast," she says.

I'm not sure if that's a question, so I focus on taking out my notebook from my shitty messenger bag. Next to me, I can feel Thalia's confusion growing when I don't answer. *It's not that I don't want to strike up a conversation with you, Thalia,* I think desperately, as loud as I can, trying to make her hear my thoughts. *It's that if I open my mouth, I don't know what's going to fall out.* My thoughts are spiders waiting to leap from my tongue and poison everything they touch.

"Good morning, everyone!" a voice trills, and thank god, because I don't know what I was about to say.

Our first teacher is Emily R. Rogers, author of the critically acclaimed but poor-selling *Mayflies in the Winter*. All of our teachers, I realized when looking over the course handbook, are of the same loved-by-critics-but-ignored-by-the-masses caliber. Emily is in her midforties, past her prime but still lovely to look at. Everyone here is like that—all of them attractive in one way or another, or at the very least, fashionably ugly.

"Right! Welcome to day one of Michaelmas." She pauses to give us all a smile. There's that term again—Michaelmas. Google told me it refers to Oxford's fall term, though why they can't just call it "fall" like every other college does is beyond me. "Today we're going to talk about prose fiction and how to keep your reader engaged. Reader engagement depends on a few factors, but the most important thing is tension. What is tension?"

I write down as much of what Emily says as I can while also being painfully aware that Thalia isn't writing anything down. When I sneak a glance at her, she's sitting back and watching Emily with a thoughtful expression. She looks so absorbed, so naturally intelligent that I have no doubt that despite the lack of notes, she will retain a lot more of the seminar than I will. By contrast, I feel silly for scribbling so furiously, afraid of missing even a single word. A child trying to play catch-up at a grown-up class.

"But before we get into all that, we're going to warm up with a freewriting session."

My pen stills. No, please. My brain is still in a wine-fug from last night, and I can barely read my own notes.

"We're going to go for five minutes. Write anything that comes to your mind. We'll read it out afterward and do a little work-shop—how does that sound?" Emily has already taken out an egg timer from her bag.

It sounds awful. Horrible. But nobody else is looking nearly as panicked as I feel. The timer starts and pens move across pages. I look around at the heads bent studiously over their notebooks, all of the hands moving smoothly. Freewriting sounds like something that requires very little effort, and yet when I look down on my empty page, I can't come up with a single word. I force my hand down, pressing the tip of my pen to paper. If I could just get the nib to touch the paper, the words would start flowing.

It's pressing so hard by now that there's an indentation in the paper, and still, the words don't come. I push the pen hard, turning the indentation into a line.

I.

I what? Please, mind. Please work. Instead, the words that come are Pam's. *I hear that every year, about a quarter of the students flunk out of the course.*

How do you flunk out of a Creative Writing course? I had asked so stupidly. Well, now I'm about to find out. You fail because your mind aborts all thought, purging it out in favor of a tangle of fear pulsing under a fog of alcohol. I can't believe that after all the hours I've worked, saving up every cent, after the enormous debt I've put myself in to be here, I'm about to crash and burn on my very first day of class.

Fucking Ani. She knew, somehow. She must've known. Last night was the first time we met, but I'd sensed it, that predatorial hunger in her, the shot of jealousy on her face when Thalia introduced us. She'd wanted to get rid of me, and like a complete patsy, I'd fallen for it. I'd let her motion the server to refill my glass over and over and over, and now here I am, about to fail a five-minute exercise, the first ever task given by my course.

A shrill shriek erupts from the egg timer and I jump; my butt actually leaves the chair for a split second. My heart stops, only to resume in a mad gallop. *Shit, shit!* It's over. All that time I'd spent worrying about being exposed, my human mask slipping and showing a glimpse of the beast beneath, and it turns out it didn't matter, because now I'm about to be exposed as a fraud, a wannabe writer who can't write after all. Life's a real bitch sometimes.

Chapter 8

TWENTY-ONE YEARS AGO

I hate waste. I don't like wasting food, or time, or money. But the thing I most hate to waste is potential. And I have so much of it. I know that; I've known that ever since I was little. And now, at the ripe age of twelve, I know that I have the potential to really make it big. You know how kids are often told the big old lie: "You can be whatever you want to be"? Ninety-nine percent of the time, it's bullshit. But not so for me. My teachers are always raving about how gifted I am, and even Aunt Claudette agrees. She'd often say, "Child, you have a busy, busy mind. Put that mind to good use." It's too bad that I was born into the wrong family. Imagine the heights I would've reached if I'd been born into a wealthy one, with parents that could afford to send me to the best private schools, then on to the Ivy Leagues. But no, I was born to this one, a single-parent home complete with a mother who's completely uninterested in me.

When I turned twelve, I decide it was time to punish my mother. Why? Too many reasons to count. For being a negligent parent. For failing to see how exceptional her daughter is. For being so fucking stupid that she has no real prospects, can only hop from one minimum wage job to another.

I've spent years studying my mother, watching her like I'm a scientist observing a rodent. My mother is a serial dater. She delights in it, plays the role of the dream girlfriend perfectly. I eavesdrop on her as she chatters on the phone each night to her friends, giggling about how infatuated her current boyfriend is. She knows just what to do to get them hooked on her, knowing exactly when to push and pull, to leave them wanting more. She loves the feeling of being desired. Then she'll get bored; maybe she senses that they're about to get bored of her, who knows? But whatever it is, my mother rarely stays with the same man for months. She'll dump them, break their hearts, and when they're gone, she'll crook one corner of her mouth up into a smile and say, "Leave 'em before they leave you, baby girl. Remember that."

To be fair, she did teach me a lot about men, so I suppose there's that.

I decide that the best way to punish her is to make sure all of her boyfriends leave her instead of her leaving them. It's the perfect punishment. She'll be left alone, with plenty of time to ruminate on how unwanted she is.

It's a lot trickier than you might think, scaring off someone's boyfriend when he's not ready to go. Most kids in my situation would start behaving badly—throw tantrums, maybe, or be a complete bitch to the boyfriend, but I know that's not going to cut it. That'll just paint me as the problem instead of Mom. For days, I wander everywhere, deep in thought, toying with one idea after another and rejecting them all.

The idea comes to me from the newspaper. Some guy one town over had been arrested for molesting some kids. Perfect. That same day, I go home and smile my way through dinner as Mom and her boyfriend du jour, Jackson, make googly eyes at each other over the pasta bake. I wait patiently for them to finish their nightly routine, watching TV and making out. Then, finally, Jackson leaves the apartment. I steal out the door, being careful to walk as quietly as I can past Aunt Claudette's apartment (I swear sometimes she just spends her time peeping out her door to catch me doing something bad), and catch up with him just as he's about to climb into his car.

"Jackson, wait."

He turns around and breaks into a smile when he sees me. "Hey, kiddo. What's up?"

Kiddo. I'm twelve and I have boobs and I bleed every month, but he's still calling me "kiddo." Guy deserves what's coming to him. "I need a favor."

He grins. "Sure, anything for you."

Don't be too sure about that, idiot. "Great," I say brightly. "I need you to stop seeing my mom."

His smile freezes on his face. "Excuse me?"

"Yeah, I need you to break up with her. Or not, whatever. Just stop seeing her."

"Uh, hang on, why—"

"I don't like you," I say. I love the simplicity of it, the undeniable clarity.

He sighs. "I think this is something you and your mom should talk about, because I'm crazy about her, and I'm willing to do whatever it takes to prove to you that I'm serious about this relationship."

"Nah." I shrug. "I just don't like you. You look like an asshole."

Now he's lost all traces of the smile. "Okay, listen here, kid—"

"If you don't break up with her by tomorrow, I'm going to tell everyone that you touched me."

"Whoa, hang on a second—".

I screw up my face and start crying, and he stops talking, his mouth hanging open as he watches my performance. I wish I could watch my performance. I bet it's stellar. Hot tears roll down my cheeks. "He asked me to go inside his car because he had a surprise for Mom, and then he—uh, he—put his hands on my—"

"Stop that!" he hisses. "Jesus fucking Christ. This is not funny!"

I stop mid-sob and look pointedly at him. "It's not a joke. I'm dead serious. Break up with her, or else." Then I turn and walk back toward the apartment.

He breaks up with Mom that very same night, and as I listen to her sobs through the thin walls, fierce joy blooms in my chest. Now, maybe, she'll give me the attention I deserve.

Chapter 9

"Time's up!" Emily says, and I wonder if she's aware of how ominous that sounds. Maybe she's a sociopath like me and she enjoys the way those two words work to slice through our dreams. Or maybe I'm just being melodramatic because I'm still staring at a blank page with the word "I" gouged into it.

Then, suddenly, a piece of paper full of words slides on top of my blank page. My head shoots up and I catch Thalia's face, a mischievous expression written—written, ha!—on it. She winks at me and gives the smallest of nods at the paper. My breath comes out in shallow, tiny gasps. A note. I've never received a note in class before. Back in high school, it seemed like everybody was passing notes. Everybody, that is, except me. The only times notes have graced my table were when they had to go through me to be passed on to the intended recipient. Passing through, DO NOT OPEN, JANE, please pass to Maura, please pass to Jake, DON'T OPEN IT, YOU FREAK, pass to Aiden.

I wonder what Thalia wants to say to me so badly that she has to say it in the middle of class. My mind jitters ahead, hope turning me into a gibbering mess. She's written to say she's sorry for not going to breakfast with me, that she was going to, but was ambushed by Ani, who had come knocking at her door in the morning—she spent the night alone, of course, just like I did—and refused to take no for an answer, and as she'd marched her down to Haygrove Hall, she'd gazed longingly at my door, wishing she had the courage to tell Ani no, that she's going to breakfast with her best friend Jane.

Then I look down at the paper and it's even better than I thought, because it's not a note for me, but what Emily had asked us to do—a little freewritten essay, done in Thalia's elegant cursive. I read it slowly, quietly, while the first student is called upon to read his work out loud. And it's good. Achingly so. Words as exquisite as the person herself. I glance up at Thalia. Her mouth quirks ever so slightly and my stomach turns soft. A little secret. Our little secret.

Fuck Ani and everyone else around us. This piece of paper is proof that Thalia is mine. Because it's not even that she's somehow managed to squeeze in double the work in the same amount of time, but she also gets me. The words she's written for me aren't just good, they're also strangely relatable, and relating to anything isn't something that happens often for me.

When it comes to my turn to read, my voice comes out with false confidence, bolstered by Thalia's words.

I am alone and not alone. I coat myself with barbed wire and broken fur, stay away, please come near, come you with bolt cutters and bran muffin and cut your way into my heart . . .

Tears prick my eyes as I read her words out loud. She sees me the way I truly am, past my human mask. With her, I don't need to wear the mask.

"Wow," Emily says when I get to the end of the passage. She's beaming at me. All around the room, I can sense everyone else adjusting their impression of me. My image is recalibrated, upgraded from the poor kid who doesn't belong to the poor kid with surprising talent despite the unfortunate upbringing. I don't know how I feel about it all, don't quite know how to handle anything warmer than polite, bland interest in me, so I duck my head and focus on my fingers as Emily lists out why "my" passage worked so well. The whole time, I go back and forth with thoughts of how to adequately thank Thalia, how to let her know that she is perfect and amazing and that she's saved me. I need her to know, above all else, that I see her the way she sees me.

Pam is right about the Creative Writing master's being intense. After Emily's seminar/workshop, we pause for a five-minute bathroom break during which Thalia goes to the bathroom, so I don't get a chance to even thank her before the next session begins. The next class is a critical seminar on fiction, and I struggle to follow as our teacher drones on and on about modernism and postmodernism. At least there's no freewriting session this time, though we are assigned homework—a five-hundred-word paper on creative trends of the twentieth century that's due the next day.

Finally, finally, we break for lunch. Thanks to the hangover and the heaviness of the course seminars, I am thoroughly defeated. I turn to Thalia, the words "thank you" halfway out of my mouth, but the sixty-year-old man's talking to her. For a second, I sit there awkwardly, wondering if there's a socially acceptable way of cutting into a conversation. Joining, I remind myself. The word I'm looking for is joining a conversation. And maybe I should just jump in? But no, I'm not built to jump into anything, so I focus on gathering my notebook and worksheets and pens, keeping half my attention on Thalia and this chatty-as-fuck old man who can't seem to shut the hell up. My last pen is in my bag now, and there's nothing left for me to tidy up, so I stand.

She stands too. She stands too! She's just as aware of me as I am of her, because our souls are two parts cut out of the same fabric. She's probably trying to extricate herself from the inane conversation just as much as I'm willing it to end. But the old man—I think his name is Peter—doesn't take a clue. He follows Thalia out of the classroom, me trailing them like a shadow. Finally, he realizes he's a senior goddamned citizen who doesn't belong with us and he says goodbye to Thalia. Good riddance. But Thalia walks on as though she doesn't see me there, as though my nearness means nothing to her.

One step, two steps away from me. I'm going to lose her. "Hey!" The word jerks out of me with more force than I intended, jarringly loud in the hallway. Heads turn toward me.

Thalia turns around, looking confused, then she smiles and all is right once more. "Jane! I'm so sorry, I didn't see you there. What's up?"

"Um, I just—" I walk up to her and lower my voice, my skin still prickling with gazes from my classmates. "I just wanted to thank you for um. You know, the freewriting thing. You saved my ass."

"Oh, that." She laughs. "It was nothing."

I shake my head. I hate that she's using that word—nothing.

It wasn't nothing, Thalia. Do not cheapen what you did. Writing something for me had proven a lot of things: that I wasn't wrong about how I felt, that she feels the same way too. I want to grip her slim shoulders and shake them hard, feel those brittle bones cutting into my palms, and tell her it's not nothing, it's not nothing, over and over until she gets it.

But before I can say anything, she says, "Anyway, I should go. I told Ani I'd meet her at the Porter's Lodge."

She might as well have punched me in the heart. Ani? At the Porter's Lodge? That means they're not lunching at Haygrove Hall. They're going someplace else, somewhere outside of the college, venturing out and exploring Oxford together like how she and I were supposed to do. My cheeks are melting with anger. I can hardly stand it. Mom's voice in my head, soft as a feather: *Baby, you gotta get used to not having anyone. People say things they think you want to hear, but at the end of the day, you're on your own.*

I came here to break away from Mom, be as far away from her poison as possible, but maybe she's right after all. No, she can't be. I won't let her. I mentally shriek at her voice until it dissipates into the wind.

"Can I come?" Those three simple words are the hardest I've had to say. *Can I come,* so pathetic, so needy.

Panic crosses Thalia's face, fleeting and gone before it even settles; she's too nice to let her reluctance show. But I catch it anyway, and my gut gurgles with acid. "Oh, um—you know what, let me check with Ani—"

"Don't bother." I brush past her. I have to get back to my room, I have to get away from everyone but especially from Thalia before this darkness bursts out of my chest and destroys everything.

"No, wait," Thalia says, grabbing my arm. Her lovely face is

88

stricken. "Sorry, it's not that I don't want you there, it's just—Ani wanted to talk about some stuff I think? Buuut!" She brightens up. "Tonight, we're going to hit a few of the local pubs, and you're very welcome to join. The more the merrier!"

Why do people say that when it's so often untrue? It's only ever said when you're lobbing out a half-hearted invitation, when you can't think of a better reason why you're asking someone along aside than that you want more warm bodies to bulk up the group. To make it look more merry.

And what's worse is that Thalia hasn't just made lunch plans with Ani, but lunch AND drinking plans. The kind of thing that best friends do. A girls' night out. I picture myself with the two of them—Thalia all shiny, her stunning face practically a beacon of light, starkly contrasted by Ani's model-sleek black hair. They'd be a hit, two girls straight out of a modeling shoot. And then me, trailing after them, skulking like a forlorn goblin, surly-faced and dowdy in my thrift store clothes. Not vintage, just thrift store. Or maybe Thalia would take pity on me and offer to lend me another outfit, and I'd be squeezed into yet another dress too tight for me to breathe in.

It's unthinkable. The night out from hell. She'd end up resenting me for glomming on to her light, clinging like a barnacle. Nobody likes barnacles.

I shake my head. "No. Thank you," I remember to add. And I hurry off before she can say anything more.

Chapter 10

PRESENT DAY
NEW YORK CITY

New York City! If ever there was a place that's the antithesis of Northern California, this is surely it. I wish I could slip into a movie montage as we walk out of the airport and into a train station. Imagine some sprightly music playing, the breeze blowing ever so slightly, just enough to give my hair that windswept look and catch a corner of my coat as though the city itself is nudging me. *Hey, you're in New York fucking City! You made it, Jane!*

Instead, what there is, is a long train ride from JFK to the city of Manhattan, where we are jostled continuously and sworn at for bringing our bags into the subway, and I'm pretty sure the guy sitting in the far corner of the subway car is dead. When we finally climb out of the dank station, we're panting and sweaty because of course these stations don't have escalators or elevators or anything that would make life slightly easier—New York isn't into easy; it loves to remind you that it's tough, and if you're not tough then you don't belong—into the sunlight, I am done. But I can't be done because it's ten more blocks of walking, dragging our luggage with us, and once again getting cussed at—"Fucking tourists"—until we get to our hotel.

Without Ted, I would've booked the cheapest little motel I could find, squirreling away as much money as I can for a rainy day. But because he has insisted on coming along and because I have claimed that my publisher is paying for it, we have to stay somewhere mildly acceptable. A three-star hotel, he pointed out, is reasonable. Something my publisher would be okay with reimbursing. Can't argue with that, so here we are. I've charged everything to my card and told Ted that Harvest would reimburse me later.

It's way past lunchtime, and after we're done checking in and going to the bathroom, Ted says, "Shall we?"

I look at him like he's just started speaking Russian.

"Lunch?" he says. "I've been dying to try all of these places in New York, and you said meals are included as part of the trip, right?"

God, he's going to make me burn through the ring money. "Actually, I have a meeting with Toni."

Ted frowns. "Now? She set up a meeting with you for today? She knows you just got off a long flight, right?"

I hate to admit it, but now that he's saying these words out loud, they do actually make some sense. Why didn't I think of it? But it's too late now. I can hardly be like, oh yeah, you're right, it wasn't today after all, silly me! Gotta dig my heels in and keep shoveling away at that grave. "Yeah, she's really busy and she can slot me in today, so . . ." I grab my purse, put my phone and a key card inside, and give Ted a bright smile. "I'll see you later."

Ted's still staring at me like he's a kid and I'm his mom and

91

I've just told him that he's adopted. "So we're not lunching together? What about dinner?"

My god, Ted. It takes a lot not to scream at him. He's doing this on purpose, I know he is. He's never ever this clingy, but now, when it actually matters, he's pulling this shit on me. Trying to distract me from following my true calling.

"I don't know," I say, trying to sound apologetic. "Toni might want to have dinner together?"

His face softens. "Yeah, of course."

I turn to leave.

"Hey, before you go . . ."

Don't scream. Do not scream. I turn around and raise my eyebrows.

"Don't like—don't set your expectations too high. I mean, I know it's exciting, meeting your agent for the first time and all, but you know, she's probably really busy and stuff, so . . ."

He can't stand that it's my success we're celebrating for once. Well, my pretend success, but he doesn't know it's pretend. He's got to shit all over it, to remind me not to have hope because all I deserve is mediocrity. I don't bother giving him a reply before I stalk out the door, slamming it shut behind me. I half hope he'd come out and ask if I'm angry because, *Wow, you slammed the door really hard, Jane.* Then I'd give an extra sweet smile and say, *Oops, it just slipped from my hand!* But he doesn't come out. I practically run down the stairs, through the lobby, and out into the street. Holy shit, I did it. I'm in New York City, sans Ted, and I'm about to meet my agent.

The problem is, Toni doesn't actually know I'm here. In all the rush to book tickets for this and that and reminding myself about what lies I'd told Ted, I'd forgotten to email her. And now it's kind of late to do so. Another shitty realization: I don't actually have a ticket to SusPens Con. But, I comfort myself, Toni probably does. And she'll be so happy to see me. She's always been so bubbly and enthusiastic, all of her emails generously sprinkled with "!!!" She adores me as a client, she's told me so many times. And given she works at one of the biggest literary agencies in the city, she'll have all the connections. Right, good plan.

I look up the address to her agency and burrow my way into the subway yet again.

Matterson and Cable Literary Agency is on 42nd Street, a street flanked by skyscrapers on both sides, so close that I get dizzy looking all the way up. All of New York is like that, designed to give you a sense of vertigo so that it can feel satisfied, like a school bully. I find the building, a behemoth of yellow brick and glass, and walk inside. Immediately, I feel all sorts of wrong. Everyone is impeccably dressed, and I do mean everyone. Suits and pencil skirts, and here I am, wearing a knee-length denim skirt and an ill-fitting cardigan, my hair messy and limp.

But that's probably to be expected from writers, right? There's a reason why we're writers and not actors. We're better on paper than in person. Toni's probably got a whole stable full of writers with sweat stains, hunched backs, and skin that's sallow and greasy from too much time spent poring over their manuscripts. I probably look better than most authors. Probably. Maybe.

I get into one of the elevators and press the button for the twenty-fifth floor. At the twenty-fifth floor, I get out and walk past a law firm and an architecture firm before finding

Matterson and Cable Literary. Here we go. This is okay. This is totally acceptable behavior from one of their longtime clients. I force my mouth to stretch into a smile before pushing open the double doors and walking inside.

The receptionist, a boy who looks like a college freshman, looks up and says, "Welcome to Matterson and Cable. Do you have an appointment?"

"Um, no. I'm looking for, um, Toni Sumida?"

"Sure, of course, that's great. Is she expecting you?"

I shake my head, and he opens his mouth, his face primed to give me a canned response, but I quickly add, "But I'm a client of hers. Jane Morgan?"

"Ah, a client. But you don't have an appointment."

"No," I say again, wondering why the hell they hired this moron to man the desk.

"Okay . . ." He stretches out the "kay" so it's more like "kayyyyyyyyyy," like he really needs the entire office to hear that, hey, you guys, look at this stupid client who's come all the way here without an appointment! Then he sighs and says, "Let me just check real quick if she's in the office." He picks up the phone and dials a number while I turn around to give him some semblance of privacy. I take the chance to look around the office.

It's a lot bigger than I expected, and a lot nicer as well. Half of it is an open-plan design, with private offices for the senior agents and an open space for the rest.

"Hi, Toni, this is Robin. I have a client of yours out here—a . . . sorry, miss, what did you say your name was?"

If I killed him, it would be a favor to humanity. "Jane Morgan."

"It's Jane Morgan. Should I—oh? Okay. Mm-hmm. No problems." He puts down the phone and leans forward. "She'll come out in a minute. Okay?" he says in a tone that says: We're done talking.

Wow, I really am not used to the sassiness of New York. I have no idea what to do with myself as I wait, so I take out my phone and try to look busy. Oh, look, there are exactly zero emails I need to answer.

I've been tapping on my phone for eight excruciating minutes when Toni finally comes out.

"Jane?" she says, and I look up to see a smiling face.

"Hi! Yes, it's me," I say, standing up quickly. Holy shit, it's really her. My agent for the last three years. The woman who sold my last two books to Harvest Publishing, who edited my books and listened to my pitches and told me over and over again what a treat my writing is. I should probably hug her. But neither of us makes a move to bridge the polite gap between us, and then she holds her hand out at the same time as I hold my arms out for a hug, and there's a moment where she realizes I'm coming in for a hug and quickly switches to hug mode, and Jesus Christ, why the hell did I go in for a hug? We end up giving each other an awkward, don't-want-to-actually-touch-you hug, and then stand uncomfortably close to each other—close enough for me to see the fine lines on her forehead and around her mouth.

"It's so nice to finally see you, Jane. Come, let's go into my office." She steps back and turns around before I can answer, and I get the feeling that she's relieved to be walking away from me. But I'm sure I'm just being silly, because of course she's happy to see me. We walk past interns and junior agents, and she leads me to a corner office and shuts the door behind me. She doesn't offer me a drink. She gestures for me to take a seat across from her desk before settling into her luxurious seat. "So, Jane! What brings you to New York? Visiting family?" She doesn't even finish the sentence before she glances over at her computer screen.

"Um, business, actually."

"Oh?" She glances at me for a second before her attention is pulled back to the computer. "Sorry, hang on . . . give me just a sec . . ." She types something rapidly before forcing her attention back to me. "Right. So you were saying?"

It takes a moment to regain my bearings. "I was saying I'm in town for business? For SusPens Con, actually."

Her eyebrows knit together. "SusPens Con? But that's for suspense/thrillers. More commercial work."

"I know, but I was hoping to attend because I'm thinking of writing a commercial suspense."

"That's—"

I can't read her expression. It's somewhere between a smile and a quizzical frown, like a polite *What the fuck?* She finally says, "That's wonderful. Yeah, adult suspense has a very healthy market, so I think it's a good, um, good move. Yeah."

Who are you trying to convince? I want to ask her. Her hesitation is coming through painfully clear. She doesn't think I could write an adult suspense. "I mean, I know it's kind of different from what I've been writing . . ."

"Yeah, pretty different." She holds up one finger and says, "Hang on, let me just pull up your file."

My file? She's only sold two of my books and she can't even remember them? But I sit there, inwardly squirming as she squints at her computer.

"Okay, here we are. Right, your debut, *Flowers That Grow in Moonlight*, lit fic, right, sold for . . . here we go, $3,500."

Yep, I know that. I don't have to be reminded of it. It rankles

96

that she has to be reminded of the details of my book deal. Aren't agents supposed to remember this stuff? I bet if I wrote young adult, she'd remember. But no, I have to write lit fic, the least commercial thing anyone could write, maybe aside from poetry. It would have done well in the nineties, before YA destroyed the entire market. With a sinking feeling, it hits me that the fact that she doesn't remember probably does mean that it was always an intern or assistant who handled me.

"And your second book, also a lit fic, *The Coldest Winter*, sold for $2,300." Her mouth stretches into a wince for a second before she recovers and turns it into a smile. Still looks like a grimace. When she looks at me again, I can see that what little interest she had has now faded. She takes a fifteen percent cut of my earnings, and fifteen percent of $5,800 is barely worth the paperwork. Worse, my advance has gone down after my first book, a sign that the first one didn't perform as well as my publisher had hoped.

But how could it have performed well when they did fuck all to promote it? Nobody even knew about its existence.

"Hmm. Yeah, going into commercial fiction could be a good move. Move away from lit fic, that's good. Did you have any pitches you wanted to share with me?"

Ah. Shit. Pitches, right. Shame curdles my gut as it hits me how unprepared I am for this meeting. And as I sit here mentally freaking out, Toni glances at her Apple Watch; I'm taking up too much of her time, she's got bigger clients to focus on, clients who make seven-figure deals and sell movie rights.

Then, surging through the turgid waters of my senses, an idea leaps out, taking form. I pounce on it. "Um, you know Thalia Ashcroft?"

That catches Toni's attention, because of course it does. Thalia's always got this effect on people. Toni turns her face toward me, no longer thinking—for now—how she can get rid of me. "The author of *A Most Pleasant Death*? Yeah, I've heard of her. Her book's at the top of the *New York Times* list. What about her?"

"Well, I know her."

Toni gives me a wan smile, the polite kind that you give to pathetic people to get them to stop talking.

"We actually went to the same MFA program together. At Oxford. In England?" I don't know why that came out as a question, but I desperately need Toni to start nodding, and she does, her eyes brightening. "Yeah, we actually lived on the same floor; we were really good friends, really close to each other."

"Wow, that's wonderful to hear." She's still got that line in between her eyebrows because even though it's nice to hear that I'm friends with publishing's next big star, she's also wondering what the hell this has to do with anything.

"And I think if I could just get to see her in person, we could reconnect and she'd probably want to help promote my books and everything. We were so tight back in Oxford."

"Why not just give her a call? Did you two lose touch?"

I shift uneasily in my seat. "Sort of. Um, something bad happened during our year, and we were all sent home for a while. I came back the next semester, but Thalia never did, so we kind of lost contact there."

"You could just send her an email, maybe slide into her DMs?" she says with a smile.

Frustration claws at my belly. She doesn't get it. "No, I'd rather see her in person—I'm sure she's inundated with emails and DMs from random people. Anyway, she's going to be at SusPens Con, so I was thinking if I could get a ticket to go there, I could go to her panel and say hi."

She nods slowly, hesitantly. "I'll ask around, see if anyone has a spare ticket. I'll give you a call once I know. Okay?"

The last "Okay?" was delivered very clearly as a placating goodbye. I'm out of ideas by now, so I just give her a nod and stand up, pretending not to see the relief on her face as she walks me out of the office.

Outside of the building, it takes a full minute before my heart recovers from the painful speed it had been galloping at. My breath releases in a long whoosh. God, I can't believe I just did that. Just showed up at Toni's office like that. What the fuck? But even as I think that, a slow smile takes over my face. For once in my life, I put myself out there. I took control of the situation. I was fucking proactive, and I'm about to be rewarded for it. I know I am.

I walk around the area for a bit, looking up at the massive buildings and searching for a bite to eat. But who am I kidding? Everything in this part of Manhattan is out of my price range; even the bottled water is six dollars each, which is insane. And here I'd thought Bay Area prices were out of control.

I've been walking aimlessly for about ten minutes when an email comes in from Toni. I open it, mouth dry. I know, as soon as I see the lack of "!" that it's not going to be good news.

Jane,
What a surprise having you show up at the office today. I made a few calls to see if I could get a hold of SusPens Con tickets. Unfortunately, I wasn't able to get any. I think

your best bet to reconnect with Thalia would be through email; I think that in general, this is a better way than showing up unannounced in person, especially since it's been quite a while since the two of you were in touch with each other.

Best,
Toni

The skyscrapers around me might as well have folded over and crumbled on top of me. I feel crushed and humiliated and above all, enraged. This email is a far cry from her usual ones, which always, always start off with "Hi!" and not just "Jane comma." And her emails have, at minimum, three exclamation marks, always. Even when they're emails containing bad news, like when I got those bad reviews from Kirkus and Publishers Weekly. She'd said: "Hi! Ugh, we got a bad review from Kirkus, but seriously, who gives a shit about them anyway, right?! They wouldn't know good writing if it hit them in the face!"

And now, all terse words and awkwardness. I could just—

I was making a gesture, turning up at her office. Aren't agents supposed to welcome their clients with open arms? Unbidden, Ted's voice rises up from the depths of my mind, like a noxious bubble popping up from a poisonous swamp. *You're small fry, Jane. Don't expect too much from her.* She's got bigger clients to tend to. I bet she wouldn't react like this if one of her bestselling authors showed up unannounced.

I can't stand it. I can't stand the thought of seeing his smug face when he finds out that he's right all along, that I shouldn't have assumed that Toni would be happy to see me. That all these years of friendly emails were nothing but lies. I wonder if they were even written by her in the first place, or if they had been something she'd delegated to an assistant, or worse, an intern. "Here," she would have said, "write an email to these clients. Make it sound like I give a damn."

And like a total idiot, I had fallen for it, thought she adored me, thought we were—ha—friends. The thought of myself, so pathetic and so foolish, makes me want to spit.

But who gives a crap about Toni? So it turns out she doesn't give a shit, so what? It doesn't matter. All that matters is that I'm here, in Manhattan, and in less than twenty-four hours, I am going to go to SusPens Con, ticket or not, and I am going to find a way to get inside, because that's where Thalia will be, and there is nothing I wouldn't do to see her again.

Nothing.

Chapter 11

NINE YEARS AGO
OXFORD, ENGLAND

I spend the rest of the day avoiding Thalia. When we get back from lunch (I get back from my room, where I spent lunchtime holed up, alternating between pacing like a caged animal and screaming into my pillow), I pick a seat farthest from her and refuse to meet her eye. As soon as classes end, I escape once more into my room. I listen behind the door, my breath coming out rapidly whenever footsteps pound through the hallway. There it is, the click and swing of her door, just a few feet away from mine, might as well be miles. I should go out there and explain—though I'm not sure what I would be explaining, maybe why I'm so warped and jagged? My hand caresses the doorknob.

Laughter.

I freeze. It's not Thalia's voice. Then I hear it, Thalia talking, followed by more throaty laughter that turns my hand into a fist. Ani. Ani's going into Thalia's room. The room I'd been in less than a day ago, where Thalia had touched my bare skin, where we had, at one point, both been undressed. And now it's being tainted by Ani's presence. Is she lending Ani an outfit too? I am frothing with jealousy. But no, says a tiny voice of logic, Ani isn't the kind of girl who needs to borrow another girl's outfit. Ani's the kind of girl who would've brought her entire wardrobe to Oxford, filling her closet to bursting with expensive silks and leathers. My heart rate slows down for a moment before speeding up again. Because if she's not here to borrow an outfit, then what the fuck is she here for? What are they doing in Thalia's room, laughing like that? Are they laughing about me? Laughing about the freak across the hallway?

A few minutes later, Thalia's door opens again, voices and more laughter flooding the hallway. I press my ear to my door, teeth gritted so hard my jaw threatens to lock, and listen to their receding footsteps. And they're off on their girls' night. How could I have been so wrong? How laughable that I should have thought myself worthy of being Thalia's friend. How quickly I've been put back in my place.

By now, I'm half-crazed with hunger and rage and pain. Mom's voice again: *Oh, sweetie, get used to it. You will never belong with these people. We're the help. Come back and work for Mrs. Crawford's niece; I hear her baby is a sweetheart, not colicky. It'll be a good job.* Shut up, Mother. Shut the fuck up. I should go out, get some food. But I've missed dinnertime at Haygrove Hall, and I don't really want to wander up and down the streets of Oxford where I might bump into Thalia and Ani and suffer the embarrassed giggles that would come from them—god, look at her, so sad and gross.

Instead, I sit down at my desk and start writing. I slit myself open and let all the darkness pour out onto the keyboard, all of my rage and all of my hunger for her. Several times, I type so hard and so fast that my hands, slick with sweat, slip from the keyboard. I keep going, writing like I'm possessed, except it's not a possession but the opposite of one. An exorcism. I'm only vaguely aware of what I've written.

> ... *her beautiful neck, as slim as the stem of a rose about to bloom* ...
>   ... *count her bones, one at the back of her neck, peeking out as she pores over the book* ...
>   ... *the way her face looks as I squeeze the air out of her, panic and ecstasy knotted together. She wants me to do this, she wants me to be the end of her, to be the final thing she sees* ...

By the time I'm done, I'm barely functional. I load the file onto the virtual classroom and click Send without thinking twice. My mind is buzzing, skittering like the legs of a centipede. I feel drunk again, a disconnect between mind and body, a deep chasm in my core. I slam my laptop shut, slump over to bed, and surrender myself to warped dreams where Thalia alternates between telling me she loves me and laughing cruelly at me.

In the morning, it takes a while for last night's events to come back to me, and when they do, they float up like noxious bubbles swirling up from a swamp of dead things, bubbling to the surface and popping to release their toxic fumes. Thalia and Ani, laughing as they head out of Thalia's room, probably arm in arm the way that girls like to walk sometimes, both of them dressed in equally expensive, fashionable clothes. Bare skin and tight jeans. Red lipstick and sensuous perfume. And me, boiling with hunger and envy, screaming silently in my room. Food. I need food. I shrug on clean clothes, rake a brush through my hair, while blinking blearily in the mirror. Plain Jane. Mediocre in every way. Not ugly, not pretty, just aggressively mediocre.

Thalia doesn't turn up to breakfast. Neither does Ani, and I picture them both squeezed into Thalia's bed, undressed, breathing slow, lazy breaths into each other's hair. I take an extra-vicious bite of my pancake. Pam appears in the doorway, and I wonder for a second if she'll join me—I half panic, hoping she won't, but then she sees another student and joins them instead. And then I'm suddenly jealous. Even fucking PAM has someone to sit with, but not me. It seems that making friends is a skill that everyone else has been born with except me. I feel like a fish who doesn't quite know how to swim and can only stay still until it sinks, slowly, into the deep and the dark, the waters getting increasingly cold as it descends.

We have each other, Mom whispers.

Shut. Up.

I gobble up the rest of my food, satiating at least one of my hungers, and escape from the noise of Haygrove Hall. Pam offers a hesitant smile as I walk past, but I pretend not to see. I don't know how you're supposed to respond to half smiles. Are they meant to initiate conversations? I shrug it off and walk out of the building. It's yet another beautiful morning; I've learned that no place else does mornings and evenings quite like Oxford does.

Back in Cali, mornings are ostentatious, the sun bursting over the horizon, Here I am! Everybody up! In Oxford, sunrise and sunsets are far gentler, the sky melting like ice cream from dark to purple, to orange, and then to a dewy haze that lines everything with gold. It's so beautiful it further enrages me. I wish I could take a knife to it, slice into this perfect moment. There's just something about perfection that makes me want to defile it. Sometimes, I fantasize going through the museum with a little razor, casually slicing apart priceless canvases as I walk past.

The day's classes start off with another workshop, this time with the theme of "How to surprise your reader." When I saw that on the syllabus, I'd snorted out loud because I'd of course imagined leaping from behind a bookshelf brandishing a knife. Bet you my reader would be surprised by that.

The weird things that my brain spits out.

I take a seat at the farthest end of the room from the door and studiously bury my head in my notebook, trying to project an air of "Fuck off." It works; my classmates mill about, chattering among themselves, but none of them tries talking to me. I'm glad, truly I am. I sense the shift in the room when Thalia enters, the way the voices stop for a second before they call out to her. How is it possible for to her to ignite such delight from others after just a day? Is this what charisma gets you—instant adoration? But no, I catch snippets of conversation like:

"—checked out that bookshop you mentioned, loved it—"

"—were right about the hot chocolate at Caffè Nero!"

What the hell? How has she had time to give people bookshop and drink recommendations? When we sat on the bus from London to Oxford, she told me she'd never been to Oxford before, that she's a complete stranger to the city. She'd been so nervous, so sweetly innocent and excited. And now here she is, giving recommendations to English people like she's the one who's a local. And I'm pushed further out of the circle, an outsider peering through a window.

I study my notebook so hard that my nose practically touches the page. Fortunately, our teacher arrives and we begin the class.

My relief is short-lived; the teacher, Taylor McKeon (also

critically acclaimed, also with fewer than ten reviews on Amazon), perches on her seat and says, "I thought it would be perfect to start today's class with a workshop session. I read through all of your short scenes, and I found one that I thought would be appropriate for today's subject matter: Surprising your reader. It's one by Jane Morgan. Jane?"

It takes a few moments to realize she's calling my name, and by then, she's had to say it twice more. Jane. Jane?

I startle back to life, my mind a mad horse, bucking and running wild. What had I handed in that could be appropriate for this? For anything? It comes back in a black rush—last night's mad raving typed with such ferocity that my fingers could barely keep up with the torrent of words. Something about strangling a young woman. Something about counting her bones. Oh my god.

I finally find my voice. "I don't think—"

Taylor smiles kindly. "Doing a reading is a harrowing experience, isn't it? Especially when it's a reading of your own work. I don't think I've quite managed to overcome that horrid sensation myself. But it's a vital skill for authors to have. So, Jane, please. The stage is yours."

There is no stage, but still, everyone's eyes are on me. I can't bear to look at them. I don't dare even glance in Thalia's direction because I have no clue what expression she'd be wearing. Encouraging? Pitying? Bored? I don't know which is worse. With shaking hands, I take out my laptop and call up the file, every passing second incredibly, painfully slow. I can hear every single noise in the room—the subtle throat clearing, the rustle of clothes as someone shifts in their seat, the scratching of a pen's nib across paper. Everyone is waiting to hear me read out my scene of rage. I might as well be undressing in front of them. I look at

Taylor again, my eyes beseeching, but she only gives me what she probably thinks is an encouraging nod. And so, with one last swallow, I begin to read.

> *We meet in the middle of a bustling city and all at once I know I will be the most important person in her life. Not her boyfriend, nor her parents or her siblings, but me. A total stranger. I shall be the defining moment in her entire life, the point at which everything will curve, because I, a total stranger, will be the one who ends it.*

Despite everything, the more I read, the less aware I am of everyone else in the room. Everyone, that is, except for Thalia. Everyone else ceases to exist; even the tables and chairs between us melt away, leaving us floating in empty space, just her and me. Her eyes are on mine, and I can feel the weight of her gaze, but still I dare not look at her. What must she be thinking? Is she repulsed? Fearful? Angry?

I come to the end of the passage and there's silence. Then someone says, "That was amazing."

And that someone was Thalia.

Things have changed for me. Ever since the day that Taylor made me read out the dark spaces in my mind, everyone's been looking at me differently. With fear, one might guess, but no. It's respect I see in their eyes. Somehow, revealing what a fucked-up mind I have has elevated me in their eyes. I'm not sure how I feel about that.

You don't want to know what people really think of you, do you, dear? Mom whispers. It's one of her favorite things to say. She would never tell me outright that people think I'm weird or crazy or unlikable; no, that would be too easy. She preferred to coax me gently into thinking that myself, so that when I asked her point-blank if people disliked me, she could widen her eyes with surprise and say, "Why would you think that, Jane?"

So I try not to dwell on it. It doesn't matter anyway. I don't care. See, the thing is, I won her over. Thalia.

Immediately after classes ended that day, Thalia had come to me and said, "We're going for lunch together." And that was that.

That was two weeks ago, two incredible weeks that I spent with Thalia. And Ani, our barnacle. I bet she doesn't think of herself as that, though. Ani probably thinks she's the main character in our story, and I want to scream at her and tell her that she isn't, she's the villain, the whiny bitch nobody loves. But it's okay. I am willing to suffer through countless hours of Ani if it means that I can be with Thalia. And I am. We're traversing Oxford together, and it's wonderful and amazing and so much more than I could have predicted, than I'd dared to hope.

In the mornings, we have greasy mushrooms and rubbery scrambled eggs at Haygrove, followed by classes where I get to sit and marvel at the words Thalia spins like gold thread. She's by far the most gifted writer on our program, and everyone has accepted it. She's always called on to read her scenes out loud, which I love and hate, because I love watching her, but I hate having to share her with others. How dare they watch her like that, their lust so open and so lascivious?

For lunch, we meet up with Ani, who is surprisingly studious. My first impression of Ani had been that of a spoiled brat who couldn't care less about school, but she's the opposite. Apparently, she's top of her class, and Thalia tells me that Ani often comes back from a night of partying to study until the following morning. Ani is powered by Red Bull and anger at the world, and she is exhausting to be around because she never stops. I have lost count of the number of times we meet up with Ani only to find her just finishing up a meeting with someone else—a Rhodes scholar, a professor, a fellow business school student. She's always making connections, such a busy butterfly. The complete opposite of me. But with Thalia as a buffer between us, I find it bearable. Each day, the three of us walk around the city and try out a different restaurant for lunch. I know Ani doesn't think much of me, just as I don't regard her as anything other than a benign tumor that has attached itself to the entity that is Thalia and me, but for Thalia's sake, we tolerate each other.

After our afternoon classes, Thalia and I go to the Bodleian Library and lose ourselves in the hushed halls, surrounded by centuries-old tomes, and there we sit and write. I steal glances at her as I type on my keyboard, and just the nearness of her is enough to transport me to that place that writers aim for. Her presence propels me through the doorway, letting the rest of the world melt away. Never before have I come up with such passionate prose, such dark, enchanting words. In class, our teachers and fellow students swoon over my compositions, marveling at the way I've managed to cut through the flowery words that writers often fall prey to and go straight to the harsh bones of human emotion. It's all thanks to Thalia, I want to say, but I keep it to myself. I don't want to share my muse with anyone.

For a few weeks, it really does feel like I've finally found my place. Something special that I never thought I could get, and I would give anything to keep this friendship with Thalia going. Anything.

PART TWO

Chapter 12

NINE YEARS AGO
OXFORD, ENGLAND

The trouble begins about three weeks into the course. We're at the Eagle and Child, leaning back in our seats with apple and pear ciders sweating in pint glasses, waiting for our food to arrive. (British pub food—steak pies, bangers and mash—because we're doing this whole English thing right.) Ani says, "What are we doing this weekend, ladies? Don't tell me we're staying in this tired old town again. I am DYING here. Literally dying."

I look at her and daydream about her literally dying, blood splashed across her skin in a fetching pattern. Ani would look good bathed in red.

Thalia smiles tenderly at her, and my heart bites at my rib cage, a petty little Jack Russell terrier.

"I've been studying way too hard," Ani grumbles.

"Yeah, you have. Why do you study so hard, anyway?"

Ani takes a sip of her pear cider. "If you had a brother and parents like mine, you'd understand why I need to excel at this stupid course. Anyway, shall we party this weekend? I've been dying to do London! I didn't come here to spend my time wasting away in this shithole."

"Oxford isn't a shithole," I mutter. I wonder what she'd call Oakland, if a city as beautiful as Oxford is considered a shithole.

Ani rolls her eyes and Thalia laughs. At me? With me? With Ani?

"You'll have to excuse Ani, Jane," Thalia says, leaning close enough to me to make breathing suddenly a challenge. "She's a spoiled, rich, big-city brat."

The left corner of Ani's mouth slices upward into a lazy smirk. I expect her to counter it and say something like, "No, I'm not that rich, don't be silly." But she doesn't. She knows what she is and she's not afraid to admit it.

Later on, after Ani leaves us to go to her afternoon classes at the Saïd Business School, Thalia tells me that Ani's family are billionaires.

"Didn't she come from Indonesia or some other country like that?" I say, and immediately regret how snarky that sounded.

"Yeah, apparently there are a ton of billionaires in Indonesia. I looked it up. They're considered the biggest emerging market, soon to be the world's fourth biggest economy."

I'm taken aback by this, and slightly, inexplicably angry too. Deep in the recesses of my guts, Mom's voice, petulant and bitchy: *Know what Grandpa used to call those third-world countries in Southeast Asia? The armpit of Asia.* But now, even someone from the armpit of Asia is wealthier than us. Laughable. Ani is a painful reminder of the kind of Asian I could have been. The kind I should have been. I'm almost overcome by an urge to eradicate her from my life.

"She's probably the richest person in Pemberton." Thalia laughs, as though reading my mind and my awful, hateful thoughts.

Yet again, I realize how out of place I am. I bet Thalia's family, if not billionaires, are at least millionaires. Just like everyone else who can afford to come here for further education.

"It might be fun to go out in London," Thalia says.

I stiffen up at the thought of going all the way to London with Thalia and Ani. Maybe if it were just Thalia. The two of us could explore the city together, at a gentle pace. Stop by the British Museum, have afternoon tea at a café tucked away from the bustling streets. But Ani would only want to do the things that are out of my reach. Shop at Harrods. Buy a ton of Burberry. And then go to the most expensive clubs.

As though sensing my reluctance, Thalia says, "How about just going for a girls' night out here in Oxford instead?" Then she adds, "Come get dressed in my room. We can do our makeup together again. What do you think? It'll be like old times."

Old times. Three weeks ago is hardly "old times," but when she mentions it, it sends an electric shiver down my spine. The thought of her fingers grazing my back as she zips me up turns my legs to water. I can't say no to that. And a night out in Oxford sounds just about doable.

I force my mouth into a smile, though I have a feeling it ends up more like a grimace. "Sure. Sounds fun."

This is not fun. This is not fun at all. Why the hell am I here, in a place called the Varsity Club where everyone looks like a young lawyer and is drinking five-year-old bottles of wine and nibbling on tiny food? I'm swept back to my first night here, and there's nothing more I want to do than skulk back to Downing and bury myself in my single bed.

The Varsity Club has four stories, including a cocktail lounge and a nightclub in case patrons weren't suffering enough. At the top level is a rooftop lounge with skyline views. Apparently. I wouldn't know, because Ani of course drags us to the nightclub part of the place, where she orders shots of something sickly sweet at the bar, shouts at us to down them, and then proceeds to strut onto the dance floor.

Please, Thalia, please hang back. Please catch my desperate eyes and roll yours so I know that you're on my side in this moment. That you hate this atmosphere—the throbbing techno music, the slick bodies writhing, working so hard to catch everyone's attention, the raised voices fighting to be heard over one another.

But she doesn't. With a slightly embarrassed laugh, Thalia lets herself get pulled into the crowd on the dance floor, and then she starts to dance as well, and I can't tear my eyes off her. I never would've thought that Thalia could move like that, not wholesome ray-of-sunshine Thalia. But she moves like oil, smooth and slow, while everybody else jerks like mad puppets around her. She flicks her blond hair over her shoulder, sways her hips sensuously, her hands trailing from her thighs up and up and, oh my god, I'm staring, I should look away, but I can't.

Ani whoops and steps close to Thalia, pressing the front of her body up against Thalia's, and begins grinding against her. No, please, push that bitch away. But Thalia doesn't. She laughs again, a girlish laugh that's half-embarrassed and half "let's go," and their thighs are kissing and kissing and I am in hell, I know it.

My head is swimming already—we'd stopped by at a nearby pub before this and grabbed a couple of pints of cider each, and now, coupled with the syrupy shot, I'm well past tipsy. I lurch toward them, vaguely aware that I'm pushing away other dancing bodies. A shout of, "Watch where you're going, sweetheart!" I ignore it. I want to wrench Ani and Thalia apart, give Ani a good shove or two to really drive in the message. Fuck off.

I'm almost there when Thalia suddenly cries out and jerks around, her shiny hair whipping in a wide arc. Before I can react, she shoves a guy who's been grinding behind her away roughly. "Bastard!" she screams.

"What happened? Are you okay?" I say, but my voice is too small and the club is too loud and it gets drowned out. I try again, a bit louder this time, but already I'm too late.

A man steps between me and Thalia, blocking her from view, and he asks the questions I did, only this time it comes from a timbre-rich voice, impossible to miss. "Are you okay?"

He shifts slightly. I see the profile of his face, the superhero jawline and the floppy blond hair and the impossibly broad shoulders, and I know he's trouble.

His name is Antoine and he's French and apparently owns a hip wine bar in Jericho, and there is no way that I can compete with him, not a handsome, wealthy French guy with a French accent so heavy it sounds like his mouth is full of cream and sugar when he talks. The chemistry between him and Thalia is hot and immediate and dangerous, and for once, Ani isn't my main concern. Ani isn't at the forefront of my mind, nor even at the back of it. Ani is nothing; I've miscalculated it, focused too much on her when I should have been focusing on the men around us. Because of course, Thalia is into them, and they are into her because there is no way that anyone with a libido isn't into Thalia.

Antoine takes Thalia by the hand and leads her upstairs, Ani fluttering around them like a drunk butterfly, and when we burst

117

out into the cold night air on the rooftop, his voice becomes even clearer, sexier now that he no longer has to shout over the music.

"What a bastard," he's saying to Thalia.

She shudders. "He grabbed my butt, just like—grabbed it—ugh."

"Gross," Ani declares.

I nod wordlessly, wanting to show my rage in solidarity, but as usual I'm flaccid, no words coming out. As useful as a glass hammer.

"Would you like a drink, maybe?" Antoine says, leading us all to an unoccupied table near the edge of the rooftop, where Oxford's incredible skyline stretches out around us. Oxford at night is jaw-droppingly beautiful, lights shining off the cathedral and the colleges, but I don't see any of that. My eyes are locked on Thalia, because the signs of my heartbreak are written so clearly on her face. The way her wide eyes never leave Antoine's face, the way her lips part ever so slightly when he's near, like he's something delectable she can't wait to taste.

When he leaves to get us a drink ("Wait eer, ladiezzz"), Ani immediately leans forward and says, "Omigod."

"I know," Thalia breathes. "Have you ever seen anyone more gorgeous?"

You, I want to say. *You are more gorgeous. You are too good for him.*

"Holy shit," Ani says. "Girl, if you don't take him, I will."

Thalia laughs. "Jesus, is he even real? Those eyelashes."

"Fuck his eyelashes, look at his biceps! That jawline, oh man. I could bite him. And I've been to Vin+. That place he mentioned he owns? It's so trendy and like, just so chic." Ani narrows her eyes. "Seriously, are you gonna go with him? 'Cause if you aren't, then I am."

Thalia bites down on her lower lip, her eyes shining with something—laughter? Desire? Then she says, "You hardly know him, you tramp."

They both laugh. My heart is thundering, hammering against my rib cage. This conversation can't be happening. I want to scream. They both look at me like they've just remembered that I'm there. Oh, it's you. Our hanger-on. "What do you think, Jane?" Thalia says kindly.

I shrug. "He seems okay."

"Okay?" Ani squawks. I really hate her. "OKAY? Girl, are you blind? Have you seen his face?"

I press my lips together and don't say anything. Ani turns her face toward Thalia and rolls her eyes. I don't know if she meant for me to see it. It makes me feel like shit. Thalia is for sure not going to invite me out again after this. The thought spurs me to say, "Yeah, I guess he's good-looking."

"Fuck yeah he is!" Ani says.

Thalia grins. "He really is ridiculously handsome, isn't he?" And then she shushes us and I turn to see Antoine walking back with a tray of wine, smiling that smile that has no doubt dazzled hundreds of women, and I wonder, fleetingly, if I could push him off the roof. Only four stories up, but they're tall stories. His skull versus the cobblestones. I'd put money on the cobblestones.

Then he's sitting down, again between me and Thalia, always between the two of us, his masculine presence thick and suffocating. I'm being squeezed out and I hate him, I truly do. I pick up one of the wineglasses and take a long, deep gulp. They talk and laugh and drink, Ani and Thalia gazing at him with shining eyes, laughing at his every word. At some point, another guy joins us, another Frenchman, pleasant to look at, though not quite as shiny. Good enough for Ani, who's pleased that she's got a Frenchman for herself; it had become clear very quickly that Antoine was only interested in Thalia.

I sit on the edge of the circle, gulping down wine so I don't have to make conversation. My head is heavy, the voices coming from all sides around me, a maddening circle of noise. There's no place for me here. Later, as we lurch back to Pemberton, Thalia clinging to Antoine's strong arm as she stumbles over the cobblestones, I wonder who I should get rid of first: Antoine or Ani?

As it turns out, I get rid of neither. The days march on, the skies turn from late-summer gold to a dreary gray, and still I do nothing. We've slumped into a comfortable routine. Classes, coursework, tea and scones. Sometimes, Thalia and I write together at a café, our fingers flying over our respective keyboards. There's just something about her presence that ignites the words inside me, and I like to think it's the same for her, that part of her aches for me in the same way and spurs her to write too.

But then classes end for the day and she disappears, leaving me with nothing but her lingering scent—mulberries and smoke—and the remnants of her hastily written scenes. While I'm left alone, replaying bits of our conversation over and over, I know she's out there with Antoine and Ani and Olivier. I know, because I often follow them, hiding behind trees and statues like a fucking creep. *This is what you've done to me, Thalia. This is what you've made me do.*

I should stop, I know I should, but I can't. Not yet. And it's not even like I'm the only pathetic one. Really, I'm not the worst out of all of us here. Ani is, because I know for sure she's not even that into Olivier. I can tell Ani's going along with it because it's the only way she gets to spend time with Thalia. Because in the end, that's what we're all vying for, isn't it? Time with Thalia. I bet Olivier, too, is secretly in love with Thalia. As I observe from behind a statue of whatever dead white guy, I often catch little looks of derision from Ani, as though she's wondering why the hell she's putting up with a greasy Frenchman like Olivier. She must know she got the short end of the stick; but maybe that's favorable to ending up like me—left out, single, alone.

But I am patient. I know Thalia well enough to know that she will soon tire of Antoine. He's just so wrong for her. That first night, they'd fallen under his spell, that heady mixture of French accent ("Dis eez ah-may-zeeng, eez it not?" No, Antoine, it fucking is not) and impossibly blue eyes. But I've gone out for meals with them twice more now—pity meals, I think, that Thalia invited me to only because she has a heart of gold and can't stand to see me suffer—and it's become painfully obvious that he is so wrong for her. He doesn't understand her sparkling wit; whether it's because of the language barrier or because he's a moron, I don't know or care, but he doesn't appreciate her for her brilliance. The only thing they share is physical lust, and while it makes me want to rip my skin off, it's also a relief because how long can lust last?

She'll get sick of him soon. She will. She must.

But the days tromp on, and now we're in proper winter wear. Ani has gotten rid of Olivier and moved on to Geraldo, and then to Jason, and still Antoine hangs around, a wart that refuses to get gone. I want to grab Thalia and shake her. What is it, Thalia? What's stopping you from seeing the truth? That you can do so much better? He calls her *ma chérie*, and I do believe any judge would acquit me for stabbing him in the ear just for that alone.

Then one day, on a quiet, dark November morning, all of us fed up of the lack of sunlight, glumly sipping our coffee in Haygrove Hall, Ani says the words that would bring our Oxford days to a bloody end: "My brother's coming for a visit."

Chapter 13

PRESENT DAY
NEW YORK CITY

As it turns out, SusPens Con is a lot bigger than I had previously thought. It's at the Javits Center, a behemoth of a building made of glass and steel with an aura that makes me think of ancient stadiums built for bloody fights. Or maybe I'm just in a dark mood. What else is new? When I finally went back to the hotel room last night, I'd told Ted that Toni took me to a fancy dinner and we talked shop all night, and then I'd immediately gone into the bathroom so he wouldn't ask me too many questions. This morning, he'd had the audacity to ask if there was a ticket for him as well. I only just managed not to laugh in his face. A ticket for him as well. As if. He, the man who reads one book every five years, thinks he should get a ticket to SusPens Con just because... what?

As I got dressed, carefully applying makeup in the bathroom mirror, Ted had leaned against the doorframe and watched me. Leaning against the doorframe is something I read about a lot of male love interests doing in books, but when Ted did it, all it did was make me nauseated. I wanted to shove him out of the doorway.

"You look nice," he said in a tone of voice that made the back of my neck crawl.

I glanced at him before muttering, "Thanks." I have given a lot of thought to what I should wear when I see Thalia. I've fantasized about this way too many times to count. One of my biggest fears is that I would bump into her while I'm running an errand in sloppy jeans and tea-stained T-shirt. Now that I'm actually getting the luxury of prepping before seeing her, I need to make sure that I look as flawless as I can.

My outfit was designed to take us back to our Oxford days—a mustard yellow dress that ends just above my knees paired with black tights, brown booties, and a black cardigan. As a finishing touch, I put on the diamond necklace to perk up the otherwise dark fall colors. Or should I say, dark Michaelmas colors? I wonder if she'll notice.

"I haven't seen you wearing that necklace before, wow," Ted said, coming inside the bathroom and tracing it with his index finger. At some point in time, my husband's touch must have warmed me. Or at the very least it must not have repulsed me. But now all I can do is remind myself not to flinch.

It was a relief to get out of that hotel room. I told Ted I was running late and rushed out, only to finish doing my makeup at a Starbucks bathroom. Of course, now that I'm actually at the Javits Center, I feel simultaneously under- and overdressed. There are people here who look like they're ready for New York Fashion Week, and then there are others who are schlepping it in baggy jeans and shirts, and I should feel happy with my outfit, but I just want to tear it off because it isn't good enough, and just what the hell was I thinking, coming out here?

I stand outside of the convention center, watching people

streaming in and out. Their bright red tickets hang from their necks, and part of me wonders if I could just reach out and snatch one off. I gnaw on my lower lip and pace back and forth. What do I do? Can I steal inside? Or—ah, I know. I'll approach one of the people coming out of the convention center and offer to buy their ticket off them. Yes! That's perfect, because presumably they're coming out of the thing because they're done anyway, right? Right.

Deep breath. Here we go. I spot a man in his forties walking out carrying a tote bag no doubt with free books, and I approach him. "Um, excuse me, sir?"

He doesn't even slow down, just brushes past me with a muttered, "No, thanks."

Okay. There's that famous New York City attitude for you. I've lived too long in the Bay Area, have become soft. Still, I straighten my back and look around for someone else to approach. A middle-aged woman walks out with the same tote bag, and I walk up to her, but before I even get close, she barks, "Not interested."

Jesus. What the hell is going on? And now it's bad because this woman was loud enough to attract the attention of one of the security guards at the door, and he comes toward me with his hands on his belt. Why do guards always walk like that? I guess because it makes them look even more intimidating. I take a small step back, my mind zipping everywhere, wondering what the hell I'm going to do if he asks me to leave. It's not like I can tell him that I NEED to see Thalia. I doubt he'd understand.

"Ma'am, do you have a ticket to this event?" he says.

"I—well, actually, I was trying to get one—" The words sound so wrong, so shady even to my own ears.

He's already shaking his head. "Sorry, ma'am, but we don't allow the sale of tickets here."

I take another step back.

"I'm afraid you're going to have to—"

And another, and my back bumps up against somebody. Warm liquid pours down my butt and the back of my thighs and I jump with a yelp.

"Dammit!" someone says in a brusque, high-pitched voice. A voice that's painfully familiar.

I turn around, an apology already halfway out of my mouth when I see her face and forget what I was about to say. The woman in front of me is busy dabbing at her pantsuit. She still hasn't seen me.

It takes a while for my brain to get a hold of my mouth again, and I say, "Ani?"

She stops dabbing and looks at me over the top of her huge Gucci sunglasses. Her eyes narrow, then widen, and her mouth drops open. "No. Janice?"

"Jane."

"Jane, of course! Oh my god!" She opens her arms wide and covers me in a hug where no part of our bodies touch and she kisses the air near my face. When we part ways, she gives the guard a once-over. "What's going on here?"

"I was just letting her know that she can't be here unless she's got a ticket," he says.

"Oh!" Ani pouts at me. "You don't have a ticket? Then what are you doing here?"

"I—" My insides are writhing, and I'm sure my face is ablaze. I want to find a hole I can jump into and die, because this is the worst outcome I could have imagined. "It was a mix-up," I say lamely. "My ticket got lost in the mail . . ."

"Oh, you poor thing!" Ani cries. "Not a problem. I have VIP passes, obviously." She rummages in her huge Louis Vuitton bag and fishes out a lanyard with a card that says "VIP" in huge gold letters. She holds it up to the guard, who waves us off with a grunt, then she hands it to me. "Here you go. Nobody wants them anyway. Who wants to come to these things, am I right?"

I'm not sure what to say to that, since I clearly want to come to these things. I make a show of being very focused on putting the lanyard on so that I won't have to answer that weird question. Speaking of weird questions, what the hell is Ani doing here?

Then Ani says something that wrenches me from my thoughts. "Hey, that's a nice necklace you're wearing."

My mind goes blank. Shit. SHIT. I'm wearing the necklace. But of course I am, because I never thought, in a million years, that I would bump into Ani, of all people. I catch hold of the pendant, the infinity symbol made out of diamonds, and slip it under my top. "Thanks, yeah. I just—my husband gave it to me. Last year. For our anniversary."

"Yeah? It's cute. He's got good taste." She smiles at me, and I can't tell if she's seen through the lie. She must. She must recognize the necklace. She—what is she thinking? I can't read her, never could.

"Yeah, anyway, it's so great to bump into you. I mean, of all people!" I say, desperate for a change of subject. We walk through the entrance and are swallowed up by the huge building. Inside is a mad bustle of chaos. There are crowds everywhere, panels and booths with bright colors, and large banners announcing their lead authors and most exciting titles. Definitely not a place for my humble books. "What brings you here?"

Ani pushes her sunglasses up into her hair. Her makeup is

flawless—her eyes smoky and lined to a sharp point, her skin aglow from years of a meticulous skin care regimen. She is as beautiful as I remember. She gives me a sidelong glance and smiles, as though she can read my thoughts. "Thalia, of course."

"Thalia?" My voice comes out choked, which makes sense because Ani's answer is basically a gut punch. She's here because of Thalia? She got VIP tickets because of Thalia? But that would mean that they've kept in touch all these years. No, that's not possible, not when Thalia's disappeared from my life so completely. I spent years looking for her and finding only a ghost, and here is Ani, telling me oh so casually that she, a nonwriter, is at SusPens Con because of Thalia?

"Yeah, I basically promised her I'd post about it on my socials or whatever. You know how it is."

No, I do not know how it is.

Ani grabs two tote bags from a booth as we walk by and hands one to me. She must see the confusion on my face because she says, "I'm an influencer. You must've seen my socials? I've got, like, over three hundred K followers on Insta."

I manage a dazed nod, which pleases her. *You fucking self-centered cunt*, I want to spit out. *I'm not impressed by your "influencer" status, I'm fucking shocked because for some reason, Thalia has decided to stay in touch with you, you parasitic brat, and not me.* I could sob with the unfairness of it all. I'd thought that Thalia had chosen me over Ani in Oxford, but maybe I was wrong all along.

"So you've kept in touch with Thalia all this time?" I say. I can barely speak above a whisper.

"Hmm?" Ani is momentarily distracted by someone giving out free books; she takes two copies and hands one to me

128

before dropping her copy in her tote bag. "Thalia? Right, yeah, of course."

Why of course? I don't even realize that I've asked it out loud until Ani gives me a strange look and says, "I thought you knew. Thalia's my sister-in-law."

Chapter 14

NINE YEARS AGO
OXFORD, ENGLAND

It's interesting, seeing the ways in which certain people react to each other, like acid and alkaline being poured into a single container, seeing which one prevails. When Ani said that her brother was coming for a visit, something in her tone of voice made me glance up and really look at her. I try not to do that; Ani's face isn't good for sanity. Too pretty in a man-made way, everything about her deliberately put together. A manufactured doll wearing a permanent sneer. If I looked at it too long, something inside me would crack and I would swipe a knife at it, just to see if she could even bleed or if there were just ice and silicone underneath.

But her voice is more bitter than usual, a half-hidden quaver underneath it, as she says, "So my brother's coming for a whole month. He'll be staying in London for most of that time, but he's insisted on spending a week in Oxford. Yay me."

"Oooh, we finally get to meet the famous Ivan," Thalia says. It hurts that Thalia knows his name, whereas I'm only now learning about his very existence.

Ani sniffs. "The famous Ivan. Right."

"Is he coming here just to see you? That's so sweet," Thalia says.

Ani's mouth curls unpleasantly for a second before it goes slack again. "Of course not. He's setting up a new office branch in London; that's why he'll be in England for a whole month. And in the meantime, he'll stay for a while in Oxford to make sure I'm actually going to classes and not fucking up as usual. Perfect Ivan. Did you know our parents have left basically everything to him in their will? They told us both that he's getting the company, like 99 percent of it, while I get Mom's jewelry and Birkins and, oh, a shitty 1 percent. Fucking patriarchal bullshit."

Poor you, I want to say. Having to make do with what is no doubt a fortune in diamonds and emeralds and branded bags. But I remain quiet, relishing the graceless way that Ani is griping. Even saintly Thalia is barely able to keep her annoyance concealed; a corner of Thalia's cheek is twitching a little, which means she's fighting to hold back her words. That's how well I know you, Thalia.

"Well, it's still nice of him to come and spend time with you," Thalia says. Why does she try so hard to be nice to Ani?

"Whatever." Ani slurps her coffee loudly, and that's when I notice that her leg is jiggling relentlessly. And I realize that Ani, take-no-prisoners Ani, foulmouthed Ani, sexpot Ani, is nervous. I would be lying if I said I wasn't enjoying it, just a little. It's nice to see someone else being pushed into a corner for a change. I, for one, can't wait for Ivan to arrive. The past few weeks haven't thawed whatever weird thing is going on between me and Ani, and it would be a nice change to see her undone. To know that I'm not the only one fighting my own inner battle all the damn time.

A week later, Ivan arrives, and it's A Whole Thing. There are

131

rooms available for guests at Downing, but he's booked a room at the Randolph instead, because according to Ani, "Prince Ivan is too good for a school dorm." I think back to how enamored I had been with my dorm room when I first arrived, swooning over the fireplace, and inside, I burn and twitch and wonder if I'll end up hating Ivan even more than his sister does.

Thalia, Ani, and I trudge through the biting English winter in turgid silence. Ani is too nervous and cranky to suffer any conversation, even between just me and Thalia. It's actually nice; Ani's snappish mood turns into an inside joke between me and Thalia. As we walk, Thalia and I sneak glances at each other, eyebrows raised in amusement, and god, I feel like I'm coming out of hibernation, like the sun's finally come out. Here we are for the first time without the fug of Antoine hanging around like a cloud of body odor. I want to shout with laughter and dance in the cold.

The Randolph is one of the oldest buildings in Oxford, and one of the fanciest. It's one of those places where the inside is decked out in old leather and rich mahogany and people automatically speak in hushed tones to show that they're wealthy and powerful enough to never have to raise their voices to get what they want. Ani sighs loudly and makes a beeline for the hotel bar. Thalia and I exchange another look—our fourth!—and follow Ani.

She's waving impatiently at the bartender. "I need wine."

"Of course, ma'am. We have a large selection—"

"Dude. Just give me a bottle of—of—whatever, a Chablis."

"Excellent choice. Which vintage would you prefer—"

"Oh my god!" Ani cries, throwing her hands up. "Just. Anything, okay? The most expensive one, whatever!"

Thalia gives the bartender a sheepish smile and opens her mouth, probably to apologize, but just then, a warm male voice behind me says, "Thirsty again, sis? Not much has changed, I see."

Ani's expression freezes, only her eyes showing a flash of horror and mortification for a fleeting second before her face melts into a simpering smile. She turns around and says, "Koko, I'm so happy you're here!" She jumps off the barstool and throws her arms around Ivan.

The lighting in the bar is dim, but even so, I can see at a glance that Ivan is devastatingly handsome. Ani's family's got amazing genes. Tall, broad shouldered, a smile that's almost as distracting as Thalia's. His heavy-lidded eyes somehow work together with his sloped nose and a jaw that would give Antoine's a run for its money, turning his face into one that speaks not just of strength, but of elegance. The kind of face that painters would cut off their ears over. His outfit is casual but obviously tailored to fit every inch of him flawlessly, showing off his swimmer's shoulders and tennis player's arms.

"Koko?" Thalia says, by way of greeting.

Ivan's smile widens—is it possible for men to not smile when they see Thalia?—and he says, "It means older brother in Indonesian. I swear my name isn't actually Koko."

Thalia giggles, and the hairs on the back of my neck prickle. Because I know this laugh of hers. Ani does too. I catch the startled glance from Ani, displeasure writhing behind her eyes, both of us probably thinking the same thing: You've got Antoine, what are you doing? On my part, of course, I'm also mentally hissing: I've been worrying over how to get rid of Antoine, and now I've got to worry about Ivan too? But isn't that just classic Thalia? She can't help being a flirt, can't help exerting her superpower over everyone. I can't blame her; we all want people to like us, and it's not her fault that she's everybody's type.

Ani detangles her arms from Ivan's neck and pats the seat next to her, away from Thalia. "Sit down, Koko. I've ordered a bottle of wine to celebrate your arrival."

"Come on, let's get a table instead. I don't much feel like sitting at the bar." He doesn't wait for Ani to agree before heading for one of the tables next to the picture windows that look out onto the Ashmolean. Thalia follows, her face glowing in a way that makes my insides churn. I catch Ani's eye—the irony! How have the tables flipped so fast? Only moments ago I was exchanging glances with Thalia, and now . . . well. She breaks the connection first, her upper lip curling like she can't believe she's at such a low point that she's having to exchange looks with me. Not Jane the help! She'd rather suffer alone.

I follow like the faithful dog I've become. If only Mom could see me now. How she'd laugh. *Are you one of them yet, Jane?*

Ani recovers quickly. It's a trick the rich have, I've noticed. They do everything with a certain confidence that the world is a clam that'll pry itself open for them. And it does. Doors are always swept open; people step aside to let them through. A constant assumption that everything they do is right. That they belong. Ani slinks away from the bar and struts to the table her brother has picked out for us and sits down like she meant to relocate to a table all along.

Thalia and Ivan are already deep in conversation when we get there, Thalia laughing, Ivan mock-grimacing.

He glances at us with a rueful smile. "I was just telling Thalia how I fell asleep on the way over here and one of the steward-esses placed a pillow behind my back while I was sleeping.

I stayed in the same position for about five hours and now my back is killing me."

"She placed a pillow behind your back? How would that even work? The seats don't even go far enough back for you to lie down on," I say without thinking. In my mind I'm recalling my flight from SFO to Heathrow, me squeezed into a seat so narrow I can't bend my arms without touching my neighbors, recoiling every time we accidentally touch one another.

There's a pause as they all look at me. A flash of pity in Thalia's eyes, right before Ani bursts out laughing.

"Oh my god, Jane," Ani says. "This is why I love you. You're so simple and sweet." Stupid, she means. I'm so stupid and poor. "In first class, your seat turns into a bed. It lies down flat and then they come and put an actual mattress on top of it."

An airplane seat that turns into an actual bed. I can't even imagine it. *Do you belong now, Jane?* Mom croons.

Ani is still giggling when the wine arrives. We're quiet while the server pours it into four glasses. Ani's shoulders are shaking, Thalia is shooting me pitiful glances, and Ivan is studying me in a half-amused way. I pretend to be very interested in the pouring of the wine, watching the pale yellow liquid splash into the glasses, wondering how much this is going to cost me. Mom's right, I realize with a twist of my stomach.

I can't look anyone in the eye as the waiter places a glass in front of each of us.

"Well," Thalia says, her attention refocused on Ivan, "let's drink to Ivan's arrival." She picks up a glass and smiles at him, flashing that naughty little dimple. A full-on assault, the kind of smile that makes even our teachers forget what they're saying mid-sentence.

135

But Ivan's still studying me, and it takes a full second before he realizes that Thalia is speaking. The spell catches him again; I see his mouth parting as Thalia's smile captures him, and I know he is hers. He picks up his glass and raises it. "Cheers," he murmurs, like he and Thalia are the only two people in the bar, like his sister isn't sitting across from him, glowering.

Ani and I pick up our glasses but don't bother to say "Cheers" before we each take a swig. I can practically sense everyone else's mind whirring, thoughts scuttling around like little insects looking for a weakness before they bite, and I think, for the first time, *I'm not the most dangerous person at this table.*

Ani tells us she can't bear to be around Ivan on her own, so we'll have to spend the whole weekend with them. Thalia agrees too readily, and in the morning, she knocks on my door bright and early. Too bright and too early for how much we've all had to drink last night (two bottles of Chablis, followed by cognac). But that's Thalia. Nothing touches her, not even alcohol. She's looking even more beautiful today, if that's possible, and if I didn't love her so much, I would hate her, this real-life Barbie who's dimpling her cheek at me, smiling like she can't smell my rank morning breath.

"Go shower," she says, striding into my room. "I'll get an outfit ready for you."

I'm too hungover to argue, not that I would argue at any other time, so I shuffle off to the bathroom, yawning and scratching the back of my neck. The shower does me good, and by the time I get back to my room, Thalia has carried out her threat and has picked out an outfit. A gray sweater (everything I own is black or gray) with my dark blue jeans, fine. What's not fine is that she's also added a bright orange silk scarf with a big "Hermès" emblazoned across it. I looked up Hermès after that first day, and if I remember right, their scarves start at $500. This one's probably above two grand. She sees me staring at it and says, "It'll look nice, don't you think? The color works well with your sweater."

I don't answer, watching her through the mirror as I towel dry my hair. She's up to something, but I don't know what. Then it hits me that she's just trying to be nice, to save me after my faux pas yesterday about the plane ride.

As though reading my mind (again! Maybe she is a mind reader after all), Thalia steps toward me and puts her arm around my shoulders, pulling me close to her. My heart stutters, forgets how to pump blood.

"I'm not like them either, you know," she says softly.

I can't manage more than a single, "What?"

"I'm not rich like they are." She gives a small, rueful laugh. "Well, I doubt any of us here at Pemberton is as rich as Ani and Ivan, but I'm not even, like, middle-class rich."

"But you—but the scarf, your dresses—"

"They're all gifts. I thought you might have guessed by now, I'm good with people. And . . ." She takes a deep breath. "I'm not above using it to get little gifts like these." She catches my gaze with those incredible eyes of hers. They're wide, so wide and so impossibly expressive. And in them, I see a sense of fear and vulnerability that makes me want to hug her. This is the first time that Thalia has admitted something like this to me, something that should make her less than perfect, but somehow ends up making her even more precious. She bites her lower lip, the movement distracting me. "Do you think I'm pathetic? Pretending to be someone I'm not?"

It takes a second to realize this is not a rhetorical question, then I jerk my head side to side. "No, of course not."

She smiles with obvious relief. "Good, because it's been killing me, keeping this to myself. I've just been so embarrassed. I guess I thought that coming here would be my chance to live like they do, you know? My parents—we've always been uh. Really poor?" she says with a bitter laugh.

"My mom's a nanny," I blurt out. I don't know why I reveal that now, and why it feels like such a huge burden has come off my shoulders. So what if my mom's a nanny?

"My mom's a dog walker," Thalia says.

We look at each other for a beat, then we both burst out laughing.

"No, seriously," she says, "that's what my mom does. She walks rich people's dogs!" And we laugh some more, because it's either that or cry.

"Well, she walked rich people's dogs," Thalia says, suddenly serious. I struggle to swallow my laughter, because now Thalia looks like she's about to cry. "She can't really walk anymore. She got sick. Bone cancer. And she doesn't have health care, so we're pretty much fucked. And I kind of was . . . hoping . . ."

By now, if she asked me to help her rob the HSBC on High Street, I would do it. I would do anything for this girl.

"Well, I was kind of hoping that Ani would help out." She grimaces and gnaws on her lower lip. "Oh god, that sounded horrible, didn't it? I just heard myself say those words, and my god, I sound like such a shit—"

"You don't," I say quickly. Because of course Ani should help out. Ani the billionaire heiress who's only here to fuck around, Ani who makes us follow her to Harrods and watch as she drops fifty grand on a mink shawl at Ferragamo, a shawl that I have since seen her drop on a sticky dance floor as she sways drunkenly in a nightclub. "Dammit!" she'd screamed, then tossed the shawl aside, forgotten. She'd staggered back to the dorms sans shawl. I think of how my mom would save her used tea bags, cut them and dry the soggy leaves before boiling them again so she didn't have to spend ninety-six cents on a new box of shitty tea. Ani is the right kind of Asian. The Crazy Rich kind. The kind that everyone loves. The kind I would kill to be. The kind that's meant to save Thalia. "I mean, it's literally nothing to her. And it would be saving your mom's life. She'd want to do that; I'm sure she would."

"I can't just ask her outright," Thalia says. "She'd think I was just being friends with her for her money. She's been telling me how growing up, she was always surrounded by these fake friends who were only with her because they expected something—money, fame, whatever."

I resist telling Thalia that Ani has nobody else because she is so intensely unlikable; that her money and status are the only things she has to offer. "This is different though; it's your mom." And your mom isn't like my mom. Your mom is worth saving.

"I've been hinting to her. The past few weeks. That's why I've been spending so much time with her. God," she sighs, her face scrunching up with shame. "Sorry, I didn't mean to dump all this on you, Jane. I know I sound horrible, but I've been getting desperate. Ani's not really taking any of my hints . . ."

"Of course she isn't," I mutter. "Ani's too self-centered."

Thalia gives me a sad smile. "Yeah, I guess so. Anyway, this isn't your or Ani's problem. It's just—well. This will probably be my first and last term here."

A wave of sickness washes over me. "What?"

"My aunt called me yesterday. We're in massive debt and she's right, I shouldn't be wasting money by attending such a fancy master's program. I've been such a selfish idiot, god." She rubs her face with her hands. "I'll probably go back once the term ends and get a job. Pay the—"

"You can't!" The words rip themselves from deep in my belly, burning as they wrench out of my mouth.

Thalia stares at me, wide-eyed.

"I—no. You can't just leave." My face is made of flames. Somehow, I manage to stop myself from grabbing her. From shaking her, or squeezing her, or doing something, anything, that would stop her from getting away from me. I imagine Thalia as a little bird; I would catch her and put her in a gilded cage, keep her safe from everything. I look around my room, desperately trying to find something—some way, of keeping her here. She's saying something, but I can't hear the words, the blood is roaring in my ears, and I have to keep her here, I can't lose her. I grab hold of something—anything—and it turns out to be the snow globe I'd bought at the Covered Market. I see myself swinging it, the snow swirling inside the globe, catching the light as I bring it down in a wide arc onto her lovely skull—

The idea strikes me just in time, hurtling out of me like a maddened horse. "Ivan!"

Thalia's still staring, and now I see that her startled gaze is on the snow globe in my hand. The walls of my room collapse onto me. "Uh. This is—I like to hold it when I need to think." I move it from one hand to another casually. Or what I estimate to be "casually," at least. It feels incriminating in my hands. I'm lobbing a live grenade to and fro, and I can't tell if

140

Thalia's buying it, or if she just saw a glimpse of the madness that skulks inside me.

She recovers her smile. "I do that, too, when I'm stressed. I like to have something for my hands to do. Anyway, what about Ivan?"

Right. Yes. "Well, he's rich, right? 'Cause he's Ani's brother." Stating the obvious. *Get to the point, Jane.* "And he seems nice . . . ish? I don't know, he seems okay. And he . . ." God, the words refuse to come out now, lodging in my throat, digging sharp little claws in and clinging tight. I cough them out. "I think he likes you."

I didn't think Thalia's eyes could get any wider, but they do, and it's almost too much. I can't keep looking at that face of hers, as trusting as a child, because otherwise I'll cave and tell her to forget it. But I don't want to lose her. I can't imagine going through the rest of the program without Thalia here, and if it means she has to belong to someone else, then so be it.

"He definitely likes you," I continue. "The way he looked at you . . ." My skin feels slimy and I want to rip it off. "You could ask him."

Thalia shakes her head. "Oh god, I couldn't. I can't ask some guy I just met—"

"You like him too." I wonder if that sounded as petulant as it did in my head. If it gave my own feelings away.

But Thalia doesn't seem to notice. Her cheeks turn rosy, from peaches and cream to strawberries and cream, and god, she is made to be devoured. "Was it that obvious?"

I shrug. It's obvious if you're watching for it. If you're ultrasensitive to it because you're obsessed with the person in front of you.

"I feel terrible. Especially since Antoine—"

I can't help snorting out loud. Antoine. Who cares about fucking Antoine? "He'll live. He's a big boy. And this is more important. Look, if it makes you feel better, you could even ask Ivan for a loan or something."

Am I solving it? Am I actually taking a huge problem from Thalia's life and offering up an actual solution?

"I think I need to get to know him better first. I just don't feel comfortable asking him for help like that." She twirls a lock of hair, and I'm distracted, for a moment, by the way it catches the light and turns almost translucent. Everything about this girl is ethereal.

"Of course you don't. Because you're a decent person." You're the best person. "How about this: this weekend, when we spend time with Ivan and Ani, I'll distract Ani so you can have some private time with Ivan? You'll have plenty of time to chat—" My insides are shriveling up as I say this, twisting and shrieking and dying. "—and hopefully get close enough to him to ask for help."

The look on her face makes my sacrifice almost worth it. It's an expression of gratefulness, mixed with disbelief. "Really? You'd do that for me?"

I would kill for you, Thalia. I shrug. "It's not a big deal. I like Ani." Oh, how the world laughs at this obvious lie.

But Thalia is without guile. She nods slowly. "I guess that could work. But, Jane, I feel so shitty about doing this. I don't know—"

"You have to. For your mom." Fuck her mom. *For my sake, Thalia. Do it for us.*

Her furrowed brow clears and she closes her eyes for a moment. When she opens them, her face turns, becomes determined. "You're right. I have to do it. It means nothing to them, right?"

"Yeah. It's the equivalent of a day's shopping spree to them."

She nods. "Okay. God, I can't believe I—we're doing this. Thank you." She grasps my hands, her eyes shining with tears, and I swear I've just died. "You're the only real friend I have, Jane."

Chapter 15

NINE YEARS AGO
OXFORD, ENGLAND

The problem with trying to give Thalia and Ivan some privacy is—well, there's more than one problem. There's Ani, first and foremost. She's always been snarky, but now that Ivan's around, she becomes so abrasive that a few times I imagine shoving her off a tall building, or stabbing her with my fork, or some other thing that would shut her up. So I might be a bit grumpy. Just a tad. I think that's understandable, given I'm basically pimping the girl I am obsessed with away. It's so that I won't lose her, I remind myself. But knowing something in theory doesn't really make that thing any easier to swallow.

We start the weekend off with a centuries-old Oxford tradition—punting. Punting consists of hiring a tiny boat and using a long stick to push your way down the River Thames. It sounds a lot more romantic than what it actually is, which is a pain in the ass. And arms. And legs. Because using a heavy wooden stick to shove your boat downstream is really freaking tiring.

Thalia has prepared a picnic basket, complete with finger sandwiches and warm bagels and champagne, but I don't get to enjoy it because I insist on doing the punting so that Thalia and Ivan can have some privacy to chat with each other while Ani guzzles the champagne and kills whatever romantic buzz there is between Thalia and Ivan. I don't know what circle of hell I'm in to have to watch Thalia turn on her charms for Ivan while I grasp this heavy stick and resist bringing it down on both Ani's and Ivan's heads.

"Ani doesn't like to talk about Jakarta," Thalia says. "Tell me more about the place."

Smart. Ani's always dismissing Jakarta—come to think of it, she's always dismissing every place; no city is big enough or fancy enough for her. Urging Ivan to talk about Jakarta is a surefire way of getting Ani to switch off. Sure enough, I spot Ani's eyes rolling behind her huge sunglasses before she turns away to watch the scenery as we float downriver.

"It's great, actually," Ivan says. "It's a huge metropolis with, like, over twenty million people."

"Wow, big city." Just like her big, big eyes. In the early Oxford morning light, they turn from brown to gold, and if I were Ivan I would propose to her right now. "The biggest city I've been to was LA."

Ivan laughs. "LA doesn't feel much like a city; it's too spread out. I love LA though; it has its own charms. Is that where you're from?"

"No, I'm from Nevada. Just outside of Vegas."

"I hate Vegas. What a fuck you to mother nature," Ani says between gulps of champagne. "Nobody should be living in the desert."

Ivan and Thalia glance at her. Thalia gives an uneasy smile. "Yeah, I guess. The Strip's kind of a weird place if you live there.

145

actually been to the Strip."

"I can see that. It's like how my friends at the Bay Area never ever go to Fisherman's Wharf," Ivan says, and just like that, Ani's caustic remark is left behind, a little verbal roadkill that they can pave over and ignore. "Anyway, I spend a lot of my time traveling. Maybe about half of my year is spent outside of Indonesia, and I swear every time I come back to Jakarta, there's a new skyscraper being built."

"Wow, sounds amazing."

Sounds like a nightmare to me, the landscape changing faster than I can adapt. Just like what's going on now. Part of me is still dazed, still wondering how the hell I ended up here, pushing this boat along. I'm tired, my shoulders ache, my belly is filled with bitterness, and I've just about had enough of everyone. I wonder if I can tip the boat over and send us all plunging into the Thames, just end it all already.

"Where do you usually travel to?" Thalia says, and I hate this, I hate her and I hate him and I hate Ani and I hate Oxford for bringing me and Thalia together and the world for keeping us apart.

"We do a lot of business with Japanese corporations, so I travel to Tokyo quite a lot, and we also have clients in Hong Kong, Singapore, Dubai, London, New York . . . all the big cities."

You know what really sucks about Ivan? It's the fact that even though he's clearly bragging, it doesn't come off as bragging. He's so used to this lifestyle that it's become natural to talk about it like it's no big deal. He lists off countries I would never be able to afford to visit like they all belong to him, like the world is truly an oyster that he holds in his manicured hand. I can't help but

146

snort out loud at this. They all glance up at me, and my heart stops beating.

"Sorry," I stammer. "I think I'm getting tired pushing the boat."

Ivan straightens up. "I'll have a go."

"Hah!" Ani snorts, jumping up. We all cry out as the boat sways dangerously.

"Oops, sorry about that," Ani laughs, not sounding at all sorry. She steps over the seats toward the end of the boat, where I'm perched. "C'mere, give me that paddle thingy. You can't do it, Koko, on account of your heart."

I glance at Ivan and he shrugs. "I'm fine."

"Like hell you are," Ani says.

She's tipsy, well on her way to being drunk, and it's not even noon yet. I look down at her and the plan forms, quick and easy, so obvious that I wonder why it didn't hit me sooner. I should get Ani drunk. So drunk that I have to escort her back to Downing, leaving Thalia and Ivan alone. Yay me, world's number one wing-woman.

I hand her the oar and sit down. Thalia meets my eye and gives me a quick smile, and I live for these moments, these little shared sparks between us that tell me our minds are in sync.

"Thanks for manning the oar like a champ, Jane," Ivan says, pouring champagne into a new glass and handing it to me. Our fingers brush as I take it and my stomach lurches. Revulsion and a guilty little coil of attraction. He holds my eye a second too long. I don't quite understand what the hell's going on. Why he would even notice my existence when Thalia is right there. I am a star and Thalia is the sun; while she's around, I am invisible.

A guilty flush taints my cheeks, and I break eye contact, muttering my thanks for the champagne. I swig the whole thing down. It's too much of a stressful situation for me to maintain, and I can't even bear to look at Thalia, too scared to see if she's noticed that strange moment between me and Ivan. I hold my glass out for a refill and Ivan obliges, then I hand it over to Ani, who's only half-heartedly pushing the stick in and out of the water.

"Thanks, this is sooo heavy," she moans, taking the champagne flute from me and taking a long swallow. "This is a lot less fun than it looks."

Touché.

She empties the glass and practically tosses it back to me. Thalia must realize what I'm up to, because she points to something in the distance and resumes chatting with Ivan. With Ivan distracted, I quickly refill the glass myself and pass it to Ani.

"Ugh, you are a lifesaver," she says. The words come out sloppy, her lipsticked mouth slightly slack. She sways a little and I jump to my feet. I don't need Ani falling into the river and causing a scene, which would surely ruin the rest of the day for Thalia and Ivan.

"Come here. I'll take that," I say, grabbing the stick and helping Ani to one of the seats on the boat. "I think maybe it's best if we return the boat now."

Thalia gives me a grateful smile, and I begin the long, arduous task of steering us back to the nearest docking bay, wondering again why I'm doing what the hell I'm doing.

I'm surprised by how weird it feels to have my feet planted back on solid ground. It's disorientating; I feel like I'm still swaying. So it's no surprise when, five seconds after we hop off the boat and onto dry land, Ani leans over to one side and vomits. Oh, Ani, so predictable.

Ivan utters a sigh. An entire history conveyed with just one breath. Impatience and anger coloring his perfect face for just a fleeting moment, the flawless facade cracking. I wonder how many years of Ani he's had to put up with, the spoiled, resentful little sister who hates that he was the one born with a cock—the key to the Pranajayas' empire. For a second, I think of a literal penis-shaped key and I have to bite down on my lip to keep from laughing. Ivan walks over toward Ani, but I'm faster because I've been waiting for this (well, minus the vomit) and already I'm there, patting Ani's shoulder and gathering her hair behind her neck.

"Let me," Ivan says, but I step between him and Ani.

"It's okay," I say. It's not okay. Take care of your goddamned sister. Take her back to Jakarta and lock her away forever. "I don't mind. I'm actually not feeling too great myself, so why don't you let me take Ani back to our dorm and we can have a bit of a rest while Thalia shows you around the city?"

He's taken aback by this. I guess he's not used to other people stepping up and offering to take care of his messy little sister. Thalia steps up beside him, her eyes shining with hope. Ivan frowns. "I don't think—"

"No, really. I mean, how often do you get to come to Oxford, right?" I say quickly. "It's one of the most beautiful cities in the world, and you're only here for a week before you go back to London. It would be such a shame to miss out on everything."

"Let me at least call you two a cab." Such a gentleman. A gentleman who can't wait to be rid of us. My heart is being ripped into two halves—one side singing happily at succeeding in my

149

quest; the other weeping, tearing things apart. I am not used to being generous, to doing things for the sole benefit of another person. I do not like this feeling, but I would do it again and again for Thalia. Thalia whose face is bright as the sun, who is staring at me like I've just saved her puppy—no, better, I've saved her mother. She mouths a thank-you as Ivan flags down a cab and gives the driver a twenty-pound note, way too much for the two-minute drive to Pemberton. We help Ani inside the cab (Ani: "I don't need help, oh my god, you guys, stop that—stop, ow!"). I slide in after her and gaze longingly out the window. The last thing I see is Thalia slipping her hand through the crook of Ivan's arm before the cab turns a corner and they disappear from my sight.

Guess what's worse than leaving Thalia with an unbelievably beautiful man who also happens to be richer than god? Well, never mind. Nothing's actually worse than that. But what makes it even worse is leaving Thalia for said beautiful man to take care of his very drunk, very angry sister.

I don't understand why Ani's so angry all the time. If I had her looks and all the money in the world, I would— well, I don't know what I would do, it's not something I've daydreamed about, but I imagine I would at least not be this bitter.

"She knows, you know," Ani slurs.

I turn my face from the window and look at her. I'm not going to take the bait. And with Ani, everything is a bait. She doesn't ever say anything without having first calculated how much it would prick at your skin. She likes to push people to the point where they're uncomfortable enough to almost tip over into anger, before she laughs and tells them she's just kidding. That's the kind of asshole she is. The world is her playground and the people in it are her toys.

"She knows you looove her."

It feels like I've been punched. The taxi driver glances at me through the rearview mirror, but I pretend not to notice. I study my hands instead.

"God, Jane, you're so fucking obsessed with her. It's sad. Why is everyone so in love with her, anyway? She's just a cute, racially ambiguous chick; there's like about a dozen of her in every Whole Foods in New York."

"You're drunk," I snap. And now I've lost, because now she knows she's managed to get under my skin.

"I see what you two are trying to do."

The taxi driver isn't even bothering to pretend that he's not listening. He's turning his head to look at Ani once every few seconds. *You should pay attention to the road*, I want to say, but my words have dried up.

"I know you're trying to get her some alone time with Ivan." She laughs, but it ends in a sigh. "I've seen it all; bitches are always using me to get to my brother. Eeevvverybody wants a piece of Ivan." The cab turns a corner and her head lolls to one side, and I wonder how much force it would take to snap her neck. Not very much at all, I don't think, especially if I use the momentum of the moving car in my favor. Wishful thinking, of course.

By the time we get to Pemberton, I'm half toying with the idea of just leaving her in the car, but in the end, I grab her arm and yank her out, not bothering to be gentle. Outside of the cab, she teeters on her stupidly high heels and I have to swing an arm over my shoulders and practically carry her into the college.

"Why're you Thalia's lapdog, Janey? I can tell you like Ivan too.

Why wouldn't you try your luck at him?" She snickers at this, and I know, I'm not delusional enough to think that me going after Ivan isn't amusing in a very pathetic way. We lumber up the stairs, and I think about how it would be so easy to get to the very top and then give her a little push. How very much like the universe, to make Ani so delectably killable. But if I were to take that prompt, everything would end. Ivan would be heartbroken—or at the very least he'd be inconvenienced, and inconvenienced people aren't the most giving. Thalia wouldn't be able to afford to continue her studies, and I'd lose her.

So I keep going. Keep on keeping on, as they say. I let her breathe her rancid alcohol fumes down my neck and I look at the myriad ways that Ani could die and I ignore each and every one of them. Love moves us to do great things, they say, and they're right.

Ani lives one floor above us. When we get to her door, I have to go through her purse to find her key, and Jesus, how many freaking pills does this girl have? There are at least three different bottles in her Prada handbag, but I don't know what they are as the labels are in Indonesian.

"Diet pills," she says, watching me under half-closed eyes.

"Why?" I can't help blurting out. I've just helped her up three flights of stairs and she weighs practically nothing, her bones sticking out under my hands, brittle bird bones.

"How do you think I manage to look like this? Give me that," she says, snatching her purse back and fishing inside it. She locates her key and stabs it at the door, missing the lock until I grab her hand and put the key in myself.

Her room looks like a fashion show has exploded in it. Mounds of clothes, shoes, and bags are strewn on every available surface.

The window is open, which is good because it smells slightly rank in here, a stench of old smoke that's going to cling to my skin even after I leave.

"You're not supposed to smoke in your room," I say.

Ani snorts. "So they'll make me pay a fine, whatever." She flops onto her bed and moans. "Ugh, my mouth tastes disgusting. Isn't that weird? Tasting your own mouth?" She laughs. "What do you think Thalia's doing with my brother right now? You think they're fucking? I bet they are. I bet she's dragged him all the way back to his hotel and they're smashing right now."

"I'm gonna go." But I don't go. I'm too busy watching Ani and daydreaming about smothering her with her pillow, or maybe one of her fancy, overpriced outfits.

"Thalia's not the angel everyone makes her out to be. Why are you so obsessed with her? She's not even a natural blonde. You haven't seen what she's like when it's just her and me. That girl is trouuuble."

I have to ask, because it's about Thalia and I can't not ask when it's about Thalia. "How is she trouble?"

"She is a sluuut."

I suppose I did ask. I don't know why I did; it's not like I was ever going to get any reliable information from this drunk bitch. "Okay, out of the two of you, she's not the one who's been sleeping around with different guys." I hate how petty I sound, how high school. But this is the effect that Ani has on me. She drags me down to her level and I'm left feeling dirty.

She laughs, her eyes closed so I can see the way her eyeshadow has smudged across her lids. "They're all guys she's sampled herself, before she gives them to me. 'He's a yummy one,' she'll say. Wink-wink."

153

Wow. Ani's even worse than I thought, and that's saying something. But what I can't figure out is why she's saying these things. Because she's drunk? Or because she wants to hurt me?

"Why are you telling me this?"

But she's already out, snoring softly as she finally falls into a drunken sleep. I stand there, watching. Why, god, why must you make it so easy to kill her? I look around her room. There are at least six different handbags in here, and two clutches, and I have no idea how many red-soled shoes, strewn about like carcasses. If I were to swipe a pair of her Louboutins, she wouldn't even notice. Then I see, on the mantelpiece above her fireplace, a careless tangle of jewelry. My cheeks grow hot, my heart thumping a manic rhythm. Pearls and diamonds and gold all twined like rat tails. I take a step toward the fireplace and glance at Ani. Still asleep. Another step, and another.

Close up, the pile is even more impressive—the pearls are perfect, smooth spheres and the stones are bigger than I thought, and there must be at least thirty different pieces here. I glance at Ani again. She won't miss one. Just one. I deserve it for putting up with her throughout the past few weeks, and for letting her live now. I try to pick out a ring lined with little diamonds like a sugar crust and a square diamond in the middle as big as my fingernail, but it's too tangled up with a necklace that has an infinity symbol made out of diamonds. Whatever, she has so many pieces of jewelry here she won't miss these. I take another quick look at her before slipping the ring and the necklace into my pocket and leaving the room, quiet as a ghost.

Chapter 16

Thalia's my sister-in-law. Sister-in-law.

The words echo in the hollow recesses of my heart, bouncing off the walls and resounding over and over and over again, until I want to cover my ears and shriek just to drown them out. Sister-in-law? Thalia is married?

But even in the storm of pain raging inside me, I realize that of course she is. Why wouldn't she be? We're in our thirties. I'm married. Of course Thalia is married too. She's never had a shortage of men and women going after her.

But it's not just the fact that she's married, a small voice whines. It's the fact that she's married to Ivan. It's been a while since I thought of Ivan, even though he was such a pivotal part of our Oxford experience. Now, his face floats back to the forefront of my memories. His flawless love-interest-in-a-romcom face. They made a stunning couple then. I'm sure they make a stunning couple now. I can't stand it.

"Yeah, she and Ivan pretty much tied the knot as soon as she

155

left Oxford," Ani says, each word a knife wound, twisting and turning in my guts. I need her to stop fucking talking already.

I can't bear it; I can't stand here and listen to this anymore. I raise my hands and shove Ani aside. She squawks and stumbles back, almost falls over, but some passerby manages to catch her just in time. "Whoa," he calls out, unnecessarily loudly.

"Sorry," I mumble. "Sorry, sorry." I'm already walking away, ducking into the crowd, ignoring the noise behind me. I can hear snatches of Ani's voice—"What the hell is her problem?"

My problem, Ani, is that Thalia was mine. All mine, before you and your brother came along and ripped her away from me. And why did she cut herself off from me but not from them? Did she only cut herself off from me? Does she still keep in touch with everybody from Oxford? I can barely remember the names of anyone else at Pemberton. Pam, or Pat, or whatever the fuck. Does Thalia keep in touch with her too? Was I the only one who was excommunicated?

The thought is too painful to bear. Already tears are burning in my eyes and I have to blink them away rapidly to stop them from falling. All this time I thought . . .

Never mind what I thought, because I've clearly been wrong about everything.

I'm stumbling blindly through the crowd, barely seeing or hearing anything. There's a cry or two as I shove people away, but I don't stop. I don't care, I can't be here, and where's the freaking exit anyway?

Then I hear it. The voice that's been haunting me all these years. It skips my ears and goes straight into the center of my nervous system, lighting up all of my synapses. My entire body reacts to it. I stop mid-stride, everything inside me pricked to attention.

Thalia.

I turn slowly, and there she is, sitting behind a desk, speaking into a microphone. A large crowd is gathered around her, a sea of humans standing between the two of us. She's so far away from me, achingly far. So many bodies in between ours. And as I stare, she continues talking: "—my first ever panel, oh my gosh. It's so wonderful to be here."

Back in Oxford, Thalia had this quality that made her, even when addressing a crowd of people, seem like she was speaking directly to you. It's still present now, everyone in the crowd staring at her with rapt attention. And how can they not? She is incandescent. Over the past nine years, her beauty has sharpened into something breathtaking, the kind that makes people do a double take to make sure she's real. It's the kind of beauty that actresses pay good money for, the kind of beauty that requires a busy mind, a mind that holds a myriad of secrets.

"Tell us about *A Most Pleasant Death*," says another woman who is sitting next to her, probably the moderator. "What's the story behind the story?"

Thalia smiles. "Well, *A Most Pleasant Death* is about an all-consuming, sort of toxic friendship between two women, and what inspired me was my own experience with various female friends. I have always found female friendship fascinating, the way that from a very young age, girls are encouraged to see one another as competition just because of how sexist many societies are, and therefore there's only ever room for one girl at the top. In school, I have always kind of felt like the other girls can't help but compete with one another: even though they may be best friends, they're also rivals. And so it becomes this extremely complicated relationship that's nurturing and yet also harmful. I wanted to show how this kind of friendship can spiral into a darker state, until it spins out of control and hurts those around it."

The moderator nods like she understands what Thalia was just talking about, but she doesn't understand. No one else understands, because what Thalia just said? That was all meant for me. Heat rises from the base of my chest. She wrote a whole book about our friendship. And that's what tips me over the edge. Because I don't understand how she could have written this, a whole book that was obviously meant for me, and yet she never once reached out to me over the years.

Before I know it, I'm wading through the crowd of listeners and calling out, "I have a question!"

Heads are turning in my direction. The moderator frowns, pausing mid-sentence, and looks at the crowd. "Wow, we have some enthusiastic listeners here," she says with a forced laugh. "We'll have a Q andA session in about half an hour, so—"

I shout the words out; I can't bear it any longer. "Why did you never come back to Oxford after your first term there?"

Silence falls, suffocating and thick. I know it's impossible, but it feels as though the entire convention center is suddenly quiet, every ear inside the building listening.

And finally, Thalia sees me. Her eyes widen, her mouth—those rose-pink lips—part slightly. For a second, something passes across her face—fear? Horror? It can't be. She's just surprised, that's all.

"Jane!" she says, and my name, amplified by her microphone, reverberates through flesh and bone and breathes life back into my whole body. Her expression is pure shock, and she turns to the moderator and mutters something.

The moderator nods and looks at me sternly. "We'll have a Q and A session after this talk. Let's get back to the program for now."

I lower my head and move to the edge of the crowd, my face in flames. Shit, what the hell is wrong with me? Why did I just blurt that out? Fortunately, the moderator moves the talk along and soon I am forgotten once more, blending into the crowd as we all fall under Thalia's spell. She got lucky with *A Most Pleasant Death*, she says, because so much in publishing depends on timing and luck. So humble, as always. Minimizing her own talent. I wish I could tell her to stop, to own that she deserves this meteoric success. It's a different form of torture to be stuck here amongst the audience, as though I'm like any of these people, a stranger to Thalia.

Nothing she says is particularly enlightening; they're all responses I've heard from other authors before, but somehow when Thalia says them, they become different, exotic, exciting. The Thalia effect.

Movement from the edge of the stage catches my eye, and I turn to see Ani aiming a serious-looking camera at Thalia. My gut sours. Shit, she's going to tell Thalia about how I went completely berserk before running away. Ani seems completely absorbed in taking photos. When she's done with the big camera, she pulls out her iPhone and takes more photos using that, before turning the phone around and posing for a few selfies with Thalia in the background. She then aims the phone at the crowd. I duck my head, but I'm not fast enough. She frowns when she sees me and rolls her eyes.

My heart rate slows to a manageable pace. She just thinks what she's always thought of me: a weirdo, just some loser that

Thalia took pity on. Nothing worth remembering. I can deal with that. I'm not here to impress Ani.

An eternity passes before the panel is finally done. With superhuman effort, I manage to stop myself from blurting out more awkward questions during the Q and A, gritting my teeth instead while listening to mundane questions like: "How long did it take you to write this book?"

"Come on," I whisper under my breath, willing the whole thing to end already. Then we're asked to stand in a single file to get an autograph. An autograph from my estranged best friend. The line that forms is impossibly long. Of course everyone wants to have a piece of her. I want to scream at them to get away, to let me have this time with her. But I am patient. I have been waiting years for this moment. I can afford to wait a few more minutes.

As it turns out, I end up waiting a whole hour. An hour spent on the sidelines, shifting from one foot to the other, biting my nails until they are ragged and bleeding. I squeeze my thumb and watch the blood well up into a fat droplet before I put it to my mouth and lick it off. The pain keeps me present, reminds me I'm not dreaming, that Thalia really is just a few feet away; after all these years, here she is in the flesh.

Then the signing is done and Thalia is waving to people and waving away her agent/editor/publicist and heading toward me. I turn into a statue. I can't move as she closes the distance between us, the expression on her face unreadable—is that a smile or a frown or something between the two? And now she's in front of me and I must be dreaming because she is here and she's so perfect I could cry. The scent of her, that familiar smell, takes me right back to Oxford. The nose is the only part of our body that can time travel, and I'm whisked back nine years to when I first landed in England, among the damp and the bus exhaust, finding Thalia for the first time. Her nearness pulling me to the surface just as it's doing now, yanking me up and up until I break through, as though the past few years I've been floating underwater, everything around me muted. Now, suddenly, everything is loud and clear, and all the colors are bursting with vibrancy.

"Jane," she murmurs, and I'm not sure who made the first move, but we're hugging now, and she feels amazing in my arms, so warm and real and—oh god—I can feel those delicate bird bones of hers and my throat thickens with my need for her. Thank god my weird outburst earlier hasn't scared her off. "Let's talk over coffee," she says, pulling back and smiling at me.

Someone clears her throat. Ani. I have to resist from lunging at her. She stands next to us with an are-you-kidding expression. "Um, not to interrupt the moment—"

She very definitely meant to interrupt the moment.

"But we've got to go, babe. You've got a photo shoot with *Elle*, remember?"

Thalia groans. "That goddamned photo shoot."

"Excuse you, 'that goddamned photo shoot' took me months to arrange, so you need to move your ass." Ani turns her gaze at me and regards me the way one would a particularly revolting insect. "How are we doing, Janet? Are you recovering well after your little"—she waves vaguely at me—"meltdown earlier? I'm fine, even though that was a really hard shove back there."

I can barely bring myself to reply, her tone of voice is so caustic. Still, I only have myself to blame. She's right; I did physically push her away. I should be grateful that she's not pressing charges against me or making an even bigger deal out of it somehow. For Ani, this reaction is surprisingly understated. Pretty sure that Oxford Ani would have reported me to somebody, and the realization that present-day Ani isn't doing that makes me swoon with relief. "I'm sorry," I say, and I actually do mean it. "I don't know what happened back there. I, uh—I'm not great with crowds."

Ani rolls her eyes. "Duh." But when she next looks at me, I'm pretty sure she's thawed a little bit. She seems less like she's about to bite my head off. She turns to Thalia. "Let's go."

The look on Thalia's face is yearning, I'm sure of it. The way her eyes widen and her mouth trembles. I know it because it's mirrored in my soul. "Jane," she says again, more of a whisper than anything. "Let's have dinner. Yes? Skye Bar on East 75th at eight."

I barely have time to nod before Ani and her agent/editor/publicist descend upon her and whisk her away, leaving me alone, the only person standing still in the throng of her fans. But for the first time in nine years, I am okay. I am alive. I have a dinner date with Thalia.

Chapter 17

NINE YEARS AGO
OXFORD, ENGLAND

Thalia doesn't waste any time. In the evening, she sends me a text: **Thank uuu!**

I look at those two words for a long time, tracing them with my index and middle fingers. I want to laugh and cry at the same time. Yay, my plan worked. Boo, my plan worked. I send her a thumbs-up emoji and it gets read, but she doesn't send anything back and my heart rips open a little bit more. I put on Ani's ring and look at it this way and that, admiring the way it catches the light before I put it in my underwear drawer and leave the room to go for dinner.

The rest of the night, I pace in my room. At the slightest noise, I jerk up and rush to my door. Is it Thalia?

It's not Thalia. It's never Thalia.

She spends the night with Ivan, and it's good, it's what we wanted. It's just how we planned it. But I can't help hating myself just a little bit more. I did this. I whored her out. I'm her pimp. The thought pushes a bitter laugh out of me and then the laugh turns into a sob and I bury my face in my hands, because I can't stop imagining Thalia in bed with Ivan, slick bodies glinting in the soft glow of lights as he takes her from various positions. Their beautiful faces purring with pleasure as they fuck. Then my brain trots out images of Thalia with other men, just as Ani described, and god, I hate Ani, I really do, and I should've killed her. With any luck, she'll choke on her own vomit. I didn't see her at the dining hall, so maybe that happened. One can hope.

I'm awakened the next morning by a loud, insistent knocking. I stumble out of bed, open the door, and it's Thalia. She's radiant. More so than usual, which I never thought possible.

"Oh my god, Jane," she says, rushing inside and throwing my curtains open.

I squint at the sudden flood of sunlight.

"He's amazing—oh my god, he's just—ahh!" she squeals and does a little hop. An actual little hop, like she's a kid who was just told she's going to Disneyland.

"Oh?" I perch on the side of my bed and rub my eyes. They're still puffy from all the crying I did yesterday. Idiot. Stupid fucking idiot.

"I can't thank you enough. I can't believe you did that. After you and Ani left, I took Ivan around the city. We went to a couple of colleges—New College, Exeter—then we went to Blackwell's, and the whole time we were talking so easily with each other like we've been friends forever. And then before we knew it, it was almost dinnertime. He tried calling Ani, but I guess she was still zonked out, so then we ended up having dinner with each other and oh my god, the dinnertime conversation—Jane, I swear it was like we were just in sync and it was like I was having a mind orgasm."

I look down when she says the O word. The thought of Thalia having orgasms of any kind with Ivan is like a drill through my head.

"He's so brilliant, oh man. He knows everything about everything. We talked about politics, economics, philosophy, everything! We were so in sync—oh, I said that already."

"Yeah," I mumble.

"And he ordered this vintage bottle of wine—oh my god, I swear it was the best thing that I ever drank. After dinner, we were so full, we decided to have a walk, and our hands just kind of found each other's and it was the most natural thing in the world. We were walking past the Radcliffe Camera when he suddenly stopped and tugged on my hand and kissed me, and oh," she sighs, fake-swooning and flopping onto my sofa with a smile. "It was some kiss. My legs actually became all weak. Have you ever had that reaction from a kiss?"

I shake my head, but already she's talking again.

"Then we kind of got carried away and hurried back to his hotel and . . ." She grins and wiggles her eyebrows at me. I feel sick. "I think he made me come like four times. I can barely walk this morning, holy shit."

Stop talking, stop talking! I want to scream. I want to clutch at my head and shriek until the whole world falls apart. Instead, I yank at my wristband and let it snap back, hard.

I don't understand this feeling myself. I don't understand any of my obsession with Thalia. My feelings for her aren't actually sexual, I don't think. I don't know. I love her body, but I don't have fantasies of having sex with her. It's just—I love the vulnerability of it, the sharp edges of it, the way that it's like priceless art. Yes, that's it. I want to just gaze at Thalia the way one admires pieces at a museum. And the thought of anyone having her, defiling that body of hers, is revolting.

Finally, Thalia notices something's off. "Are you okay? What's wrong?"

I shake my head. "It's fine." It's not fine. "So when are you going to ask him for help?"

The excitement leaks from her face. "I don't know. I kind of don't want to now. I just—it feels so slimy doing that, and what we had yesterday, that was real, and I don't want to ruin it."

I stare at her. At her pale, slim neck. I imagine putting my hands around it. "But your mom," I say dumbly.

"I know," she sighs. "I'll tell him about her soon. I just—not yet. It's too soon."

Great. I guess I just have to grin and bear it as she continues seducing him for the rest of his stay here. What could possibly go wrong?

If I thought that Antoine was bad, Ivan is worse. So much worse. Because Antoine is your stereotypical French dudebro—oozing sex appeal and romantic quotes, which is bad, but reeks of short-term fling. Burns hot and fast before dying out. She breaks up with him without any preamble, a task on her to-do list crossed off just like that.

I wonder at her ruthless efficiency when she tells me about it the night after her magical day with Ivan.

"He was so angry," she says with a slight shiver. "It was so unattractive. Ugh. The way he spoke. I'm just glad I'm no longer with him."

I try to imagine Antoine radiating with spurned anger, and I'm surprised to find that the image comes to me easily. His handsome features contorting, turning him ugly with hate. His big hands turning into fists. Yeah, I can imagine it easily enough.

Meanwhile, Ivan is *husband material*. This is what Thalia actually says to me after spending a second day with him. Husband material, like men are made of different ingredients and this one happens to have the organic, wholesome ones she's been looking for all along.

It sickens me to the point where I almost hate her. Almost. But I am spineless, so the following week, I merely watch from the sidelines as she traipses around Oxford with her future husband (because let's face it, once Thalia decides she's going to marry you, you're going to walk down that aisle with her). When his week in Oxford is up, he returns to London, but my relief is short-lived. Instead of staying on in London as planned, he comes back after just one day. ("He said he just couldn't bear to stay away from me!" Thalia squeals.) And his second week here, they're even more in love, entwined even tighter.

And she's right, Ivan *is* husband material. Romantic but not too romantic, so you know he isn't just being carried away by the newness of their relationship. Calm, so he'll make a good husband and father. And a bit of a workaholic, so if he turns out to be a terrible husband, at least she won't have to see too much of him. The occasions that the four of us spend together, Ivan has to excuse himself a couple of times to take a work-related call. Tonight is no different.

"Poor Koko, having to run an empire must be sooo hard," Ani purrs when he comes back to our table. "You know what would help? Letting your own blood relation have company shares so she can assist you."

"We'll talk about that when you're done with your MBA," Ivan says in a tone that makes me look up, because there's a quiet rage simmering underneath it. So he has a bit of a temper when it comes to Ani. What else is new? I can barely keep myself from choking the girl.

Thalia and Ivan share a look and a soft smile, so I push my fork off the table and bend down to pick it up. I glance under the table as I bend down, and sure enough, she's found his hand and is squeezing it. A secret message, an alliance against Ani. It's this small gesture that plunges the knife deep in my gut and twists. They've only been going out for about two weeks, but already they're close enough to have secret gestures, and she's offering him support over his bratty sister. Thalia is no longer Ani's and my friend first, but Ivan's girlfriend first, our friend second. And I can't forgive her for that. I cannot, not after everything.

I'm changing the plan. The plan is shit. The plan needs to die a swift death. I could just about tolerate the plan when it was about Thalia playing a part to get some quick cash from Ivan so she could stay in Oxford with me. She wasn't supposed to actually fall for the guy. This has gone too far. It's time to put a stop to it. She'll thank me for it later, when she's no longer under Ivan's spell.

After dinner, I tell them I'm too tired to go pub-hopping with them and walk in the direction of Pemberton, hoping madly that none of them will try to follow. I turn the corner and wait. None of them follows. Disappointment clutches my chest, then relief. This is okay. This is exactly what I wanted.

I go in the opposite direction, down St. Giles', until I reach Jericho, where there's a cluster of hip bars and nightclubs. I check Google Maps, just to make sure I've got the right place. Thalia and Ani have gone to Antoine's bar several times, but I could never make myself go. I'd imagined it being as sleazy as Antoine, low lights, throbbing music, and date rape drugs. But as it turns out, Vin+ is a classier place than that. The lights are low, but so is the music, and the crowd in here trends older; post-grads instead of undergrads. I wrap my coat around myself tight, feeling massively out of place, and skirt the edges until I get near the bar, where I spot Antoine.

I watch him for a while as he chats with customers and pours different drinks for them. How strange to be watching him in his own element, minus the Thalia effect. He's less disgusting now, on his own. I almost turn around and go back to Pemberton, but I make myself walk up to the bar. When he sees me, a look of such naked hope appears that I want to scratch him.

"Janice!" he says, delighted.

"Jane," I say, but he's not even listening, he's so excited.

"This is a nice surprise. Are you with . . ."

"No," I say quickly, and he deflates.

"Oh." He picks up a towel and starts wiping down the bar. "Did you want something to drink, or . . ." Clearly, without Thalia accompanying me, the conversation might as well be done.

"Uh. Just water. No, white wine. The house white." I need some liquid courage for what I'm about to say.

I watch as he pours the white wine, the sides of the glass turning frosty from condensation. When he slides the glass over, I take a long swallow.

"So what can I do for you?" There's that French accent.

"Um, actually, I'm worried about Thalia."

His handsome face darkens, the corners of his mouth pulling down into a sad-face emoji. This man is a walking cartoon character. "Oh, Janice, I am so glad you bring her up. I haven't

169

been able to stop thinking about her, you know? The way she broke up with me was so abrupt—"

"I know, but trust me when I say she's still not over you. She's kind of . . . easily influenced. She's been pushed into getting together with this guy—god, he's bad news, Antoine. He's horrible, a monster, and Thalia—you know how she is, so kind and such a pushover—"

"What do you mean a monster?" He plants both hands on the bar and leans over it, training his baby blue eyes on me. It's like having stage lights focused on me. Lights, camera, action. I want to quail, but I'm doing this for Thalia, so I lean into the light and perform my lines like an actress with the Oscars on her mind.

"I don't know exactly what he does to her, of course. In front of us he's the perfect gentleman. But there are bruises on Thalia's arms and legs, and one time I went to her room and she was crying like she's really scared." I even manage to make my voice quaver, that's how dedicated I am to saving Thalia from Ivan.

Antoine's face is a study in barely restrained rage. "What—but—" He shakes his head. "I don't understand. Who is he? Why doesn't she just leave him?"

"That's the thing, he's so charismatic, I don't think she sees how toxic he is. Will you talk to her? Please? I know that she still misses you. She's just blinded by this guy or something. I think if she just sees you—if you remind her of how good you two were—she'll wake up."

"She misses me?"

I give an empathic nod, my eyes wide. "Very much. She talks to me about you all the time. Said you're the best she's ever had. In, uh, in every way." It's like gargling acid in my mouth, saying these words.

Antoine laps them up, because of course he does. What is it about men and their need to be the knight in shining armor? He loves the image so much he doesn't pause to ask why Thalia, a grown, able woman, could possibly allow herself to get into such a bad situation over a matter of weeks. Months, years, I can see how someone can be worn down slowly, layers peeled away until there's nothing left. But weeks? Come on.

But Antoine is too blinded by the blaze of glory.

"I miss her, too, of course. How can you not? She is magnificent, no?"

I nod. She is magnificent, yes. That's the whole reason I'm here, asshole. "And, um, maybe it would be best if you didn't tell her that I was the one who told you about Ivan. We should make it look like you just knew because you're so in sync with her."

"Ah yes. Good point. I'll win her back, Janice. I promise you."

I don't bother correcting him this time. It doesn't matter; I've achieved what I came here to do.

First thing I do when I walk out of Vin+ is to run down a side street and try to slow down my heart rate. What the hell have I done? Sociopathic tendency #17: Brash.

But I couldn't just stand by and watch as Thalia ties herself down to Ivan, quite possibly for the rest of her life. We're too young, only in our early twenties. It's too soon! Our brains aren't even fully formed yet. She'll regret it. I'm only saving her from a lifetime of disappointment.

When my heart feels like it's no longer about to rip itself out of my chest, I walk back to Pemberton. My mind is still spinning, wondering what Antoine is going to do. Some over-the-top romantic gesture? An old-fashioned fight with Ivan? Maybe I should've given him some pointers. But it's too late now. I've done my part to try and save Thalia; now I just have to sit back and watch as Antoine does the rest. Who would've thought that in the end, I would be turning to him for help? How's that for irony?

The second week passes; one long, excruciating week where Thalia and Ivan wrap even tighter into each other, folding around each other so that there's absolutely no space for the rest of the world. It feels as though they've been in love for years. They now have their own secret code, their little inside jokes. All it takes is a seemingly nonsensical phrase here and there: "Like the squid," Thalia says as we tour the beautiful grounds of Trinity College, and Ivan will burst out laughing and pull her close. *What squid?* Ani and I would ask each other silently before shrugging and rolling our eyes.

How strange that Ani should now be my reluctant ally. Though she's not much of an ally; she seems content to stay back, spitting out barbed comments here and there, but mostly a passive bystander. She drinks more, splurges on more luxury clothing, which I didn't think was possible, but aside from that she's mostly harmless. A shame.

Fortunately, it's all about to come to an end. Ivan's due to leave the morning after our formal college ball. It's the biggest night of Michaelmas; everybody's been twittering about it for weeks now. The local dress shops have been filled with students trying on ball gowns. Ani's already bought five gowns. She tells me with sloppy generosity that I am allowed to wear her least favorite one. I'm so anxious/looking forward to Ivan leaving that I ignore the slight in Ani's comment.

But that morning, Thalia bursts into my room, cheeks ablaze. "I think he's going to propose," she squeals.

No. What? NO.

Somehow, I manage to keep from screaming. "What? But—what?"

"I know!" she cries. "It's so fast, but oh god, it feels so right. I—he asked me how I felt about possibly living in Jakarta, and all these questions like did I want kids, how do I feel about him needing to travel throughout the year . . . things a smart, down-to-earth guy would consider before popping the question."

Of course he's the type to ask these questions before popping the question. Wise Ivan. Kind Ivan. Down-to-earth Ivan.

"And then he took my hand and was like—well, I swear he was measuring my ring finger. Oh my god, Jane! Can you imagine? If he proposed tonight?" She hops and squeals again. "Is this the most romantic thing you've ever heard or what?"

I make myself nod slowly.

Thalia finally notices that All Does Not Seem Right and stops chattering. "Are you okay?"

"Yeah. It's just—it seems really fast, don't you think?" *It's been barely a fortnight,* I want to scream at her. I've had rashes older than this relationship.

"I know, but I've never felt this way about anyone before—"

Wow, that stings.

"—and when you know, you know. You know?"

I shrug. "Sure, I guess. Have you told Ani?"

Her smile loses a bit of wattage. "No. I don't really know how she'll take it. Does she seem slightly off to you the past few weeks?"

You mean while you and her brother wrap tentacles around each other in front of her? Instead, I shrug again. "I don't know, maybe."

"I think there's a lot of history between the two of them. Like, a lot of tension or something. I'll let Ivan break the news to her. He'll know how to deal with it." She says this with such confidence that it makes me want to stab her. Already she sounds like a wife, a good Christian wife who adores and respects her husband and trusts that he'll be able to handle everything. I can hardly believe this is the girl I've been obsessed with for the past three months. I really, really need Ivan to disappear from her life.

Once she's out of my room—imagine that, me wanting Thalia out of my room—I call Antoine. Come on, you useless prick. He picks up on the second ring.

"Allo?"

"Antoine, it's getting worse," I say.

"Janet?"

This fucking guy, I swear. "Jane. Listen, Thalia is so—so dominated by this guy, she's not even thinking straight anymore. I think he might propose to her, and if he does, you know what she's like; she's too nice to say no. And the way he is with her, it's like he's controlling all her thoughts and actions. Antoine, please, you need to help."

He makes a sound that sounds suspiciously like a whine. "She won't pick up my calls, Janet. I must have called over ten times, and she won't pick up." His words come out thick around the edges, like he's been drinking. I guess the guy does own a bar.

She won't pick up his calls, so he's done trying? I grind my teeth with frustration. Another thought prickles at the edge of my mind: Thalia never mentioned Antoine calling her. It hurts. Isn't that what friends do? Share things like this with each other? Have I been relegated to even less than a friend? I wonder if she shares such things with Ivan, if she's confided in him about

Antoine so he can wrap her in his tennis-muscled arms and coo at her comfortingly.

"Janet, I'll talk to you later. I have to take care of this shipment," he says, and as he hangs up I can hear him shouting in French at someone in the background.

I knock on Thalia's door, my mind whirring. She carries a curling iron in one hand as she opens the door. "What's up, girlie? Do you need anything?" She doesn't wait for me to reply before going back to the mirror and wrapping a lock of hair around the iron.

"I ran into Antoine, and he mentioned that he's been calling you?" I blurt out.

She freezes for a few seconds, then her hair starts steaming and she curses and quickly unwraps it from the iron. She puts the iron down with a sigh and turns to face me. "When did you see Antoine?"

I think fast. "Uh, this morning, when I was out for . . . a walk."

Thalia frowns, and I wonder if I've blown it. If she can read me as easily as she used to be able to. "Where?"

"Just outside the college."

A look of concern creases her lovely features. "Oh my god, do you think he's stalking me? Why would he be here? His bar's all the way in Jericho and his apartment's in Summertown. He has no reason to be anywhere near here except me."

Try to save the situation, Jane. "Um, well, don't you think it's kind of romantic?"

Thalia looks at me like I've lost my mind. Can't say I blame her. "No! My god, can you imagine if he ran into me and Ivan? I would be mortified. Ivan has no patience for any drama. He comes from a huge Chinese-Indonesian family and he says they've got enough drama to last a lifetime. He's broken up with past girlfriends over less drama. He'll dump me for sure."

For sure? I almost ask hopefully. I manage to stop myself in time. "I see. Well, I'm sure it was nothing. Antoine's a good guy."

"But he talked to you? He mentioned he's been calling? I've been avoiding his calls because I've been with Ivan this whole time and—" She shrugs. "I guess I don't really have much else to say to Antoine."

"He only mentioned it in passing. I'm sure he's fine. I'll leave you to it." I can't leave her room fast enough. My whole body is wound up tight with nervous energy. This is it. I can break her and Ivan up while at the same time making her so angry with Antoine that there's no way they'd get back together.

Back in my room, I dial his number again, pacing as I wait for him to answer. When he does, I don't even bother with a greeting. "Come to our ball tonight. At Pemberton. Thalia will be there and she misses you. When she sees you in a tux, she's going to lose it. She'll leave him for sure."

He actually laughs at this, his voice going a bit high from excitement. "I love balls." I hate all men, I really do. Why do we let them roam around freely?

"Great," I manage to bite out. "Dress nicely. Be your handsome self. Break this awful spell she's been under."

"I will try. Thank you, Jane. Thank you." So the prick knows my name after all.

Thalia and I have agreed to meet up ahead of the ball, so fifteen minutes before the ball, I knock at her door. The sight of her. It's too much. She's wearing a dress the color of crushed sapphires, and it makes her skin look luminous. Her hair is done up in intricate braids, with a few loose tresses framing her face. She's gone for smoky eyes, and it's transformed her into something enchanting. A work of art.

"What do you think?" she says, twirling like I'm her date, like she did all this for me.

"You look amazing," I manage to say.

"Thank you, so do you!" She grins at me. What a lie. I'm wearing a five-year-old dress I'd bought at Macy's that had looked emerald green under the shop lights but as it turns out is more frog green. "Oh my god, I'm so excited. I can't believe this is going to happen." Before I can react, she reaches out and hugs me. "Jane, thank you."

"Huh?" I'm too stunned by everything—by the way she looks, by the sudden hug, by the overwhelming scent of her—to understand fully what's going on.

"Jane, my sweet, sweet Jane." Thalia grasps my hands, her eyes shining bright. "You've been my friend from the very first day. You've made this entire semester wonderful. You are my best friend."

Best friend. A part of me cackles with glee. I'm her best friend! Yes! Me!

The rest of me is dying a long, excruciating death. Guilt is crushing the air out of me. She's radiant with happiness because she thinks Ivan will propose tonight, and meanwhile, her supposed best friend has put into motion a last-ditch effort to stop her dreams from coming true.

You're doing it for her own good, I remind myself. She's just being carried away by her infatuation. She'll thank me for it later.

We walk down to the Chapel Quad, which has been transformed—majestic white tents erected on the lawn, a full bar, and bursts of flowers, flowers everywhere. Everyone is there and everyone is beautiful, shiny lips and shinier dresses, coiffed hair and diamond watches. Ani waves to us and sashays over, looking decadent in a low-cut dress the color of blood. A short while later, Ivan arrives, wearing a bespoke tux that fits him perfectly. He looks like an Asian James Bond. It's impossible not to stare when he and Thalia stand next to each other. Everyone watches them with open envy and admiration. I may as well be a frog in the dewy grass.

I scan the crowd, trying to find Antoine. Where the hell is he?

My phone buzzes and my heart leaps to see his name on it. I excuse myself from Thalia and Ani and pick up the phone.

"Where are you?" I hiss.

"I'm here. At the Old Quad."

I tell Thalia that I have to go to the bathroom and hurry through Highgate Hall. The entire time, my heart is beating a staccato rhythm. I can't wait to see Ivan's expression when Antoine shows up.

As promised, Antoine is at the Old Quad, standing near the Porter's Lodge. I give him a once-over; he's looking dashing in a well-fitting tux, with his hair slicked back, there's no denying that. But he also reeks of alcohol fumes, and as I walk toward him, I see him sway ever so slightly on his feet. Is he drunk? I'm about to snap at him for turning up drunk, but then I realize that the alcohol would probably make him even more dramatic, which is great.

"Hey," I say.

"Yooo," he says. Okay, definitely drunk. "You look great, Janet."

I don't even bother correcting him. "Yeah, so do you. You ready to win back Thalia?"

"Of course!" He grins at me and I have to look away because he's just so disgusting.

"Great, let's go." We make our way across the Old Quad toward the ball.

But when we get to Highgate Hall, I tell him to stop. "We can't go through to the Chapel Quad together. Wait like ten minutes after I go in before making your big romantic gesture. Remember, you have to make it convincing. Good luck."

Antoine gives me a sloppy grin—just how much has this idiot been drinking?

My blood roars in my ears as I walk through the gates and out onto the Chapel Quad. It's finally time for the Thalia and Ivan show to end.

Chapter 18

Of course, fucking Ted has a fucking problem with me having made dinner plans without him. When I finally get back from SusPens Con, he's all over me, abandoning his laptop and clattering about like an excited dog. How was it? Did you meet anyone famous? Did your publisher set up a booth for you? Did you get to speak? Sign books?

Each question is an assault. He knows damn well Harvest wouldn't have bothered to set up a booth for me; they barely have one for the entire publishing house. And he knows better than anyone else that my books haven't done well, that they were released and pretty much immediately sank into obscurity. No reader has ever emailed me about them; no one has ever asked me for an autograph. On the launch date of my debut, Ted had given me a copy that he had bought at our local bookstore and asked me to sign it, and I'd very nearly burst into tears at his cruelty, the way he was mocking me for my failure as a writer.

I can barely restrain the bitterness and anger seething inside me for this man as he fires question after question, none of which I can answer to his satisfaction. *No, Ted, they didn't set up a booth specifically for me. No, Ted, I didn't sign any books.* Why? Then why bother sending you to the con at all?

Why indeed.

I close my eyes, massaging my temples. "Stop."

The questions stop abruptly, a surprised look fleeting across his face. "Are you okay?"

I hadn't meant to say "stop" quite like that, with so much acidity in it.

"Geez, Jane. I thought you'd be in a good mood. I mean, it's your first ever author event—"

"It's not MY author event, it's a bloody convention for all writers." All writers except me, apparently. I struggle to restrain my temper. It's not his fault that he doesn't understand. It's not his fault that he thinks I'm a big enough author to score a ticket to SusPens Con. He doesn't know that I basically barged my way into the convention center with Ani's help. Fuck, I'm a mess. And it's not his fault that he doesn't know any of it.

"Sorry," I manage to push out. "I've just—it's been a long day. I don't like crowds, and the con was—heh, it was very crowded."

Ted's shoulders slump a little. "Aw, sweetie. You should've told me." He reaches out and places a meaty hand on each of my shoulders, and I remind myself I mustn't recoil, because that's not how wives react when their husbands touch them. "Tell you what," he says, lightly massaging my shoulders, "how about we have a nice night out? We're in New York, let's live it up a little, huh? A nice romantic meal, just you and me, how about that?"

The thought of it fills me with dread. A night out with Ted, dinner over candlelight; what the hell would we talk about to each other? When we first dated, I made a huge amount of effort

181

with him. I don't remember why now, but I do recall those days, where I'd read up on the news in the daytime, or scour Twitter for the most amusing, most shocking pieces of news. I would actually jot them down in a little notebook so I wouldn't forget them, and I would carry these news pieces, like little pieces of delicious candy in my pockets, where I would feed them to Ted over candlelit dinners. *Did you know that scientists may have found the God particle—the Higgs boson?* Fascinating. *They uncovered a two-thousand-year-old mummy today, perfectly preserved.* Wow, no way! *I read an interesting article today about the widening wealth gap and why it happens.* Gosh, you are so interesting, Jane.

I was so interesting because I gave a damn. I made an effort. I was never caught unprepared. I had to do it to cover up the fact that I am, in fact, without personality. All those news stories are only meant to paper over the bleak, empty hole where a personality should've been. I've read that this is something many sociopaths have—a lack of authenticity. We're empty inside, a monster pretending to be human.

I don't know when I stopped trying, when our dinners went from the two of us at the table, discussing physics and philosophy, to us talking about seeing Kimiko and her husband out walking their dog, to us struggling to even find anything worth saying. And finally, the death knell of dinnertime conversation—to us sitting in front of the TV, slurping our linguine without having to look at each other. I'm fine with that dinnertime arrangement; it's a lot easier on me, not having to pretend to care about Kimiko and her dog or our other neighbor, Frances, and her two-year-old kid who has a penchant for climbing up trees and then jumping out of them. And so it's very unfair for Ted to suddenly demand the old Jane back, the Jane who had something to say. I need time to prepare, to bring that Jane back to the surface. And I don't have the energy to do that.

And plus I can't do that; I have dinner plans with Thalia.

"Actually," I say in as casual a way as I can manage, "I can't. I have to have dinner with—" My voice falters. If I say "a friend," he'll ask me who it is, and I don't want to go into the whole thing. Oxford is mine, and mine only. He doesn't have a right to it. "Toni. And my editor."

His face lights up. "Oh, wow! That's amazing. Wow, so they're really going all out to woo you, huh?"

The bastard. He knows they're not. I study him, looking for the glint of steel underneath the happy facade. He can't be that clueless. Can he? "Um, yeah, I guess? I think it's pretty standard, probably something they do for all their authors when they happen to be in town."

"No, I don't think so. They're making an effort for you because they see your potential."

He's got to be doing it on purpose, rubbing my lie in my face. Yes, that's it. He knows I'm lying and he's pushing to see when I will break. Well, I won't break. Two can play at that game.

"Would it be okay if I came along?" he says, and there it is. His final blow. "I want to see my wife being schmoozed up by her agent and editor." He moves closer, until our faces are only inches apart, and gives me what he probably thinks is a seductive smile. "It's kind of hot."

Bile rushes up my throat, and I have to swallow it back down. *No, Ted, it's not hot in the least.* "It's a business dinner, not a social arrangement. It wouldn't be appropriate. And anyway, you hate book news."

He frowns. "But it's not just any book news, it's *your* book news." My breath catches, and I hate him. In that moment I truly do hate him, my cruel, vindictive husband who knows damn well that there is no book news when it comes to me. I'm still struggling to come up with a third book, knowing at the back of my mind that neither Toni nor Harvest Publishing is that interested in getting more books from me. Writer's block, Ted calls it, except I don't feel like I'm writer enough to have writer's block. And now that my second book has been out for months, everyone knows nothing's going to happen. No news, no surprise book club picks, no celebrity live-tweeting it and getting their millions of followers to pick it up. It's done, and I'm done, and we both know it.

It takes a whole lot of self-restraint to bite back the caustic retort burning its way up my throat. Instead, I say, "Tomorrow? Tomorrow morning, we can go for a nice breakfast."

Ted sags, disappointment lining his face. When did we get old? His whole face looks gray, a detail that surprises me. It snuck up on us. I wonder if I've turned old without knowing it too; if he sees me and sees a "ma'am" instead of a young woman. "Sure, tomorrow." He gives me a smile to show that he's being gener-ous—*look how understanding I'm being, Jane; don't I deserve at least a hand job?* I turn away so I don't have to keep looking at that expectant smile. "I'll look up brunch places on Yelp."

I nod. "Great." Then I escape to the bathroom and start getting ready for tonight.

Skye Bar is a glitzy restaurant at the top of a boutique hotel. It's very definitely outside of my comfort zone, but fortunately, I'd had the foresight to Google it beforehand, so I've come dressed for the occasion. I'm wearing my only nice dress—an LBD I'd splurged on years ago for this very moment, for when I do see Thalia and spend a night out with her. It's as though I have always known that we'd end up meeting again, because the thought that we might not was simply unbearable. It's an off-shoulder dress that calls out for a necklace, so I put on Ani's necklace. Seems fitting, somehow. I hid the outfit under an understated coat so that Ted wouldn't see how dressed up I am. Still, when I came out of the bathroom, he noticed the amount of makeup and said, "Wow, you went all out. You look nice." He started walking toward me, but I quickly headed for the door.

"Thanks," I said. "I'll probably be back late, so . . ." I let the rest of the sentence hang in the air. I didn't want to be the one who said, "Don't wait up," to my husband. That seemed a bit too aggressive, and he'd probably bring that up when we bickered down the road.

"Gotcha," he said with another valiant smile. "Have fun. You're gonna do great."

Could he be any more patronizing? I didn't bother looking back before leaving the room.

But never mind Ted. Who cares about that right now? Right now I'm in a swanky New York City restaurant and I'm about to be reunited with Thalia and I look amazing, I know I do. The hostess gives me a once-over, nodding a little when she sees the necklace I'm wearing, then smiles at me. "Welcome to Skye. Do you have a reservation?"

I give her Thalia's name and her smile widens. "Ah, Ms. Ashcroft! Yes, of course. Follow me."

She leads me through the restaurant, and I try not to stare at my glamorous surroundings. Everyone here looks like they belong at some fashion show—the suits all bespoke and the dresses glittery and the jewelry ostentatious. She leads us to a table at the corner of the rooftop with a breathtaking view of the Manhattan skyline, and there she is. Thalia. She looks like a star, a burst of light and energy so beautiful it's blinding.

"Jane!" Thalia says, standing up and giving me a hug. I'm dizzy from the nearness of her. "So glad you made it."

"Shall I bring you the usual wine, Ms. Ashcroft?" the hostess says to Thalia.

"I think a champagne tonight. We're celebrating." Thalia grins at me. "Maybe a Dom?"

"Wonderful. I'll be back in a bit with your amuse-bouche."

I wait until she leaves and then lean forward in my seat. "Do you come here often? She seems to know you."

Thalia smiles. "A bit, yeah. It's one of our favorite places in New York. But enough about me—how are you? It's been what—nine years since we last saw each other?"

Here it is. I hadn't expected her to dive into it, but okay. I'm ready. I've been ready for this moment for years now. "Since that night that we—"

She sucks in a breath through her teeth sharply, her smile frozen in place. "Yeah," she says quickly. "Right, yeah. Since that—the incident." For a moment, neither of us speaks, both of us lost in that terrible, beautiful night. A night of death, a night of endings. A night that I had thought would've cemented our bond to each other, but had ripped it apart instead. "So anyway," she rallies, regaining her poise, "what have you been up to ever since?"

"Well, I came back the next semester. I finished the program. I was hoping that you'd be back, too, but . . ."

"I couldn't afford to come back after everything," she says, looking sad. "I think you know about my financial situation."

I nod. How could I forget? A waiter comes back with a bottle of champagne, which he opens and pours out for both of us. We wait until he leaves before Thalia holds up her glass and says, "To new beginnings."

My chest flutters with hope. New beginnings, yes. That's perfect. The champagne goes down like electricity, bringing me back to life.

"So, um." I don't want to bring this up, but I have to. I need to know. "You're married to Ivan? How—tell me everything." I mentally go over the words I just said to make sure they're okay and don't give away my obsession. No, they sound like perfectly normal words that a perfectly normal, non-sociopathic person might say.

Her mouth curls into a strange, mirthless smile. "Yeah," she says, taking another swig of champagne. "We kept in touch after that first semester, and he visited me back in Nevada."

"Wow, he went all the way to Nevada just for you?" The minute I say that, I realize that, well, yeah, he's a billionaire. Vegas is probably one of his favorite spots. The old hatred toward him flares up.

"Yeah." She refills her glass and tops off mine. "We were seeing each other pretty seriously, and he's got a private jet, so it's easy for him to fly anywhere he wants."

Everything she's saying sounds glamorous, but her voice is flat and slightly bitter.

"We got married a year later, and that's the story of my life."

I'm missing something here. "Is that where you live now?"

She snorts. "No, of course not! Ivan can't possibly live in

a sleepy town like that. We live all over, really. We're based in Jakarta because that's where his company is headquartered, but we spend our time flying back and forth to Singapore, Shenzhen, Dubai, London, et cetera. Wherever business takes him."

"Wow, Thalia, that sounds amazing." I hate how much of a fangirl I seem like, but really, I can't hide my amazement. This is exactly the sort of life she deserves, and I'm happy that she's living it. Happy for her, at least. Part of me is crying for myself, curling up in a dark corner and licking my wounds and sorrowful that it can't be me she's spending her life with. I drain my glass again to try and numb the pain.

"Yeah. Well, actually, things have been kind of difficult—Ivan's been having some health problems that we're trying to deal with."

I've studied enough human interaction to know that this calls for empathy, so I frown and say, "Oh no, what kind of health problems?"

"It's his heart. He's got a genetic condition, and his work is making it worse."

I shake my head and the world spins with me. I grip the edge of the table to steady myself. Dimly, I recall Ani had mentioned something about Ivan's heart back in Oxford, though of course I thought nothing of it at the time. "That sounds terrible. Is he okay?" Even in my inebriated state, I know that's a stupid question because she literally just said he's got heart problems, so he's obviously not okay.

Luckily, Thalia doesn't seem to mind my idiocy. "He's hanging in there, but it's been hard on him. He's such a workaholic. I mean, he's used to being able to work twelve-hour days and then go out drinking with his clients until three in the morning, you know?

All the doctors we went to told him to take it easy. That's part of the reason why we're here, actually. I had to come here for SusPens Con and my book launch party, and we decided it would be good for him to come along and get away from everything. I've taken away his laptop and work phone. Gotta force the guy to relax somehow."

"Wow, so Ivan's here in New York?" I can't seem to stop myself from spewing stupid shit.

"Yeah, he's back at the apartment with Ani."

"Ani."

"Yep, Ani. We're sisters-in-law now."

We stare at each other for a beat, and then we both burst out laughing. I don't know why we're laughing, exactly, aside from the fact that we've drunk way too much, but hey, here they come with yet another bottle of Dom, and neither of us is saying no.

"I feel bad for laughing!" Thalia cries. "Sorry, I mean, I love her, but she's always around! Even back in Indonesia, she's always hanging around the office, and she insists on going with us to the doctors and everywhere." She replenishes her glass and drinks deeply. "God, Jane, you have no idea how glad I am to see you. The last few years—they've been a LOT. Ivan's family . . . they're—you know, he warned me about them. He told me that they're really big and tight-knit and his parents are very controlling, so I can't even blame him for it, really—but holy shit, they're like a whole other level of controlling. That's why I couldn't reach out to you."

Everything stops spinning, and I'm suddenly hearing every word clearly, as though she's speaking right in my ear. This is it, the reason I haven't heard from her in so long.

"I wanted to, so many times. You can't even imagine. But his parents heard about what happened at Oxford—of course they did—and they forbid me from having any contact with anyone from Pemberton. They made me sign all these NDAs; it was crazy."

"NDA?" I can barely keep up.

"Nondisclosure agreement."

"What—why?"

Thalia shakes her head. "Because of the family company, of course. It's a huge media and tech corporation, so they need to uphold a good reputation. No scandals allowed. Not even for in-laws. Especially not for *bule* in-laws—*bule* means white person, by the way. The direct translation is 'faded.' That's what they call me. The faded person." She snorts again.

"Thalia, that sounds terrible." It's a struggle keeping my voice even. In my mind I'm lining up all of Ivan's faceless family members and stabbing them one by one. I can hear the wet thud of their bodies so vividly that it makes me lick my lips.

"Whatever, fuck them. I can't believe I'm here with you. Tell me about yourself. What have you been up to?"

If we'd spent the last hour only talking about her brilliant debut, I wouldn't mention my writing at all. But since she's revealed her less-than-wonderful marriage to me, I feel like I owe it to her to reveal my less-than-wonderful career. "I've been writing, actually," I say.

"Writing?" Thalia cries, delighted. "What do you write? Are you published? You must be! You were one of the best writers at that program."

I shrug and take a longer swallow of champagne. It's painful, revealing how unremarkable my life is. How, without the sheen of her brilliance, I have sunk into mediocrity these past few years. "Just a couple of lit fic."

"Oh, I love that! I can totally see you writing lit fic. You've always been so deep."

"Your book—*A Most Pleasant Death*—it sounds . . ." I want to say that it sounds like it's about us, but I have no idea how to say it without sounding completely desperate.

Thalia purses her lips and looks down on her lap. "Um, this may sound a bit crazy, but it was kind of inspired by us."

A warm glow spreads from the middle of my chest all the way to my fingertips and toes. I almost burst into tears and hug Thalia, but somehow manage to stop myself and drink more champagne instead.

"I knew I wanted to write about our friendship for the longest time, but I just never had the right plot, or the right—I don't know. I guess I just never had the guts to." She gives me a sheepish grin. "So the years before I worked up the courage to write *A Most Pleasant Death*, I'd actually been writing a few YAs."

I snort. "Yeah, right." I can't see brilliant, deep, incredibly complex Thalia writing YA.

"No, really! Look them up. I wrote under the pen name Ali Pemberton." She laughs. "Kind of on the nose, but what can I say? I missed our Pemberton days."

She can't possibly be serious, can she? But I take out my phone and Google the name, and sure enough, Ali Pemberton has published four YA books, and they've all done significantly better, especially the latest one. I look at the shiny "Junior Library Guild Gold Standard Selection" and "National Book Award Longlist" stickers on the cover of the latest book. Getting picked for those are a feat that most authors long for. Then I see the publication dates and I look up, wide-eyed. "These books were all published in the last two years."

She nods, taking another sip of champagne.

"You published two books a year? That's amazing!" Most writers chug along at a single book per year. Or rather, most writers are like me and struggle to come up with one book a year. Publishing schedules are geared toward releasing one book a year; a good pace at which to properly set up a known brand without putting too much of a strain on authors. But of course Thalia is too fast for such schedules, whereas I am the turtle, forever doomed to struggle to even keep up. Even if I were to miraculously finish a new book by next week, due to the slowness of publishing, the earliest it would hit the shelves is in two years' time. Most people don't know that it takes two years on average from the time a book is sold to a publisher to the time it's available to consumers.

"It's not so hard, once you get the hang of writing fast. If you want, we can do a few writing exercises to get your juices flowing," she says. "I actually feel like the MFA course kind of screwed us over in that sense. They were so focused on writing flawlessly instead of writing fast. Such pretentious assholes."

That shocks a laugh out of me, and I stare at her in wonderment, because how can a person like Thalia exist? I drain my glass and she refills it for me, and I've lost count of how many glasses I've had but I don't care; I don't care because I'm with Thalia and it's just like old times.

"In fact," Thalia says, "I'm going on a writing retreat tomorrow in the Hamptons. You should come. There are eight of us going, and we've rented an incredible house there. It'll be good for you and me—we'll do nothing but drink and write and I could show you all of my secrets."

I know she's talking about writing secrets, but I can't help the thrill of excitement that shoots up the length of my spine. The way she's smiling at me as though she's talking more than just about writing.

"But—tomorrow? That's too soon. I haven't—don't you have to, like, pay or something? Make reservations?"

She shrugs. "Sure, of course. But one of the few perks of marrying into Ivan's nightmare of a family is that I do have access to a disgusting amount of money. Call it my repayment for having to put up with all of their shit. And as for rooms, don't even worry about it; you can just stay in my room. It'll be a bit of a squeeze in bed, but we'll make it work!" She winks at me. She *winks* at me. I've stopped breathing completely.

"I can't take that, Thalia, it's too generous." I would literally give up everything to be able to go on a writing retreat with Thalia where we would have to share a bed with each other after a day of wining and writing.

"Nonsense! You're coming. Where are you staying?"

"Domino Inn in Brooklyn."

"Oh, Brooklyn! I know the area well; my aunt lives there. Great, I'll pick you up first thing tomorrow morning."

And just like that, it's been decided.

Chapter 19

NINE YEARS AGO
OXFORD, ENGLAND

When I get back to Chapel Quad, everyone is streaming slowly toward the entrance of Haygrove Hall. Shit, I guess it's time for the meal to be served. I hurry across the quad and find Thalia, Ivan, and Ani.

"Jane, there you are!" Thalia says, her face shining with joy.

Have I missed it? Did he propose already? But her ring finger is still empty, thank god. I force a smile at her and follow after the group, my mind and heart both racing. This is okay. I'll text Antoine and let him know we're going to the dining hall. If he confronts Thalia indoors, it'll make for even more drama, right? Yes, that's okay. That's good. I'm doing this for her own good. Yes.

But as we cross the grass, Thalia suddenly stumbles forward with a cry. Ivan grabs her arm in time to keep her from falling over. She looks down at her feet in dismay; one of her heels has stabbed into the grass and broken off her shoe.

"Crap," she groans. "I'm going to go up to my room to change into a different pair. You guys go ahead."

"Are you sure?" Ivan says. "I could come with you—"

"No, it's totally fine!" she says, forcing a laugh, still playing the easy-going, drama-free girl of his dreams. "You guys go. I'll meet you all at Haygrove." With that she walks away, leaving the three of us looking at one another awkwardly.

"Oh well," Ani says with a shrug, making her way to the dining hall.

Ivan gives a small laugh and shakes his head. We walk slowly, a few paces behind Ani. "She's so independent, isn't she?" he muses to me.

I nod slowly. "Uh-huh."

"I really, uh, I really love her," he says.

A thousand fire ants crawl and prick at my skin. Why is he telling me this?

As though reading my mind, Ivan says, "I'm telling you this because, um, I know it sounds really rushed, but I'm planning on asking Thalia a very important question later tonight . . . and I wanted your help to make sure everything goes smoothly."

I refuse to look at him. "You're right, it's too rushed."

"I know, but . . ." He sighs dreamily. "There's no one quite like her, is there? I would be a fool to let her go."

I suppose he is not wrong. "Well, good luck with it." I gather my dress in my hands and hasten my steps so I won't have to keep talking to him.

Haygrove Hall was already beautiful to begin with, but now, with huge flower arrangements and fancy plates and glasses decorating the long tables, it's been transformed into something that looks out of this world. As it turns out, there are placards on each plate, and I find myself sandwiched between Pam and Ani. Across the table is Ivan, who is—thank god—hidden behind a ridiculously tall tower of hydrangeas and peonies. The seat next to him is empty, awaiting the queen of the ball.

Fortunately, both Ani and Pam are too busy talking to other people, so I take the chance to check my phone. No messages from anyone. I try calling Antoine, but he doesn't pick up. I steal glances at the doorway, wondering who'll show up first. Antoine or Thalia? It doesn't matter, as long as they both end up here, causing a scene in front of Ivan. I'm filled with so much anticipation that I actually feel my mouth watering.

Minutes trickle by and still no sign of either of them. I peer round the flowers, sneaking a glance at Ivan. He's busy texting, probably yet another business-related thing. The servers stream out of the kitchen and place our appetizer on our gold-edged plates. A single fat scallop, gleaming atop a bed of crushed peas, topped with a dollop of caviar.

It should taste amazing, but it might as well be plain bread for all that I notice.

"This is exquisite, isn't it?" Pam says. She's the only person I've ever heard using the word "exquisite" in casual conversation.

"Uh-huh." I glance at the doorway again.

I can barely choke down the remaining bite of scallop, grimacing as it makes its gelatinous way down my throat. Where the hell are they? Has something gone wrong? What if—oh shit—what if Antoine runs into Thalia outside, at the Chapel Quad? They'd have their talk in private then, and Ivan would never know about it. Thalia would ply Antoine with her usual charm and tell him to go home, and he would. He doesn't stand a chance against her intelligence, her eloquence.

Just then, my phone buzzes with a phone call. Antoine? I turn it over and my breath catches when I see Thalia's name flashing on the screen.

"Hello?"

"Jane?" Her voice sounds strange. "Hi, could you—um, can you please come up to my room?"

"Huh? Now?" She's still up in her room? Fuck. Antoine must be pacing about the Chapel Quad, wondering where the hell everyone is. Or worse, maybe he's just given up and gone back to his bar.

"Yeah. Don't bring anyone else with you. Just you, okay?" The strange note in her voice is clearer now, a giant crack running through glass. All thoughts of Antoine and Ivan leave me. Something's wrong. I grab my purse and stand.

"Where are you going?" Ani says.

"Bathroom."

"I'll come with you," she says, already getting up.

"No!" I half shout it. Pam and Ani stare at me. "Sorry, I just—I'm not feeling well and I, uh, I get self-conscious if there's someone else in the bathroom."

Pam's mouth drops open. "Oh nooo, is it the scallop? I ate it too!"

"I'm sure the scallop's fine." I rush away from the table, the noise of the ball receding as I hurry across the marble floor. Out in the hallway, I take off my heels and run all the way to Downing. Up the stairs, panting, my hair coming loose from the bun I'd painstakingly twisted it into. Finally, I'm at Thalia's door. I don't even get to make a second knock before the door is wrenched open.

"Thali—"

She grabs me by the arm in a painful grip and yanks me inside before slamming the door shut.

"What is it?" I've never seen Thalia like this before. Undone. Her eyes wild with fear. I taste a metallic tang at the back of my mouth. Bile. Fear.

"Jane," she babbles. "He attacked me. He was—he was waiting in here when I came in, and I didn't see, I—"

"What?"

She's not even looking at me. She's looking at something over my shoulder, in the far corner. The hairs on the back of my neck rise. *Don't turn around*, Mom says in my ear. *Just leave, now. You don't want any part of this.*

But I can't not turn around. I can't, because this is Thalia who needs my help, Thalia whose happily-ever-after I just sabotaged, and I know what's there before I even turn around. I know it because I've orchestrated everything. Everything up to the moment that led to this. Why did he come up here instead of confronting Thalia at the ball like we planned?

Too late, I realize that Antoine must have been so drunk that he must have decided to—to attack her. The thought is unbearable.

Antoine looks massive inside Thalia's room, a toppled, broken giant. He lies on the rug, a letter opener sticking out of his throat. His eyes are still open, as is his mouth, caught in a surprised O. It looks obscene somehow, his lips so pink, his eyes so blue, and all that dark blood coating his throat and chest. My legs lose all sensation and I crumple to the floor. It feels as though all of my insides are coming out, my body turning itself inside out, revealing all of my dirty secrets. The whole time, my mind is a continuous, shrieking chant: *He's dead! He's dead! He's dead!*

It's my fault. I did this. I goaded him into coming here, and then he lost control and he nearly attacked her—she was nearly—

I almost pass out at the thought of it, the image of Thalia, frightened and sobbing, shoved up against a wall by Antoine. Somehow, though, it gives me a bit of strength. I need to make things right. She doesn't deserve this.

Somehow, I manage to pull myself up and stagger to the sink to splash some cold water on my face. In the mirror's reflection, I see Thalia's silhouette, standing very, very still. I wonder what's going through her lovely, brilliant mind then. I splash more water on my forehead, my cheeks. I need to stay calm. With trembling fingers, I snap the rubber band so hard that it makes me wince. It helps to clear my mind slightly.

I turn around, averting my eyes from Antoine's body. *You stupid fuck*, I hurl mentally in the general direction of his feet. I focus on Thalia. She's just staring at him, obviously in shock. And so am I, surprisingly. The number of times I've fantasized about killing someone, but now when I'm faced with an actual dead body, it's startlingly different from anything I could have ever imagined. He's just so there. So fleshy.

"It's going to be okay," I say.

Her gaze flicks to my face, and she utters a mirthless, awful laugh. "How can it be okay?"

"We'll call the cops, tell them what happened. He ambushed you in your room, he attacked you, you—what did happen, exactly?" The thought of Antoine—good-natured himbo Antoine—attacking Thalia feels wrong. So wrong. But maybe that's just my guilt talking. Because I know that in a very real way, I caused this to happen. I was the one who pushed and instigated him to the boiling point.

She shakes her head. "I don't know, it was all a rush. He was rambling, I think he was drunk, and then he came at me and oh god, his hands were all over me—"

She moves her shoulders back, showing me where her dress has ripped near the bodice. A ripple of revulsion and rage curdles my skin. If Antoine weren't dead, I would have killed him myself.

"I pushed him off and he came at me again and he was on top of me, his hands were pawing at me, and I reached for something, anything—" Her words dissolve into a sob. "I need you, Jane. I can't—you've got to—I can't, I can't."

I did this. I broke her. Not only did I ruin her happily-ever-after with Ivan, I may have ended her freedom. "No, it'll be fine," I say, weakly. "It's self-defense. He clearly attacked you, and you were just defending yourself. You'll be okay."

"I won't be okay!" she half shrieks, half sobs. "It looks so weird, don't you see? I panicked. After that, I washed my hands. Who does that, right?" She holds out her hands toward me, and sure enough, they're clean. "I just wasn't thinking. I saw all that blood on them and I thought, 'Ivan can't see this, Ivan can't know,' and before I knew it I was washing it off and it's going to look so suspicious! It's going to look all premeditated!"

I shake my head. "No, it doesn't . . ." My words can't convince even me. Does it look weird? Maybe it does? Who the fuck knows anymore? All I know is, I caused this. It was all my fault. And I can't let Thalia shoulder the burden of the blame. "We'll say I did it," I blurt out so fast that it takes a second for my mind to catch up with what I just said.

But once it's out, I get it. I get my role in this thing, and it is perfect. Just like our friendship, it's dark and lovely, and I am finally going to get to save the girl I love. For once, I get to be

200

the knight in shining armor. And, a small, dark voice whispers from deep in the underbelly of my mind: *Once you do this, she will owe you for life.*

As Thalia stares at me, mouth open, eyes wide, I say it again, twining our life paths into a single knot. "We'll say I did it."

We're creative writers, we know how to set a scene, and so we do.

Antoine was waiting in Thalia's room when she came inside. He was obsessed with her. He attacked her, would have raped her if I hadn't come in to check on her. There was a struggle (here we make sure that there are more signs of struggle for the cops to find). We're two young women trying to stop a crazed, muscled bull. We were overpowered. He was choking Thalia; he was going to kill her. I yanked him off her and he came after me and that was when I grabbed the letter opener.

"You have to choke me," Thalia says.

My mouth turns into sandpaper and I stand there uselessly as she twines a thin scarf around her slim neck and hands me the ends.

"Do it."

And so I do. I pull and pull as her face turns pink, and then red, and then purple, and my pulse is one with hers, her life like a little bird in the palm of my hand. Such trust. She wouldn't put her trust in just anyone. She knows we belong together; this is why I'm pulling, choking the life out of her.

She flaps at me and I break out of my trance. I release the scarf and she stumbles back, coughing, gasping like a fish. There's something almost erotic about her wheezing, and I have to turn away, my face burning at the excitement inside me. What the hell is wrong with me?

Sociopathic tendency #27: Does dangerous things to feel alive.

I've gone too far. I know it. Thalia must have seen it, too: that little evil spark behind my eyes. But when I turn around, she gives me a little smile. So brave. My heart goes out to her. She is too pure for this world.

"You should probably have a few bruises on your face," she says.

So pure, but also such a realist. I nod and she takes a deep breath. "Ready?" she says.

I close my eyes.

When she smacks me, the pain is blinding. Deafening. Stars explode behind my left eyelid, the insides of my head sloshing sickeningly. I fall backward and bump my elbow on a piece of furniture. Holy fuck, it hurts. Then, somehow, we're laughing. A mad laugh filled with tears.

When we're done, we look at each other, and for a while, neither of us speaks.

"I can't thank you enough, Jane," she says, taking my hand in hers. Her voice is hoarse. "You're my best friend. Forever."

My voice catches in my throat. I look deep into her beautiful eyes and say, "Forever."

Chapter 20

PRESENT DAY
NEW YORK CITY

"Wakey, wakey!"

The words grate against my eardrums, and I wince, turning away from them.

"Sweetie, time for our fancy New York City brunch."

It takes a while for the words to sink in, but when they finally reach the part of my brain that digests verbal information, my entire body curls up and I let out a groan.

"Did we imbibe a little bit too much last night?"

I resist the urge to wrap a pillow around my head to drown out Ted's voice. I can't bear that playful, wheedling tone. And then last night comes rushing back like a fist to my gut and I sit up, suddenly awake. "Shit, Ted. I can't go to brunch."

He stares at me for a moment before smiling. "Very funny. You got me good."

"No, I'm not kidding. I—uh, I've been invited to go to a writing retreat in the Hamptons and we're leaving today." I glance at the clock on the wall. "Uh, in an hour, actually."

Ted's smile slips off his face and hardens, sharpening into

something else. "A writing retreat?" There's something ugly in his voice now, something that makes my stomach tighten.

"Um, yeah. Sorry, I didn't have a chance to tell you last night. But it's a really good opportunity for me—it'll allow me to get to know other writers who are at the top of their game." I'm rambling and he's going to know something's going on.

"How long will you be gone?"

"Only two nights."

"But we're supposed to go back to the Bay Area tomorrow." I wish he'd stop walking toward me. He stops short of being within touching distance, and all of my instincts are alert, on standby. "And how much is this going to cost?" And just like that, The Sigh comes out, long and slow. "Look, sweetie, I know how exciting it must be to be sent to your first ever convention. I mean, I agree it's a huge change of pace from what we're used to, but we can't afford to get swept up in all this hobby of yours."

"Hobby?"

He must have detected the dangerous tone in my voice because he stiffens and straightens up. "I didn't mean to say hobby. Sorry, it's obviously more serious than a hobby, but like—" The Sigh again, this time a quick one. "It's not really a job, is it? It's not like it's earning much money at all, and I have faith that you'll earn more, with time," he adds quickly, "but I just don't think that now's the time to be splurging on things like a fancy retreat in the Hamptons. I mean, Christ, Jane, it's probably going to cost like a grand or something. We can't justify it!"

I hate him. I despise him, this small man who's trying to make me smaller so I can fit him, so I won't ever outgrow him. "Well," I say, getting up and walking away from him, "that's fine, because this is being paid for by Harvest Publishing. I guess unlike you, they see my potential and think it's worth investing in me." The lie burns coming out, sizzling in the air with its falsehood. I don't see how anyone could possibly believe this; it's just so far-fetched. I've never even heard of publishers sending their authors on writing retreats, unless maybe said author is of Stephen King status. A small part of me wants him to call me out on it so that we can spiral into a proper fight, finally, one where I unleash all of my fury on him, breakable objects whizzing through the air and shattering against the walls.

Instead, there is a long silence, during which I busy myself packing and refusing to look him in the eye.

"They're paying for it?" he says finally. "Is this a retreat organized by them?"

I don't have a moment to consider what would be the most believable answer, so I just say, "Yes."

"Huh." Silence again. I stuff more clothes into my bag. "So I'll just . . . wait here for you then?"

"If you want. Or you could go back to the Bay Area first and I'll be back in a couple of days."

"Oh." It comes out so small and so sad that before I can stop myself, I look at him. He looks even smaller than before, all of the bluster gone, leaving just my husband behind, old and saggy and sad.

"Ted," I sigh.

"No, it's fine. This is really good. I'm happy for you; you deserve it." He turns away from me and looks out the window. "Yeah, I'll just . . . yeah, you're right, I'll fly back myself. I've got a ton of work to do anyway. So. Yeah."

"Great."

"Yep."

I wonder, fleetingly, if this is the end of my marriage. The thought is a surprisingly painful one, though as soon as Thalia texts to let me know she's here, the pain disappears, fading like the San Franciscan fog in sunlight.

I'm in a dream. This can't be real, this can't be my life. I'm not really here, in Thalia's convertible, driving out of Manhattan toward the Hamptons. The entire drive there, we glance at each other and grin like, *holy shit, can you believe that we're finally reunited after all this time?* And we've shed our baggage, left both our husbands behind in the city while we drive out into the sunlight and ocean breeze. We talk about nothing and everything. Books, agents, things about publishing that I have never discussed with anyone because no one in my life is that interested in the nitty gritty details, and I'm not big into the book community, which consists of people who are too cheerful and too wired for my liking.

Before I know it, we're entering into the driveway of an incredible property. How incredible? Well, so amazing that it has its own name: Graystone House. The name is displayed proudly on a bronze plaque at the gate.

"Isn't it crazy?" Thalia says as the wrought-iron gate swings open. "Six bedrooms, plus a guesthouse. There's even a heated pool and a Jacuzzi. We went all out for this retreat." She drives slowly up the driveway and stops a little ways from the front door. "Hey, so."

Something in the tone of her voice leeches the easygoing mood from the air. I turn to face her.

"I haven't told the others that you're coming yet. I'm kind of waiting for the right moment. You know how writers can be so precious about their retreats," she says with a roll of the eyes, followed by a smile.

A knot tightens in my stomach. "But—" I don't even know where to begin. They don't know I'm here? Me, someone who's already an outsider, is now about to show up unannounced? This feels bad. The kind of thing that makes me want to burrow into a deep, dark hole and never come out again.

"Don't worry about it!" Thalia says. "Look at me, Jane."

I do so, and am lost in those deep brown eyes of hers.

"They're going to love you," she says. "But maybe give me like ten minutes to prep them before coming inside?"

If it were anyone but Thalia telling me this, I would not be okay. I would beg them to let me drive the car out of here. And if they didn't agree, I would run all the way back to the city. Okay, I wouldn't actually run, but really, all of my insides are shriveling up and I just want to hide away. But then it strikes me that all my life, I've just wanted to hide from everything, and I can't do that now, not when it's taken so long to find Thalia and she's invited me to, of all things, a writers' retreat! Who gives a fuck about all these other writers, right? I'm not here for them; I'm here for Thalia. For my own writing. I'm here to soak up her presence and everything she can teach me about writing, and it's obvious she has a lot of knowledge to impart.

I nod and watch as she gets out of the car and takes her bags from the trunk. She waves at me through the window with what I think is supposed to be a reassuring smile, then she walks up the steps and through the front door and is swallowed up by the house.

If I ran now, no one would be the wiser. Or maybe I could drive the car back to the city. Thalia wouldn't mind. Or she would, but she wouldn't hold a grudge. She's not the type to. I could make something up, send her a text about a "family emergency" halfway back to Manhattan. But then I'd be going back to Ted, and on his face I'd see—what? Relief? A knowing smirk. *I knew you'd come back, Jane. You don't belong with those hoity-toity writers. Come back to our comfortable, safe lives.* Our lives of mediocrity, where we do the same, mediocre things every day and got paid a mediocre amount for it and then had mediocre meals over mediocre conversation.

The thought of going back to my old life, after just one evening spent with Thalia, is unbearable. It makes my jaw clench. I make myself take a deep inhale. It comes in shaky and releases in an audible gasp. God, I'm so nervous. But these things are always worse in my mind than they are in reality. Yeah. I always build them up in my head and then it turns out to be okay. I watch as the clock on my phone ticks away. When it's been exactly nine minutes, I get out of the car and grab my bags, then walk toward the house.

Ten minutes.

I raise my hand and ring the doorbell.

It is as bad as I thought. Worse, actually. Everyone here is either a *New York Times* bestselling author or a prize winner. I recognize Rebecca Young, a Hugo Award winner who recently sold the rights to her books to HBO. They'd called her series "a feminist take on *Game of Thrones*." Then there's Kurt Fenton, *New York Times* darling whose love stories (not romance; when men write romance, it's classified as "love stories" so they're taken much more seriously than those silly things women write) always, always top the lists. Basically, everybody here is Somebody, and I'm the only Nobody, and they all know and act like it.

Even Thalia.

When she opened the door and let me in, I thought I sensed something off about her, something stiff about her smile, but I'd shrugged it off as my own nerves. But now, I'm in the stunning living room with everyone else, and I think it's pretty clear that Thalia doesn't want me here. She's introduced me in the most awkward way possible, taking me to the living room and saying in a falsely cheerful voice: "Everyone, this is Jane, the woman I was telling you about." A couple of the writers barely glanced up before continuing their whispered conversation, while the rest looked at me warily. Why had she said "woman" and not "friend"? Maybe I'm just reading too much into it. She'd led me to a seat at the farthest end from everyone else and told me to sit, before leaving the room.

And so here I am, looking around awkwardly and picking furiously at my fingernails. Nobody is even looking my way, so I can't really catch anyone's eye to make small talk. Kurt glances at me and I quickly smile, but it only seems to offend him. A crease appears between his eyebrows and he looks away. My stomach drops. I want to disappear. The fact that everyone here is very, very white does not escape me. Ani would relish that she's the only Asian in the room, revel in her difference and use it to stand out, but all I want to do is blend in, to pretend that I belong.

Thalia comes back, wheeling a drinks cart. Eyebrows are raised, but she grins at everyone and they can't help but smile at her.

"Hello, everyone! I'm your server for the day." The others laugh. "A bit early, I know," Thalia says, "but you know what they say—write drunk, edit sober."

One of the women, a thriller author named Siobhan, laughs

and says, "Hey, I'm not complaining. The last retreat I went to was a dry retreat." She rolls her eyes and everybody groans along with her.

"God, was it the agency retreat?" someone else says.

She nods. "Yep."

The others groan again. "I hate those things."

Toni's agency holds a yearly retreat, but I've never been invited. Of course not; not I, sad little midlister. Such retreats are only for their biggest clients. Here I've been lusting after these retreats, and here are the big clients, grousing about them like they're a chore.

"Honestly, if they're going to hold a yearly agency retreat for all their agents and clients, they should at least ply us with alcohol."

"You need to fire them," Rebecca says. "If they're not even sensible enough to provide alcohol, you don't want them representing you. I'll call my agent; she's great. She'll represent you no problem."

Siobhan shrugs like switching agents is no biggie. Is this how they move in these circles? I live in fear of Toni dropping me as a client. Before signing with her, I'd been stuck for years in the query trenches, collecting hundreds—literally hundreds—of rejections. When Toni offered, she wasn't as successful an agent as she is now. She still had room on her list for writers like me. I'd gotten so lucky. If she fired me, it would end me. But I guess these writers can afford to agent-hop, firing their agents over the most frivolous reasons.

Thalia goes around, taking drink orders. Of course, she makes the drinks with perfect precision. She even shakes the shaker like a professional bartender. With each drink she serves, she does so with exaggerated flourish, saying things like, "Enjoy, madame."

Everyone's gaze is riveted on her, the way she moves with such grace and confidence. She trundles the cart to me last.

"And what will it be for you?" she says.

"Um, it's a bit early to start drinking—" I check my phone and hold it up to show her it's not even noon yet.

Thalia gives me a concerned smile. "You okay? Come on, this will help you loosen up a little."

My cheeks burn. She's right. She's trying to help me fit in. I shouldn't have questioned her. I give her a small smile and say, "Just the white wine, please."

"Great choice." She pours heavily, filling my glass to the brim, before pushing the cart to one side of the room.

Please sit next to me. Please, please—

She goes over and joins Siobhan and Rebecca. I hear her say, "Ladies, what are we talking about?" and a wave of anger rushes over me. Why did she invite me here if she's just going to ignore me? And what am I supposed to do, just sit here sipping my wine?

"So what do you write?" someone says.

I look up to see Kurt towering over me. I shift in my seat, making room for him on the couch, and he sits down next to me. "Um, lit fic." It comes out apologetic, somehow, like I'm a hack trying to write highbrow novels.

Kurt nods and takes a mouthful of his drink. "Anything I might've heard of?"

I tell him my book title, the words feeling small, like grit, in my mouth.

"Never heard of it."

My skin crawls with embarrassment. Of course he hasn't heard of it. I would never presume that Kurt fucking Fenton would've heard of my little book, but the way he says it, dismissing me like a fly, stings more than expected. I focus on my wineglass, wrapping both hands around it and feeling the drops of condensation.

"So you've known Thalia for a long time, huh?" he says, and there's something in his voice that makes my ears prick. Something that reaches deep into the primordial instincts of my body, a whisper of danger that sidesteps my brain and goes straight for my muscles, tensing them.

"Um, you could say that, I guess. We got to know each other at our MFA program."

"In Oxford? That was where she met Ivan, right?"

I nod. Take another sip of wine to keep from having to reply. Then I realize I should redirect, turn the questions back on him. "And you? How do you know Thalia?"

Kurt smiles, and it's not a pleasant one. "Oh, everybody who's anybody in publishing knows Thalia. You know that."

There's a sourness in the back of my mouth, because no, I don't know that, and I am in publishing, but I guess I'm a nobody in publishing and he's a somebody and so is Thalia.

"I got to know her a few years back, at some con or another; I don't remember, there are so fucking many of the things."

Yet another one of those things that plebs like me had to beg and scrape to attend and superstars like him think are a chore. I force a smile and say, "Tell me about it."

"We hit it off right away. She's got a way with people, doesn't she?" He empties his glass, and I get a whiff of whiskey breath.

I wonder if it's just me or if he's talking about her in a weird way. I get like this sometimes. Too in my own head—that's what Ted says. I'd think that someone said or did something weird, and Ted would say, *Nah, it's just you; you're too in your own head.*

A shadow crosses over us, and I look up to see Thalia, carrying two full glasses, one with a refill of Kurt's whiskey drink and the other with white wine. She hands them to us and smiles. "What are you two talking about?"

"You," Kurt says, and that one word is so loaded and so heavy with meaning I feel it like a physical blow.

Thalia's smile freezes for just a second before she recovers. "Nothing interesting about that. Tell us about your current work in progress, Kurt. I'm dying to hear all about it."

She's touched on the right note. Kurt settles back, taking a long, slow gulp of his drink, and starts telling us about his latest work, which he evidently thinks of as his masterpiece, a blessing to the literary world.

The rest of the afternoon passes by in a blur. There isn't a lunch per se; a lush, abundant grazing table has been laid out on the kitchen counter, and everyone goes back and forth throughout the day, taking bits of cheese and cured meats onto their plates. They chat about books and other writers, and as the drinks are steadily refilled, the talk turns nasty. Which writer is a hack, which writer is a snob, which writer is "problematic." I don't partake in the conversation, because I don't know any other writers; I'm not part of the #WritingCommunity, and even if I were, I wouldn't be part of *their* #WritingCommunity. They're A-list and I'm barely on any list. So I sit a little bit outside of the group, losing count of how many glasses of wine I've had.

At some point, the group breaks up as everyone staggers away to their rooms to write. A couple of people choose to write in the common areas. I skulk off into the room I'm supposed to share with Thalia and wait for her to come up. She does so after a while, and now I'm nervous because I have no idea what she'll be like toward me. I want to ask her why she's been so cold and

213

stiff the whole day, but it doesn't seem right to ask such things. Too confrontational.

"Hey, you okay?" she says, and I almost burst into tears because her voice is now the soft, warm Thalia voice I know. She sees my expression and her face softens. "I'm sorry if I was a bit standoff-ish downstairs. I just get so nervous around these people, you know? Like, we chat with one another online everyday, but seeing them in person is like, whoa."

I nod, the room swaying along with me. "I understand."

"I'm so glad you're here. It's just like old times."

"Yeah." I wish I could say something more interesting, but after all the wine, my brain is slush.

"I'm going to write downstairs. Are you going to write up here?"

My throat thickens. I find it hard to swallow. I'd fantasized about us writing together, glancing up at each other once in a while and smiling, knowing that we're creating worlds with only a few feet between us. We'd do writing sprints, maybe, race each other to get to five hundred words. But now she's abandoning me. I could come downstairs with her, but god, writing in the same room as those A-listers? Me? What a fucking joke. They'd eye me with open derision; they've been eyeing me with barely concealed distaste the entire day, their expressions making it clear that I don't belong.

"You go ahead. I'll write up here."

"Okay." And just like that, she's gone. Leaving me up here alone. I open up my laptop and stare at the blank page and the blinking cursor. Then, as though of their own accord, my hands float up over the keyboard and then they're flying across it, words flowing out of me the way they haven't been for months. It's the kind of state that writers are forever chasing, the one where the world around you melts away and you drop into this hole where there's nothing between you and the words. It's just you and the story and your fingers aren't even yours anymore, they're just bypassing your mind and doing the story's bidding, typing out words that you weren't even aware were inside you all along. At some point, Thalia must have come back up, because I become half-aware of a new glass of wine being placed next to me. At some point, I drank it. I don't stop writing.

It's the Thalia effect; I know it. I haven't felt this way since Oxford. Since those afternoons she and I spent in the cozy darkness of the Bodleian Library, tapping away at our keyboards, pausing only to share with each other little snippets of our work. Even though I'm barely aware what I'm writing, I know it's good. I know because I'm no longer held back by my own self-conscious thoughts, that little inner editor who's always nagging at me and telling me that what I'm writing is shit. Just being near Thalia is enough to silence that voice.

When I next look up, the sky has darkened to a deep purple and voices are floating up from downstairs. People are done writing, and so am I. I've somehow pounded out two thousand words. I don't dare read them yet, not now while I'm still woozy from the booze and the writing. I stumble down and everyone's there and I guess they've all been drinking throughout the day like I have, because they're all just on the edge of drunkenness; some of them maybe well beyond drunk. We all crowd around the kitchen counter and paw at the boxes of takeout.

The boxes say: *Green Village, Clean Body, Clean Mind*. And when we open them, we find steamed vegetables and lightly seasoned white fish. Not a single carb hiding amongst them.

Thalia frowns at the anemic boxes. "They must have gotten

our order mixed up with someone else's. I ordered their party set. I'll call them and ask them to come pick these up."

"Eh, don't bother," Rebecca says, nibbling on a long stalk of asparagus. "I'm too hungry to wait for them to come and switch the food and blah, blah, blah. Let's just eat these."

"Okay," Thalia says. "I'm so sorry for the confusion."

"It's not your fault," Rebecca says.

We eat in the living room, and there's so little food that I feel hungrier after dinner than before it, but there's plenty to drink, and by the time we're done, I'm too woozy to think about eating. The chat resumes—just how many authors can these people bash?—then we finally, finally retire for the night. By the time I get back into the bedroom, I've drunk so much wine that whenever I roll over in bed, the entire bed rolls with me. I'm not even aware of Thalia's presence. At times I think she's there, but when I call out her name, there's no answer, and I can't tell if I actually did call out her name. The last thing I remember thinking before I fall into oblivion is: I shouldn't have drunk so much.

Morning comes abruptly. When I open my eyes, it's bright, blindingly, painfully so. Neither of us had thought to close the curtains. I turn my head gingerly and wince at the way the slight movement makes it throb. Thalia is sound asleep in the bed next to me, and god, what a sight it is, to wake up and be staring at her. Even this early in the morning, after a whole day of drinking, she looks gorgeous. I take in all of her, noticing little details I'd missed before, like the tiny freckle on her right eyelid, and the way that the roots of her hair are surprisingly dark in color. I forget my headache, just for a bit. I could stay here all day and gaze at her, I really could.

A frantic knock pounds on the door one second before it bursts open. Siobhan stands there, a horrified look on her face.

"Wake up," she cries. "Thalia, get up!"

Thalia mumbles something and blinks slowly. "Mmh?"

"Shit, get up! The cops are here."

"What?" Thalia and I say it at the same time.

Siobhan's face is deathfully pale as she says, "There's been an accident. Kurt was—uh." Her voice catches and tears fill her eyes. "He was walking out on the cliffs and he—he fell and—" She starts crying then. "He's dead. Kurt's dead."

What?

I'm looking at Thalia when Siobhan says this, because of course I am; I am always watching, too afraid to miss even one second of her beauty. And that's how I catch the flicker going across her face. It's not shock, or horror, or anything that would've been appropriate in that moment.

It's relief.

And in that moment, something cold ripples over my bones. I know Thalia, I know all of her facial expressions, all of her quirks. I know what I saw.

I think back to that night in Oxford, when she'd called me to her room and I'd come rushing up to see Antoine bathed in blood and Thalia shaking with fear. He'd attacked her, she'd said. It was self-defense, she'd said. And I'd simply believed her even though none of it felt right. So many pieces not fitting in. But I'd wanted to believe her. I'd loved her—I still do, and I would've believed anything she told me.

And now, Kurt is dead, and for the first time, I wonder if maybe I don't know Thalia that well after all.

PART THREE

Chapter 21

THALIA

Jane knows. She knows that I have something to do with Kurt's little accident.

She's not saying anything, of course, but she knows, and that's a bit of a shame. Rather spoils the surprise a bit. She's always been like that, so hopeless with the social cues, which I found amusing when we first met. There were so many things about Jane that amused me at first. Like the way she was so obviously obsessed with me from that moment I saved her at the bus station. My god, the way she'd gazed at me, like a leper being allowed to touch Jesus's robes, or a fan at a BTS concert. It was exhilarating. It was the whole reason why I started flirting with her, asking her to come to my room and try on dresses. I thought she was going to have a heart attack when I started undressing in front of her. I suppose that was somewhat cruel of me, teasing her like that. But I adore the feeling of being adored, don't you?

And before I could get bored of it, she told me, in a drunken stupor, that she's a sociopath, which piqued my interest, because you see, when I was fifteen, Aunt Claudette finally convinced my idiot mother to take me to a clinical psychologist, where I was actually properly diagnosed with APD—antisocial personality disorder. So can you blame me for being curious when I came across Jane? What are the odds of two people with APD coming across each other in this vast world? And oof, that little essay she wrote about wanting to strangle a beautiful woman. That was so clearly a love letter written for me. Very romantic, isn't it? She really shouldn't call people like us sociopaths, though.

Terms like "sociopath" and "psychopath" are very nineties and not politically correct anymore. I'm very careful to be politically correct at all times. On social media, my political views lean left (BLM! No TERFs!) because I have learned that this is what's currently acceptable. Don't worry, you can still like me; I'm not secretly a Republican.

I just don't give a shit.

The psychologist referred me to some specialist or another, who tried their best with interventions—I have always hated that word "intervention" because it is a lie, and what they were doing was more of an interruption, a distraction. I went along with it anyway, just to get them off my back, and plus it was quite fun toying with them and seeing if they bought my act. If anything, the treatment they put me on taught me how to become a better actress, how to guess what the other person is thinking and wrap that knowledge around my finger, so that when I crooked it, they would do my bidding. I'm not sure if I ever fooled them completely, but no matter, because your average person isn't quite as intuitive as a professional psychologist, even though they'd like to think they are.

Take Kurt, for example. Oh, Kurt. Named after Vonnegut, which should tell you something about his fucked-up parents. Kurt writes love stories—he'd get so riled up if you called

222

them romances—about dying people. His characters are always suffering from some form of cancer that's terminal but not the kind that turns them ugly and unmarketable. Because of this, Kurt thinks he knows love, and he resents that his wife doesn't love him the way that his characters do, the kind of love that only exists when both people know that their time is limited. He thinks she doesn't deserve him (he's right; she deserves someone better). Enter me.

I do not want sex; I mean, I do, but not from Kurt, for god's sake, with his pale, skinny-fat author's body. I have plenty of lovers, one in every city, in fact, and all I wanted from Kurt was his agent. Most writers love to recommend their agents, as though the fact that they were fortunate enough to land a good agent is somehow a reflection of them, but not Kurt. Kurt was represented by the legendary Beatrice McHale, an agent whose smallest deals are at the very least "significant" (this is Publishers Marketplace speak for "$250,000 to $499,000"). Rumor has it that the clients whose books do not sell for at least $250,000 get dropped. It might sound heartless, but to me it speaks of efficiency and, well, probably someone who also has APD. Imagine me being represented by a fellow psychopath. Unfortunately, Beatrice only takes clients by referrals, so I figured I'd schmooze up to Kurt until he referred me to her.

But it turned out that Kurt, fed on a steady diet of his own clichéd love stories, believed in True Love, just not with his own wife. So I pretended to be attracted to him, smiling as he droned on and on about his latest project, telling him how beautiful his shit-brown eyes were, how gentle his limp fingers were, how much I longed for his flaccid touch. I have done more, and would do more. Anything it takes to advance my career. You're wondering why. You're thinking: Why not just write better?

Anyone who thinks that publishing is a meritocracy is not in publishing.

Because yes, to a certain extent it does depend on writing well, but that's only half the battle won. It also depends on the "market," though what the "market" actually is, no one can tell you. All they can tell you is that despite the "powerful prose" or the "riveting characters" or "exciting plot," they still can't buy your book because it's just "not marketable." And it depends on knowing the right people—being represented by the right agent. For the longest time, I was with Ruth Steinwell, a middling agent who doesn't even live in Manhattan; she lives in Seattle and is a bored suburban housewife who thought agenting would be good for a laugh. She sold my debut YA for a piddling sum of money and told me it was about as good as could be expected, given "the market." Ruth's clients were all midlisters, all bored housewives who thought dabbling in publishing would be good for a laugh. I have nothing against these women, but they kindly need to move the fuck out of my way.

I didn't want another Ruth for an agent. I wanted a shark. Because only a shark of an agent would be able to get me the kind of book deal I deserve, and only a shark of an agent would be able to prod and nudge and cajole my publisher into giving me the kind of marketing I deserve. (Everything.) We all know what I've been through—being attacked at my MFA program, marrying into Ivan's family; something that I will get into in a bit. I've been through hell, am still living through it, and after enduring all of these things, I deserve everything, wouldn't you agree?

Anyone with a heart would agree. But not Kurt, because all Kurt cared about was himself.

After months of exchanging raunchy phone calls and two cons during which we had sex and I pretended it wasn't mediocre and was so overwhelmingly good that I cried a little, Kurt finally introduced me to his agent. Beatrice, oh Beatrice! The two of us combined were basically unstoppable. In less than one month after signing me on, she'd read and edited my latest manuscript. When she finally submitted it to publishers, her pitch was so incisive and so glowing that we started getting offers right away. She quickly turned down the bottom two, telling them that they'd offended her by coming in with an insultingly low number, which created even more of an uproar. By the time she set up my book auction, publishers were practically frothing at the mouth. The auction was swift and ugly in the best possible way, with editors going behind one another's backs to make me promises of publicity while also bad-mouthing their competition. Finally, I was getting what I deserved—an all-out fight over me.

But Kurt had to go and ruin everything by declaring that he was in love with me (I suppose I couldn't blame him) and that he was leaving his wife (wait) because unlike me, she didn't fully appreciate him (oh no) and I would agree, wouldn't I? Surely, I also wanted to leave my abusive, tyrannical husband (Ivan has never abused me in the traditional sense, but he might as well have, for all the shit I've had to go through).

When I told Kurt that no, I did not in fact want to leave my husband, he turned sour. Told me I was a brainwashed, abused woman, and that if I didn't leave Ivan, he was going to go public with our affair. That was why Kurt had to die. That was why I had to lure Jane back into my life, because I needed a fall guy in case

I didn't succeed at making his death look like an accident. I didn't want to have to use Jane like that, but needs must, and she's the perfect fall guy, what with her history of violence (poor Antoine).

If you're wondering about Antoine, the idiot ambushed me at the college formal, thinking he'd march into the dining hall to make some sort of grand announcement, to brand me as his. (Really, what is wrong with men?) I couldn't let him ruin what I had with Ivan. I begged him to leave, which only made him angrier—*you're so afraid of that man, ma chérie, what has he done to you?*—and so at the last, desperate second, I kissed him and then led him up to my room. I tried to placate him, I really did, but he insisted that I stay there with him for the rest of the evening. That just wouldn't do. So in the end, the letter opener became the key to my freedom, the knife that fully severed Antoine's grasp on me. And Jane, good old loyal Jane. I knew she'd help me. I almost laughed when she offered to take the blame for killing Antoine. I thought I would have to suggest it to her, but nope. Didn't even have to hint.

I really think that Jane was quite happy to do it for me. Like Antoine and Kurt, she saw herself as my savior. I know she definitely saw herself as that when I came to her with my sad mommy story. That was hilarious. *Oh, Jane, my mother is sick! I need money to pay for her treatment!* Honestly, who in their right mind would fall for it? But this is Jane we're talking about. My most loyal doggo. You know, I don't actually know if Jane has APD. She's a bit of an armchair psychologist, diagnosing herself like that. But whatever she is, she is definitely obsessed with me.

There wasn't even a sliver of doubt in her mind when I told her my sob story. And I saw the look in her eyes when she suggested that I get close to Ivan. She was so pleased with herself for coming up with the most obvious idea in the world. Good job, Jane. I got exactly what I wanted: Jane distracting Ani so that I could have some alone time with Ivan.

Jane was so excited to be able to help me like that, so I decided to let her do it again. Serve herself up on a platter for Kurt's death, should I need someone to blame it on.

I called Beatrice and asked her to have my author name changed from my pen name back to my real name. Pretty ironic, because the reason I used a pen name in the first place was to keep Jane away. After the whole thing with Antoine, I thought it best to simply disappear from Jane's radar, just in case she got any funny ideas about coming clean or whatever.

Unfortunately, Beatrice told me that it was too late in the game to change my pseudonym. The book was already out, and that was that. Bit of a blow; I'd had higher expectations from Beatrice. But never mind. I took things into my own hands. I created social media accounts under my real name and connected it with my pen name. On every available outlet, I made sure that I was known as "Thalia Ashcroft, writing as May Pierce." Whenever I had interviews or guest articles, I made sure I was known as "Thalia Ashcroft, writing as May Pierce." I created a fake *New York Times* email account (if Jane had bothered to read the sender's address properly, she would have seen that it says newsletter@ newyorktinnes.com and not newyorktimes.com) and sent Jane a newsletter with a doctored bestseller list that showed my name as "Thalia Ashcroft, writing as May Pierce," knowing she would see my name and be so swept up that she wouldn't pause to wonder why the *New York Times* had bothered listing my real name. Then, having set my trap, I waited for Jane to turn up. The day of my panel at SusPens Con, I kept coming up with reasons to send Ani to the entrance of Javits. I told her she should take selfies at the entrance, under the huge "Welcome to SusPens Con!" sign. I told her she should try the delectable coffee at the pop-up drinks cart near the entrance. All sorts of stupid reasons I came up with just to keep her there in case small-fry writer Jane couldn't score a ticket to SusPens Con. And if that were to fail, I would've posted other events I would be at.

Honestly, I've kind of missed Jane after all these years apart from her. I missed that intensity of hers, the way she'd watch me in what she probably thought was a subtle way. There is literally nothing subtle about Jane. As Ivan's wife in Indonesia, I was respected, even admired, but I wasn't the object of any-one's obsession, which is honestly quite offensive, if you ask me. I deserve to have rabid fans, to take up as much space as possible in people's brains. Why not? It's not like most people have anything better to think about. Might as well be thinking about me.

To be clear, I really didn't want to do it. I begged Kurt not to go public with our affair, but he dug his heels in. It's all those fucking love stories. They'd gotten into his head; he thought that like his dying female characters, I, too, was in need of a savior.

The thought of needing to be saved by a pathetic male like Kurt. When I pushed him off one of Montauk's cliffs, he had felt so light, like a doll. Couldn't even save himself, yet he thought he could save me. What is it about men that blinds them to their own mediocrity and allows them to think of themselves as heroes?

Chapter 22

JANE

The cop interviewing me is wearing a name tag that says Howe. Midforties, small wrinkles around the eyes that deepen whenever I give her an answer that she thinks is a lie. Which is a lot of them, for some reason. Detective Howe thinks I'm lying, and I don't know why.

"So you weren't invited—"

"I was," I say for the third time. "Thalia Ashcroft invited me here."

"Right . . ." Those lines become stark. She obviously doesn't believe me. "Okay, so Thalia invited you here, but you don't know anyone else here?"

I shake my head.

"Kind of awkward, don't you think? To be invited to a gathering of writers where you don't know anyone else?"

We're sitting in the living room, in an opposite corner of the room from Thalia and the cop who's interviewing her. Siobhan and another writer are also there, though Siobhan I think has had her interview; she's just walking around and going, "Oh my god, can you believe it?" to anyone who will listen. The other

229

writer, someone named Monday, I believe, is just staring out the window with a dazed expression, an expensive-looking shawl wrapped around her. The others are all being interviewed somewhere else in the house. No, I hardly know any of these people.

"I suppose. But Thalia said it would be fine, and it's been so long since we saw each other, I guess we thought it would be a good chance to catch up."

"Really? Huh." She nods slowly, and my instincts are reacting, telling me I'm in very dangerous territory, but I don't know why. I have nothing to hide, but somehow I feel guilty, I feel like a suspect. "When was the last time you saw her?"

"Oxford. We attended the same MFA program. About nine years ago."

She writes this down in her notepad. "And you didn't have any contact with her between then and now?"

"No."

I can practically feel the waves of disbelief radiating from her.

"That's a long time ago. You didn't find it strange that she invited you to such an exclusive retreat after so many years apart?"

The back of my neck tingles. Is Thalia a suspect? That would be bad. Or good? I don't know. I need to talk to Thalia, but I haven't had a chance to; after Siobhan woke us up, everything had turned into a whirlwind. We barely even had enough time to brush our teeth before we had to go downstairs, which was when the cops took us aside to interview us one by one. And a huge part of me is internally screaming: *Thalia, what have you done? What have you done to Kurt? To Antoine?* But I won't betray her to the police, and even if I wanted to, what would I tell them? There's literally nothing to tell, nothing but a hunch. I know how well that would go over.

"No, we used to be really close in Oxford. We were best friends, and when we bumped into each other at the con, we picked up right where we left off."

Detective Howe smiles. "That's nice. I have friends like that too. We could go for months without talking to each other, but when we do, we pick up right away like we've been talking every day."

I nod, not buying for a second that she has any friends. I, a loner, can tell another loner right away.

"What kinds of things did you talk about with Thalia when you reconnected?"

It takes a second for me to digest what she's just asked because it seems so out there. "Um, I don't know, all sorts I guess? Our books . . ." I try to think of what we had talked about, and then race ahead to try and figure out if these things are safe topics to share with Detective Howe. Then I end up questioning why I need to figure out if they're safe or not. Everything should be safe because I did nothing wrong. And yet everything inside me is holding me back from telling Detective Howe anything. "Just life in general," I say finally.

"Right. Stuff like your marriage? Did she share anything about her marriage? When I get together with my girlfriends, we're always bitching about our husbands." Another smile appears.

"Just the usual stuff, nothing that stuck out." What is she trying to get at? Why would our marriages factor into this conversation?

"So while you're here, you're rooming with Thalia?"

I nod.

"That's very interesting."

Why is that interesting?

"Who suggested the sleeping arrangements?"

She's fucking with me. She must be. "Thalia, of course. She was the one who invited me here."

"Right, of course. Did you leave the room at any point during the night?"

"No, I was sleeping. We'd all drunk a lot." My mouth is painfully dry. I can barely get the words out.

"Right," she says, clearly not believing me. "And Thalia? Did she leave the room at any point during the night?"

"No. I don't know. Like I said, I was sleeping," I snap. Shit. The anger slipped out before I could control it, like an embarrassing burp.

Something changes in Detective Howe's face. A trap clicking shut.

She's seen the sharp edges, the gaping red maw of me. She knows the kind of monster I am. My insides go cold.

"Sorry, I'm just a bit jumpy because, uh, holy shit?" I gesture vaguely around me and give an uneasy laugh, then I hate myself for laughing, because what the fuck kind of person would laugh at a time like this? A sociopath, that's what.

"Don't worry about it. I'm used to people being jumpy around me," Detective Howe says, her beady eyes trained on me. "Did you notice anything strange about Kurt's behavior yesterday?"

It's a struggle to keep breathing, to keep my voice level. "It was the first time I'd met him, so I wouldn't know what's strange and what's not." Did that come out sympathetic? I hope so.

"What about Thalia? Notice anything strange about her behavior?"

From across the room, I see Thalia talking to another cop, and I wish I could just walk over there and pull her aside and talk to her. Find out what she's thinking, what really happened last night, and what really happened all those years ago in Oxford. But even now, I feel the need to cover up for her, to protect her. She looks so frail and so frightened. Are they being tough on her? I can't stand the thought of Thalia as a suspect. What if they take her into the station for questioning? She doesn't belong in such places.

I shake my head. "No, she seemed fine."

"Anything feel off between her and Kurt?"

A flash of Kurt, questioning me about Thalia. The way his face had darkened when he mentioned Ivan.

I shake my head again. I need this interview to be over. "They seemed like okay friends."

Howe nods, clearly not buying anything I tell her. "Okay, thank you for your time."

"Wait," I say, and then I wish I hadn't said that. But it's too late now, so I might as well spit it out. "How did he—it was an accident, right?" My voice comes out wrong. Desperate and stilted and just plain wrong. Detective Howe catches it too; I see it in the glint of her eyes. Very much not the kind of question an innocent person would have asked.

"We're still trying to figure it out. But don't worry, we've got the forensics team out on the cliffside, doing their magic. They'll figure out exactly what happened." She grins at me, and I get the sense that I've just been given a challenge, or maybe a threat. As she leaves to interview the next person, I have to stuff my hands in my pockets to keep them from shaking visibly.

Chapter 23

JANE

It is forever before I can get Thalia alone. Even after Detective Howe is done with me, I'm accosted by yet another cop wanting a statement, asking me adjacent questions—where was I last night? In bed. The whole night? Yes. Didn't wake up at any point to go to the bathroom? No.

Unlike me, the others aren't getting the same amount of grilling. It's not just my imagination. Monday, for example, is only questioned for about fifteen minutes before being dismissed. And Rebecca even less than that. Questions are fired my way, though, for over forty-five minutes. It feels like an assault, and halfway through I feel as though my mind has been stabbed through from all directions. Nothing makes sense. I don't under-stand it. I feel like a hunted animal surrounded by hounds who have caught my scent. *But I didn't do anything wrong*, I want to scream. *I didn't, I swear. It was—*

No, I can't think that. Not my sweet Thalia. But she isn't mine, is she? Never has been.

It's nearly noon by the time I manage to get to Thalia. She's talking to Rebecca and one of the male writers, the three of them with their heads bowed, speaking in low murmurs. When I approach, they jump apart and Rebecca stares at me with open hostility while the male writer studies me carefully, like an interesting but dangerous specimen.

"Hey," I say in a low voice. Then I wonder why I'm speaking in a low voice, wonder if it makes me look even more suspicious, then I wonder why I'm caring about looking suspicious because I did nothing wrong, god damn it. "Can I talk to you real quick?"

I expected Rebecca and the male author to, you know, fuck off like normal people would at this, but instead, they both look at Thalia with a questioning expression. What the hell? I get the feeling that if she were to say no, these two would forcibly remove me. Which is absurd. Right? My imagination is just getting the better of me, right? What the hell is going on?

Thalia nods at them and says, "Sure," and they very reluctantly move away, but they stay in the room, hovering a few steps away like protective guards.

"I need to speak with you in private."

"I don't think it's a good idea to leave the room," Thalia says, glancing over her shoulder at Rebecca, who's still watching us.

"Okay . . ." *Not okay*, I want to scream. I cock my head at a far corner of the living room instead, hoping like hell she'll follow. I almost start crying when she does. It's not perfect, as there are still people around, but I guess it's the best I can get for now. I lower my voice until it's barely above a whisper. "Thalia, what the hell happened?"

She looks at me with those round doe eyes. Eyes that brim with innocence and fear. "I don't know what you mean. A horrible accident, it sounds like." A sob lurches out of her, and she covers her mouth and looks up at the ceiling, blinking rapidly. "I'm sorry, I just—it's kind of hard to digest that my friend is gone."

Uncertainty catches hold of my chest, weighing down on it like a boulder. I'd been so sure that—

That what? I hadn't been sure of anything. I just had a . . . an inkling? A worry. A gnawing sensation that she might have been involved somehow. Because that's two men who were in her proximity who are gone now, and surely, that can't have been a coincidence? When it comes to deaths, what number is too many?

"Last night, did you uh—" I don't even really know what I'm trying to ask. "Did you leave the bedroom?"

Thalia's eyes lock on mine, and now, beneath the lake of fear, I sense something lurking in the deep. Some dark, slouched beast with teeth and claws. I blink, and the beast is gone. I'm losing my mind.

"What are you asking, Jane?" she says, clearly hurt. I can't stand it, even now, to see that look of betrayal on her beautiful face. "You can't be—" She chokes on the rest of the sentence, as if the words are too painful to say.

"No," I say quickly, unable to bear her pain. "I just wanted to know if you heard anything."

She lets out her breath slowly, still eyeing me like I've just kicked her in the heart. "No. I was asleep next to you. I was dead drunk. We all drank way too much."

"Yes, of course. Yeah." I nod vigorously when what I really want to do is apologize, tell her the panic and anxiety are getting to me. "Um, I'm sure I'm just imagining it, but the cops—what sort of questions did they ask you?"

"Just routine ones, I think?"

"Okay, because they were asking me all these questions like I had—god, I don't know, like they thought that maybe I had something to do with it. Do you know why they might think that?"

Thalia's eyes widen for a second before she frowns. "No, god. Jane, what are you asking me?" Her voice rises; she's clearly upset. "Why are you asking me these things?" She stops herself abruptly and takes a deep breath.

"Everything okay?" Rebecca calls out.

She looks over her shoulder and flashes a small, reassuring smile at Rebecca. When she turns back to face me, she's wearing a frown again. "Listen, Jane, I think it may have been a mistake to invite you here . . ."

She means because someone freaking died, my mind chitters nervously. But I know what she really meant by that. She said it because I don't belong, and even if Kurt hadn't died, it had become painfully clear that I don't fit in with her circle of A-list writers. It shouldn't surprise me. It shouldn't. And yet.

I nod, unable to speak.

"I think it's best if you go back to Manhattan," she says.

"I just—I—are we okay?" Are you going to disappear again for another nine years? Or is it forever this time? Will I only be watching you from afar, telling anyone who will listen that I used to be friends with you?

Thalia sighs. "I'm just a bit hurt that you would—I don't know, suspect me of something? After everything we've been through, Jane. I mean, I trusted you fully at Oxford when I was—I was assaulted." Her voice breaks then, and to my horror, tears roll down her porcelain cheeks. People are looking over. Rebecca leaps into action, crossing the room quickly with a deadly look on her face.

"I didn't mean it like that," I say hurriedly. "Of course I don't suspect you of anything."

"I think it's best if you leave now," Rebecca says in a cold voice. She wraps an arm around Thalia's thin, shaking shoulders and leads her away with one last glare thrown my way.

Another writer peels away to join them, murmuring to Thalia. The rest of them glare at me. There's a couple of officers left, and they both watch the scene, looking back and forth between me and Thalia, before exchanging looks with each other. My insides are knotted so tight that I think I might vomit. I'm sweating through my clothes, my palms slick, my hair sticking to the back of my neck. For a few painful moments, I'm rooted to the spot, their glares pinning me down like a butterfly struggling as pin after pin is stabbed through its wings. Then something snaps and I stumble away, half running. I hurry up the stairs and into my shared room with Thalia. I pack in a frenzy, stuffing everything I see into my bag, and don't spare the room a second glance before rushing back down, the weight of the house suffocating me. I don't look at anyone as I pass by the living room, but I know they're all still watching. A thought flashes through my mind—you're going to look so guilty if you run now—but I'm beyond caring. I don't hesitate before wrenching the front door open and running out into the blinding sunlight.

The memory of Thalia and me driving up here, so carefree, the wind in our hair, smiling at each other, is like a knife wound. It actually makes me take in a sharp, hitching breath. I shove the mental image out of my head and order a Lyft to the train station. I breathe easier as the miles are eaten up, as I gain distance from

Montauk, from those cold stares—god, I swear I can feel them, even now. A sudden rip of pain startles me, and I look down to see that I've ripped my thumbnail to the quick and drawn blood. I suck on it, and the tang of blood takes me back to that night in Oxford, the way it always does. But now, instead of the usual sensation of longing that I've always felt with a memory associated with Thalia, all I feel is nausea. That look of hurt on Thalia's face—god. I take my thumb out of my mouth and wipe the blood off on my jeans instead.

I send Thalia text after text:

Are you ok?

Please answer me.

We need to talk.

No replies come. My rib cage has turned into a vise that is crushing the air from my lungs, the life out of my heart.

My mind is a mess by the time I get back to the city. I stumble out of the train into Penn Station, find my way to the right subway train, and make the rest of the trip back to the hotel in a daze. It's only when I walk into the lobby, closing my eyes with relief at the cool, soothing air in the hotel, that it hits me. What the hell am I doing back at this hotel? I no longer have a reservation here. Ted would've checked out already.

The thought is too much to bear. I can't stand it. I sense the tears coming and I rush into the elevator before any of the receptionists notices me. Maybe they haven't reset my key card yet. Maybe I can still go inside our room and take a hot shower before booking a flight back to SFO. Yes, one could hope. Oh god, please. I need it to happen so badly that I mutter to myself as I make my way down the hallway, my bag dragging on the carpeted floor behind me.

I tap the key card against the door lock and the light turns red. My stomach plummets. "God, no!" The words come out in a harsh whisper. I try the card again even though I know it won't work. The light turns red again.

Everything inside me plummets to the floor. I'm done. I am so tired that I actually sink to my knees, letting my head slump forward and thump against the door. I feel thoroughly and utterly defeated. What happened at Montauk? What happened at Oxford? I thought I knew, but now I realize I know nothing. What really happened with Thalia? But even now, the thought is a painful one. I don't want to think of her as anything but the Thalia I knew. The perfect angel. I don't know what to do with this growing stain that's tainting the image of her in my mind. I'm untethered and directionless. My eyes flutter closed and I let out a long, exhausted sigh.

Then the door swings open, and there's Ted.

"Jane!" His eyes are wide with surprise.

I scramble to my feet, staring at him, wondering if it's a mirage. If I blink, maybe he'll disappear. I do so, but he remains in front of me, solid as ever. "Why—I thought—wait. Aren't you supposed to be back in the Bay Area now?" An ugly thought rises, a noxious bubble bobbing to the surface of a toxic swamp—he's cheating. He's got another woman in there. Maybe he hired a sex worker.

He smiles sheepishly. "Okay, so this is going to sound stupid, but I thought it would be nice to surprise you. We haven't had a chance to explore the city, just the two of us, so I extended

240

our stay for another week. I thought it would be nice—Jane? What's wrong?"

He'd extended our stay so we could explore the city, just the two of us, and here I'd jumped to the conclusion that he'd extended his stay to fuck around. Here I'd gone off and left him, seen him as nothing more than a burden I have to bear while I went off chasing the dream of Thalia. A dream that had ended in a nightmare. And for the first time in so long, I realize that I'm glad to see Ted. Relieved to be back with him. For the first time, I long for the boring, predictable comfort of our home. I feel my heart cracking, the gray wall around it crumbling, and I fall into my husband's arms and cry.

Chapter 24

THALIA

Poor Jane. It's honestly like kicking a puppy. Something I have never done before, just to clarify. I really am not a monster. Killing men, I believe, is a much more forgivable transgression than kicking a puppy, wouldn't you agree? And honestly, the men I've killed—it's a gift to humanity to erase them from this world. Kurt Fenton, your typical lazy, entitled, straight, white male author who has mistaken his success for brilliance. Antoine Deveraux, your typical straight, white male who likened himself to a romantic savior. Ha, it just hit me that if Antoine had been alive today, he'd probably love Kurt's books. (I'm smiling at the thought. What a hoot.) How's that for irony?

But Jane, the poor thing, I really didn't enjoy doing that to her. My goodness, the way she'd looked at me when I'd asked her to leave! Those kicked-puppy eyes. They're a study in pitifulness. I took a mental picture of them and shall practice in the mirror later on. Everything I do, I do very seriously, because I must excel at everything I am interested in. I do this with writing, cooking, fashion, and my most masterful craftwork of all: human behavior.

It's not easy for me, you know, having APD. It's like there's a bridge missing and all I can do is stand on one side of a deep ravine and watch as other people—the normals—mix with one another and go through emotions as easily as changing clothes. I hope you can see that I was the victim all along. It felt like everybody was feeling things at me to taunt me: *Ha, look at pathetic little Thalia who doesn't understand why birthday cakes are a cause for delight, and why people coo at babies or dogs, and why people cry when you tell them, with all sincerity, that they're ugly/worthless/stupid.* It's honestly quite rude of other people to parade their emotions in my face, I think. Would you jump up and down in front of someone in a wheelchair? Didn't think so. But somehow, it's okay to rub things like joy or pain in my face.

Anyway. Where was I? Right, Jane's hurt expression. Must remember the angle of her eyebrows and the way her mouth had parted ever so slightly. Not just hurt, but a little hint of surprise—*how could you?*—as well. Chef's kiss. I can't wait to try that particular mask on. But for now, I must mill about with the rest of my writer friends and allow them to fuss over me. And they're fussing over me because, poor me, to have my stalker classmate reappear after all those years and follow me all the way to Montauk! How awful. How terrifying. How delicious.

It's the kind of thing this crowd can't have enough of. I can see the hunger in their eyes as they mine me for more information about Jane. Mining—that's exactly what they're doing—using me for research for their next manuscript. I wonder how many of them are going to go away from here and start pitching their next book—a story about a stalker. Rebecca for sure is going to write a stalker novel. Now that sci-fi/fantasy is going through a rough patch, she's been talking endlessly about venturing out into writing thrillers, an evergreen genre. She's so predictable, hovering about me, her breath a disgusting hot blanket of sour tequila as she plies me with questions. *How long did you know Jane? Did you know back in Oxford that there was something wrong with her? What was she like then?* I have to resist shoving her away. I wish she'd at least make more of an effort to disguise her opportunistic research as concern.

I stay long enough to make sure that the story takes flight; quite easy to do with this bunch, obviously. They're so wrapped up in storytelling that everything is a fucking prompt to them.

Prompt 1: One of our own, a gifted writer, a dear friend, a loving husband, has been found dead at the bottom of a nearby cliff. The police are still investigating. Was it an accident or something more sinister?

One hundred percent of the people here would go for "something sinister," because that makes for a better story.

Prompt 2: If it was indeed "something sinister," who did it? Perhaps a vagrant who somehow stumbled upon Kurt while he was out on his nightly wanderings, pondering his work in progress? Or was it (dun dun dun!) someone he knew?

Again, one hundred percent of writers here would pick the latter, because of course that makes for the better story. And they would be right. It was someone he knew (*c'est moi!*) and it was no accident. I just have to do a bit of redirecting so that their attention will stay far, far away from me. Not that anyone would suspect me; for all they know, Kurt and I were just friends. We were discreet about our affair, both of us being happily married and all, but I don't like taking my chances. I've been so careful about this whole setup. I paid attention to all the little details, down to things like changing our dinner order to the restaurant's lightest menu, ensuring that there isn't a single carb in the meal so that nobody has a chance to sober up. The whole damn day, I went around refilling everyone's glass so that by the time we retired for the night, everyone would be drunk out of their minds. Layers and layers of preparation, that's me. I almost giggled out loud this morning, listening to the police interviews around me. The useless answers everyone gave. "I didn't hear anything. I was passed out..." "We drank way too much. I can't remember what happened last night..."

If only they gave out awards for attention to detail. I should have been a wedding planner, or a neurosurgeon, or a war strategist.

"Do you think Jane..." Siobhan says to me in a stage whisper loud enough for everyone else in the living room to hear. The way she let the rest of the sentence trail off, letting everyone fill in the rest themselves, is really quite brilliant. Siobhan is probably the most masterful storyteller out of this bunch, a living example of Show, Don't Tell. I could've stood up and applauded her right then and there.

"Oh, it's too awful to think about!" I cry, burying my face in my hands.

And now here comes Rebecca with her alcohol breath, wrapping her limp arms around me like an octopus. "Oh, you poor thing. It must be terrifying. To think, your stalker might've killed Kurt." Rebecca is not a believer of Show, Don't Tell.

"But why would she have done that though?" Thomas says. He swills the brandy in his glass and frowns. He probably thinks he looks very thoughtful.

"Who knows why crazy people do anything?" Rebecca snaps.

"I don't think you should use 'crazy' in that way," Alicia says.

245

Alicia is a YA writer and very much involved in the woke YA sphere. I hate Alicia.

"Yeah, don't wanna be canceled," someone snarks. A couple others snort-laugh their agreement.

Being canceled is always at the edge of our minds, always a gnawing fear.

"My guess is," Rebecca says, raising her voice, "it's because Jane was obsessed with Thalia, and she saw how close Thalia was to him."

I stiffen under her embrace, because excuse me? I wasn't close to Kurt. I mean, I was, but no one else was supposed to know it. We were always formal when we texted or emailed each other, leaving the raunchy stuff for the phone calls. I sneak a glance at Rebecca, trying to get a gauge on her. Does she know something? Is she trying to needle me? And then a chilling thought: What if Kurt had told her something?

Oh god, of course he fucking did. He must've been so proud of it, secretly. Maybe he got drunk one night and spilled it all over DMs.

How much does Rebecca know? The bitch, all this time I thought she was just trying to lap up extra attention, but maybe she's putting down the pieces needed to make a move against me after all. She's never liked me; I know it. Ugly women rarely do.

"I don't think so," I say in a small, shaky voice. "I wasn't that close to Kurt. I mean, I'm closer to you than I was to him, Rebecca." Ingratiating myself to this bitch, ugh.

Rebecca gives me a small smile, smug to have been acknowledged as a better friend than poor dead Kurt.

"Oh, I think we all know that Kurt had a little crush on you, Thalia," Thomas says with a smirk.

I'm about to deny this when it hits me that it's fine by me if they want to think that Kurt had a crush on me. After all, who could blame him? I take care of myself. And it would probably add to my allure without soiling my reputation, to know that he'd been lusting over me.

"I'm sure he didn't," I say demurely. "He loved his wife very much, I've heard." (The ungrateful bitch, he'd called her.)

"I'm not saying he would've cheated on his wife. I think it was just a harmless crush. But maybe Jane noticed him looking at you and it made her angry," Thomas said.

Good dog.

I let out a small sob. How terrible to think that me being a beauty has unwittingly led a man to his death. Very Greek tragedy. I approve.

"It's not your fault," Siobhan says. I hate her the least out of everyone here, have I mentioned that? She is the best dog.

Someone else snorts. It's Monday (yes, her parents really did name her that). "I don't think it's useful to sit here and make up stories about what might've happened." Not useful to make up stories? It's like she's not even bothering to pretend to be a writer. "I mean, the cops said it might've been an accident. And this is real life, not a novel. In real life, the simplest answer is usually the truth. Kurt was drunk and decided to wander outside—he probably thought it was romantic and deep; sorry not sorry, but Kurt was the kind of guy who'd totally do that—and he fell off by accident." Guess what genre Monday writes. Guess! Yeah, you're right, she sells self-help books. Her latest book was titled: *Zero Drama Mama! How to get rid of all the drama and #LiveYourBestLife*. (Yes, with the "!" and the "#". The book has been on the *New York Times* list for twenty-three weeks. I should've killed her instead.)

Despite myself, I kind of have to agree with Monday. Kurt was very definitely the kind of idiot who'd go for a night walk on a cliffside while drunk. Case in point: It didn't even occur to him to say no when I suggested it. I think he was expecting some kind of al fresco drunk sex thing, as though any woman thinks getting fucked in the wilderness while branches stabbed at your skin and mosquitoes feasted on your blood is sexy.

"Yeah," I say in a wobbly but brave voice, "I think you're right, Monday." Monday simpers. Why is she so repulsive and why does she have 1.2 million followers on Insta? "I mean, Jane is—there's something off about her for sure—but it might have just been an accident." See? Not a monster. I *am* trying to pin Kurt's death on his own idiocy. Jane is just a fail-safe.

I take a deep breath. I've mastered the art of the Heroic Inhale. Mine lasts for a full second and is done with eyes closed and a resigned look on my face. It's supposed to convey: I hate to do this, but I will because I am a trooper. "I'm going back to the city. I can't stay in this house, knowing what happened."

"Oh, honey, I don't know—you drove here, right? You'd be driving in the dark," Rebecca says. What is her obsession with me? Never mind Jane; I should've told everyone Rebecca's my stalker.

"No, it's fine. I'm fine," I say in the I'm-not-really-fine-but-I-will-be-because-I'm-so-brave voice. "I just can't stay here any longer. How can you all stomach it? The thought of Kurt—" I finish the sentence in a sob.

Everyone shifts uncomfortably. That's right, assholes, I am purposefully trying to make you uncomfortable about staying here. I want everyone to disperse like ants. Only about half of this crowd lives in New York; the rest are strewn all over the country. If I can get the group to break up, it'll make it just that little bit harder for the cops to ask follow-up questions in case they have any.

"Yeah, I'm gonna head back too," Monday says. "Too much drama here for my mental health."

"Would anyone like to hitch a ride back to the city?" I say. Ugh, I hope none of them takes me up on the offer. But whatever it takes to get them the hell out of here.

"Sure," Rebecca says.

The things I do to get away with murder.

After that, everyone else does decide to leave Montauk (phew). If not for Rebecca and her revolting breath stinking up my car, I would've breathed a huge sigh of relief as I drove away from the house. But like beggars, murderers can't be choosers. I put up with her yammering the entire drive back to Manhattan about her latest WIP and how wonderful her agent thinks she is ("I'm her star client, she tells me every day!") and how useless her publicist is ("Couldn't even get me a cover reveal on EW, what the hell? It's like, you have one job, Mikayla!").

Finally, we're back in the city and I can make up an excuse to drop her off at the nearest subway station. I grin all the way back to my penthouse apartment. I did it! They were right when they said that hard work pays off! So many obstacles in my climb to the top—my useless mother, Antoine, Kurt—but I've done it. I am now a bona fide *New York Times* bestselling author with a magnificent agent and a glittering career ahead of me. My plan isn't done yet, there are still a couple of steps ahead of me to secure the life I deserve, but the hardest part—killing Kurt—is over. Tomorrow, Ivan and I will go back to Indonesia, where the rest of my plan can unfold in as effortless a way as possible.

Shall I tell you the rest of my plan? No, I shall leave it as a surprise. I hate surprises, but I do love springing them on people, because my surprises are actually good ones.

After handing the car key to the valet, I practically dance my way to the private elevator. Inside, I tap my foot impatiently as I watch the numbers go up. I am so jubilant, so incandescent with victory, that when the doors slide open and I spot Ani at the picture window overlooking Central Park, I don't get the stab of annoyance that I usually do when I see her. Then she turns around and my interest is piqued, because her expression is an awful mix of everything—fear, alarm, sorrow. Ooh, maybe her mother is dead. Or her father? Or better yet, both.

"Ani, what is it?" I say in a concerned voice as I step out of the elevator.

"Where have you been? I've been calling you nonstop."

I'd turned my phone off because one must focus when killing a man. "Oh, sorry, I must've turned my phone off. What is it?"

"It's Ivan," she says, her voice catching. Tears well up in her eyes. "He had a heart attack. I don't know if he's going to make it."

And with that, she pitches herself at me and bursts into tears as I stand there, stunned to silence. Because, oh, irony of ironies, I might have gotten away with Kurt's murder, but I think I'm about to go down for my husband's.

Chapter 25

JANE

If someone had told me just a day ago that I would be genuinely glad for Ted's company, I would've cackled out loud. But here I am, ever so grateful that my husband ignored me and made his own decision to remain in Manhattan. He's borrowed money from his parents to help pay to extend our stay, telling them it's for our upcoming five-year anniversary. Normally, I would've balked at that, tying myself up into knots about being indebted to them. But I can't afford to tie myself into any more knots right now. I'm out of string; every available length is well and truly tangled up. I'm barely coherent as Ted gently pries what happened in Montauk out of me. When I'm finally out of words, he leans back on the sofa with a huge sigh.

"Jesus, Jane. That's massively fucked-up."

I stiffen, readying myself for him to blame me somehow. Maybe he'll tell me that I'm just being too sensitive, that I imagined all of those accusatory glares and questions. Or maybe he'll tell me that I shouldn't have gone, remind me that he tried to keep me here, that he knew all along that going to a retreat with a group of strangers wasn't the best idea.

"And the cops haven't said either way? If it was an accident or ..."

I shake my head. Here it comes. *I told you, Jane, you shouldn't have gone, you should've listened to me, you should've ...*

"Shit. I'm sorry this happened to you."

I brace myself, but he doesn't say anything else. Wait. That's it? That can't be it. This is my husband we're talking about. He never lets an opportunity to prove me wrong go. "You can just say it," I mutter.

"Say what?" He frowns at me.

"I told you so, I told you not to go there," I say, mimicking his voice.

The creases on his face deepen. "Why would I say that? You've obviously been through a lot of shit."

I stare at him, and it's like I'm seeing him in a new light. Part of me wants to fight, to prod him into arguing with me because that's all I know to do in these situations. But the other part of me is just exhausted. "Never mind."

"No, I think we should talk about that, because—" Ted takes a deep breath. "For a while now, I feel like you take everything I say in the worst possible way, and I don't think that's healthy for either of us."

I bristle, but before I can come up with some bitter retort, he says, "I care about you. I want us to be able to work it out. And I realize that I often say the wrong things, but it's really because I want to be included. I want to be able to celebrate your achievements, all your publishing news—I feel like you've been wanting to keep me apart from that, like maybe you don't think I care about it, but I do. I really, really do."

"But you're always . . ." The rest of the sentence fades away as I go through our past interactions. Everything he had said or asked that I had seen as a put-down. I'd thought they were moments where he was twisting the knife, but with an awful rush, it hits me now that he was showing genuine interest. He'd asked if he could come to dinner with me and Toni, and it wasn't because he'd thought I was lying, but because he'd really wanted to partake in what he thought was a celebration of my career.

The realization nearly knocks me over. For as long as I can remember, I stopped seeing him as my ally and started seeing him as the enemy. All of our interactions have been tainted with the purpose of winning, and to win, the other person needs to lose. All of those questions he'd asked about my books, about Toni, about Harvest, hadn't been because he wanted to be cruel. They'd been because he wanted to be included, and maybe he's just as awkward as I am when it comes to making conversation, and maybe, yes, I have been interpreting everything he says in the worst possible way.

My eyes start filling again, and I say, more to the floor than to him, "I'm sorry. I don't know why I'm like this. I don't want to be." More tears come. "I'm so tired of being myself, Ted. I don't know what to do! I don't! I just—"

"Hey, it's okay. It's going to be okay. We can talk to someone. Whatever you need." He wraps his arms around me and murmurs into my hair as I break.

That same night, over a glass of wine, we sit down with my laptop and look up online counselors, because I decided that an in-person session would be too much. My mind is a mess. Part of me wants to do this as quickly as possible, rip off the Band-Aid before I have a chance to chicken out. If we were to wait until we got back to the Bay Area, I would probably lose my nerve. Years ago, after a particularly bad fight, Ted had suggested that we see a couples counselor, but my whole body had rejected it immediately. My muscles spasmed; my scalp tightened like it was trying to crush my skull. Mom's voice, whispering at the back of my mind: *Therapists are all fakes, making up imaginary problems so people give them money to fix them. You're either crazy, or you're normal. If you're crazy, then you go to a mental hospital. If you're normal, then deal with your own problems. Why do people insist on wasting money just to have a stranger listen to their problems? Why is your generation so soft?* I mentally scream at Mom to shut up, but as soon as she does, another part of me whispers: *What if Ted finds out I'm a sociopath?* He'd leave me for sure. Days ago, I would've said I'm fine with it, but now I realize it would devastate me. Somehow, bolstered by the wine and Ted's reassurance and the absolute fucking mess I've made of everything, I manage to agree to an appointment for the next day.

The following morning, we sit stiffly on the love couch inside our hotel room, my phone propped up in front of us, both of us smiling nervously as the mental health app logs us into our session. The session begins, and the counselor isn't at all the way I'd pictured counselors to be. She's in her forties with pink hair, wearing a button-down blouse that shows off the intricate tattoos on her arms. Her appearance disarms me enough that I feel my walls shifting ever so slightly.

"Good morning, Jane and Ted," she says. Her voice is soothing, like a librarian during story time. "I'm Kathryn. What brings you here today? Jane, would you like to start?"

I stare mutely.

Kathryn smiles reassuringly. "Well, how about telling me a little about yourself?"

Still, I can't find the ability to speak. Ted squeezes my arm and I flinch.

"Maybe I can start," he says. Thank fuck, because I don't know what the hell is wrong with me. I sit there, half listening as he spills everything, about how fraught our marriage has become, how he feels like I take everything he says as an attack, how on edge we both feel at all times. And with everything he reveals, I feel more and more emotions piling up—frustration, anger, sorrow—leaping from the ether and turning into a giant ball of feelings that I have to fight to hold back.

Kathryn nods like she understands, but she doesn't. No one does, and how could they? They don't know the kind of monster I truly am, the sick thoughts crawling like spiders inside my head. "You'd be surprised," she says, when Ted's done, "to know that many couples go through the same struggles you do . . ."

It's too much. The monster bursts out of me. "No they don't, because most people aren't married to sociopaths!"

Kathryn falls silent. Ted stares at me. "Um," he says after a beat. "I understand that I've probably not been the best husband, but calling me a sociopath is a bit much—"

"No, not you," I say through gritted teeth. "It's me. I'm a sociopath. I've done all these tests and it's what I am. I hid it from everyone else because—I don't know—I guess I just wanted to fit in, and I'm sorry I tricked you into marrying a monster, but . . . yeah."

Ted's staring at me like I've just grown an extra eye.

"Jane," Kathryn says, "when you say you've done tests, do you mean you were tested by a professional and given a medical diagnosis of APD?"

"No. I just—I found tests online—"

"There aren't any official tests you can take online, as far as I know. What kinds of questions did these tests ask you, do you remember?"

I try to ignore Ted's stare and recount as many questions as I can. Kathryn nods encouragingly. If she's judging me, she hides it well.

"Interesting," she says after a while. "Can I ask you a few questions, Jane?"

I shrug.

"Do you often feel fear that others would judge you for whatever reason?"

"Yes, you definitely do," Ted says, nodding at me.

Kathryn smiles. "Ted, maybe we can let Jane speak for herself."

"Sorry." He deflates.

I don't even feel satisfaction; I'm too absorbed in what Kathryn just asked me. Slowly, I open up my box of memories, cautiously, as though it's Pandora's box. "Uh. Yeah." My voice comes out soft at first, but the deeper I go into the box, the more I see it. How I'd felt about going to Montauk, the way I felt at SusPens Con, always lost, always an outsider. "Yes. Always."

Kathryn nods. "Do you have intense fear of interacting with strangers?" When I hesitate, she says, "This fear may manifest itself in different ways that might not seem like fear. For example, on the surface you might feel intense exhaustion, or stress, or in some cases, even anger."

I find myself nodding along before I even realize it. "Angry, yes. I often feel angry when it comes to other people. But isn't that anger because of my sociopathy?"

"Let's put the possibility of sociopathy—or antisocial

personality disorder—aside for now. I'm just trying to gather more information for now, no labels, okay?"

I don't know what I am without the label of a sociopath, so I just shrug.

"Do you spend time after a social interaction hyper-analyzing your behavior and finding flaws in the way you behaved?"

"Yes. All the time. I do it during the interaction too." I almost add, *because I'm a sociopath and I don't know how to behave normally*, but I stop myself.

She asks me a few more questions, and I'm sure, so sure that when this is all done, she'll tell me that yes, I'm right, I'm a sociopath and there's no saving my marriage. But when she finishes with her questions, she gives me an empathetic smile and says, "Jane, you don't have APD. You're not a sociopath."

"What?" Panic laps at the edges of my consciousness. "But everything I've said—the anger, not knowing how to interact—"

"Yes, I believe you have social anxiety, Jane. Keep in mind I can't formally diagnose you without doing a proper evaluation in person, but—" She shakes her head. "I'm very sure you don't have APD. My guess—and I encourage you to come in for a proper evaluation—is that you have social anxiety disorder that manifests in anger toward yourself and others. In fact, I would say that your strong belief that you have APD is a way for yourself to cope with your anxiety—you have intense fear around social interactions and other everyday activities, so you tell yourself that you don't care, and that you're perhaps not as good with social interaction as you want to be because you're a sociopath. It gives you back some semblance of control, thinking that it's because you're apathetic and don't care about others instead of the truth, which is that you're scared of people."

"I—what?" I'm shaking my head, my voice unrecognizable. "No, you're wrong, I took all those tests—"

"Like I said, there are no online tests that have been approved by the DSM-5 that can diagnose APD. Not to mention that self-diagnosis is very hard and discouraged by most health professionals. Evaluating and identifying mental health issues can be a long and confusing process."

She might as well be speaking Russian. I don't understand what she's saying. I can't. I stare blankly at the computer screen, mouth agape. I'm not a sociopath? But all those thoughts I've grown up having, all the anger and malevolence. It feels as though she's just broken a part of my identity. I want to scream at her.

But underneath the whirlwind of emotions, a small part of me is nodding its head and agreeing. A small voice at the back of my head is sighing with relief that after all this time, it's finally being understood. My eyes fill with tears, and I take a shuddery breath. I am unmade, shattered, yet I'm also relieved.

I'm not a sociopath. I don't have APD.

Maybe.

I'm not ready yet to fully embrace this new identity. She could be wrong. Couldn't she? Of the two of us, she's the one with a degree in psychology. My mind swims.

I look at Ted. He's regarding me with concern. "So all this time," he says, "you thought you were—what, *American Psycho*?"

"I would encourage you not to use such incendiary terms," Kathryn says.

Ted closes his mouth. Then he says, "I'm sorry. It's just kind of a lot."

"Yes. But proper evaluation is the first step to healing, and I think the two of you have a lot to think about after this session.

I'm going to give you some homework. Ted, your homework is to wear a rubber band around your wrist and snap it every time you talk over or talk for Jane. Make a mental note whenever you do it."

Ted gives a sheepish smile. "I guess I do that quite a bit."

Kathryn smiles. "And Jane, your homework is to wear a rubber band around your wrist as well—"

I lift my hand toward the phone to show that I already wear one, and she laughs. "Great! What have you been wearing it for?"

My cheeks burn with shame, though why I feel ashamed, I don't quite understand. Because I'd foolishly thought I could do the work of a trained psychologist by evaluating myself? Because I'd thought that I could control whatever it was I had all on my own? "To uh—control my anger."

Ted's mouth drops open. "I thought it was just to tie up your hair."

If I weren't so mortified over everything, I would've laughed at that.

She nods. "I see. It's actually very astute of you. But let's shift the focus so that you snap it whenever you start feeling that fear. Remember, in your case, it might feel like anger, so when you feel angry, snap the rubber band and remind yourself that you're not actually angry, it's just anxiety manifesting itself as anger. Over the next few weeks, we'll use some known cognitive behavioral therapy methods to cope with your anxiety. And some extra homework—I want you to look in the mirror every morning and every evening and say these words out loud: *I am not a sociopath. I do not have antisocial personality disorder. I have some anxiety around social interactions, which I will learn to cope with.* Okay?"

Everything inside me wants to fight it. I want to reject

everything she's said and pretend that none of this has happened, so I can go back to the familiar identity I've been wearing all these years. But the burden of that identity is going through life alone, feeling like a complete outsider while everyone else is celebrating life, a party I'm never invited to. And I'm tired of it. I've had enough.

I look at Ted and meet his eyes. They're filled with kindness, sorrow, and a small glimmer of hope. A tentative smile touches the corners of my mouth, and together, we nod.

Chapter 26

THALIA

My husband is dead, and I am bereft. I am a grieving widow. I am beside myself.

No, I am not acting. I am genuinely distressed, though perhaps not for the obvious reason. No, I'm devastated because Ivan died too soon. About a year too soon, I would say. And now we (me and Ivan's body, that is) are stuck in New York, unable to go back to Indonesia because of his cunt of a sister. Let me catch you up. Go back in time, to that awful, horrific night in Oxford, where I was very nearly raped by an angry Frenchman.

After the cops came and took our statements, etc., I spent the night at Ivan's hotel room, being very gently cuddled by him. I made it clear that Antoine didn't manage to actually rape me before Jane came into the room and pushed him off me. Because I knew Ivan; he liked that I was a damsel in distress, but it would have been too much for him if I had actually been defiled. He didn't propose that night. I suppose he thought that proposing the same night some guy was killed in my room would be in bad taste. Or maybe he wasn't planning to propose that night at all.

It didn't matter. As it was, Antoine's attack turned into the perfect catalyst for my relationship with Ivan. I told him I was too traumatized to stay in Oxford, and he whisked me away to London, where we spent the next few days dining at Heston Blumenthal and Gordon Ramsay's Michelin-starred restaurants. He seemed to think that the key to recovering after a traumatic experience was to eat foie gras and langoustines and shop at Burberry and Gucci. I mean, I don't disagree. It's a fine strategy.

By the time I "recovered," he was besotted with me. I'd made it easy for him to fall in love with me. I was the perfect girl, one who challenged him in a coy, playful way that led to both of us tumbling into bed amongst shriek-giggles. I was vulnerable enough for him to feel like a big man, but not needy, not at all. Stable enough for him to want to take me home to see his family. I created a dream of us as a married couple—me, always happy to see him when he came home from work, running toward him—"Baby! You're home!"—and jumping into his arms. I said I loved to cook and wanted to cook for him every day, morning and night. I would wear nothing but an apron so that when he came home, I would be the ideal wife: a sex slave who cooks.

He fell for it. He was so into this image of me as his forever-slave that at the end of the week, he asked me to go with him to Jakarta.

By then, I knew that Ivan was my ticket to the kind of lifestyle I deserved. Hard work may turn you into a modest millionaire, but it sure as hell isn't going to give you access to mega yachts and private jets and mansions guarded by military police. So I said yes. We flew to Indonesia, and that was where I met his family.

His family, oh my. Where do I begin? I've watched *Crazy Rich Asians*, I thought I knew what to expect, but Chinese-Indonesians

262

are an entirely different breed. First of all, they are extremely tight-knit. When I say extremely tight-knit, I mean Ivan still lives with his parents. Oh yes. This is common in Chinese-Indonesian cultures. These people own several mansions and luxury apartments in Jakarta alone, but do they utilize them? Nope. They choose to live in the biggest one in North Jakarta, a behemoth of a mansion with eight bedrooms, a fully equipped gym, a ballroom, a home theater, and two Olympic-size pools, one indoors and one outdoors. It's staggeringly luxurious, but I saw it for what it truly was: a gilded cage.

Ivan's parents are incredibly controlling. You think you know controlling? You haven't met these people. They control everything from Ivan's diet ("He must eat bird's nest soup every day!") to Ivan's bowel movements ("Have you been regular, dear?" they ask every morning, as if I wanted to hear about literal shit over my breakfast). From mouth to anus, they had to know what was going on.

No wonder Ani was half-insane by the time I met her in Oxford. Who wouldn't be driven mad by these people? Ani in Jakarta was a shell of the person I knew in Oxford. It would've been funny if it wasn't so pathetic. In Oxford, she had been wild and carefree, switching boyfriends as often as she switched expensive purses. In Jakarta, she became unrecognizable; even her makeup was different. She was a good, pious Chinese-Indonesian girl—she went to church every Sunday, her outfits were stylish but above all modest, and she never, ever spoke back to her parents. Sometimes, I'd catch her regarding me with a calculating look. I'd tried, one night, to pry her open and find the real Ani, but she'd locked Oxford Ani up in a steel box. I didn't blame her. I would've probably done the same if I had Ivan's parents.

And oh, how his parents hated me. The dirty foreigner come to colonize their precious son. They tolerated me until Ivan announced one year in that we were going to be married, then they tried everything to break us up. They even tried to pay me off to disappear. A measly two million dollars they offered me to dump their son. As if anyone in her right mind would have taken that, after seeing their true net worth. I took the two million dollars and gave the money, tears streaming down my face, to Ivan. He stormed into their room and told them they were repulsive, then he gave them the ultimatum: Let us be married, or else he would move out (gasp!). They quickly relented after that, though they did make me sign a prenup.

Contrary to what Hollywood would have you believe, people with APD don't necessarily like killing. I, for one, find it rather bothersome. Unhygienic. All that blood. (Between you and me, I feel that Antoine bled so much just to get back at me; that was exactly the sort of petty man he was.) I didn't go into the marriage planning to kill Ivan. I didn't have anything against him; he was always perfectly benign. That's a very deliberate word choice, by the way. I'm a writer; I think hard about these things, and "benign" describes Ivan most accurately. He's inoffensive, unthreatening, and I didn't mind his presence much for the first few years of marriage. How many married couples can say that? Everyone is always so obsessed about being #blessed and #livingyourbestlife, and here I am, modest little Thalia, perfectly satisfied with benign. And I could have tolerated Ivan for a much longer time if not for his abhorrent family. I'm the true victim here; I was given no choice but to kill him, because of the prenup.

Prenups. Aren't they just the worst? They're only there to

protect the rich from the rest of us. But I saw the loophole right away: If Ivan and I had a divorce, I would get nothing, but if Ivan were to die . . . well, they failed to specify that in the prenup. So there was my answer, clear as day. All I had to do was wait until Ivan passed away.

I'm very good at waiting.

It took a while to figure out how to kill Ivan. For months after I decided to kill him, I continued playing my role as a dutiful Chinese-Indonesian wife. I followed him on his business trips to Shanghai and Dubai and bought decadent souvenirs for his parents—dates as fat as scarab beetles, ginseng more expensive than gold bars. Every gift I gave them, they came up with some reason to push aside. They only drank ginseng from South Korea, not from China. They found dates sickeningly sweet, never mind the fact that they inhaled sticky-sweet palm sugar syrup like it was water.

I accompanied his mother everywhere, carrying her snakeskin Birkin for her like a handmaid. I called her "Mama" and I called his father "Papa" and I called Ani "Saosao," which means sister-in-law in Mandarin. Imagine being Ani's sister. The sheer horror. Luckily, Mama and Papa didn't much care for Ani either. They were all about Ivan.

My patience was rewarded when I was allowed to accompany Ivan on his annual checkup at the Mount Elizabeth Hospital in Singapore. Mount Elizabeth is the most overpriced hospital in Singapore, so naturally, it's teeming with Chinese-Indonesians. Chinese-Indonesians adore coming here for annual checkups. They're paranoid and have too much money to know what to do with, so every year, they subject themselves to extensive blood tests and scans to get reassurance that no, they're not about to randomly drop dead. Ivan was no exception to this rule, but Ivan actually had something to worry about, because apparently, my husband had some hereditary heart condition that required a bit of monitoring. Belatedly, I recalled Ani's comment all those years ago in Oxford, when she told Ivan not to punt because of his heart. I'd dismissed it as a stupid barb then, because of course, everything that came out Ani's mouth was a barb.

"It's fine," his doctor assured Mama, Papa, Ivan, Ani, and me. (Of course, Mama and Papa and Ani had come with us on this trip. They, too, had a series of unnecessary tests to undergo at Mount Elizabeth.) "Still seeing a little bit of arrhythmia, but overall you're in good condition." He prescribed some medication and charged us three thousand six hundred dollars for this. Mama and Papa fussed over Ivan. *My sweet baby, oh my poor darling. Talia* (This was how they pronounced my beautiful name, butchering it so the Th-sound turned into a harsh T. Just one of the many transgressions that I dutifully jotted down into my little notebook.), *you must take better care of him!*

I nodded and kept my head lowered so they wouldn't see my smile. A hereditary heart condition. Interesting. As soon as we got back to their apartment in Singapore—a penthouse off Orchard Road, one of the most sought-after districts in a city of wealthy expats—I nagged Ivan into bed and told his parents I was going to the pharmacist to find the best supplements for him. They nodded, satisfied at this over-the-top show of concern, and off I went. Once I was out of the apartment, I logged on to a VPN and did a search on his heart condition.

He had some sort of hereditary arrhythmia, which was basically just a fancy way of saying that his heart didn't beat to the correct rhythm. For a rule follower like Ivan, this seemed a tad ironic. Fortunately for Ivan, thanks to his gaggle of attentive, well-paid doctors, his condition was kept under control. Unfortunately for Ivan, his poor, long-suffering wife was about to take what was rightfully hers.

At the pharmacist, I asked for "heart healthy vitamins and supplements" and selected the most expensive ones. Then I asked for a bottle of caffeine pills. I've just been so tired nowadays, I told the shopkeeper, and I hate the taste of coffee. The shopkeeper shrugged and gave me a bottle of their strongest caffeine pills. I asked if they had anything stronger, and they shrugged again and told me to Google it. Which I did. I found out that while caffeine pills held a comparable amount of caffeine to a cup of coffee, pure caffeine powder is a whole other story. A teaspoon of caffeine powder is equivalent to twenty cups of coffee. And, oh look, I could easily order them online. How very convenient. I practically skipped all the way back to the apartment.

I had to be very, very careful. Indonesia has capital punishment, and the police are largely in the pockets of the rich and powerful, i.e., Ivan's family. If they even suspected foul play that involved me, I would either rot in an Indonesian prison cell or be killed quickly in the dead of night. No one would miss me; I didn't have any close friends, and my only remaining relative is Aunt Claudette, who would be torn between sadness and relief at the news of my demise. The precarious position I'd put myself in, to be married into this tyrannical family.

So I did what I do best. I planned meticulously. And it was a plan that would take years. I couldn't just cram a whole bottle of caffeine powder into Ivan's mouth and call it done. No, I started off small. A sprinkle here and there. He started sleeping badly, tossing and turning in bed, waking up in the morning looking disheveled. I visited him at his office, where I'd subtly sabotage him—misplace an important document, change the numbers on his spreadsheet. Nothing that would actually derail and bankrupt the company (hey, I wanted that money), just little things that I knew would stress him out, so that when he came home in a bad mood, I could cluck over him, in front of Mama and Papa, and tell him he was working too hard, that it wouldn't be good for his health. This was trickier to pull off than it should be, because Ani was always hovering around like a wraith. Often, when I dropped by the office, I'd find her there, skulking around, butting into conversations and just generally trying to insert herself in Ivan's business, so desperate to become relevant within the company. It was honestly pathetic, and very irritating as I would have to make sure she wasn't paying attention to me while I changed numbers around.

Then I would hold off for a couple of months, helping out at his office to make sure things ran smoothly. No more caffeine. Just to make a clear connection that it was his work that was causing him stress and definitely not his loving, helpful wife. Then back to more powder, mixing it into his morning kale smoothies, his maguro salad bowl, his chicken soup, until he was worried enough to fly back to Singapore for another checkup. The doctor put him on a heart monitor for three days, which showed nothing of concern (I eased up on the caffeine then) and cost us over twenty thousand dollars. You know how bloody hard it was to pull it off? I had publishing deadlines to meet, not to mention cons that I tried my best to attend, though at times I did have to turn them down, yet another reason I had to punish this awful family.

Once we came back to Jakarta, I started him back on the

caffeine. It was actually rather fun, like a little game we were playing with each other. When the palpitations happened again, Mama and Papa insisted he fly to Japan for a checkup. Another doctor, another heart monitor. *He's fine*, the doctor said. *Is anything stressing him out?*

His work, I piped up. *I wish he'd take more time off from it.*

Listen to your wife, the doctor said.

Good dog.

Yes, listen to Talia, Mama and Papa said.

I almost cried at that. Finally, all those years of hard work, trying to prove myself, that I was a good wife, had paid off. In fact, I was so moved by this that I decided to postpone killing Ivan. I wanted to bask a little in his parents' approval. How crazy is that? The Chinese-Indonesian culture of sacrificing everything for your parents' approval had actually managed to sink its claws under my skin. Mama and Papa's approval was like a drug; they doled it out in stingy little pinches, and the more I got, the more I wanted. This part was my fault—I fully admit to it. I should've just gone ahead and killed him when I'd planned, but I let myself be distracted.

Obviously, it didn't last long. After a few months of it, I got bored and resumed my plan. But by then, Kurt had started talking about leaving his wife for me. It soon became clear that I had to get rid of Kurt first. If anyone in Indonesia got wind of my affair, it would be all over for me. I tried, I really did, not to have to resort to killing him. I tried to break things off, plying him with all of the charms I had (which is a lot), but nope. Surly, selfish Kurt. If he couldn't have me, then he'd make sure no one else could. Of course, killing Kurt meant that I probably shouldn't kill anyone else for at least another year. It meant postponing

Ivan's death, which I wasn't thrilled about, but I could stomach it. I told you I was very good at being patient.

But now, somehow, Ivan's dead. A mere day after Kurt's fatal accident, which looks bad. Very bad.

I pace about the penthouse. I go through the papers from the hospital, all those medical terms, the numbers that mean nothing, and I ask myself: *Where did I go wrong?* I'd let up on the caffeine powder for over two months now, since I decided to kill Kurt. Yes, I realize that all those years spent messing around with Ivan's heart probably worsened his condition, but surely, it wasn't enough to actually kill him this fast? No, it couldn't be. Whenever I eased up on the caffeine, he'd quickly bounce back to normal. Unless his heart was still bothering him but he kept it from me, because men can't help but lie.

A surge of anger stabs through me, and I crush the hospital document and fling it at the wall.

"Knock-knock," Ani says, popping her head in. She actually says the words instead of knocking. "How are you doing?"

"What do you think? My husband's dead." It's surprisingly easy for me to allow a small sob to escape. I am upset, after all. He really was taken away from me too soon.

Ani stretches the corners of her mouth and eyebrows down, making a literal sad-face emoji. "And my brother's dead. You're not the only one who lost someone here."

Typical Ani. Of course she'd make this about herself. I stop moving and just stare at her until she looks away.

"Sorry, I didn't mean it that way," she says finally. "I just—I don't even know what to do. He's been there my entire life, and now he's not, and I don't understand why." At this, she breaks down sobbing, sinking gracefully onto the chaise longue. I roll my eyes and grit my teeth before sitting down next to her and putting my arm around her shaking shoulders.

I count to ten and then say, "Okay, enough of that. We need to be strong, Ani. We need to make arrangements." We need to get Ivan's body the fuck out of America and back to Indonesia, hopefully outrun any suspicions that might be cast on me after Kurt and Ivan's deaths. One day apart! I could cry at the thought of my unbelievably bad luck. "Don't you worry about a thing. I'll take care of everything. I'll see to it that he's flown back ASAP and buried in your family plot—"

"No!" Ani cries, pulling away from me.

I blink at her, confused.

"No, are you kidding? His body is not leaving this country until we know exactly what happened."

My stomach turns to ice. "What do you mean?"

"Mama and Papa are on their way here right now."

I'm so shocked by this that I almost miss the glint in Ani's eyes. Almost. As I stare at her in mute horror, her lips tremble like she's fighting back a smile, and she says, "Don't you worry, my sweet sister-in-law. We are going to get to the bottom of this."

And I know, then, that I've made a terrible mistake. All those years of planning, all those careful moves I'd made, and I'd missed a crucial factor: Ani. Like everyone else, I never even spared a thought for her. I assumed that I was the only predator around, when all this while, there was another more dangerous creature in the family, and now she's standing right in front of me, smiling a smile that says: *I got you.*

Chapter 27

JANE

Every day feels like a dream. Okay, granted, it's only been two days since Ted and I had our session with Kathryn, but it feels like something huge has shifted. After that session, I went to the bathroom and cried until my eyes ran out of tears, then I just dry-sobbed until I was completely and utterly empty. I thought of myself as a little kid, and myself as a teen, and myself in my twenties and now, thirties, the whole time believing that I was a sociopath just because I happened to take some stupid online quizzes that told me I was. Just because I thought I was smart enough to do the work of trained psychologists. Just because I had social anxiety and didn't know how to deal with it. I spent the next hour or so going through my memories, reliving all the social interactions I could think of and identifying all those feelings of apathy and anger for what they truly were—fear and anxiety. How could I have been so wrong about myself? I looked up antisocial personality disorder, and this time, I saw many, many traits that didn't fit my personality. Traits that I had dismissed years ago, telling myself that of course I wouldn't have all the symptoms of sociopathy, that I was an individual and not a statistic.

Surprisingly, Ted had left me to cry for as long as I wanted, and only when I came out of the bathroom of my own accord did he approach me, with a plate of cheese and crackers and a glass of wine. He gave me a hesitant smile and said, "Thought you might be hungry."

And I looked at my husband and didn't hate him.

We spent the rest of the day in Central Park, just walking through the lush greenery holding hands and talking about anything and everything. He asked me how I felt, and I told him "Like a mess," but after a beat, I added, "But also hopeful." And that was enough for him. And it was enough for me too.

The next day, we went and did the tourist thing. Went to the Statue of Liberty, got the hats, went up the Empire State Building. We didn't kiss or hug—we weren't ready for that yet—but we held hands, and I snapped my rubber band whenever I felt angry and I reminded myself it wasn't anger but fear that I was feeling. And he snapped his rubber band whenever he talked over me, and then gave me a sheepish smile and said, "Wow, I do that a lot, huh?" After a full day of this, I was tired but like I said, hopeful.

We're in the midst of packing up for the airport when there's a knock on the door. I immediately know something's wrong, because it's not the kind of knock that precedes the words, "Room service." It's the kind of insistent knock that precedes the words, "Open up, we know you're in there!"

In fact, what the person opposite the door says is worse. "Jane Morgan? It's Detective Howe. Please open the door."

Detective Howe. Why's she here? The old anger resurfaces and I snap the rubber band, but knowing that the emotion is actually fear doesn't make me feel any better in this moment.

Ted looks at me with brows raised, his face largely unconcerned. "You okay?" he says.

I nod. I am okay, I remind myself. There's absolutely no reason why I wouldn't be okay. No reason at all. I didn't do anything wrong.

"Yeah, I'm fine." I flash him a small smile and head for the door, taking a deep inhale before opening it. "Hi, Detective."

She doesn't return my polite smile. Instead, she frowns at the scene behind my shoulder. "Are you leaving town?"

"Uh. Yeah? We're flying back to the Bay Area today."

"Yeah?" she says, and it comes out like a challenge, like, *Yeah? You think so, do you? Well, you have another think coming.* "What time's your flight?"

Ted comes up to the door, standing just behind me. "Hi, I'm Ted. Jane's husband."

"Detective Howe." They shake hands.

"Is everything okay here?" Ted says, and I feel the old irritation starting to scrape at my nerves. He's doing that thing again, inserting himself where he's not needed, playing at being The Man of the Household. I remind myself that he's probably doing this to reassure me, to remind me that he's on my side. But I bristle anyway, because I'm used to not having anyone on my side.

I expect Detective Howe to say yes, of course everything's okay, but instead, she says, "We have a few follow-up questions for you, Jane. Can you come back with us to the station? It would be really helpful if you did. It would only take an hour."

"But we're flying out—" Ted says.

"I can spare an hour to answer some questions," I say. I don't know what made me say that, except that I feel an urgent, overwhelming need to show that I'm trustworthy, that I'm here to help. Good old Plain Jane, always here to help! I desperately need to prove that I'm innocent, and to do that I must surely agree with anything and everything they ask of me.

"Great."

"Just let me grab my stuff first."

"Of course."

I go back into the room and shove random things into my purse, half in a daze. I keep having that out-of-body sensation like I'm floating above myself and wondering, *How would an innocent person behave? What would an innocent person bring to the police station for an interview?* Which is strange, because I am an innocent person, so I shouldn't need to think about this. I'm vaguely aware of Ted fussing around me, asking things like, "Are you sure this is a good idea? Should I call a lawyer?"

"Only guilty people need lawyers," I bite out.

Ted stops short. "That's not—I don't think that's true. I—"

"I'll be fine." Maybe the last two days have been a dream after all. It's surprisingly easy to slip back into the old ways, wearing my resentment at him like an old sweater, wrapping it tight around me. I don't give him a second glance before walking out the door. I can feel the hurt radiating from him in thick, slow waves, and it's a relief when the door finally clicks shut, cutting me off from Ted's gaze. I let out my breath.

"Thanks for agreeing to come with us," Detective Howe says.

I nod, not trusting myself to say anything. Never mind my stomach, everything inside me is knotted up, even my muscles. It's almost next to impossible for me to keep walking. I'm actually relieved when we get out of the hotel and her car's right outside, a gray, nondescript sedan. I'd been half expecting a black-and-white police car with flashing lights, Howe placing her hand on my head as she "helped" me into the car. But nothing like that happens. I get in normally, like I'm sliding into an Uber.

The station, at least, is reminiscent of TV police stations, all gray walls and stark fluorescent lights and a dozen cops going about their day, filing paperwork, talking to one another. A couple of them are walking some guy in handcuffs in, and the sight puts me on edge. Howe waves and greets other officers and leads me into a room marked as "Interview Room 4."

"Can I get you a drink? Coffee, tea? Coke?"

I shake my head. I just want to get this over with. "I'm fine."

"Great. Have a seat and let me just . . ." She takes out her phone and then pauses. "It's okay if I record this, yeah?"

That catches me off guard. The way she asked that, so casually, like it's something she's just remembered at the last minute. "Yeah." It's not like I could say no.

She unlocks her phone and calls up the voice recording app. Presses the big red button. "Okay, great. I'm Detective Tricia Howe, speaking with Jane Morgan. Can you confirm that's your name?"

I nod, and she says, "Can you please give me verbal confirmation that your name is Jane Morgan?"

"Oh, yes. It's Jane Morgan." My stomach lurches unpleasantly. This feels way too official for what I was prepared for.

She gives me an encouraging smile. "So first of all, thank you for coming to the station with me, Jane."

I press my lips together, wondering what to say to that. It's not like she's asked me a question.

"I'd like to go over a few more details about what happened at Montauk."

I nod. "Sure."

"So you said that Thalia Ashcroft invited you to this retreat?"

"Yes."

"Do you remember what she said to you that made you think she invited you there?"

That made me *think* she invited me there? Beneath the table, my hands are wringing each other, my fingers writhing like snakes, pinching and strangling. "Um. She said, 'Come with me to this writers retreat.'"

"In those exact words?"

I stare at her. "No, I don't know, that was days ago. Of course I don't remember her exact words, but I remember the gist of it, and it's that she invited me." *Careful, Jane.* I'm letting my temper overwhelm me again. Again, I remind myself it's not my temper, but my fear. But it's really not actually helpful at all in this moment.

Detective Howe nods, and it's clear she doesn't believe me. "Is there anyone that can corroborate this?"

I claw at my memories and come up with nothing. "No."

"Hmm. Okay. Can we talk for a moment about how you know Thalia? You said you guys were friends in college."

You guys. She's trying to put me at ease—*look, Jane, I'm just a pal!* I nod. "Yeah. Well, not college. Grad school."

"Ah yes, of course. In Oxford, right? That's pretty fancy. So you two were classmates?"

We were much more than just classmates, I almost tell her, but I don't. "Yeah. Like I said, we were friends."

"But you mentioned that you lost touch after the first semester there. Would that have anything to do with what happened to . . ." She makes a big show of glancing at her notes. "Antoine Deveraux?"

My mouth snaps shut. I don't know why this surprises me. It shouldn't; I should've known the moment she brought up Oxford that she would've done her homework and that she must've known about Antoine. But I guess I'm not as cunning as I thought I was, because damn, that catches me off guard, and now I don't know what to say. "Yeah, well. What happened was—you know, it was very traumatic. Thalia left the program and didn't come back. I don't like to talk about it. Hell, I haven't even told my husband about it," I say with a small laugh.

She doesn't return the laugh. "What happened then? Can you fill me in?"

"The Oxford police didn't give you any details?" God, I'm way too acerbic. I need to be more pliant, more pleasant.

"They gave me a summary of what happened. Let's see . . ." Another glance at her notes, which I'm sure she's actually got memorized. "They said Antoine had stolen into the college and hid in Thalia's room, and when she went up halfway through the ball, he attacked her. Fortunately, you came into her room and were able to save her by"—she clears her throat—"stabbing him with a letter opener. Is that accurate?"

I look down at my hands. That awful night flashes through my head. Me going inside Thalia's room and finding Antoine covered in blood. Me, the besotted idiot, coming to Thalia's rescue. Offering to take the blame. God, I was so fucking stupid. Fleetingly, I wonder if I should tell Detective Howe the truth about what happened. But that would just come off crazy. She'd think I was making it up, and she'd probably become even more suspicious.

"Yeah." My voice comes out as a whisper.

"Can you walk me through how that happened? Because the

angle seemed a bit . . . off." She mimes grabbing someone with her hands. "If you were to grab him from the back and throw him off, then he would've been at this angle."

"There was a lot of struggling involved," I say quickly. "Thalia was there and she was fighting him, too, and he was just kind of, you know, fighting both of us."

"Sure, yeah, of course. Huh." She refers to her notes again. "Okay . . . And the Oxford police, did they do any sort of investigation?"

"I'm not sure? I mean, they interviewed everyone there. They reviewed the security tapes at the common areas, I think? But I also know that the university was keen to shut it down. There were a lot of whispers in the dorm afterward about how the university basically got the cops to close the case."

Detective Howe nods slowly. "Uh-huh. I can see that. A wealthy, powerful college like that, they wouldn't want the bad press. Especially since this guy stole in and nearly raped one of their students."

I nod, keeping my eyes on my lap.

"And ever since then, you never heard from Thalia?"

"Yeah, she kind of just went off the radar."

"Not even social media?"

I shake my head.

"Don't you think that's strange? I mean, we're on everything nowadays. Hell, I'm on TikTok. You know TikTok?"

"Sure." A lot of authors are on TikTok, doing all sorts of videos to convince people to BUY MY BOOK, GUYS!

"So you never tried looking for her on social media?"

"Once in a while." So many times. "I don't know, she was never on it."

"And you don't find that strange?"

"I don't know. I mean, I know people who're not on social media. My husband's not big on it."

"Oh, Ted doesn't have a Facebook account?"

I frown. "Well, he does, obviously. But he's not, like, on it, on it. He never checks it." As soon as I say that, I realize it's not true, because Ted checks Facebook about once a week.

"Right, that's common. But what you're saying is that Thalia doesn't even have a Facebook, or a Twitter, or an Instagram account, which is not normal."

I gape at her, opening and closing my mouth. "I mean—yeah, I guess it's not very common. But I don't understand what that has to do with me. Why am I getting grilled because Thalia's not on TikTok?"

I'm met with a long, drawn-out sigh. Detective Howe leans forward, clasping her hands in front of her, and looks me straight in the eye. "Have you ever wondered why she might have disappeared so completely after you killed Antoine?"

The way she said "you killed Antoine" sends a chill down my spine. "Uh, hang on—"

"Because I have a statement from Thalia Ashcroft saying that you were obsessed with her. You were stalking her in Oxford, and yes, you did save her from Antoine, but she also felt like you weren't—hmm, how to say this delicately—like you were glad that you were given this opportunity to kill him and get away with it."

"What?" The blood in my veins stops flowing. Everything inside me has turned to jagged ice. "No, wait—"

"Obviously, she didn't tell any of this to the Oxford police; she said she was so terrified that she just wanted to get away from it all, and she took the chance to leave the city and escape your attention."

"Hang on—"

Detective Howe holds up a hand. "There's more. Thalia said after leaving Oxford, she deleted all of her social media profiles to ensure that you wouldn't be able to track her down. She even released her first few books under a pen name to avoid you. Then she said that when she got her big book deal, she felt so strongly about using her real name that she was willing to risk it, especially since it's been years since Oxford. She thought there was a good chance that you'd moved on. Kind of a silly risk to take, if you ask me." She actually winks at me then, like she's still trying to get me on her side even though she's lobbing these insane accusations at me. "And that was when you tracked her down again. Showed up at some book convention she was at? We've got a couple of witnesses saying you were behaving somewhat aggressively during her talk."

Behaving aggressively? I see a flash of myself at SusPens Con, overwhelmed by emotions at seeing Thalia again after all these years, shouting out a question at her. How I must have come off to onlookers. Unhinged. Like a stalker. "I don't like crowds."

She crooks her mouth into a mirthless smile. "We also spoke to Ani Pranajaya about you, and she swore that you stole a necklace from her? Erratic behavior, Jane. Everyone we talked to can attest to that."

Ani's necklace. God, who would've thought that it would come back to bite me like this?

"And of course, the other writers at the retreat all attest to you inviting yourself to Montauk. They said Thalia was obviously uncomfortable around you, but that she was too kind to tell you to go away."

Another flash of me and Thalia at Montauk, the way she'd gone inside first to let everyone know that I was there. What must she have told them? *Oh my god, my college stalker is here. Please be nice to her; she's dangerous and I'm so scared.* I can picture it so easily in my mind's eye, the way that Thalia's beautiful face would've looked then, tight with fear. No wonder they'd all been so quietly furious toward me. All those glares. The look on Kurt's face.

Kurt.

Realization smashes into me like a hammer. This is why. This is why she lured me back to her. Because she wanted me to go down for Kurt's murder.

"Why are you asking me these questions? Do they have to do with Kurt's accident?"

"Was it an accident, Jane?"

I glare back at her. I'm not going to be the one who looks away first, because I'm not guilty. I'm not the one who's failing to do my job. "Isn't it your job to find out if it was an accident?"

"You're right." She blinks. I win. But it's an empty victory. "We're still looking into it. It's just that some details are showing up and I thought it would be best to talk to people, cover our bases."

"So this is all just covering your bases? Asking me if I wanted to kill Antoine?" It's too much. All of it. I feel the truth bubbling inside me, hitting its boiling point before erupting. I can no longer keep it inside me. "I didn't kill Antoine!" I cry. "It was Thalia. She was the one who did it." The words sear themselves out of my mouth, leaving me breathless. There, my deep, dark secret is out.

But Detective Howe only looks smug. "Yes, Thalia did warn us that you might say that."

"She's fucking lying!" My voice comes out harsh with rage,

and yes, it is rage, fuck what Kathryn says, because I know what anger feels like and it is this, hot and pulsing and animalistic.

Detective Howe's eyebrows shoot up into her hairline. She's looking at me like I'm a dangerous criminal, like she's this close to reaching for her gun. Somehow, by sheer teeth-gritting power, I manage to will myself to breathe. BREATHE. I suck in a breath through my teeth, clenching the armrests of my chair.

"I've been talking to many people, Jane," Detective Howe says. "They all say you're—you've got quite a temper, don't you? Your neighbors commented on it."

My neighbors? A flash of Kimiko, seeing me angry at Ted over his remark about me being untidy. I could kill Kimiko.

I flinch at the thought and look at Detective Howe guiltily, as though she could read my mind. I'm losing it. I need to get out of here.

"Am I under arrest?" I ask thickly.

"No. We're just talking, hoping to get more answers."

"I'm done talking." I'm done being helpful Jane. I'm done being anything. I'm buzzing with fear, I don't know what I'm doing, but I know I need to not be here anymore.

Detective Howe frowns. "Jane, I really advise you to—"

I jump out of my chair, out of breath, everything inside me screaming at me to run, and I just about manage to spit out, "Next time you want to speak to me, go through my lawyer."

Chapter 28

THALIA

How the hell did I get outplayed by Ani of all people, for god's sake? As Mama and Papa land at a private airport in New Jersey, I pace about in my bedroom, going through all of the steps that led to Ivan's death. Ani has something to do with it, of that I am sure. And once I realize it, I could kick myself for missing it. All those years, living under the same roof with her and Ivan. The way she would sometimes watch him as he did the most mundane things—eating, swimming, watching TV. The way she often came with us to doctor appointments under the guise of being a caring sister. How she would often make a snarky remark about how everything is being passed down to Ivan purely on the basis of him being born a boy. The way Mama and Papa ignored her, tuning her out at mealtimes as though she weren't there. I never thought much of it, because obviously, Ani is unbearable. I can't blame Mama and Papa for ignoring her; it's probably the only way you can keep your sanity with a daughter like her around.

I'd just dismissed her as an insignificant little brat with the maturity of a five-year-old. But now, too late, I realize that this persona of hers—the flighty, party animal Ani—is a carefully curated one. I'd sometimes wondered why she bothered to do certain things—shop for branded bags and shoes, for example, when she couldn't be bothered to even wear them. Now I see them for what they truly are—a facade. The real her is far more calculating and horrifyingly more intelligent. I recall now how I once walked in on her at the office, on one of my visits there to sabotage Ivan. She'd been looking through his ledgers, and when I walked in, she'd looked up with a guilty flush. I'd thought she was just guilty because she was caught snooping, but now I see that it was something more sinister. She'd been planning.

I go back even further. To our Oxford days. How she portrayed this image of a party girl, but underneath that, she was always studying, always making connections with people she found useful. Forging business relationships, I realize. All this while, she'd been preparing herself for the eventuality of Ivan's death, so she could take over. And she'd developed this dumb fashionista persona so no one would even think of suspecting. Not even me. Fuck, I was so stupid.

Okay, enough of the self-hatred. This is what most people don't realize: self-hatred is indulgent. I know how contradictory it sounds, but trust me, hating yourself is not the opposite of narcissism. In fact, it's just another facet of it, because at the end of the day, the attention is still placed on you.

Sorry for the derail. I'm just a bit thrown off by the complexity of it all. I'm not used to feeling self-hatred. I hope I don't get used to it, because quite honestly? I'm pretty fucking amazing. And I hate Ani even more for making me feel even an ounce of self-hatred.

Okay. Think. Ivan (RIP) died of a heart attack. Did Ani trigger a heart attack somehow? Why not, right? It's the most obvious way of killing him. So how would she have done it? I pace faster around the room, gnawing at my fingernails. In my eagerness to figure it out, I almost Google "how to trigger a heart attack" but manage to stop myself in time. Shit. I must remember that the stakes are different now. I can't just Google whatever I want.

Fortunately, I always have a couple of burner phones with me. Perks of being rich: your burner phones are iPhones. I take out one of them now, log on to a VPN because I'm always careful, always putting as many layers between me and the truth as possible. Then I look it up.

Okay, so basically everything can lead to a heart attack. Amphetamines. Cocaine. Mercury. Too much alcohol. And of course, caffeine.

That tells me nothing. Except . . .

Ani was so fucking eager for an autopsy to be done. Which means whatever the results of the autopsy, it would be in her favor. What does that mean?

Cold dread spreads through my limbs as I make another realization. In case of Ivan's death, his wealth would go to the next of kin, which would be me, his wife. Which means that Ani doesn't just need to get rid of Ivan in order to get control over the family company. She also needs to get rid of me.

Shit, shit! I take in a sharp breath and force myself to calm down. I'm usually so good at being calm. But having all those years of meticulous planning and sacrifice go down the drain like this is infuriating. Not to mention the fact that I might actually end up going to prison for a crime I haven't had the chance to commit. How's that for irony? I hate irony.

Okay, so to frame me, Ani would have to—

What? What would she have done? I close my eyes, try to

put myself in her shoes. How would she have done it? Once more, I go back to the previous months, the previous year, and this time, I think of Ani, sitting at the sidelines, watching me carefully as I went about my day. Watching me prepare Ivan's kale smoothies in the morning. I'd been so careful. I'd mixed some caffeine powder in with his protein supplements, so that in the mornings, I could simply add in the protein supplement in front of everyone without causing any suspicion. Or so I thought.

Now, I see myself through Ani's eyes, and god, I was so smug I could smack myself. I see the way she watched me, and then she would've watched Ivan as he drank the smoothie. The way he became jittery, hyper. Each smoothie would've contained the equivalent of ten cups of coffee. Ani would've seen that. She would've made a note of it, his strange behavior, my behavior.

What else?

She would've kept watching. Maybe even kept a journal of Ivan's moods. It wouldn't have taken her long at all to figure out that there was a correlation between the days where I put in protein supplement powder and his jitters. His heart palpitations.

Ani, for fuck's sake. Of all people.

But just because she knows I was poisoning him doesn't mean she figured out what it was I was using. I could've been dosing him with cocaine, or a million other drugs. Not that it would make me any more innocent, but if she doesn't know, then she might not have used caffeine to kill him off.

My reverie is interrupted by the arrival of Mama and Papa. I hear them through even the thick bedroom walls, they're so fucking loud. They barge into the penthouse crying and wailing, and I hear Ani wailing back at them out in the living room. I can picture them now, clutching one another, finally acknowledging

Ani's existence now that their son is dead. Belatedly, I realize I've made a mistake. I should've been waiting out there for them, should've been ready to play the role of dutiful daughter-in-law. Shit. Once again, I've been outplayed.

Too late to salvage that now, so I do the only thing I can think of. I quickly make my way to the darkest corner of the bedroom and crouch there. I run my fingers through my hair, messing it up. Then I start to sob. Minutes later, there's a knock on the door and I manage a teary "Yes?" Mama comes in and sees me, and I see the flash of satisfaction crossing her face at my disheveled state. I'm mourning her son the way I should, with all my being. I quickly cross the room and rush at her, flinging myself at her like she's a life raft. "Mama!" I cry, burying my face in her shoulder and letting loose another violent round of tears. I need her to think that Ivan's death has broken me, that I am nothing without her insipid son. Her shoulders shake with sobs, and gingerly, she pats me on the back.

"I don't know what to do without him," I wail. To them, women are incomplete without their husbands. "I might as well die!"

Mama sniffs. "Don't let yourself be destroyed by grief," she says. "You still have a whole life ahead of you. I'm the one who has lost my son. I'm the one who has lost her life."

That's right, mustn't upstage her grief. I lean back from her so I can give a small, brave smile. "You're right, Mama. I'm so sorry for your loss. I can't—I'm so sorry. I know how much you loved him. You're the best mother."

This brings forth more tears as she nods and cries. She agrees that she had been the best mother, even though the truth is that she'd been such an awful parent that one might say it was her fault that Ivan was killed. By her own daughter. To have raised such a monster and not realize it, that's a whole new level of negligence.

After a while, we both stumble out into the living room, clutching each other and taking turns sniffling. Ani is with Papa, who looks so shrunken and aged that I almost feel bad for him. He's almost unrecognizable. Just days ago, he'd been a healthy, strapping seventy-year-old man. Now he looks like he's one step away from his own grave. Ani, on the other hand, is pacing madly about the living room. She's glowing with triumph, though she disguises it well as rage.

"We need to know exactly what happened," she says. "Wouldn't you agree?" She aims this at me, chin raised, eyes blazing. A challenge.

"I—I don't know," I say softly. *Tread very, very carefully, Thalia.* "I'm just—the thought of them cutting him up—" I feel Mama stiffen next to me. Good. She's getting an image of her beautiful son being sliced into like a pound of meat on a cold metal slab.

"Yes, but somewhere, somehow, someone did something wrong," Ani argues. "How many doctors have we taken him to? And all of them said he was fine, and then suddenly he has a heart attack? These doctors deserve to lose their medical license, and that's not going to happen unless we can prove there was malpractice. That they missed something. I mean—" She pauses, choking back a loud sob. "They might as well have killed him themselves."

Mama and Papa straighten up at this, a light entering their eyes. Shit. Ani is good. Their grief is so overwhelming right now that they'd jump at any cause to distract them from the endless sorrow. And what better cause than revenge for their dead son?

I think fast. "It's next to impossible to prove medical

289

malpractice. I don't want you to put yourselves through that for years and years. It's not—"

"No," Ani says, nodding her head. "I agree with you, Thalia. It's too much on Mama and Papa." She gives them both a sad smile. "I will do this. I'm not going to stop until we find out who killed my brother."

I can only watch, unable to say a thing, as Ani whips out her phone and calls the hospital to make arrangements for an autopsy to be done.

My blood chills. She's so insistent about it that I know then, whatever they find, it's going to be bad for me.

Chapter 29

JANE

I walk out of the police station in a daze. When I check my phone, I see seven missed calls and a dozen messages from Ted, asking me if I'm okay. It's been almost two hours since I left for the station. I hit Return Call. He picks up on the first ring.

"Jesus, Jane. Are you okay? I've been going crazy here. What happened?"

The concern in his voice is heartbreaking. Or it would be, if I weren't in shock. I want to tell him what happened, that I seem to be the suspect in Kurt's death, but as soon as I start to say it, my throat clamps up and the words won't come out. Because how ridiculous do they sound? It makes no sense. So instead, I say, "Yeah, it's fine. They just had a few follow-up questions that they've been asking everyone." How easy it is to lie to my husband.

"Okay . . ." He sounds unsure. I guess I'm not that great a liar. "Well, do you want to meet me at the airport? Because I don't think there's time for you to get back to the hotel. I've packed up everything—"

The airport. God. I'd completely forgotten about our flight. And as soon as he mentions it, I realize that there is no possible way I'm getting on that flight today. There's too much unfinished business left in New York. And how would it look to Howe if I were to fly back to California now? She'd think I was trying to run away.

"Um, actually, I think I'm gonna stay here for a while longer."

"What?"

"I just—there are some things I need to do." Like clear my name.

"Well—" He struggles to speak for a few moments before sighing. "Okay. I'll extend our room."

"No, I think you should go home, Ted," I say without realizing what I'm really saying until the words are out. But as soon as they're spoken, I know I meant them. I don't want him here. The past couple of days, we've been inching back toward each other, but now I'm about to do something I don't want him to know about. "Go home; don't bother checking out because I'm going to be staying on for another couple of days at least."

"But—" The word comes out sharp with so much pain that I have to close my eyes for a second.

"Go home." The words come out heavy with finality. I don't wait for an answer before hanging up. As soon as I end the call, I tap on his number and add it to my Blocked Contacts list. I can't afford to be distracted by Ted no doubt calling and texting me nonstop, demanding an explanation, wheedling, begging me to talk.

I go into a nearby café and buy myself a hot coffee. I need time to think about what just happened. I sit down in a far corner and start ripping up napkins into narrow strips to give myself a bit of a distraction while I work out the giant ball of shit that Thalia has somehow plopped into my life. Right. So this goes back years. Oxford. She's always been someone different. Beautiful on the outside; something repulsive and dangerous on the inside. I think about how, at Oxford, she'd fooled me into thinking she was a socially anxious person, and I realize with a kick of bitterness that she must have read me well, must've figured out that I have social anxiety and so pretended to have it as well to get my guard down. The thought of it is so overwhelming that I almost crush my coffee cup. I have to will myself to keep breathing, snapping the rubber band over and over.

Doesn't matter that she was a conniving little bitch, that she'd fooled me all this time, that she'd tricked me into claiming responsibility for Antoine's death. Oh god, Antoine. I'd believed her without any second thought, but now I know, without a doubt, that she'd killed him for no good reason. Maybe she was bored; maybe she was angry that he'd shown up unannounced—shit. He wouldn't have shown up if it wasn't for me. For years, I'd tortured myself, thinking that it was my fault that Thalia was assaulted, that she'd had no choice but to defend herself by killing him. But now, I'm overcome by guilt because it was my fault that Antoine was killed.

Okay, focus. I need to prove that Thalia was behind everything all along. That she'd planned it so that she could kill Kurt and pin the blame on me. But how? I'm a pawn in a game I hadn't even realized was being played. What move would she make next? What weaknesses does she have?

I rack my mind, trying to remember every little detail she'd once shared with me. All the life stories she'd told me. All of them were lies, probably. I sift through them anyway. She'd hated her mom and never knew her dad, just like me. Was that real? Maybe. What else? Her mom was neglectful. Always leaving her to be looked after by someone else while she went out with a different guy every night. Someone else. Her neighbor. She'd mentioned her name three, four times, back when we were in Oxford. Aunt Claudine. Claudia? Claudette. That's it. And she'd said—what had she said about Aunt Claudette? That she wasn't actually related, but that she was the only family Thalia had, and that she was closer to her than she ever was to her own mother. She's mentioned her last name before, something starting with a Cl-. She'd joked that it made her sound like a porn star even though she looked nothing like one. And that night, at Skye Bar, she'd mentioned a relative who lives in Brooklyn. It's a long shot, but maybe she was referring to Aunt Claudette?

I take out my phone and do a search for "Claudette Brooklyn." Google spits out the results, and ugh, there are a ton of Claudettes in Brooklyn. I scroll down the page and—

Claudette Clovis. That's it. That's her. It's a Facebook page of hers. I click on it, and bless her heart, Aunt Claudette is one of those old women who overshare. She lives in a retirement home in New Jersey, a swanky place called Golden Years Estate. I order a Lyft and drain my coffee before going outside.

I have no idea what I'm going to say to Aunt Claudette. I know I'm grasping at straws, but know what's worse than grasping at straws? Grasping at thin fucking air. The whole drive there, I go over and over what I might say to her, but by the time I get to Golden Years, I still have no clue. The driver drops me off at the front, a thoroughly impressive grand entrance complete with a fountain and a massive doorway.

I walk inside and approach the receptionist, an altogether too-shiny young man who looks like a living, breathing Ken doll, which is a lot more creepy than it sounds.

"Good afternoon, are you here to visit one of our residents?"

"Um. Yes. Claudette Clovis?"

His face breaks into a smile, and I'm half-blinded by the whiteness of his teeth. "Oh, Ms. Clo, of course. May I ask who's visiting?"

For a moment, I freeze. Then I manage to spit out, "Uh. Jane. Just Jane."

"Okay, I'll let her know you're here." He picks up the phone and dials a number. After a few moments, he says, "Hi Ms. Clo, it's Aaron." He gives a simpering laugh. "Oh, Ms. Clo, you're so bad. I have a visitor here for you, a young woman named Jane. Yes." He glances at me and my stomach lurches. She's going to refuse to see me. "Jane, what's your last name?"

"Morgan."

He tells Aunt Claudette this and nods. "Okay, I'll send her right up."

Relief floods through me, followed quickly by suspicion. Why did she agree to meet with me? Maybe she's bored, I tell myself as I walk after Aaron. Yeah, she's probably just bored out of her mind in this place. We walk past a living room that opens up to a beautiful courtyard where I can see a handful of old men and women playing croquet, and a game room where more people are playing chess and other board games. My mind is half-wild with anxiety by the time we get to Aunt Claudette's room. Aaron knocks on the door, and when she calls for us to come in, he smiles at me and says, "Go ahead. Just call the front desk if you need anything."

With a deep breath, I check on my phone in my bag, making sure it's recording. I'm not sure why I'm doing this, keeping a record like this. What am I expecting to hear? I open the door and step inside.

Aunt Claudette's room is exactly as I pictured it would

be—bright and airy and beautiful, but with a smell of death about it. I don't know what it is, exactly, but despite the canary yellow walls and the bright turquoise touches, there's a sense of heaviness in the air. Aunt Claudette, the large, white-haired old woman sitting in a wheelchair with her papery hands folded on her lap, is dying. I know this immediately.

"Hi, Ms. Clovis, I'm Jane."

"Jane," Aunt Claudette says, smiling warmly at me. Behind her glasses, her eyes are overly bright, and I wonder if she's been put on medication. "Please, call me Aunt C. That's what Thalia calls me. I assume you're here because of her."

The back of my neck prickles. It's the way she says it. Not a question. More a resigned statement, like she always knew that I would one day show up.

"I am, actually. Yeah." I move closer, peering at her carefully.

Aunt Claudette's mouth puckers with displeasure and she nods. "None of the others ever showed up, you know. I kept waiting, and waiting, so certain that one day, one of you would come here asking about her."

"The others?" I say, sitting down.

"Her 'friends.'" She puts air quotes around the word, and I know then that she knows exactly what Thalia is. The question is: Is she on Thalia's side? I don't say anything, and she fills in the silence. "She has so many of them, you know. Well, I'm sure you do." She sighs and gestures to her dresser. "Do me a favor, will you? Open that—yes. And take out that box down there, yes, that's right. Lovely. Now let's see . . ." She takes the box from me and opens it. Inside are photo albums and a yearbook. I'm getting impatient, jittery. I'm not here to look at old photos.

"I actually have a few questions—"

"Here she is," Aunt Claudette says, opening the yearbook and pointing at a photo. "Beautiful, wasn't she?"

I hold back a sigh and look at where she's pointing. Eighteen-year-old Thalia. She was gorgeous, but I can't help noticing that her hair is a very dark brown. It looks strange on her. "Yeah."

"That was the year that her mother's boyfriend was reported missing."

All of my instincts prick up, my mind going from bored to a high-pitched alarm. "Missing?"

Aunt Claudette closes the yearbook with a sigh. "Her mother tried so hard with her. But Joanne wasn't a very bright woman, bless her soul. From when Thalia was little, you could already tell Joanne was outmatched. She loved Thalia in her own way. Wanted to do right by her. She didn't have much, but she was beautiful—oh, movie-star good looks. Where do you think Thalia got her looks from? She was always on the hunt for a husband. A dad for Thalia, she said. I tried telling her that what Thalia needed wasn't a dad, but one of them brain doctors, but she just couldn't see it." She opens one of the photo albums and flips through the pages. "Ah, here he was. Jackson Giles."

I frown down at a photo of a woman resembling Thalia, her arms around a blond man.

"Dated Joanne for—hmm, three months? Before he abruptly broke up with her and disappeared. Thalia was twelve at the time." She flips through more pages. "And this one . . . Matthew something or other. Went out with Joanne for almost a year before leaving suddenly."

There's an ugly sensation unfurling in my guts.

"We both assumed these men were cads. What you kids would call 'players,' or 'fuckboys.'" She snorts at my raised eyebrows.

"What, you think I don't know the way you kids talk nowadays? Anyway, so. Fuckboys, they existed back then, too, so we just thought, ah, he got bored of Joanne and just stopped calling, stopped coming round. Joanne would cry and then she'd get over it and move on. See, I always had my suspicions. I thought that maybe Thalia had said something to these men to drive them away. But I told myself that was, well, maybe not quite normal, but it wasn't illegal. Kids rebel against the people their parents are dating all the time, don't they?" Her tone is almost pleading.

I shrug. I wouldn't know. My mom never dated anyone after my father passed, shrouding herself in unhappiness, reveling in her self-imposed loneliness so she could blame it on me.

"It wasn't until him—" Aunt Claudette points to a balding man who looked somewhere in his midforties. "Freddy Somer. He disappeared like all the rest, but unlike the others, he had people who loved him. People who reported him missing. It all came back to Joanne, and the cops found nothing on her, of course, because she was innocent. She was horrified, actually. But I remember being there when the cops came to the apartment to question her, and I saw Thalia—she was listening in from the next room, and that look on her face—" She shudders.

"You think she did something to all these men?" I don't even recognize my own voice. "But that's impossible. You said the first one disappeared when she was twelve? How could she have—"

"I don't know about the other men. I—when the cops came asking about Freddy, I thought maybe—I don't know. But I kept a closer eye on Thalia. I love Thalia like my own kid, I do, and she's done so much for me—she paid for all this, you know? I wouldn't have managed to retire in a place like this on my teacher's salary. I didn't want to—I didn't want anything bad to happen to her.

But—" Her voice wavers and she takes a shaky breath. When she speaks again, the words come out as a whisper. "A couple years ago, they found him."

"Freddy?" I don't get why she's looking at me like that, with her eyes all wide and burning with fear. "I think I'm missing something . . ."

"They found his body. He's been dead for years. Some hikers found the—ah, the remnants."

Horror crawls, like a spider, from the base of my spine all the way up my neck. My scalp prickles, everything inside me curling up into a tight ball. *Thalia, what have you done?*

Her hands twist in her lap, fingers squeezing and writhing. "I want to believe that it was a coincidence. Maybe he was out hiking and fell? Freak accidents, they happen more often than we think, right?" She squeezes her eyes shut, and for a few moments, there's silence, except for the sounds of our breathing, deafening in the dead air. "All I know is, my time's coming to an end. I'm going to see my own judgment day, and I told myself, if someone were to come one day, asking about Thalia, I'm going to tell them everything. I know it sounds crazy, and it's all probably going to turn out to be nothing, but . . ." She swallows. Takes another deep breath. "The point is, I love that girl, but there's something broken inside her, and she scares the hell out of me sometimes."

Hope blooms inside my chest, bright and burning. "I need to talk to her. Do you know how I can get a hold of her?"

At this, Aunt Claudette's mouth tightens, and I realize with a sinking feeling that even though she says she knows what a monster Thalia is, she's not quite ready to give her up just yet. I've miscalculated, been too forward. I should've taken more time to listen, nudge Thalia's address or phone number out of her gently.

That's what Thalia would've done. Still, I can't judge Aunt Claudette too harshly, I know, especially since Thalia is apparently footing the bill for this place. And she knows where Aunt Claudette lives. If I were Aunt Claudette, I wouldn't be in a hurry to sell Thalia out either. She turns away from me slightly and says, "I'm quite tired now, dear. Maybe we can continue this another time?"

I wipe my face, trying to ignore the tightness in my chest. I want to shake her and tell her how Thalia's made me out to be a stalker, a murderer. But the last thing I want is for her to call for help. It would be yet more evidence of my so-called erratic behavior. "Okay," I say in a small voice. "Thank you, Aunt Claudette."

She's already turning her wheelchair away from me, probably can't stomach another moment of looking at me. As I pick up my purse to leave, I see a notebook sitting atop a stack of letters on a side table. I don't even hesitate before taking the entire pile and hiding them behind my purse. Aunt Claudette turns around then, and my heart jams its way up my throat, but she only gives me a sad smile. "I'm sorry I couldn't be of more help."

"You've done enough," I mumble, and hurry out of her room.

Outside of the facility, I look through the pieces of Aunt Claudette's mail. Two of them are spam and the third is a credit card bill. Gritting my teeth with frustration, I stuff them into my bag and flip through the notebook. My heart soars, because as it turns out, I've managed to steal Aunt Claudette's address book. I go through the pages until I find Thalia's name. There are four different addresses listed in here, one in Jakarta, one in Singapore, one in Dubai, and one in—bingo!—Manhattan. I take out my phone and order a Lyft, my breath coming out ragged

300

as I key in the address. Once it's ordered, I briskly walk out of the driveway and down the street, eager to put some distance between me and Aunt Claudette before she realizes that I've stolen her things. When the Lyft arrives, my breath releases in a whoosh. I spend the entire car ride wringing my hands, working out different scenarios, a multitude of ways in which my confrontation with Thalia could go.

I don't know what I was expecting from the address, but when the Lyft arrives at my destination, I get out and look up. And up. And up.

So Thalia lives in a bloody skyscraper right next to Central Park. So what? She married Ivan, so they're rolling in dough. I knew that. Still, as I walk toward the imposing building and the doorman nods and opens the door for me, I can't help but feel intimidated. It's probably the desired effect. I feel completely out of place, dwarfed and fraudulent. The inside of the lobby is all shiny marble and gilded edges and lush carpet. A receptionist stands to attention and, after giving me a once-over, puts on the bare minimum of a smile; she knows I don't belong here.

"Good evening," she says. "Visiting someone?"

I try to look as imperious as I can. "Yes. Thalia Ashcroft. Or she might go by her married name, Pranajaya."

"Ah yes, Mrs. Pranajaya. And your name is?"

"Jane," I say without thinking. Then I realize I should've given her a fake name, but it's too late.

"I'll let her know you're here." She picks up the phone.

"Oh, don't bother. I'll just go straight up. She's expecting me." The words sound like a lie even to my own ears.

She looks at me like: *Who're you kidding?* And I can't blame her.

"I was going to surprise her," I say lamely.

She gives me an icy smile. "Our residents don't like surprises." She punches a number into the phone and waits. "Hello, Mrs. Pranajaya, sorry to bother you, but there's a guest here for you? Jane. Yes." She glances at me and she's no longer bothering to smile, not even a little. "Of course. I'm so sorry to bother you, ma'am." She hangs up, and when she turns to face me, her face is cold. "I'm afraid you'll have to leave the premises."

I hate myself. I should've been better prepared. What the hell was I expecting? To just be able to barge into her apartment? Actually, yes, that was exactly what I expected. For Thalia to live like a normal person, without security manning the lobby of her apartment. For me to be able to randomly press buttons on the front of the building until someone buzzed me in.

"Ma'am, did you hear me? Please leave the premises or I will call security."

I glare at her balefully before turning for the front door. I dip my head and look down at the marble floors, so shiny that I can see the lights reflected in them. I'll wait outside, I decide. I don't care how long it takes. Thalia can't possibly stay in her apartment forever.

Behind me, one of the elevators dings and opens. For a split second, I wonder if I can rush into the elevator and hit the button before the receptionist can stop me. But before I can do anything, someone calls out, "Jane, wait!"

I freeze. Thalia's come down here to see me after all. But when I turn around, it's not Thalia who's hurrying after me, but Ani. The receptionist is watching us with wide eyes, probably confused. That makes two of us, I want to tell her.

"Ani, I need to see Thalia, I—"

"For fuck's sake, Jane," Ani snaps, "could you please stop the Thalia obsession, just for one fucking second? My brother is dead."

She might as well have smacked me in the face. For a few seconds, all sounds are muted, as though I'm listening to them underwater. Everything moves slowly. I see Ivan the way he had been in Oxford, full of life, sunshine coursing through his veins. "Ivan's dead?"

Ani's eyes fill with tears and her chin trembles. "Come on," she says hoarsely, leading me out of the building. Outside, next to the heavy New York City traffic, she turns to me and says, "Yes. Ivan's dead. And I think Thalia had something to do with it."

It shouldn't surprise me, but it does, and I hate that it does. I hate that despite everything, Thalia still shocks me. Dimly, I'm aware that Ani is leading me down the block and onto a side street. The noise of the traffic recedes dramatically as we stand in the alleyway.

"Sorry, I don't know where else to go to have this conversation," Ani says.

A shocked laugh burps out of me. She's right; I mean, it's not really the kind of conversation you have over a pumpkin spice latte at Starbucks. "I—yeah. Wait, so. Uh. Ivan's dead?" I know I've asked this already, but my mind is still refusing to comprehend it. "And Thalia? You think she . . ."

"Yes. She fucking killed him, Jane!" Ani cries, grabbing my arm.

My mouth opens but nothing comes out.

"You need to help me," Ani says. She's gripping my arm so tight that it's starting to hurt, but I cling to the pain because it's the only thing anchoring me at this moment.

"Help you?" I echo uselessly.

"Look," she says, sighing. "I know you're part of the Thalia fan club—god, why do people fall for her act?"

"I'm not." My cheeks burn. "I mean, I used to be, but not anymore."

Ani pauses, and slowly, like honey, her lips stretch into a smile. "She did something to you."

I swallow the lump in my throat and nod. "I think—um, I think she killed Kurt." It sounds so ridiculous. Alien words tumbling out of my mouth, unrecognizable. "And she's framing me for it. I think," I add. How many times can I say "I think"? But it just sounds so crazy I can't help but try to soften it. Despite what Ani said earlier about Ivan being dead and Thalia possibly having something to do with it, I still half expect her to laugh at this and tell me I'm nuts, that my obsession toward Thalia has led to me completely going the other way.

Instead, she nods solemnly. "I believe you."

Those three words are so far from what I'm expecting that I feel a surge of warmth toward her, this woman I have hated for so long. I look at her, dressed impeccably as usual, her hair sleek, her makeup flawless, and I see the anger simmering behind it. She's lost her brother, and I suddenly feel such sorrow for her. We're both Thalia's victims. "What can I do to help?"

Ani takes in a shaky breath. "I need to find evidence of her killing Ivan. I think I know how she did it. She's been poisoning him for years—"

"What?" I try to wrap my head around it, try to digest the words, but they sit like a rock in the center of my brain, defying all logic. "Poison?"

"I'm pretty sure she's been slipping him caffeine without him knowing it."

"Caffeine? That's not poison."

"It is in the right amount. And my brother has—had—a heart condition. The caffeine triggered a heart attack."

"Oh my god." I shake my head, blinking several times. This can't be real. But then I think of Thalia, past that gorgeous, innocent facade she wears so well. I think of the little glimpses of her that I've caught, the way she sometimes smiled just a split second too late, as though she only just realized that something was meant to be humorous. And then I think of her using those long, elegant fingers to sprinkle caffeine into Ivan's food, and my body turns cold. I can picture it all too easily. "But I don't know how I can help. She's blocked my number, she didn't allow me to go up to the apartment—"

"Yeah." Ani nods. "I was hoping we could brainstorm something together, maybe find out where she keeps the caffeine, or how she even got it to begin with. It's not like you could get it over the counter, you know? So she must've ordered it online. I tried looking through her credit card bills, but I couldn't find anything."

A sense of hopelessness washes over me. Thalia's been ahead of us by so many steps this whole time. We're two beginners playing against a master. "She would've thought of everything. She—" Then the thought strikes me. "Wait, you got access to her credit card bills?"

"Yeah, in Indonesia, we have a family account and all our cards are registered to the same account, so we can see each other's purchases. There are no secrets in my family," she says with a bitter laugh.

"Did you see a charge for Golden Years Estate?"

She frowns and takes her phone out of her pocket. "Hang on,

let me open up the bill—" She taps on it and scrolls down. After a while, she shakes her head. "Nope. What is it?"

"It's a retirement home that Thalia's been paying because her aunt lives there. And her aunt said the bill is paid every month, so if it's not in here, that means she has a different credit card." As soon as I say it, it sounds so obvious. Of course she wouldn't have used the family credit card to buy the stuff she was using to kill one of them.

To kill one of them. God, the thought is still so shocking, a jagged shard through my brain. Then I recall the stack of papers I'd taken from Aunt Claudette's room.

I rip open my purse and rummage through it.

"What're you doing?" Ani says, but I ignore her, digging until I locate the right envelope. I tear it open and look at the bill. It's for a credit card belonging to Claudette Clovis. My heart sinks, but still I scan the list of purchases anyway, because maybe . . .

And there it is.

A purchase from Burn Fast for $72. I Google "Burn Fast" and find a weight-loss site whose number one product is "Pure Caffeine Powder." The description reads: "Pharmaceutical-grade pure caffeine anhydrous powder! Watch as the fat literally melts from your waistline! Each teaspoon of our caffeine powder has the equivalent of 28 cups of coffee!"

"I found it," I whisper.

Ani's eyes widen, and I feel the blood roar in my ears. We may be new to Thalia's game, but somehow, I think we've managed to stumble on her only weakness.

Chapter 30

THALIA

It will take less than a day for the autopsy to be done, because apparently, money gets you expedited service even in death. I watch helplessly as Ani orders the autopsy to be done, requesting a full blood work including—and this is key—the amount of alcohol or caffeine in his system. My fists clench and unclench, as though longing for her neck to be in their grasp, and still I cannot say a word; I can only stand on the sidelines and nod, pretending to agree with this farce. What will they find? The only thing in my favor is the fact that I don't have any caffeine powder on me, not in New York, at least. Because, god damn it, I hadn't planned on killing him here. So if they do a search, I will be clean. I remind myself of this fact over and over, caressing it in my mind, my own little mental talisman.

But now I need to make my move. I need to figure out what Ani knows and what Ani has done and outmaneuver her. The house phone rings and I hurry to pick it up, leaving Mama and Papa sobbing quietly in the living room with their reptilian daughter. It's the lobby receptionist, telling me I have a guest. The last thing I want is a guest. I snap, "Well? Who is it?"

"Jane."

Jane. My sad, pathetic, little clinger-on. My god, Jane. Have some self fucking respect. I just framed you for murder and yet still you come, begging me for attention. "Jane?"

"Yes."

"I don't want any visitors. Do your job, get rid of her, or I'll lodge a complaint."

"Of course," she says hurriedly. "I'm so sorry to bother you, ma'am."

I hang up the phone and turn around, only to run into Ani. Jesus. She moves as silently as the snake she is. She narrows her eyes at me. "Everything okay?"

"No, everything's not okay, my husband's dead." I brush past her and stalk off. Moments later, I hear the elevator ding and I breathe out. Good. Ani's left the apartment. I need time to think. Fortunately, Mama and Papa have retired to the master bedroom, so I don't have to deal with them. I go into my room and start pacing again. I need to—what do I need to do? I need to go through Ani's belongings, see if I can find anything incriminating. Yes. Hope flutters in my chest, a lonely butterfly. At her heart, Ani's a dumb bitch, she's careless, she—

No. I can't afford to think like that anymore. She's outplayed me. I can't keep underestimating her. I take a deep breath and walk out of my room. For a few moments, I listen hard, but aside from the muffled sobs coming out of the master bedroom, there's no sound in the apartment. No clue where Ani went, no idea when she'll be back. I need to do this fast.

For the first time, I'm grateful for the suffocating tightness of Ivan's family, for the fact that we're all sharing an apartment even though they could easily have bought a separate one for

Ani. Ani's room is slightly smaller than the one Ivan and I shared. I go inside and leave the door open just a crack, so that I'll be able to hear the elevator's ding when Ani comes back. I move fast, letting my instincts take over. I open drawers, dig my hands into mounds of lacy underwear, search under her bed and her chaise longue. I go into her bathroom and rummage through all the cabinets. I read all of the labels on the bottles she has, and I hate how unsure I feel. Is this bottle of pills really Advil? Or has she switched it with something else? What should I take? And even if I were to take any of it, what would I do with it? In the end, I leave them all alone. I figure if any of them were incriminating, she wouldn't have left them in her medicine cabinet like that. I go back to the walk-in closet, and this time, I search harder. I dip into every shoe, grimacing at the thought that I'm putting my hands where Ani puts her disgusting feet. I open up her Louis Vuitton luggage one by one, searching the inner linings, then I move on to her handbags. There are over a dozen of them. The more I search, the angrier I become. I'm breathing hard, panting like an animal, so unlike myself. I can't stand it, the thought that I'm being outsmarted by someone like Ani.

I'm so absorbed by my search that I fail to hear the elevator's ding. I fail to hear the footsteps padding down the hallway, the sound of Mama and Papa's door opening. There must have been a hushed conversation, but I miss that too. And suddenly, the door to Ani's room bursts open, and I am caught with my hands buried in a Gucci bag. Ani and Mama and Papa stand before me, their faces a mix of horror and shock and disgust.

Explanations crowd my head. "I was just—"

Ani holds up her phone, a look of triumph on her face. I can't quite see what's on the screen, but based on that smug smile of hers, I know it's nothing good. "You're a murderer," she says, simply. Just like that, *you're a murderer.*

I snort. "What?" I glance at Mama and Papa, who are still staring at me like they can't quite comprehend what they're seeing. "This is—you're crazy. Mama, don't believe anything she says—"

"Don't talk to my mother," Ani snaps. "This is your credit card bill. Your secret credit card bill."

I forget how to breathe. "What are you talking about?"

"Your aunt? Claudette Clovis? I know you registered a credit card under her name and used it to buy caffeine powder, which you used to poison my brother."

Aunt Claudette? Did the bitch betray me?

"And," Ani continues, her eyes glinting madly, "I just got the call from the coroner's office. My brother died of cardiac arrest, triggered by caffeine overdose."

"No, wait—" I drop the handbag and start forward.

Ani steps back, her expression switching seamlessly into exaggerated fear and alarm. "Stay back, Thalia! Don't move. I've called the cops. Don't do anything stupid."

"I'm not—Jesus, I didn't do it."

"Just stay away from me and my family," she spits out, backing away, herding her parents away from me. Right before she shuts the door, she flashes me a smile. One that says: *Checkmate.* And I know, then, that I have well and truly lost.

My bail is denied. My lawyer, provided by the state, warned me before my arraignment that bail would likely be denied since this is a murder case, but when it comes, it still hits hard. Yet another blow I wasn't ready for. I can only stare silently ahead as I am led back to my cell, ignoring the shouts from the paparazzi and the flashes of their cameras. Back in the silence of my jail cell, I look into the mirror. Regardless of what Netflix tries to tell you, orange is definitely not the new black. This isn't an Hermès orange that I'm wearing, but a neon one, against which my skin looks sallow. Despite that, I still look rather beautiful. This is a fact; I'm not being narcissistic. I haven't had much of an appetite, which is understandable given the disgusting slop they serve in here, and over the past few days, I have lost enough weight to make my cheekbones even more prominent. It gives me a sort of vulnerable, haunted look, which I understand is quite trendy at the moment. I make a note to myself to decrease my caloric intake even after I get out of here.

And make no mistake, I will get out of this place. Jail isn't for me, much less prison. I do not deserve to be here, locked up with the rest of society's filthiest dregs. I turn my head to one side, admiring the sharp angles. No, I am made to be seen, not locked away. It would be like keeping the *Mona Lisa* buried. A crime against nature's art.

I don't know how I will get out of here yet, though. My lawyer, she of the ill-fitting suit and frizzy hair, tells me that the prosecutor has gathered all sorts of damning evidence against me. The caffeine powder that I had bought for the last two years, charged to Aunt Claudette's card, a card I have been paying off for years. I suppose that is pretty damning indeed. And, of course, the autopsy results. Rather irrefutable.

The clang of my jail cell rouses me from my plotting. A guard is standing there, somber and burly. I wonder if this is a requirement for prison guards. "You've got a visitor."

I frown. "Is it my lawyer?" Maybe she's found something after all. Nah. She's about as smart as a box of hair.

311

"Nope. Come on, we don't got all day."

I resist the urge to correct his grammar and let him cuff me, noting with satisfaction how huge the cuffs are on my slender wrists. We walk toward the visitors room. I wonder who—ugh, I hope it's not Ani, come to gloat. I might just leap across the desk and shove my thumbs into her eyeballs, just for the satisfaction of wiping that smirk off her face. But when we get there, I see a dark-haired woman sitting across the table. Jane.

My heart softens at the sight of her. What? Just because I have APD, doesn't mean I can't feel genuine affection for someone. Okay, yes, it means exactly that. But Jane really does have a special place in my heart. Like a favorite coat, comfortable and worn. And she's just so pathetic; look at her sitting here even after everything I did to her.

"Jane!" I sit down across from her and shake my head in disbelief. The smile on my face is as genuine a smile as I have ever worn. "I wasn't expecting to see you here."

She looks surprised by the warm reception and quickly looks down at her hands. "Um. Yeah." She sneaks another glance at me. Poor Jane. Some people are just built to be prey, and she is the worst of them. She reminds me of a rodent, small and twitchy, made to be hunted and killed with a wet squeak. Still, I've been so bored, I find myself looking forward to knowing what brought her here.

"Thank you for coming," I say, making my voice warm. A verbal hug, because physical contact isn't allowed. I wonder if it's time for tears and decide against it. "I'm so glad to see you."

"Are you?" There's a flash of anger on her face that quickly fizzles out, replaced once more by the anxiety I'd quickly come to associate with her all those years ago.

312

"What do you mean? Of course I am."

Her mouth twists. I want to tell her to stop sneering like that; it's so unbecoming. "Funny you should say that, given how you tried to frame me for Kurt's death."

I let my mouth drop open in a shocked O. "What? There must've been some kind of—no. Kurt—he died in an accident. What are you saying?" My voice trembles a little. "Please, I can't stand it, Jane. My husband's dead and they're saying I killed him when I didn't; I had nothing to do with it. Now you're here, you're my best friend, the only person in the world who understands me, and you're saying—what are you saying?" I whisper, blinking so that the tears won't fall.

She hesitates. Always so quick to be pushed off-balance. "You told everyone I was stalking you."

I raise my eyebrows. *Look at how shocked I am!* "No. I would never. I told everyone we're best friends, that we—" I stop myself and mentally count to three before gasping. "Oh my god. I think I know what's going on." I pause, waiting.

And because she is Jane and she can't help herself, she goes, "What?"

"The cops," I say. "It's what they do, right? They get you alone and then they feed you all sorts of crazy stories to make you confide in them. I mean, they told me all sorts of things about you. They wanted me to throw you under the bus, but I didn't. I told them you're an amazing person, you'd never do anything like that." I pause again and look at her with sad puppy eyes. "Did you tell them that I would hurt Kurt?" My voice ends in a pained squeak. Got to drive home to Jane what a fucking betrayal it would've been to throw me under like that.

"No," she cries. "No, I couldn't—they were so—they said that

313

the other writers at the retreat said you told them I was stalking you, and . . ." She shakes her head. "It doesn't matter, anyway. You killed Ivan."

"I didn't," I say, and here I infuse some indignation into my voice. "I swear to you, I did not kill him." I don't break eye contact. I let her in to see my truth.

She blinks again, confused. Poor little rodent Jane. Must I do all the work for her? One despairs. "Ani did," I say finally, when it becomes clear she's not going to get there.

"But—" She gnaws on her bottom lip. Her lips are disgusting, all chapped, bits of skin peeling off. I wish she'd put some Vaseline on them. "The—he died of caffeine overdose and you'd been buying all that caffeine—"

"I was being abused." I let out a single, short sob. An idea is beginning to take form. My mind rushes ahead, spinning a whole new narrative. One that relies on me leaning into the whole Asian stereotype of an overbearing family. The best stories, after all, contain grains of truth. "You don't know what it was like to be married to Ivan, to be living in his country. I couldn't turn to anyone. His family controls the police, the whole justice system. I couldn't divorce him. I was trapped. They told me if I ever humiliated them by divorcing Ivan, they'd kill me and my family—Aunt Claudette—that's why I hid her existence. I was—you don't know what I've been through." Now I let the tears fall, though not too much, don't want to look all puffy. "I was—he raped me every night. I tried telling Ani and she just laughed and told me it was my fault for marrying him."

Jane looks so horrified I wonder if she's going to fall off her seat. The more I tell her, the more the story comes alive. And it's a good one, I can feel it in my bones. I know stories; I'm an author

314

after all. And this one has all the makings of a hit. Me, a beautiful, intelligent, modern woman. This new thinness of mine makes me look so vulnerable, almost ethereal. Ivan, a handsome prince with a dark secret. I dare anyone to try resisting it. I can already see how it'll take flight. The media will lap it up. Women's rights groups will clamor for my freedom. I will become the face of their movement, the poor, broken woman who escaped her captor. I will be a heroine.

"You know what Ani's like. She'd been vying for Ivan's position in the company even when we were in Oxford. She was always so resentful, so jealous about it. Remember?"

After a second, Jane nods.

"She did it. She killed him to get control of the company, and she framed me for it. You must find out how she did it," I say through my tears.

She's so torn between wanting to believe me and the string of irrefutable evidence behind me. All she needs is a little nudge. And I know exactly what Jane wants, what her life has been all about ever since the first time we met. Me.

"Please, Jane. You're my only hope. You're my best friend."

At this, her face brightens, a righteous flame burning behind her eyes. I almost laugh at how easily she fell for it. She nods and says, "I'll do it. I'll find out how she killed him. I'll set you free."

I smile at her. Good dog.

Chapter 31

JANE

After I visit Thalia, I walk for hours, only half-aware of where I'm going. My mind is a jumble of emotions. I want to cry and laugh and scream and hide, all at the same time. I want to hug Thalia, put my arms around her and squeeze. I want to strangle Thalia, put my hands around her throat and squeeze. I remember that night in Oxford, when she'd asked me to strangle her so she'd have marks on her throat. I go back to that moment and I don't let go. I watch as the light goes out of her eyes and she turns from a living, breathing being into a rag doll. A dead thing. A sob escapes me, and I wipe away the tears that trickle down my cheeks. I don't know why I'm crying. Thalia is exactly where she belongs, and I should be out celebrating. The cops are off my back. I don't know what's going on with the investigation of Kurt's death, but I'm sure that since Thalia is being charged with Ivan's murder, she would also be the number one suspect behind Kurt's death, if they decide it was murder, that is.

So why do I feel like part of me is slowly dying? Why do I feel like I've left the most beautiful bird in the world to rot in a tiny cage, its vibrant wings clipped, its sonorous chirps silenced?

She belongs there, I tell myself. She's dangerous, the most dangerous creature there is. A serpent.

But I can't forget that look on her face. Haunted, broken, as she begged me to help her. Could she really be lying? She looked shattered. And what she told me made sense. Ani has always been bitter about the whole family company. The number of times she ranted to us back in Oxford about how Ivan only got his position because he had a dick. Could she have done it?

I close my eyes and try to picture Ani poisoning her own brother, and the image clicks into place all too easily. I shudder and open my eyes once more. The problem is, I can also very easily think of Thalia doing it. Both of them are deadly. I should forget all of this and just go. I'm caught in a game between two apex predators.

And yet. The thought of going back to Ted, to my mediocre, safe life, grates at my nerves. What the hell is wrong with me? Social anxiety, Kathryn had told me. I can see that. It fits. I should go back home and just curl up and hide away from the world. Do that cognitive behavioral thing Kathryn wants me to do. Learn to cope. Live with the knowledge that Thalia is in prison and I'm outside of it, safe and sound.

Should, should, should. How long have I lived my life according to "should"?

I take my phone out of my bag and call Ani. When she picks up, I say, "Want to get drinks?"

Chances are, Ani has changed from the girl I knew back in Oxford. Chances are, she's a lot wiser now, less of a loose cannon. But she's also just coming down off a real roller coaster; I mean, there's a possibility she just framed Thalia for Ivan's murder and

317

got away with it. I'm guessing she's in real need of a good, stiff drink and someone to celebrate it with.

We agree to meet at Doorway, a quiet restaurant with outdoor seating, where we can drink and chat without her feeling claustrophobic. When she arrives, she looks as fashionable as usual, not at all like a woman who's recently lost her dearest brother. No eye bags; she hasn't been crying.

I've arrived early and ordered us a bottle of wine, asked for them to pour it out into a decanter. I poured myself a glass, and when no one was looking, I added a sprinkling of Ambien into the decanter. Not too much, not enough to actually knock her out. Just enough to lower her inhibitions. I've set my phone to record and put it facedown on the table. I'm ready.

"Ani," I say, standing up and giving her a hug. She's all tight cords of muscle. It's like hugging a lizard. I have to stop myself from shuddering as I step away and sit back down. I pour her a generous helping of wine and push the glass toward her before lifting my own glass.

"To putting away the evil cunt," she says, lifting her glass.

I grit my teeth and force myself to say the words. "To putting away the evil cunt." I watch as she takes huge gulps of the wine. "So how are things with you and your family?" I hope I sound sympathetic. My heart is beating so hard I wonder if she can see its silhouette pressing against my top. I resist the almost overwhelming urge to wring my hands under the table. I can do this. I must do this.

Ani scoffs. "How do you think? My parents are a mess. Ivan was always their favorite, you know."

Like she'd ever let us forget that. I put on a sad face and nod, lifting my glass to my lips and taking the smallest sip. She mirrors

318

me, except she gulps instead of sips, and I refill her glass as soon as she lowers it.

"They're lucky they have me. I've been taking care of everything. The funeral arrangements, the company—oh man, the company." She snorts and takes another long swallow of wine. "Let me tell you, Jane, it would all be going down the shithole if it weren't for me."

"Yeah, I can believe that. They're so lucky to have you." She must know I'm faking it. I'm not that good a liar. I take a bigger swallow of my own wine. The more we talk, the worse I feel. It feels like I'm betraying more than just Ani, but parts of myself as well. I don't want to feel a kinship with Ani, of all people.

But by now, the spiked wine is taking its effect. I can see it in the way Ani's eyes become heavy-lidded, the way her bright red lips go slack, the slurring of her words. It takes me right back to our time at Oxford, those wine-drenched days where Ani swung wildly from competitive student to drunk dancer, hopping from books to boys and back again. I guess some things never change. The memory of it loosens my nerves. I know this Ani. I tolerated her for months, gritted my teeth and pretended to like her just so I could be close to Thalia. I can do this.

"But," I say, leaning forward, "you must find it hard, to take over the company so suddenly? I mean, have you been involved in the company all these years?"

She glances at me sharply and frowns, or tries to, anyway. The drink and drug have softened her. Without them, Ani would've probably leapt up and leaned so close I could smell her rank breath and hissed to me about how valuable she is to the company. As it is, she merely leans back and laughs. "Uh, ya think?"

"I thought your parents didn't really trust you to work there?

319

Didn't you say they're pretty sexist and everything?" I don't actually remember her specifically saying that they're sexist, but I know enough from my mother how deeply ingrained traditional gender roles are in many Asian countries.

She rolls her eyes and takes another big swig. "Yeah. Misogyny in da house!" she crows. God, I hate her. And I know it's hate, not fear or anxiety, Kathryn. "Yeah, my parents are total fucking misogynists. Didn't think I could handle it. But I'm showing them. They're pretty fucking impressed with me right now, I can tell you that."

"I'm sure they are." I laugh along with her, then widen my eyes so I look impressed. "How are you managing everything? It must be so tough jumping in when you know nothing about the company. I mean, I don't even know the first thing about running a company, and with one as large as yours—"

"Girl, I've been preparing for this moment for all of my fucking life!" she hoots.

My heart stutters, screeching to a halt. Oh god. I try not to show it, try to recover. "Um, what do you mean? Preparing for what?" Quickly, I lean forward and refill her drink. She's almost finished the whole bottle. Two whole Ambiens plus wine. This is it.

"Every goddamned day I go to the office. He thought I was just there to gossip with the employees." She snorts. "Like I would ever be friends with those nobodies. I went in for years, learning as much as I could. Taking control of projects behind his back. Did he notice?" Another swallow of wine. "Fuck no. My idiot brother. He thought he was soooo great. Didn't even know his own fucking wife was poisoning him." She laughs, an ugly, jagged sound.

I frown. This isn't what I came here for. Thalia, were you lying after all? The thought is a cold one. I flinch away from it. Ani's lying. But she can't be, not when she's this drunk. This drugged. She can barely even keep her eyes open. Only the adrenaline of finally telling her story to someone is keeping her awake. "What do you mean, poisoning him?" I say in as calm a voice as I can muster. Mustn't alarm her now.

She gives me a cunning sideways glance. "Jane, Jane, keep up," she says in a singsong voice. "Didn't I tell you? Didn't we go over this already? Caffeine, Jane!" she cries at my blank face. "Remember?"

My stomach plummets. Thalia was lying. She'd sent me out on a wild-goose chase, and for what? Just for fun, I guess. One last practical joke from prison. Ha, very funny. I'm ready to call it a night. I put my glass down and start fiddling with my purse.

"So I just gave the final push," Ani says.

My head shoots up, my breath caught in my throat. "What?"

She gave a sloppy shrug. "She was taking so. Fucking. Long. I had known from, like, a year ago what she was doing, and I kept waiting for her to seal the deal, but she never did. What the fuck, right?" she says angrily. "So I got a bit impatient—you get it, don't you? She was just stringing me along, teasing me the way she loved to tease those guys in Oxford. Do you remember those days? God, she was such a slut."

"Stringing you along? Did she—did you two plan this?"

"God no. But part of her must have known that I knew. It wasn't like she was being that subtle about it. She always thought she was so smart." In a high-pitched, squeaky voice, Ani says, "Look at me, I'm Thalia, I'm Miss Perfect!" She laughs again and drains her glass.

"So you—you killed—you, uh—"

"I gave him an extra big dose of caffeine, right before Thalia left for her stupid writers' retreat. He had his heart attack pretty quickly after that. Went into a coma, blah blah blah. Well, you know the rest. RIP Koko."

I can hardly believe what I'm hearing, the words are so horrifying, coming out of her lipsticked mouth so casually. She's sick, her mind nothing but a twist of vipers. I can't get away fast enough. But somehow, I manage to make myself stay, gripping the stem of my wineglass so hard that my skin is stretched taut over my knuckles. I nod and smile, smile and nod as though she hasn't just admitted to murdering her own blood, her only brother.

Then I think about the other beautiful monster, the one who is currently behind bars, the one I've been obsessed with for so long. I think about how Thalia has played me, pulling my strings so expertly, a puppet master putting on a show for everybody. I should hate her, and part of me does, but the other part of me can't deny how alive she makes me feel. Even when she's using me and discarding me like an old toy, the nearness of her alone is enough to ignite something inside me. I think about what I wrote that day in Montauk, after just a couple of days of being near Thalia. I'd read the words over and over again, and I can't believe that they were written by me. So powerful and incisive. Not the writings of a midlist author.

No, this situation isn't as straightforward as I had thought, and my opponents are both deadly and probably slightly insane in their own ways. But, with a start, I realize that I have something over both of them.

All my life, I've grappled with my identity. Always different. Never fitting in, not even into my own skin. But maybe that doesn't have to be a bad thing. I'm not my mother nor my father.

I am neither like Thalia, nor am I like Ani. In this deadly game of cat and mouse, I am neither cat nor mouse, but something else entirely. Something unexpected. My own person. I feel the change spreading over me like warm honey, settling my bones into my new skin. I look down and gently swill the wine in my glass.

And I think hard about my next move.

Chapter 32

THALIA

Jane came through. I can't quite believe it myself, and I'm still not sure how she did it, but there you go. Sometimes, old dogs can learn new tricks. The moment I'm freed, I slip back into my old clothes with a sigh of relief—there is no silk or cotton in prison wear—and order an Uber back to the penthouse. I'm already imagining a long, hot shower with the most luxurious soaps and ultra-moisturizing conditioners, but when I get there, I'm faced with Mama and Papa, tearstained and shaking with rage.

"What have you done?" Mama shrieks the moment I walk out of the private elevator. Behind her, two men in bespoke suits start forward. Mama and Papa's lawyers, I guess.

I stand there and frown at her. As I expected, they rush to fill the lack of response.

"You," Papa thunders, pointing a stubby finger at me, "you framed her. You framed our only daughter."

At this, I raise my hands and twist my expression into a mixture of hurt and horror. "I didn't. I'm sorry, Papa, Mama, I know this is hard for you, but the truth is that Ani poisoned Ivan. Your daughter killed your only son." I know I didn't have to say it quite like that, but it's honestly a treat to be able to spell it out for them, to twist that knife in their chests. And the look on their faces at those words . . . chef's kiss.

"You framed her. You killed our son and then you framed our daughter!" Papa says. He is very repetitive, which bores me. Now that I've dealt the final blow, I'm ready for them to be out of my sight.

"Please don't fling around such accusations," I say. "I understand you're hurting right now, but I must protect myself." I glance at their lawyers, who catch my drift and whisper urgently in their ears. That's right, motherfuckers, I can be a litigious bastard, too, now that I'm about to inherit Ivan's massive wealth.

Mama scoffs and shoots her lawyer a murderous glare before turning her fiery gaze back to me. "You are not getting a single cent of Ivan's money."

I almost laugh out loud at her, but somehow, I manage to keep a straight face. "I think it's best to leave that to the law. I don't want to fight you over such things, but I am his next of kin . . ." I let the words trail away because I can't help it; I am one for dramatic pauses.

And in the silence that follows, I see the unearned triumph on their faces, and I have to bite my lip to keep from smiling. They still think they have the upper hand, that they can bribe and threaten their way to victory. They don't know that I've spent years studying them, following Ivan to meetings where he delicately felt out whether the other party was open to bribes and how much would be an appropriate amount. They have no idea that I have built a contact list of my own, filled with politicians and businessmen, people who run the world. And the cherry on top: I might not even have to use them, because the law is on my side. I am Ivan's next of kin, his wealth is rightfully mine. We can play this nicely or we can get dirty; either way, I have won.

"I'll just pack a few things and stay at a hotel," I say kindly. So gracious, so generous. "You can stay here until you figure out other accommodations."

Their faces blanch at the reminder that this penthouse, like all the other assets, will soon become mine. I quickly turn and walk away then, because I can no longer keep the elated grin off my face.

I sit back in my leather seat at the bar of the Plaza Hotel with a glass of their best whiskey and sigh with contentment. Lifting my glass, I inhale the woody scent of the amber liquid and gaze out the window at the city. After so many years of planning, of inhuman levels of patience, I deserve this.

Footsteps approach, and I know without even looking up that she's here. Only Jane can make even her footsteps sound apologetic. The smile on my face as I stand to greet her is genuine; after what she's done for me, I am actually happy to see her. She looks different tonight, more beautiful somehow, her face glowing with something I can't quite put my finger on. I embrace her and pretend not to notice her sniffing me. Once a dog, always a dog. But at least she's a faithful dog.

"I've ordered for you, something to remember Oxford by," I say, because I know this will delight her, the knowledge that I care enough to remember her favorite drink.

I was right; her smile takes over her face, dimpling her cheeks. She looks ten years younger than when I last saw her. But more than that, she looks somehow more herself, like she's finally settled into her skin. It's made her really quite stunning. I wonder what's different now. Careful, Thalia. This is a new game. A different game. I need to figure out what she wants now that she has rescued me. And I need to figure out how to win.

"How are you doing?" she says. The waiter arrives then, placing a pint of English apple cider in front of Jane, and she smiles again.

After he leaves, I let out a long sigh. "I mean, I don't know, really. It's been a whirlwind. I'm so—Jane, I can't thank you enough for helping me. On top of losing my husband, being accused for his death was—" My voice wobbles very convincingly. "Well, let's just say I wouldn't be here if it wasn't for you." I put down my snifter and reach out for her hand. Her eyes widen, and a flash of uncertainty flits across her face, like she can't believe that I want to touch her limp, clammy palms. Well, I *don't* want to, Jane. But one must show gratitude when appropriate, so here I am. She trembles ever so slightly as she reaches out for mine, and then I'm clasping it, and it's just as damp as I remember, like holding a frog in the palm of my hand. I fight down the wave of disgust and smile at her. "Jane, my best friend in the world." She gazes back at me, completely under my spell. "You saved me."

Tears shine in her eyes. She looks grateful, and rightfully so. In a very meaningful way, I have given her the best gift—to be able to say that she saved me. It is the one defining moment of her miserable, unremarkable life. A highlight that every other moment will fail to live up to. After this, she will go back to her very average home and her very average husband and continue writing her very average books, and she will look back on this and know that she has peaked, thanks to me.

Then she says, "I know," and those two words come out so quiet that I wonder if I've misheard.

"Sorry?" I say, leaning closer.

"I said I know," she says, louder now. Her hold on my hands tightens. "I know I saved you, Thalia."

I cock my head to one side. I'm a little confused, slightly taken by surprise. I don't like surprises. I try for a smile, but it fights me all the way.

"Because," she continues, "I know the truth. You were poisoning Ivan. I have a recording of Ani saying that."

I lean back and try to pull my hand away, but her grip is now a vise, and I can't yank my hand away without causing a scene. "You have a recording of Ani confessing to Ivan's murder." That was what my lawyer had told me, anyway.

"I do, yes. But that was just a snippet of everything that Ani told me. I only gave the cops what they needed to arrest her and let you go. The rest of the recording, where she said all sorts of damning things about you . . . it's safe somewhere."

A small laugh wobbles its way out of my mouth. "That's so—do you realize how ridiculous it all sounds? Nobody's going to believe Ani, especially now that she's admitted to killing her own brother."

"I know." She looks down and caresses my hand with a thumb. My skin erupts into gooseflesh. "But I also have Aunt Claudette on record, telling me what you were like as a child, as a teen."

I snort. "The ramblings of a senile, old—"

"I looked up your mom's old boyfriends. I managed to find a couple of them. They said you threatened them, said you'd accuse them of raping you unless they broke up with your mother."

My mouth twitches, itching to come up with a retort to refute her, but my mind comes up with blanks.

"And then I saw that the last boyfriend—what was his name?

328

Freddy Somer. See, unlike the others, he disappeared without a trace. His family filed a missing person report on him." She leans closer, close enough for me to see all of the minute differences on her face, the way she's changed from a dog into a wolf. How did I miss all of the signs before? "What did you do to him, Thalia?"

I lean toward her, too, until a single, lonely inch separates us. "The same thing I'm going to do to you if you insist on playing this game with me," I whisper. I don't do well with threats.

She grins then, and releases my hand. She leans back, still grinning, and flips her hair over her shoulder. "I love it. I knew you'd say that." Her breath releases in a sigh. "I always wondered why I was so obsessed with you. And now I know. It's because you make me feel alive. Maybe some part of me knew that you were this dangerous monster, and it triggered an instinctive reaction inside me—whatever it is, I just—I am addicted to this feeling. I want to be near you. I know—" She holds up a hand when she sees that I'm about to say something. "I know you're a psychopath or whatever, and you probably don't understand what love is. I don't care. I've driven myself crazy all this time, wondering why I'm so into you. I don't think I'm sexually attracted to women. Who knows? But anyway, I think I've finally figured it out. Did you know, as it turns out, I have social anxiety? I think I do, anyway. I've always been scared, always felt this, like, resentment toward others for whatever reason. But I don't feel it with you, and I think it's because when I'm with you, everything is shaved down to the bone—to basic survival instincts. It's crazy, I know, but it's true. I write so much better with you around. You're my muse. All those years when you were gone, I felt like a part of me had died. You can see it in my books. They were just . . . dead. And then you came back and, my god, Thalia, you need to read what I've written these past few days. I swear it's like I've been possessed."

I have to admit, what she's saying is a lot to process. I mean, it's insane, but it's also really flattering. Because yes, of course I should be a muse. Anyone who's been lucky enough to come across me knows I ignite something in others.

Jane leans forward, her eyes burning into mine. "So here's what I want, Thalia: I want to be with you. You're a killer, a monster, but we belong together."

For once in my life, I have no idea what to say. She's not turning me in. She wants to . . . be with me. I stare at her, my mind zipping ahead as it always does, making multiple moves across the chessboard. Already I'm plotting her murder.

"You're probably wondering how you're going to kill me, aren't you?" she says, and my expression must betray me because she laughs. "I knew you would. I've put safeguards in place. If I were to suddenly disappear, there are quite a few damning files that would be sent to the police. But I'm sure you'll figure out some way to outsmart me. And that's exactly why I love you. I'll be doing the same. Don't you see? We make each other into the best version that we can possibly be."

And despite everything, she's sort of winning me over. Because, when I let myself think of the life ahead of me, filled with Ivan's incredible wealth and privilege, a part of me wants to cry with boredom. I am my best self when I have something to fight for. Maybe that was the real reason I took years to kill Ivan, because I knew that once I did, I would have nothing else to aim for, nothing to take up my busy, busy mind. And now, looking at the new and improved Jane, I realize that here's something that will occupy me for the next handful of years, at least. For so long, I've seen her as nothing more than an obedient dog, but here it turns out she's outfoxed me. Only temporarily, of course. I'll find a way to outwit her over time. But what she's done is still impressive. And, more importantly than that, she's outfoxed Ani. I'm not sure if this makes her a worthy adversary, since it's been years of me seeing her as something less, but it certainly makes her interesting. Different. Someone who knows exactly who and what I am. Someone who has seen the thing that lurks deep inside me and wants to play with it. Is this what true friendship is? It's not completely awful.

A slow smile spreads across my face, and I lift my glass.

"Okay, Jane. You're right. We're not done with each other yet."

Epilogue

Know what's funny about prison? Actually, never mind. There's nothing funny about prison, especially when you're on the wrong side of the bars. Let me rephrase. Know what's curious about prison?

The library.

It actually does not suck. I mean, prison itself sucks. Very, very much. But the library is surprisingly decent. We've even got John Green in here. His books, I mean. Not the actual author. On Wednesdays and Fridays, I rush through my assigned duties because those are the days I'm allowed to go to the library, as long as I'm done scrubbing the day's dishes or mopping up the dining hall. I hear that in the men's federal prison, they don't have a library because the inmates kept destroying the books. Men, I tell you. Good thing for me, women are far more civilized. Our books are generally in good condition. One time, I caught my roommate Lulu tearing a page out of a library book. My lawyer massaged his temple as he explained to me, later, that I couldn't go around breaking people's noses just because they mistreated a library book.

"It was our only copy of *The Unhoneymooners*!"

He remained unmoved. Fucking lawyers. Mama and Papa

332

assured me this one's the best defense lawyer in all of New York City, but I have my doubts. Still, he did get me a pretty light sentence, all things considered. He worked some magic; came up with a viable strategy to present me as an airhead/bimbo who didn't think it would be possible to actually harm someone with caffeine. I mean, we all drink it every day, for gosh's sakes—how would I have known that it would kill my brother? I loved him, I looked up to him, anyone could see that. I just wanted to help him because he was complaining about being tired all the time.

Manslaughter in the second degree, out in four years, two with good behavior. I'd thought that "good behavior" would be pretty easy to achieve, but that was before I met Lulu the Destroyer of Books.

Anyway, as I was saying, prison libraries. Who would've thought? Today, like all Wednesdays, I hop to the brightly lit room in a good mood. Because today is the first Wednesday of the month, and that's when we usually get our shipment of donated books. New Yorkers love donating books. I think it makes them feel like good people or something. I wish they'd donate Starbucks lattes, too, but I'm not complaining. I'm trying to be a better person, really I am. I even took up yoga.

"Four minutes early." Elsie, the library guard, glances at the clock. "You must be really looking forward to the new books."

"Well, it's not like I've got HBO to look forward to, so new books it is." I smile wide and shrug. See? I'm sweet, I'm cheerful, I am a totally new person.

Elsie snorts. "True that. Well, it's your lucky day. We got that latest *New York Times* bestseller everyone's been yammering about."

My excitement isn't faked. Elsie's been talking up this book for weeks now. "You mean the one you've been yammering about?"

"Ha, yes. I can't wait for you to read it and tell me what you think." As far as prison guards go, Elsie's cool. She and I have formed a little book club, encouraging a handful other inmates (not Lulu, obviously) to join in. "I've put a hold on it for you." She takes the book out from behind the desk. I reach for it eagerly.

And freeze.

"Ani? You okay?" Elsie's voice sounds so far away. Small and tinny, like it's coming through a tunnel. I barely register it. All I see are the words in front of me.

THE #1 *NEW YORK TIMES* BESTSELLER

Best Left Buried

by Jane Morgan

A choked sound claws its way out of my throat. Jane fucking Morgan. No, it can't be her. There must be a million Jane Morgans out there. It could be anyone. It's not her. It can't be her. I force myself to exhale. Then I turn the book over, and there's her face, those drab, undistinguished features of hers, except they're no longer drab, nor undistinguished. She must've hired a great photographer to take her author photo, because Jane looks—there are no other words for it—stunning. I am literally stunned. Her normally dull skin is positively glowing, her lips curved into a shy, knowing smile. But it's her eyes that arrest my attention. Jane's always had this intense look about her, like a fucking creep. You could totally imagine her as some middle-aged man who likes to linger outside women's bathrooms. Her gaze is still intense now, but it's the kind of intensity that says she's got a secret. A real good one. And it would be very, very alluring if I didn't know just what that secret was.

I don't realize I'm crushing the book until Elsie says, "Hey, knock it off!" and yanks it out of my hands. I blink at her stupidly. It takes me a moment to recover myself, to snap back to reality, to leave the wine-hazy memories of that last night with Jane. I've lost count of the number of times I've replayed that night. Each mental rewind is a confused jumble with a multitude of time skips and gaping black holes. I recall snatches here and there. Jane refilling my glass over and over. Jane asking questions about Ivan. I had my guard down because it was Jane, harmless tagalong Jane. Even after they presented the recording she took of me to the judge, I still didn't blame her. I'd assumed it was all Thalia's idea. My brilliant, deadly sister-in-law.

But now, looking at this photo of the new and improved Jane, it hits me that I've gravely miscalculated. That I don't just have one, but two bitches that need taking down. I need to read Jane's book. I need to know just what Jane is capable of. I've underestimated her, but not anymore. I've got plans for when I get out of here. They only included Thalia before, with Jane as an afterthought, but I think I might just move Jane up my VIP list.

I force myself to take a deep inhale. Stretch the corners of my mouth painfully up into a reassuring smile. I make sure my voice comes out even.

"Can I have that back? Please?" I add. I will never get used to saying "please."

Elsie narrows her eyes at me, still hugging the book to her ample chest like it's a baby and not a thing written by a lying bitch. "You sure you're okay?"

335

"Yeah, I just got too excited at the thought of finally reading this book you've been raving about." My teeth are clenched so tight I almost hear them crack. A book. That Elsie's been raving about. Written by Jane. I have to suppress a strong urge to lunge for it.

"Okay . . ." Elsie sighs. "Just. Be careful with it, okay? It's prison—"

"Property. I know."

"And I would hate to have to report you for—"

"You won't have to. I'll be careful with it. I promise." I'm ever so gentle when she finally hands me the book. Her frown eases into a smile.

"You're going to love it."

I grin. "I'm sure I will. And when I get out of here, I'll make sure to tell the author just how much I did."

Acknowledgments

As I mentioned in my dedication, this book would not have been written if not for the encouragement of my writing bestie, Laurie Elizabeth Flynn. Laurie is the queen of psychological suspense, which is hands down my favorite genre to read. I'd been wishing to write one for a very long time, but didn't think I had what it took to achieve it. Laurie was the one who coaxed me gently to dip my toes into the genre, and that was how I started on one of the most thrilling writing journeys of my life.

I'm also so grateful to my husband, Mike, who unlike Ted has never referred to my writing as a "hobby." I did use a couple of our real-life tiffs in this book, and for that I apologize, but they were too good to not take advantage of.

This journey would not have been possible without the brilliant hand of my agent, Katelyn Detweiler, guiding my career path. Katelyn's vision has turned my humble journey into one I could only have dreamt about years ago.

I am beyond amazed and thankful that I am able to work once again with my editor, Cindy Hwang. Think of the best editor that has ever editored—one who is kind, patient, insightful, and attentive, Cindy is that editor and more. I am spoiled, I know. Cindy has set the bar so incredibly high.

Along with Cindy comes what is surely the best publishing team an author could dream of. Thank you to my Berkley team—Jin Yu, Angela Kim, Erin Galloway, Dache' Rogers, and Danielle Keir.

As always, I would've quit a long time ago without the support of my writing friends. My beloved menagerie—Elaine Aliment, S. L. Huang (whose epic fantasy is about to take the world by storm), Toria Hegedus, Tilly Latimer, Rob Livermore, Maddox Hahn, Lani Frank, Mel Melcer, and Emma Maree. My wonderful writing friends—Nicole Lesperance, Grace Shim, May Cobb, and Kate Dylan.

I think it's next to impossible to exist in this world as someone who identifies as a woman and not be enraged time and again. This book is the result of all the anger and bitterness at the inequalities of our society. I was fully submerged in Jane's and Thalia's mind, and what deliciously twisted minds they were. Writers are often chasing that moment of falling into the darkest depths of their book. I had so many of those amazing moments while writing this book, because it was a chance for me to pour out all of the rage inside me. And so this book is for anyone who identifies with Jane's and Thalia's anger. Thank you for reading it. Totally unbiased opinion here: I have the best readers. And I'm sorry to those who might have been expecting something lighthearted like *Dial A For Aunties*, LOL!

Want more unputdownable page-turning reads from Jesse Sutanto?

Put the kettle on, there's a mystery brewing . . .

Sixty-year-old self-proclaimed tea expert Vera Wong enjoys nothing more than sipping a good cup of Wulong and doing some healthy 'detective' work on the internet (AKA checking up on her son to see if he's dating anybody yet).

But when Vera wakes up one morning to find a dead man in the middle of her tea shop, it's going to take more than a strong Longjing to fix things. Knowing she'll do a better job than the police possibly could – because nobody sniffs out a wrongdoing quite like a suspicious Chinese mother with time on her hands – Vera decides it's down to her to catch the killer.

Nobody spills the tea like this amateur sleuth.

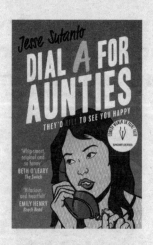

'ARE YOU . . . DEAD?'
OH MY GOD. I THINK HE IS.

When Meddy Chan accidentally kills her blind date, she turns to her aunties for help. Their meddling set her up on the date so they kind of owe her.

WELL, THAT DIDN'T QUITE GO TO PLAN.

Although hiding this goddamn dead body is going to be harder than they thought especially when her family's wedding business has THE biggest wedding of the year happening right now.

IT'S PRETTY BAD TIMING REALLY.

It turns out the wedding venue just happens to be managed by Meddy's ex, aka the one who got away. It's the worst time to see him again, or . . . is it? Can Meddy finally find love and make her overbearing family happy?

It's supposed to be the perfect day . . .

After getting away with literal murder, Meddy can't wait to
settle down and marry the love of her life, Nathan. She's
found the dress, got the dream venue at Christ Church
College, Oxford, plus having a destination wedding comes
with the added bonus of not having to invite her very large
extended family.

. . . But is it even a wedding if nobody gets killed?

Although when her meddling aunties get involved, Meddy
knows her wedding is going to be anything but quiet. Even
though there's no dead body hidden in the freezer this time,
for better or worse, it's certainly going to be a day she's never
going to forget . . .